*contin*

# MASTER OF THE NIGHT

"Her novels are spicy, extremely sexy, and truly fabulous . . . complex and intriguing . . . loads of possibilities for future sensual adventures."                     —*Romantic Times*

"A terrific paranormal romantic suspense thriller that never slows down until the final confrontation between good and evil. The action-packed story line moves at a fast clip."
                                        —*Midwest Book Reviews*

### *Further praise for the novels of Angela Knight*

#### "A WRITING TALENT HEADED FOR THE STARS."
**—*Midwest Book Review***

"Nicely written, quickly paced, and definitely on the erotic side."                                  —*Library Journal*

"Get ready for the adrenaline-rushing read of your life . . . the cream of the crop!"       —*ParaNormal Romance Reviews*

"The sex scenes were explosive and should have come with a warning for the reader to have a fire extinguisher handy during reading."                          —*Euro-Reviews*

"Delicious . . . wonderfully crafted . . . Angela Knight brings such life to her characters and to the world she's created for them that readers can't help but believe in magic."
                                        —*Romance Reviews Today*

"If you like alpha heroes, wild rides, and pages that sizzle in your hand, you're going to love [Angela Knight]!"
                                        —*J. R. Ward*

# WARRIOR

### THE TIME HUNTERS

## Angela Knight

BERKLEY SENSATION, NEW YORK

**THE BERKLEY PUBLISHING GROUP**
**Published by the Penguin Group**
**Penguin Group (USA) Inc.**
**375 Hudson Street, New York, New York 10014, USA**
Penguin Group (Canada), 90 Eglinton Avenue East, Suite 700, Toronto, Ontario M4P 2Y3, Canada
(a division of Pearson Penguin Canada Inc.)
Penguin Books Ltd., 80 Strand, London WC2R 0RL, England
Penguin Group Ireland, 25 St. Stephen's Green, Dublin 2, Ireland
(a division of Penguin Books Ltd.)
Penguin Group (Australia), 250 Camberwell Road, Camberwell, Victoria 3124, Australia
(a division of Pearson Australia Group Pty. Ltd.)
Penguin Books India Pvt. Ltd., 11 Community Centre, Panchsheel Park, New Delhi—110 017, India
Penguin Group (NZ), 67 Apollo Drive, Rosedale, North Shore 0632, New Zealand
(a division of Pearson New Zealand Ltd.)
Penguin Books (South Africa) (Pty.) Ltd., 24 Sturdee Avenue, Rosebank, Johannesburg 2196,
South Africa

Penguin Books Ltd., Registered Offices: 80 Strand, London WC2R 0RL, England

This is a work of fiction. Names, characters, places, and incidents either are the product of the author's imagination or are used fictitiously, and any resemblance to actual persons, living or dead, business establishments, events, or locales is entirely coincidental. The publisher does not have any control over and does not assume any responsibility for author or third-party websites or their content.

WARRIOR: THE TIME HUNTERS

A Berkley Sensation Book / published by arrangement with the author

PRINTING HISTORY
Berkley Sensation mass-market edition / July 2008

ISBN: 978-0-425-22084-9

BERKLEY® SENSATION
Berkley Sensation Books are published by The Berkley Publishing Group,
a division of Penguin Group (USA) Inc.,
375 Hudson Street, New York, New York 10014.
BERKLEY SENSATION and the "B" design are trademarks of Penguin Group (USA) Inc.

PRINTED IN THE UNITED STATES OF AMERICA

10  9  8  7  6  5  4  3  2  1

# WARRIOR

## THE TIME HUNTERS

# · 1 ·

July 10, 2008
The outskirts of Atlanta, Georgia

**Galar Arvid hated time travel.**

First came the electric tingle that built almost instantly to white-hot pain. Then the sickening wrench of the Jump—the nauseating feeling of being ripped apart and reassembled in the blink of an eye. His ears rang from the sonic boom of displacing air, but worse was the blinding blue-white light that left him unable to see for several crucial seconds.

Galar was moving well before his sight cleared, putting space between himself and the spot where he'd materialized. If the killer opened fire, he'd just as soon not be standing around waiting to get hit.

*Any sign of temporal aliens?* he demanded.

Sensor implants throughout his body did their work, the results processed by the computer that wound throughout his brain in fine strands no thicker than a molecule. The comp gave him access to bursts of great strength, as well as sensor data, any information he cared to know, and an uncanny accuracy with weapons. *No indication of non-natives in the area,* it told him.

Good. Maybe they'd beaten the Jump thief to the scene.

His sight finally clearing of purple afterimages, Galar turned to look for his fellow Temporal Enforcers. He quickly spotted the two as they moved to safety through the dark, tree-ringed clearing. His comp relayed his snapped mental command over the TE communication channel as he strode toward them. *"Report!"*

*"I hate time travel,"* the timber wolf said. A hundred kilos of fur, fangs, and computerized intelligence, the big beast plunked his furry butt down on the leaves to scratch vigorously at his T-collar. Vocalizer lights flashed around his neck in time with the words.

*"You hate everything, Frieka,"* Enforcer Riane Arvid put in. *"Except bitching."*

*"That was* not *the report I had in mind,"* Galar said drily.

*"Well, I seem to have all my paws,"* Frieka replied, contemplating them thoughtfully. *"And I don't want to yark up my dinner, which is a real improvement over some Jumps I've made."* To Riane, he added, *"Did I ever tell you about the time your father and I . . . ?"*

*"Yes,"* Riane interrupted. *"At least six dozen times."* She was a tall woman dressed in temporal armor that clung to her lean, muscled body. The T-suit's tiny matte navy scales rendered her all but invisible, as well as virtually invulnerable. Only her pretty face showed clearly to Galar's acute night vision: wide, dark eyes, a lushly sensual mouth, red hair falling around her shoulders, a single jeweled braid swinging beside her cheek. An intricate tattoo swirled down one side of her face in shades of red and blue. Like Galar, she was a genetically engineered Vardonese Warrior, complete with computer, sensors, and fantastic strength.

And, like Galar, she was armed. A belt studded with weapons and pouches rode her narrow waist, including a shard pistol, several knives, restraints, a fist-sized courier 'bot, and other assorted gear. Temporal Enforcers had to be ready for anything.

The cyborg wolf peeled his lips back from his teeth, an intimidating display in a creature the approximate size of a pony. *"You, brat, are a smart-ass."*

*"Better than being a dumbass,"* she shot back. Despite the acid words, genuine affection warmed the look the two exchanged.

*"I hate to interrupt your customary banter,"* Galar growled. *"But we do have a potential murder victim to save. Frieka, patrol the perimeter and give the area a good sniff. I want to know if the Jump thief has been here."* He looked through the stand of trees. Just beyond it, across a neatly trimmed square of yard, lay a long, narrow brick box of a house, looking deceptively peaceful in the moonlight. *"Riane, you take the rear of the victim's home, I'll take the front. Full camouflage. The natives don't need to know we're here."*

The smile faded from Riane's face, and she straightened, almost throwing Galar a salute before his cold gaze stopped her.

*"You're not in the military now,"* he reminded her. *"Enforcers don't salute."* Riane had been in Temporal Enforcement less than a year, after three years with the Vardonese Space Fleet. Old habits died hard.

She nodded jerkily, pivoted with a soldierly snap, and strode away. Galar's gaze lingered involuntarily on her swaying ass. To his relief, Riane chose that moment to activate her suit's camouflage field and disappear from view.

He glowered. The instinctive glance at her butt told him it was time to find a woman once this mission was over. It wouldn't, however, be Riane. He didn't get involved with those he worked with. Not emotionally, not sexually, not in any way at all. Ever. That lesson had been seared indelibly into his brain a decade before.

Galar turned away, gaze colliding with the wolf's reproachful ice-blue stare. *"She may be a little green, but she's a good kid, Master Enforcer,"* Frieka told him stiffly. *"You didn't have to bite a hunk out of her."*

*"Yeah, she is a good kid. So good that if somebody gets killed because you two are busy dicking around, she'll never get over it. If I have to rip a strip off her to keep that from happening, I'll do it."* He lifted a brow. *"By the way—didn't I just give you an order?"*

The wolf flicked an ear and stalked off, hackles bristling with canine affront.

Galar watched him go. *Well, my reputation as a son of a bitch is secure.* He activated his own suit's camo field and headed for the house. Time to do a scan of its layout and find out what the hell was going on.

His computer pronounced the building an example of the twenty-first-century style called a "two-bedroom ranch." It was constructed of the red brick favored by builders of the period, though its front door and shutters were white-painted wood. Filmy lace curtains hung over the windows.

Come morning, the police would find the house splattered with Jessica Kelly's blood. Yet there was no sign of that violence now. It seemed Galar's team had beaten the killer to the scene.

His neuronet computer confirmed that, its voice murmuring in his mind. *The house's residents are in good health.*

Something moved inside the house, just beyond one curtain. Wary, alert, Galar moved closer. Through the window, he saw a woman standing at an easel, a paintbrush in her hand. Must be Jessica Kelly, the victim they'd come to save.

*Affirmative,* his computer whispered in his mind.

*Anybody else in the house?* Invisible, he stepped up to the window to watch as she worked.

*Charlotte Holt, her roommate. Currently reading in her bedroom.*

*Is she a human of this era?*

*Affirmative. Sensors indicate no alien chemical traces present in her body.* Molecules of the foods and materials of the future couldn't be disguised.

A native, then. Galar grunted. Charlotte would disappear at the same time as Jessica, though none of her blood would be found. Police would never be sure whether she'd been the killer or another victim. Historians would argue the topic endlessly over the coming centuries.

He'd do his best to save Charlotte if she was a victim. If she was Jessica's killer—well, he'd be able to do nothing at all, not even save the artist herself. His team was forbidden to interfere in crimes between temporal natives.

Brooding, Galar watched Jessica work. She was tall for a woman of the twenty-first century, leggy in her paint-stained jeans and T-shirt. Dark hair lay around her narrow shoulders, straight and thick and shining. Her eyes were a smoky, intense blue under angular dark brows, her features delicately rounded, her lips full, wide, red as rose petals. The sensuality of her face was matched by a lush body with curvy hips and breasts that looked like delectable handfuls.

She stepped back from the massive wooden easel, the brush held poised and ready in her right hand as she stared at the painting, her expression fierce with concentration. Small, white teeth bit her lower lip, and she turned away to pace. Her body seemed to vibrate with energy and passion as she moved in catlike strides from one end of the room to the other. He really did like those legs.

*Yeah, definitely time to find a woman.*

Turning back to the easel, she began painting again, using her brush with delicate, careful strokes. Her eyes narrowed, and a flush climbed the soft curve of her cheeks. Full lips parted. The rosy tip of her tongue slipped out, moved over the curve of her upper lip. Sensuality seemed to pour from her like heat from a star as she worked, a product of some intense inner energy.

Long minutes passed before she stopped and closed her eyes, weariness on her face. Arching her back, she stretched her slender arms over her head as if to relieve tensed muscles. The gesture thrust out her full breasts.

Galar wanted to cup them, thumb the tight nipples. Taste. He hardened in a long, sweet rush, and grimaced at the inconvenient hunger. *Keep your mind on the job, Arvid, not on her ass.*

Jessica returned to work, her face lit by that intent sensuality. Galar began to feel as if he were intruding on something far more intimate than a woman working on a painting. Almost as though she were naked, with one of those pretty hands busy between her thighs.

Actually, if he *had* caught her masturbating, he suspected it would have affected him with less searing potency. He'd love to be the object of all that intense passion, that ferocious energy. The thought made his cock harden even more.

What was it about this girl? He was usually better at controlling his hunger than this. Not that it was ever exactly easy. Being a Warlord meant far more than genetically engineered strength, more than sensors and computer implants. The males of his kind were intensely sexual, with a ferocious instinct to protect and defend women in general. And lovers in particular.

*Unless they try to kill me first . . .*

The rumble of an approaching car jolted him from his uncomfortable preoccupation. He turned, tense and ready, as a battered Ford came around the corner and slewed gravel as it turned up the ranch's short driveway.

*Identify,* he demanded.

*Jessica's sister, Ruby Kelly,* his comp replied.

Another suspect—and this one, too, was definitely from this time. Galar glowered at the thin blonde as she shoved open the car door and ran toward the house's brick steps.

Sweet Goddess, he really didn't want to have to stand by and watch Jessica Kelly die. . . .

**Inside the house,** Jessica stroked cadmium red across the canvas, painting rays of blazing energy around the writhing female figure. Dark memories seethed through her, bleeding from her brush like poison being squeezed from a snakebite. She knew from experience that when she was done, she'd feel light, boneless. At peace.

Peace she knew so rarely, and craved so much.

"Hey!" Knuckles rattled on the screen door. "You in there, Jess?"

Jessica muttered a soft curse. It had been just cool enough this July night to seduce her into leaving the front door open. Now she was going to pay for it. "I'm working, Ruby."

"Yeah, I knew that from the paint stink." Her sister shouldered open the door and sauntered inside, the butt of a cigarette dangling from her mouth. Like Jessica, she was tall, but drug use had rendered her long body gaunt and her skin sallow. A cropped T-shirt with a Confederate flag spread proudly across her meager breasts, and a pair of stained blue jeans flapped loosely around too-thin legs. Her blond hair hung lank around a face marked with fading bruises. She had been pretty once, but hard living had etched bitter lines around her mouth and eyes. She looked a good decade older than Jessica's twenty-five, though she was actually a year younger.

Ruby ran a bored gaze over the painting on the easel. "Jesus, that's ugly. You don't think you're gonna sell that piece of shit?"

Jessica could feel her shoulders knotting, but she didn't look away from her work. She needed to finish if she was going to make her deadline. "I've got an appointment with an Atlanta gallery owner Saturday morning."

Ruby snorted. "You always have an appointment with some fuckin' gallery owner. Only they never buy your little pictures, do they?"

Familiar, impotent anger sizzled through her. Pointless. Her sister was what she was. "What do you want, Ruby?"

Bloodshot blue eyes flickered, and the younger woman's tongue flicked over lips that looked chapped under a coat of bright red lipstick. "I need cash."

Jessica tossed her brush into the mason jar of turpentine. "Let me get this straight—you come into my house, insult my work, and then beg money so you can go buy crack?"

"Not a buy. I owe Billy Dean." True fear flashed in Ruby's eyes. She looked around vaguely for an ashtray, found one on an end table beside the room's single couch, and stubbed out the lipstick-stained butt. Her thin hand shook. "He's such a mean son of a bitch. If I don't pay him, he's gonna beat the crap out of me again. You know he put me in the hospital the last time."

"I also know you didn't show up in court to testify so the judge could throw his ass in jail." Wearily, Jessica raked her fingers through her hair, knowing perfectly well she was leaving streaks of paint through it. "He's going to kill you one of these days."

"Maybe tonight." Her sister dug into a pocket for a battered pack of Virginia Slims and a box of matches. The box slipped from shaking fingers as she lit the cigarette, but typically, she didn't bother to pick it up. "Look, just give me the two hundred. I swear, I'll stay away from him from here on . . ."

"Two hundred? What the hell did you buy from Billy Dean that cost two hundred dollars? I still have to pay my half of the rent! If I give you that much, I'm going to be seriously short!"

Ruby snorted a plume of smoke. "And if you don't, I'm going to be seriously dead."

"Dammit, you can't run a tab with Billy Dean. He'd kill

you over a two-hundred-dollar debt as soon as spit." If only to send a warning to all his other crack-addict customers.

"Yeah, I know, it was stupid, but—I needed it bad."

"You always 'need it bad.' Why in the hell did he give you that much rock to begin with?"

Bruised eyes flickered. "He didn't exactly give it to me. I was over at his place last night. You know. Partying. He got real drunk. . . ."

"And you smoked all his crack when he passed out." Jessica swore in a long, ripe roll. "You're lucky he didn't kill you when he came to."

Ruby gave her a sickly smile. "I wasn't exactly there when he came to."

"Shit." Her stomach slid into an anxious tumble. Ruby was right. If her sister didn't have the money by the time Billy Dean tracked her down, he really would beat her to death.

Jessica stalked across the living room to her purse and dug for her billfold with paint-stained fingers. She pulled out the roll of tips she'd carefully hoarded over the past week from her job at the restaurant. She'd have to find some other way to make up the difference in her half of the rent.

Maybe that gallery dealer would buy a painting. . . .

**Galar stood wrapped** in darkness and tension as he watched the house. He relaxed only slightly as Ruby pushed open the front door, clattered down the brick steps, and jumped back into her battered car. Tires slung gravel as she sped away.

She'd later tell the cops she'd gone off to visit her drug dealer.

*Time?*

*2100 hours.*

Nine p.m. He grunted. According to the police report he'd seen, the attack would come sometime around 2300, or eleven o'clock. That estimate could be off by a couple of hours either way, which was why Galar and his team had arrived so early to stake out the scene. If they meant to save Jessica Kelly's life, they had to be ready for anything, anytime.

The blood the police would find splashed all over the living room tomorrow would be identified as Jessica's, and the coroner would report that the woman couldn't have survived. She would never be seen again. Everyone from law enforcement to art historians would believe she'd ended up in an unmarked grave.

Galar's team was the only hope she had of survival—assuming the would-be murderer was indeed a time traveler. If sensors indicated the killer was a native of 2008, there would be nothing they could do. They'd be forbidden to interfere.

Actually, had police already found Jessica's body, Galar and his partners would have been forbidden even to make the attempt to save her. And if they had tried, they'd have failed. You couldn't change history.

Still, he thought there was a chance. When he'd run across the police report while scanning the Outpost's historical records, his gut had told him this was a temporal crime. A twenty-third-century collector would pay a great deal of money for historically unknown Jessica Kelly originals. Which was one hell of a motive for a time-Jumping art thief with a taste for murder. Goddess knew there were plenty of them out there—ruthless men and women, skilled in the use of the primitive weapons that were all you could take on a Jump. The tachyon blazers of the twenty-third century had an ugly habit of exploding if you attempted a temporal leap with one. That left blades, projectile weapons, or fists.

It was Galar's duty to catch such criminals. Whether or not their crimes were part of history, you couldn't just let time travelers Jump around preying on helpless natives. If there was any possibility a victim could be saved, agents of Temporal Enforcement were honor-bound to make the attempt.

If Galar's team succeeded, Jessica would be given a new life in the future.

If.

**Jessica stood in** front of the canvas, the brush limp in her hand. All the boiling creative energy she'd enjoyed earlier had been drained away by her sister's visit. Now there was nothing left but helpless worry and angry frustration.

"Think you were suckered?"

She looked around to find her housemate leaning a shoulder against the frame of her bedroom door, watching her with sympathy in those big green eyes. Charlotte Holt was a petite woman, her build lush rather than leanly muscled. Her hair was a tumble of red curls that irritated her with its tendency to frizz in the Georgia humidity. She wore a skirt and a silky black top, as if ready for a night on the town.

Jessica turned back to her canvas. "I'll still pay my chunk of the rent, if that's what you're worried about."

"Don't be insulting." Charlotte moved closer and slipped an arm around her waist in a half hug. "Of course you had to give her the money. You couldn't let your sister get killed. Even if she is an idiot."

Jessica snorted and hugged her back. "What I really need to do is drop a dime on Billy Dean. Unfortunately, whenever the police bust him, he never seems to have any drugs. Ruby says he's got dirty cops in his pocket."

"Maybe." Charlotte tilted her head, considering the painting. "That girl truly is a moron. This is good. Amazing, in fact."

"You really think so?"

Charlotte met her gaze, her own steady. "This is the kind

of painting you'll find answers in, when you're ready to look for them."

Jessica blinked. "Wow. And here I thought it was a picture of a naked lady."

Her friend snorted. "Twit. You know, you've got the least ego of any genius I've ever met."

"Genius, my ass." Uncomfortable, she stepped away from her friend and started capping the tubes of paint. "Anyway, if I'd ever even thought about developing an ego, my mother beat it out of me years ago. She and Ruby never understood my stuff." Jessica reached for the jar of turpentine and started cleaning her brushes. "Mom's idea of art was Elvis on black velvet. You know, I gave her one of those when I was ten. I think it was the only thing I ever painted that she actually liked."

"Just because your mother didn't get it, that doesn't mean nobody else will." Charlotte moved to the couch to open the portfolio Jessica had put there in preparation for the upcoming interview. Her clever fingers flipped through the canvasses, pausing now and again. Skillful swirls of paint depicted a dirty child with hollow eyes, looking up warily from a mud puddle. Next a prostitute, standing hipshot and defiant in a sweatshirt and ripped jeans, face hard and hungry. A homeless drunk, his face weathered from decades of cheap booze. And in between, the nude studies Jessica did to lighten her mood, long-limbed and clean, surging with energy. "Anything this gorgeous is going to get attention."

"I don't know about that." Jessica stirred her brush in the turpentine, watching red paint swirl from the bristles like blood. She pulled the brush out of the jar and wiped it on a clean rag, then set it aside on the taboret. "Nobody has yet."

"That's because real art isn't always comfortable or pretty," her friend told her quietly. "It's not the kind of thing you pick out because it matches your couch."

Jessica sighed and screwed the cap back on the jar of

turpentine. "Trouble is, it's not the kind of thing that pays the rent either."

*Any sign of* the killer? Riane asked Frieka on their private frequency. She scanned the woods, then turned her sensors on the house for the twentieth time in the past three hours.

*Nope.* The wolf's paws whispered through the leaves. Then again, the soft rustle might have been the wind. Thanks to the genetic engineering that had extended his life, Frieka had almost thirty years of combat experience, much of it with her father. He could be silent as a ghost when he wanted to be.

*"You think the Master Enforcer's right—that the killer will turn out to be a time traveler?"*

*"Probably. The man may be a dickhole, but he's got a good reputation."*

Riane snorted. *"Except for the part about him being a killer."*

*"We're all killers, Riane."*

*"Yeah, but they say she was his lover."*

*"They say all kinds of crap. You can't believe half of it."*

Riane wasn't worried about being overheard; they were using the private com code they'd employed since she was a two-year-old and Frieka was her furry nursemaid. Even her father hadn't managed to crack it, and Baran Arvid was damned good. Neither had a succession of commanders in both the Vardonese Military and Galactic Union Temporal Enforcement.

Riane gave the house another scan. Still nothing. *"You think it's true—that the traitor really was his lover?"*

*"You mean up until she tried to blow a beamer hole in my chest?"*

Galar's icy question made Riane's cheeks flood with burning blood. *"Master Enforcer! I didn't mean . . ."*

*". . . To be overheard? Yeah, I gathered that. I'm very*

*good at cracking code. You may want to keep that in mind."*

**The woman who** called herself Charlotte Holt sat in the darkness of the living room, listening to her roommate's breathing settle into sleep. She'd enjoyed the past six months, getting to know Jessica Kelly, with her blazing, unrecognized talent, dark family past, and driven insecurities. Too, the respite from the chase had been welcome.

But the Xeran assassin would make his attack in half an hour. She had to be gone before that, and there was much to do in the meantime.

Restlessly, Charlotte rose and moved to the window to push aside the lace curtains. Though there was nothing visible beyond darkness and moonlit trees, her special senses detected the Temporal Enforcement agents waiting with varying degrees of patience around the house.

Good. The pieces were in place, just as she'd foreseen.

Pivoting with military precision, she walked into the tiny kitchen where she'd shared so many meals with Jessica. Charlotte knew the room would have been pitch black to her friend, but she could see the butcher block knife rack clearly.

She drew the blade she wanted with a soft, metallic hiss, then walked to her roommate's door and pushed it quietly open.

## · 2 ·

✿

**Jessica lay deeply asleep, curled in a cotton sleep**
shirt under a sheet covered with tiny roses. Her dark hair
spilled across her pillow, shining softly in the moonlight.

Charlotte paused in the doorway and closed her eyes,
feeling alien forces gather deep inside her with a hot electric
tingle. Blowing out a breath, she sent the wave of energy
rolling over Jessica.

There. She'd sleep through this now.

Silent as an assassin, Charlotte moved to stand over the
girl, raised her left hand, and swiftly ran the razored blade
across the pad of her own index finger. She didn't even flinch
at the pain. Tilting her hand, she watched fat drops of blood
fall on her roommate's forehead.

As she watched, the drops pooled there for a moment,
then slowly disappeared, sinking into Jessica's skin. Dark
brows drew down as if in discomfort, and the girl moaned in
her sleep.

"I'm sorry," Charlotte told her softly. "I just don't have a choice."

Turning away, she strode from the room, moving fast now, leaving her former roommate alone, asleep. And changing.

In the living room, Charlotte stopped to snatch up the leather purse she kept packed in case she had to make an emergency Jump. She paused and glanced out the window. Though she couldn't see him, she could sense the leader of the Enforcers waiting right outside, patient as a sentinel, invisible in the dark.

She frowned. He was a little too close, he and his partners. If she tried to Jump now, they'd realize she was far more than a temporal native. On the other hand, if she attempted to simply leave and find another place to Jump, one of them might follow her. She couldn't take the chance.

And she was running out of time. The assassin would be here soon.

Closing her eyes, Charlotte reached for the three minds around the house—the man, the woman's, and the wolf's. She let her power gather, sent it rolling toward them. . . .

And all three dropped, stunned unconscious, to the ground.

Charlotte sagged against the window a moment, then shook off the momentary weakness and made for the door. She clattered down the stairs, strode past the male agent's unconscious body, and started across the yard. She'd Jump as soon as she was far enough away not to leave suspicious energy traces for the agents to detect.

She hadn't quite reached the road when she sensed the roiling field of a temporal Jump spilling from the house. Charlotte spun around in horror.

A blue blaze of light lit up Jessica's window. Charlotte's mouth shaped a silent curse. The Xeran assassin had arrived.

She shot a desperate glance at the TE agents, but knew she didn't dare wake them yet. She had to put some distance between herself and the house before she could let them go. "God, Jess, I'm sorry!"

Whirling, Charlotte broke into a hard, pounding run.

*Jessica'll survive,* she told herself desperately. *Jessica will make it. Just a little farther, and then I'll let them save her.*

*A little farther . . .*


"Get up!" A huge hand locked in Jess's hair and jerked her off her bed, white-hot agony flaring through her scalp. Jarred violently awake, she yelped and grabbed at the fist tangled in her long mane. Through tears of shock and confusion, she saw a man looming over her, the silhouette of immense shoulders blocking the dim light from the window. Teeth flashed in a snarl. "Where is she? Where's the heretic?"

He flung her against the wall so hard, she felt the Sheetrock crack. Stars exploded behind her eyes as her head snapped back against the wall. "What?" Jess yelled. "Who the hell are—"

"Shut up!" Hot breath flooded against her skin as a face shoved inches from her own. Something cold pricked her throat as a massive body pinned her. Whatever he was wearing felt oddly slick and scaly, more like snakeskin than fabric. "Where is she?"

"Who?" She swung at him with all the ferocity her trailer park childhood had taught her.

Light flared behind her eyes again. She tasted blood, heard a metallic ringing. He'd punched her. "Your roommate! Where did she go?"

Like she'd tell him a damn thing. "Get off me!"

The sting of cold pain intensified against her throat. "Do

you want to die?" He bared his teeth in her face. "Do you want me to slit your throat? Because unless you tell me everything you know about Charlotte Holt, you're dead!"

Knife. He had a knife. The cold prick she felt against her neck was a blade. Jess grabbed for his wrist with both hands, tried to force his hand back. She might as well have been pushing a forklift. "I don't know anything! She left! She's not here!" She had no idea whether Charlotte was still home or not—for all she knew, her roommate was hiding in a closet—but if this bastard didn't know where she was, Jessica wasn't going to give her away.

**Galar snapped to** consciousness with his computer howling a warning in his skull. *Victim under assault!* He shot up off the leafy ground even as Frieka and Riane rolled to their feet.

The Warfem was white-faced, the wolf snarling. "What the Seven Hells . . ."

"He's got her!" Galar plunged toward the front door. "Go, go, go!"

"What happened? How the hell did he knock us out without us seeing him?" Riane demanded as they ran.

Galar didn't bother with an answer as he cleared the steps in one leap. *Give me* riaat*!* he snapped to his computer implant.

Fire flooded his veins in a wave of euphoria as the comp pumped biochemicals from reservoirs throughout his body, increasing his already considerable strength by a factor of ten even as it made him almost impervious to pain.

One thrust of his foot shattered both the wooden door and the metal and glass storm door beyond it. He ignored the broken fragments, though they raked at his T-suit as he bulled through them.

*Where?* he snapped at his computer.

*Back bedroom. Down the hall to the right.*

Lips peeling back from his teeth, he charged through the living room and down the short corridor.

*Sweet Goddess, let us be in time. . . .*

**Jessica struggled fruitlessly** as the thug thrust his face closer. She recoiled. His breath smelled strange. Some weird metallic taint she couldn't identify. And what were those glinting shapes protruding from his shaved head? Horns?

He sniffed at her like a bear. "Blood—I can smell her blood on you." Was that fear in his eyes? "She's made you one of *them*!"

The man drew back the knife from her throat, lowered his aim. He meant to plunge it into her belly. Jess screamed, bucking helplessly against his hold. . . .

Wood broke with a thunderous crash in the next room. Voices roared something incomprehensible. The cops! Relief washed through her like a sun-warmed tide. Maybe she'd make it out of this after—

Her captor snarled words she didn't understand and shoved her violently away. She reeled sideways, hit the bed, and fell across it as he reached for his waist.

Shadowed figures burst into the room to slam into her attacker, driving him back into the wall. Voices bellowed in a language she didn't understand.

Okay, this new bunch sure weren't cops.

Out. She had to get *out* of here. Jessica tried to roll off the bed, but her knees gave under her. She crashed to the floor as pain detonated in her guts.

She looked down.

*Oh, fuck. Fuck, fuck, fuck.*

His knife was buried in her belly.

*Get it out!* The words screamed in her head. She wrapped her hand around the hilt as a wave of cold nausea rolled through her. The knife slid free from her flesh, slowly, obscenely. Blood flooded hot down her belly. She fell back against the side of the bed and slid down until her butt hit the floor.

Her attacker was exchanging hammer blows with two others. And—a dog? She could hear snarls, see shadowed shapes writhing on the ground, a tangle of kicking legs and swinging arms.

An ambulance. Help. She had to get help. Phone in the kitchen. *Call 911.*

Crawling seemed safest. She rolled onto her hands and knees and headed for the doorway. Somebody's foot slammed into her calf, and she bit her lip against a yelp.

*Don't attract attention. Get away.*

Weak. So weak . . . Dying.

*Hell, no. I am not going to die!* Determination rose in her, the same fierce refusal to give up that had driven her to paint when everyone told her a white-trash girl could never be an artist.

*I am* not *going to die.*


**Well, this was** a planet-fuck of galactic proportions.

The supposed art thief Jumper—who should have been easy prey for the three of them—was actually a Xeran heavy-combat cyborg. He was well over two meters tall, with cybernetic implants that gave him strength greater than Galar's even in *riaat.*

Galar ducked a punch that would have taken his head off, and drove one of his own at the 'borg's belly. The impact jarred his teeth. The bastard's T-suit was so heavily armored, nothing could get through it, not even projectile weapons like the shard pistols the agents carried. Worse, the metal shards would probably ricochet, posing a risk to Jessica. Their only chance was to hit the 'borg so hard from so many directions that his suit's protection broke down under the barrage. Then Galar might be able to get a knife blade in and finish him off.

A kick blurred out of nowhere, catching him across the jaw and spinning him into the wall. Thanks to *riaat*, he didn't feel it; the berserker state his computer induced gave him fantastic strength and a near-immunity to pain.

At least until after the fight.

Galar whirled back into the battle, hungry to pay the bastard back with a sucker shot of his own.

Riane had engaged the Xeran, trading flat-footed punches with him despite the fact that he outweighed her by a hundred kilos. Frieka darted around the pair, trying to get his fangs through the 'borg's T-suit for a good bite. Defeated by the armor, the wolf cursed steadily in frustration.

Galar stepped in and swung. The blow landed with every erg of his *riaat*-enhanced strength behind it, sending the battleborg reeling back.

For an instant, the Xeran crouched against the wall and panted, eyeing them with the crazed glitter of desperation in his eyes. "You don't know what you're involved in!" He licked the blood off his lip. "That little primitive is dangerous!"

Galar bared his teeth. "Yeah, all sixty kilos of her. Why don't you surrender and explain it to us?"

The cyborg made an anatomically impossible suggestion and lunged, swinging his knife in a blurring arc. Galar ducked and drove a punch upward, catching the 'borg's wrist. The knife went flying.

Seeing his chance, Galar bulled into him, trying to throw the big Xeran. Riane crashed into the man's thighs, adding her weight. With a howl of victory, Frieka locked his jaws around one of the battleborg's ankles.

The Xeran crashed onto his belly, Galar riding him down. Jerking a pair of force cuffs from his weapons belt, he grabbed for the 'borg's left arm and started wrestling it back.

The cyborg kicked out viciously, sending the wolf flying into the wall with a yelp of pain.

"Frieka!" Riane, straddling the Xeran's ass now, jerked around to stare after her injured partner.

Which was when the 'borg twisted and buried a bloody knife in her thigh, slicing right through her T-suit as if it were paper. That shouldn't even have been possible.

Riane screamed in pain, grabbing desperately at the hilt.

*Warning!* Galar's comp shrilled. *Weapon hit the femoral artery. . . .*

*Sweet Goddess, she'll bleed out in minutes!*

Something slammed into his head, knocking him sideways. The Xeran gave him a kick in the gut for good measure and scrambled away.

Cursing, dazed, Galar did the only thing he could—grabbed for Riane and jerked the knife from her leg, then clamped a hard grip over the wound. He needed to maintain pressure until her system's medibots could seal the injury.

*Comp, Riane's medibots?*

*Responding. Three-point-four minutes to wound closure.*

Jessica might not have three minutes. He threw a desperate glance at the limp, furred figure against the wall. *Frieka's status?*

*Stunned,* his computer replied.

"Dammit, dog!" Nothing would rouse the wolf faster than the hated insult of being called a dog. "Get your furry ass up! I need you to get to Jessica before that bastard kills her!"

But Frieka didn't even twitch.

Cursing, Galar kept his grip on the wound with one hand while he reached for his belt with the other. He found one of the pouches, opened it, and jerked out a fist-sized silver globe. After broadcasting a quick message to it, he opened his fingers. The ball floated up off his palm toward the ceiling. A temporal field built around it with an electric tingle, and the courier flared blue and disappeared, off to get help from the Outpost. Com messages couldn't be sent through time; you had to send a messenger.

Blood pouring from the wound under his palm, Galar counted the seconds until he could save the artist himself. "Just stay alive, Jessica. Stay alive a little longer."

**Cold. Jessica felt** so cold. The hall stretched ahead of her, an endless corridor in the dark.

*Sliding into shock.*

She gritted her teeth and kept crawling. Her arms trembled, the muscles in her thighs jumping. Jesus, it was like being stark naked in the snow.

*Forget that. Phone. Get to the damned phone! 911, 911, 911 . . .* The desperate mental chant drove her forward.

In the living room now. Easel off to her left. Something lying in a patch of moonlight on the floor. She blinked at it, forced her blurring eyes to focus. The box of matches Ruby had dropped. *Light a match to see the phone.* She closed her hand around the box and kept crawling.

"Do you really think you can escape *me*?" The ugly words—and an even uglier laugh—made her head jerk up in terror. A sudden wash of adrenaline catapulted her to her feet, and she reeled around.

Her attacker leaned against the hallway wall, his face twisted in a snarl. As he staggered forward again, blood glinted wetly across his scaled suit. "I will not let your heretic taint spread any further!" He lowered his horned head and charged her like a bull, rage twisting his brutal features.

Crazy. This guy was batshit crazy.

Jess jumped back and knocked against the easel. It toppled with a crash. On sheer instinct, she grabbed a jar from her art taboret and hurled it at his head. It shattered on the metal projections protruding from his skull, filling the air with the reek of turpentine.

"Heretic slut!" He jerked a knife from his belt. Jesus, how many of them did he have?

And all she had . . .

. . . was the matches.

Frantically, Jessica fumbled the box open, grabbed one, raked it across the striker. By the grace of God, it burst into flame on the first try. "Stay back!" Surely the dumb bastard would know better than to jump her when he was covered in turpentine. . . .

He roared a bestial battle cry and dove at her.

She tossed the match. It hit him and ignited with a hot *whoosh*. He bellowed in startled pain and batted at the flames.

Something big and dark charged past her. A man, damn near as tall and muscled as her hulking attacker, snarling in an alien language. Her attacker danced away, narrowly avoiding being tackled as he fumbled for his waist. Searing blue light exploded in Jessica's vision with a thunderous boom, blinding and deafening her. The smell of ozone flooded the air.

When Jess blinked away the purple afterimages, her attacker had vanished. "What the hell?" She fell back against the wall behind her and slid down it, staring at the singed spot in the carpet. Her ears rang. "Did he blow himself up? Why are we still alive?"

"No, he just Jumped." It was the big man who spoke. He was using English now, not whatever the hell he'd been speaking earlier. He walked over and flipped on the light switch somewhere far over her head.

Jessica blinked, bracing her back against the wall as she looked up at him in dazed exhaustion. He crouched beside her, a frown of concern on his face. A very handsome face.

He pulled off his gloves—they were covered in blood—then clamped both hands over her stomach.

She sucked in a breath of pain. "What . . . are you doing?"

"Putting pressure on your wound." His face was grim as he leaned into her. His grip tore a yelp of agony from her lips. "Sorry, but I've got to keep you from bleeding to death. There's a doctor on the way. Just hold on."

"Are you . . . a cop?" Talking hurt. Everything hurt.

"Something like that." His hair was short and very blond, shining under the overhead light.

She stared at it dreamily, concentrating on it through the waves of pain. Shades of sunlight yellow, ocher, gold. *I'd like to paint his hair,* she thought. Her eyes fluttered, tried to close.

"Hey!" His voice turned sharp. "Stay with me, Jessica."

She licked dry lips. "Tired."

"I know, but you need to stay awake. Don't let go. Help's almost here." His eyes were pale amber, reminding her of sun-kissed honey, warm and unusual. And worried.

She could feel herself drifting away, and shook her head hard, fighting to concentrate. "Talk to me. Keep me awake. What's your name?"

"Galar. Galar Arvid."

"Galar." Funny name. She'd never heard anything like it. "You're not from around here, are you?"

"Not really, no." He wore a dark blue one-piece suit of some kind, made of tiny scales and piped in silver along the arms and across the width of his chest. Splashes of blood marked it, presumably not his own. The suit, whatever it was, appeared hard, dully gleaming, more like armor than fabric. It hugged every powerful inch of him so tightly, she could make out the impressive musculature that lay beneath it, from broad, brawny chest all the way down to powerful thighs and gleaming boots. A weapons belt rode his narrow waist, with a holstered gun, a couple of knives, and an array of pouches of different sizes.

Okay, so maybe he *was* some kind of cop.

The room rotated slowly to the left. "May . . . I paint you, Galar?"

Golden eyes met hers, urgent, demanding. "I'll be happy to let you do anything you want. Just stay with me."

She fought to concentrate on those remarkable eyes. The

pain was intensifying, and with it the cold, radiating from her belly as if she'd been stabbed with a frozen ice pick. She gritted her teeth against the need to scream. "It . . . hurts!"

"I know, but they'll be here any minute." He gave her a smile, but it was a little tight, a little fixed. "You know, it was really clever, the way you got rid of the Xeran. Took guts too."

"Xeran?" Her voice sounded slurred. "What the hell is a Xeran?"

"Long story." He lifted his head, alert. "Here they come, Jessica. Just a little longer, and it'll be all right."

She smelled ozone, dimly felt every hair stand up on her body, heard a faint crackle.

A lightning bolt struck right in front of her with a deafening crack and a quivering static shock. She yelped and tried to jerk upright, but Galar held her still as the room filled with people. They just *appeared* there like something out of a science fiction film. Men, women—all of them in the same dark blue suit he wore, except for two people dressed in cherry red.

The first, a woman, hurried toward Jessica and Galar, towing a man-sized transparent cylinder. A second red-clad person, a man, veered down the hall leading another cylinder. Both tubes floated three feet off the ground with no visible means of support whatsoever.

Three impossible feet.

What the hell?

The woman crouched before her, exchanged urgent words with the cop in that alien language.

*Alien,* Jessica thought, stunned, as the pieces came together with an almost audible click. *They're aliens.*

Darkness flooded in and swept her away.


**Colonel Cyrek Marcin** materialized a kilometer away, his nerve endings shrieking in pain. He could smell his skin burning. Even as he fought not to scream, foam sprayed from his suit, coating his face, cool and soothing. *Medibots en route to injury,* his computer purred in his mind.

The burns would be a distant memory in minutes. He'd suffered worse, though never from such a humiliating source. Marcin couldn't believe he'd let a primitive hurt him like this. He ached to go back and kill her for the stain to his honor. Gut her slowly in a fitting sacrifice to the Victor.

Marcin considered the idea, greatly tempted, then reluctantly decided against it. The primitive was, at best, only a distraction from his real target: the heretic. She was the true menace to the Faith. She had to be stopped.

She had to die.

Yes, she'd infected the primitive, which meant Jessica Kelly, too, would have to be eliminated. Unfortunately, Kelly was currently surrounded by Enforcers, which made killing her a high-risk mission. There were others who could do that job—assassins her protectors would never even see coming.

He had to keep his focus on his own heretic target. The first step was finding out where she'd gone, which meant he'd have to return to the house she'd shared with the girl.

Carefully, very carefully. Temporal Enforcement would still be there, and he didn't need to attract their attention.

Marcin scanned his surroundings, taking stock. His comp had chosen a nearby meadow for the emergency Jump. He raised his camo shield and started back toward the house the two women had shared.

And what was that all about? Why would the heretic choose to live as an ordinary primitive? According to the warrior priest, she could bounce through time without need of a T-suit. And that was the least of her deadly abilities.

Yet she'd apparently lived with Kelly for months. Why?

Marcin frowned. Had she intended to infect the artist all

along? If so, that implied all this was part of some larger plan.

Whatever it was, they had to put a stop to it, and quickly.

He reached for one of the pouches on his knife belt and drew out a fist-sized silver ball. Holding it up in front of his eyes, he composed the message he wanted to send and broadcast it at the ball, then tossed it lightly into the air.

He watched as the courier-bot soared skyward, then flared blue-white and vanished. It would carry his progress to the Cathedral Fortress.

Or rather, his lack of progress.

Marcin winced, imagining Tarik ge Lothar's reaction. He'd damned better find the heretic in a hurry, if he didn't want to face his leader's rage.

Breaking into a ground-eating lope he could maintain indefinitely, Marcin headed back toward the women's home, considering hunting strategies as he went. He'd have to avoid the Enforcers if he didn't want another . . .

A scent came to him, female and subtly alien. He stopped in his tracks, his heartbeat accelerating with excitement. It was the woman who called herself Charlotte Holt. She'd been here within the past half hour.

He drew in a deep breath, tasting the air like a wolf even as his comp scanned his surroundings for any trace of the heretic.

There.

A faint energy trace.

He cursed softly, recognizing the pattern of forces. She'd Jumped.

Marcin's lips pulled back from his teeth in a feral, snarling grin. If the little bitch thought she could get away from him, she was sadly mistaken.

He scanned the energy trace and fed the data to his computer. It was possible to take the strength of energy remnants and calculate a Jump's destination. Unfortunately, that only gave you a range of possibilities, a series of times and places where your target could be. To find out for sure, he'd have to search. And get lucky.

But considering the stakes, he had to try. Killing the heretic was all that mattered. That, and finding the Abominations before their taint spread.

# · 3 ·

**Grimly, Galar surveyed the wreckage. A blood trail** snaked down the hall and halfway through the living room. Jessica's easel lay toppled on its side, and a blackened scorch mark on the carpet marked where she'd set the battleborg on fire.

Sweet Goddess, she had guts. Not just when she'd fought the Xeran, though that had been striking enough. She'd demonstrated even greater courage when he'd clamped her wound. His sensors had told him how much it hurt, but she'd scarcely made a sound.

By the time the medtechs had arrived, Galar was just aching to kick the Xeran's ass. As soon as Chogan had Jessica safely in a regenerator, he'd gone after the battleborg. Using his sensors to collect data, his computer had determined a series of likely destinations, and he'd started making his Jumps.

Galar found the first materialization point easily

enough, since it was only a short distance from Jessica's house. The Xeran's next destination had been a filthy alley in seventeenth-century London, while the third was an isolated mountain valley high in the Canadian Rockies around 1923. He'd just missed the battleborg that time.

Next Galar had tried a fourteenth-century Chinese village, but there was no sign of the Xeran's Jump energies there at all. His computer had attempted another calculation, suggesting a little Alabama town in 1953, but the Xeran hadn't been there either.

Two more fruitless Jumps convinced Galar he'd lost the trail. He wasn't really surprised. Tracking someone through time was a crapshoot at best.

Frustrated, he'd returned to Jessica's house to help with the mopping up.

Now Galar watched Dr. Chogan bustle around the regenerator tube that held the artist's unconscious form. According to his sensors, her wound had closed, and her blood volume was increasing at a rate that would have been impossible without twenty-third-century medicine.

Just in time too. Much longer and even a regenerator wouldn't have been able to repair the brain damage caused by blood loss.

Next to Galar's booted foot, a collector stopped to graze on a tuft of wolf fur. A dozen of the fist-sized floating 'bots were busily swarming over the house, gathering every scrap of evidence that anyone from the future had ever been here. It wouldn't do to leave the Claremont County Sheriff's Department with forensic evidence of genetically engineered time travelers. When the 'bots were done, only the artist's blood trail would remain.

"Dammit, let me out of this thing!" Riane growled from the next room. She, too, was in a regenerator, but from the sound of it, her healing was even further along than Jessica's.

"Step foot out of that tube without the doc's permission,

and I'll bite you on the ass!" Frieka snapped. Despite the blow he'd taken, he was obviously none the worse for wear.

Galar breathed a deep breath in pure, singing relief. And promptly frowned at the intensity of his own reaction. What was with him lately? First the girl had gotten to him, now these two.

True, it was his duty to lead his subordinates safely through their missions. And Riane had real potential as an Enforcer. Galar had been impressed by her willingness to go toe-to-toe with the Xeran, despite his greater size and power. Then there'd been Frieka's frantic efforts to protect her. The big cyborg beast loved his partner with an intensity that was more paternal than canine.

Anybody would find that touching. It didn't mean Galar was losing his protective edge.

He stepped closer to Jessica's regenerator and looked down through the pink healing mist that filled the tube. The girl's delicate features still looked far too pale. Blood matted her dark hair and covered her slim body, left bare when the doc had stripped off her nightshirt. Galar, no stranger to nudity, didn't let his gaze linger.

She looked so fragile—but in her case, looks were deceiving.

A smile twitched his lips as he remembered charging into the hall just in time to see her throw the jar of turpentine on the battleborg, then follow it with a lit match. There was obviously more to the little artist than met the eye.

"How's she doing, Doc?" he asked.

Dr. Sakari Chogan looked up from the regenerator and pushed a long strand of iridescent green hair back from her face. She was a lovely woman, but her air of fragility was belied by a fierce intelligence and sardonic wit. "Our nasty Xeran friend did a lot of damage. His knife left a three-centimeter gash in the large intestine, which bled. A lot. Must have hurt like a son of a bitch." She turned to eye the blood trail. "But Ms. Kelly apparently isn't the type to lay down and die."

"So she *will* recover?" His computer had predicted as much, but he wanted it confirmed.

"Oh, yeah. I've patched you up from worse." She appraised his face. "Speaking of, you could use a session in the tube yourself. Nice collection of bruises there. Anything more interesting?"

He shrugged. "As you said, it's just bruises."

"Schedule a session in the tube anyway." The voice that issued that order was deep and commanding, rumbling with a natural power that brooked no disobedience. Galar looked around as Chief Enforcer Alerio Dyami strode into the room. The Outpost's commander had been checking on Riane and supervising the cleanup in the rest of the house.

A Viking Class Warlord, Dyami was even bigger and more powerfully built than Galar. He wore his black hair long in the traditional Warlord style, with glittering combat decorations worked into the single braid that hung beside his face. A tattoo in intricate lines of green and gold ran down the left side of his face—the symbol of House Dyami, which had genetically engineered him.

Unlike Galar, who wore neither tattoos nor beads. He hadn't even adopted the last name of his House; he'd taken his father's House name instead. He owed those Kasi bitches nothing after what they'd done to him and his family.

"Well, you called this one right on the money," Dyami told Galar as he joined the two beside the regenerator. "You said that police report looked like Jumper work, and it was."

"Yeah, but I thought it was your standard art thief. Which it wasn't."

The chief Enforcer's black eyes narrowed. "But why would a Xeran battleborg try to murder some twenty-first-century artist? He's certainly no run-of-the mill thief looking to make a fast galactor."

Galar turned a grim look toward the tube. "That's the question, isn't it?"

January 3, 1824
New York City

**A thunderous crack** and a flare of blue light made the carriage horses shy and toss their heads. The hack driver swore and hauled at the reins, bringing them back under control before they could bolt.

A flicker of movement drew his attention, and he glanced around. A woman stepped from the alley between two buildings, breathing hard, her face pale, red hair tangled and wild. For a moment she seemed to be wearing a strange, scandalously short skirt that bared the entire length of her legs from well above the knee. A strange leather bag swung from one arm.

The cabby blinked, shocked. Must be some kind of doxy . . .

She met his gaze, and just like that, she was properly attired in a forest green redingote pelisse in fine velvet, a matching feathered bonnet framing demure red curls. She hurried toward his cab.

He must have imagined that outlandish costume.

Automatically, the cabby swung down to open the door for her. So well-dressed and prosperous a lady would obviously have the funds to hire a hack. Though he did wonder what had happened to the ladies' maid who should be escorting her. . . .

"The Carlisle Arms, please," she told him in a soft, cultured voice as he handed her inside the cab.

He touched the brim of his hat and nodded. "Yes, miss," and closed the door with a thump.

Charlotte sat back against the leather squabs with a sigh of weary relief. She thought she'd finally lost Marcin, though it had cost her five Jumps to do it. She was running dangerously low on power, especially now that she had to project an illusion of being a lady of 1824.

Luckily, she'd known she was probably going to have to do some Jumps when she left the house. She had coins and paper money from several time periods tucked in her handbag, along with gemstones she could easily convert to cash.

Now if only Marcin would leave her alone long enough to rest and recharge her waning powers.

Still, she'd do whatever she had to. All that mattered was keeping Marcin from getting his hands on *them*.

*"Tell me it's not true."*

*"It's not true." His sensors picked up the spike in brain activity in the clear pattern of a formulating lie. She hadn't even bothered to try to conceal the reaction.*

*She smiled at him, catlike and feline, her eyes laughing. Laughing at his gullibility, at the way she'd so thoroughly played him to gain access to his investigation of the Xeran plot. Offering her "help," working with him for weeks, then seducing him, slowly, carefully, distracting him with her lush body and drugging sexuality. It had never occurred to him that she could be a double agent, that she could have infiltrated Vardonese Military Intelligence with intent to betray and kill.*

*He'd believed every lie out of her mouth. Especially when she'd told him she loved him.*

*The rage he felt was almost enough to drown out the pain.*

*"Do you know what you've done?" To Vardon. To the Galactic Union.*

*To him.*

*"Oh, yeah." She went for the tachyon pistol holstered at her hip. He grabbed for his own, but pain made him slow.*

*Agony exploded in his chest as she seared away his heart*

*with a blast of hot-white energy. The last thing he saw was her taunting smile.*

**Galar jerked upright** with the echo of his own hoarse scream in his ears. Panting, he fell back to his elbows against the mound of pillows.

The dream. He hadn't had it in two years. He wasn't really surprised he'd had it tonight.

Restlessly, he rolled from the bed and padded naked to the darkened window that took up most of one wall. *Polarization off,* he ordered the Outpost computer, and the window went fully transparent.

The light of the rising sun spilled across what would one day be called the Blue Ridge Mountains of Georgia. Mist cloaked their tree-covered flanks, painted now in the reds and oranges and vivid yellows of autumn. A hawk circled, gliding on rising thermals, great dark wings outspread.

The beauty of the mountains did its customary job. Galar felt the furious rhythm of his heart settle. He braced a bare shoulder against the cool glass and wiped his sweating forehead with the back of a wrist.

Tlain Morey always killed him in the dream. In reality, he'd been faster, but he'd still spent a month in regeneration, healing the left arm she'd almost seared away.

Jessica Kelly must have gotten to him more than he'd thought, if he was dreaming about Tlain again.

He'd always had a weakness for victims. Their vulnerability and pain never failed to get under his skin, no matter how hard he tried to armor himself against them.

He straightened his shoulders. Well, Kelly wouldn't be a problem for long. They'd be shipping her off to Temporal Rehab in a day or two. He'd just keep his distance until then.

*Morning briefing in sixty-five minutes,* his comp whispered in his mind.

Galar sighed and rubbed his hands over his face. He'd

only slept a couple of hours, but it would have to do. He moved to make his sprawling bed with the precision drummed into him at the Vardonese Military Academy years before. One of the Outpost's 'bots could have done the job, but he considered picking up after himself an exercise in personal discipline.

Tlain had taught him that maintaining discipline was the only way to avoid pain.

Job done, he gave the room a quick scan. Dark, gleaming shelving ran along the wall opposite the window, a match for the bed's heavy headboard and the wall panels that concealed his clothes and weapons. The shelves held mementoes from his temporal travels—a few books bound in calfskin, beeswax candles in massive golden candlesticks, a rapier with an intricate basket hilt. Trids of his parents, one of him standing with them at his Vardonese Academy graduation. Baird, his Comanche Class Warlord father, tall and dark and massive, with the red and blue of a House Arvid tattoo spilling down his face. His mother, Alina, blond and lithe, with the build of a Samurai Class Warfem, the colors of Kasi House marking her cheek. They both looked so proud.

He'd damned near destroyed them both. The son of the vice admiral of Vardonese Military Intelligence and one of its most decorated senior officers, played for a fool by a double agent. A scandal like that could have ended his parents' careers, as well as his own. It was a good thing Galar had managed to turn the situation around before it exploded in their collective faces.

It all began when a communications officer in the Vardonese Interstellar Fleet had attracted the interest of Galar's superiors in military intelligence. Galar had been assigned to investigate whether the man was indeed selling information on ship movements to the Xerans.

Senior Femmat Agent Tlain Morey promptly volunteered her assistance. Since Galar had known her for years—they worked in the same intelligence division—he'd gratefully accepted. Over the months that followed, he'd become entranced by the Femmat's sensuality, beauty, and intelligence.

Luckily she wasn't as smart as either of them thought.

Three months later, Galar had the officer under surveillance when the spy met with Tlain one dark night in a city park. They'd acted so transparently suspicious, Galar had found himself hoping they were having an affair. After all, the Femmat knew Galar was watching the suspected spy in a variety of imagizer disguises. Why would she be so stupid?

He'd later realized Tlain simply enjoyed the risk that he might be watching. Taunting him was all part of the fun.

Driven to discover the truth one way or another, Galar had cracked Tlain's secret computer unit, kept hidden in a diamond bracelet. He would never forget the cold horror he'd felt as he'd read her matter-of-fact account of her espionage activities. She'd been working for the Xerans for years as a leader of the spy ring, which was even larger than Galar and his superiors had thought.

Sickened, he'd shot the file to headquarters and confronted her with the evidence before killing her in that last explosive confrontation.

Thus, instead of getting cashiered for stupidity above and beyond the call of duty, he'd received a commendation.

Yet Galar had known he could no longer serve in Vardonese Military Intelligence. He couldn't risk another mistake that might destroy his parents' careers, so he'd sought a post as an Enforcer in the Galactic Union's Temporal Enforcement Agency. He'd spent the last decade working his way up the ranks.

Atoning for his gullibility.


**As Galar strode** along the labyrinth of corridors toward the main briefing hall, he downloaded the Outpost's DNA results on the Xeran. He'd be expected to present a report on the night's events, and he needed to pin down a few more details.

A moment later, his heart sank. Seven Hells, it was worse than he'd thought.

He stalked into the main briefing hall with five minutes to spare. After ordering a cup of stimchai from the wall vend-ser, Galar dropped into one of the seats mounted on curving risers surrounding the central stage. The dark blue cushions shifted around his body, adjusting to his height and weight until the chair cradled him comfortably. He sipped his stim-chai and brooded.

Fifty Enforcers of various ranks filled the seats around him. Most were either human or close enough to the root stock to fake it. A few, like Frieka, could pass themselves off as Terran animals. To work undercover as a time traveler on old Earth, you couldn't appear visibly alien.

"I did it! I finally got the murderous son of a bitch!"

Galar looked up as Enforcer Jiri Cadell half-danced up the aisle and threw herself into the seat next to him, a broad grin on her long, elegant face. Senior Enforcer Ando Cadell, looking tolerant, dropped beside her.

"It took me six hours of interrogation, but Usko Vappu finally admitted he killed all those women. The prick." An expression of catlike satisfaction lit her tilted green eyes.

"She's going to be insufferable for at least a month." Cadell rolled his eyes, but there was love in the smile he sent his wife. He was a big, broad-shouldered cyborg, a patient investigator who was painstaking rather than brilliant. Gray salted his brush-cut cobalt hair, though at seventy he was just barely middle aged.

"Nah." Jiri folded her arms behind her head. "I figure this is worth a good two months of insufferability. At least." She was fifteen years younger than her husband, fit and strongly muscled. There was no gray at all in her own long sable braid.

"All right, folks, quiet down." Chief Enforcer Dyami stepped up to the massive transparent podium. "I want to get this briefing on the road." He couldn't have had much more sleep than Galar, but he looked as fresh and bright-eyed as a recruiting trid.

Dyami ticked through the agenda with his usual efficiency. The Outpost mainframe spent its considerable computing power chewing over reams of data on historical crimes to determine which ones were likely to have been committed by time travelers. Each week it generated a list for Dyami's consideration. He, in turn, used the daily briefing to assign the most likely of those cases to various Enforcers, who would investigate further to determine whether some morally challenged Jumper had indeed been responsible. If not, it was up to officials of that particular time period to catch the perpetrator.

Next came the reports on confirmed temporal crimes. Jiri stood up to brief the group on her Jumpkiller investigation. Galar couldn't blame her for the obvious triumph in her voice. She'd worked the case for over a year before finally tracking Vappu down.

The Itaran, who made historical documentaries, had confessed to killing fifty-two women during Jumps spanning four centuries and three continents. Jiri curled a disgusted lip as she recounted the sick bastard's smug description of his crimes.

"The Galactic Union Temporal Prosecutor tells me Vappu'll spend the rest of his life on the Gorgon penal colony," she finished with grim satisfaction. "May he rot there."

As Jiri seated herself, her husband rose to recount his own progress. Ando was working a string of fires he believed had been set to cover up jewel heists. "I've found traces of twenty-third-century accelerants at each scene," the Senior Enforcer said with a grim smile of satisfaction. "When I finally catch the dickhole, I should have no problem getting a conviction."

Enforcer Clar Vanda was next, describing the murders of fifteen temporal tourists who'd gone to Philadelphia for the signing of the Declaration of Independence. All fifteen had been shot with a shard rifle—not exactly a weapon common in the eighteenth century. Their tour guide had gone on the run after looting their respective financial accounts. Vanda was working with Galactic Union Interstellar Investigations on tracking the woman down.

Finally Dyami gave Galar a faint nod, and he stood to report on his own case. He outlined the events of the night before in terse, pointedly unemotional terms. Even so, an angry mutter rumbled over the Enforcer crowd when he described the Xeran's knifing Riane.

Regen or no regen, nothing pissed off TE agents like an attack on their own. One rule had remained the same over the centuries: you kept your hands off law enforcement. If you didn't, they'd hunt you down like soji dragons after a snakebird.

"The Outpost computer has completed its analysis of the subject's DNA." A three-dimensional image of the Xeran appeared in the center of the stage, twice life-sized, rotating slowly in the air as Galar spoke. He was a big bastard, of course—that went without saying. He had the aggressively masculine kind of face Xeran genetic engineers favored, all cheekbones and chin, so that his head sat on his thick neck like a stone block. His eyes were a demonic red, with thin slit pupils. Two sets of skull implants jutted from his shaved head, a larger pair curving out like a bull's horns, two shorter ones protruding from his forehead. Both were heavily engraved with fine, intricate designs in a glittering blood red.

Xerans had a taste for melodrama.

"Colonel Cyrek Marcin is a heavy combat battleborg with Xeran Interstellar Intelligence," Galar said. "According to our own Galactic Union Interstellar Intelligence, he specializes in the assassination of political and military targets.

GUII has been sending agents after him for years, but he keeps killing them."

Dyami lifted a brow. "Yet our little artist stopped him in his tracks. Smart girl."

"Lucky girl. Unfortunately, that kind of luck doesn't last. And I have a feeling he's not after her because she paints very expensive, very pretty pictures. This isn't a simple art theft. Something else is going on here."

The chief's expression turned grim. "I suspect you're right, Master Enforcer."

The meeting wrapped up ten minutes later. Galar gestured to catch Dyami's attention, then walked over to join him off to the side for a low-voiced conversation.

"We can't afford to send Kelly to the Rehab Center," he told the commander. "Security at that facility won't have a prayer of stopping Marcin if he comes after her again."

Dyami folded his powerful arms and frowned. "And he's not the kind to give up on a target."

Galar nodded. "He'd find it a lot more difficult to get to her here, behind the Outpost's shields."

The chief gave him a sharp, cool look. "This isn't a halfway house, Master Enforcer. We need to bounce this one to GUII. Let them protect her."

A chill of pure, elemental fear crept down Galar's spine, not for himself but for Jessica. With an effort, he managed a cool tone. "They've lost a dozen agents to Marcin, Chief. Kelly would be dead inside a week."

"You think you can do better?"

Galar blinked. "Me?"

"We can't let her run around loose. And if you're right, Marcin's going to try for her."

He shifted uneasily. "I thought Dona Astryr and Ivar Terje could keep an eye on her. Given their cybernetic enhancements . . ."

"Sorry, Master Enforcer, this is your job," Dyami interrupted. "From what I saw in that house when we Jumped in last night, you already have a rapport with the girl. She's going to need a friendly face to help her get through this with her sanity intact."

Every instinct Galar had howled a warning, but he knew a direct order when he heard one. "Aye, sir."

Dyami sighed. "You're a damned good investigator, Galar. Steady, coolheaded, disciplined. And there's no other officer I'd rather have leading my people into a combat situation."

Galar's brows flew up as he stared at his commander. Where had this conversational detour come from? "Thank you, sir."

"However, you do have one serious flaw. A good leader engages his people's loyalty, and you don't. In fact, you've got a reputation for being an icy son of a bitch."

He stiffened. "I wasn't aware winning popularity contests was part of my job."

"No, dammit, but you do have to be open enough to your people to understand what makes them tick. You've got emotional shields three feet thick, and until you can learn to drop them, you'll only be half the leader you could be."

The statement stung just enough to show it had an element of truth. "What does this have to do with guarding Jessica Kelly?"

Dyami gave him a slight, wintry smile. "You'll figure it out. Now, I suggest you swing by the infirmary and check on your new charge."

Galar gave him a stiff nod, turned on his heel, and stalked away.

Just what he didn't need. Too much time with a woman who was already too far under his skin.

# · 4 ·

**Sometimes he liked to entertain himself by imagin-**
ing how they'd all react if they knew what he was. That
rigid fuck Galar, for example, or Chief Enforcer Dyami.

He could just imagine their incredulous rage, their fury
that he'd fooled them all so throughly for so long. Just the
thought of it put a grin on his face.

They'd destroy him if they could, arrest him, charge him.
Shame him. He'd be paraded before the public, branded a
traitor and a spy. If, that is, he survived to go to trial. The
Xer would do their damnedest to see him dead in an effort
to protect both themselves and the spy ring they'd so pains-
takingly created.

His life balanced on a knife blade. And he loved it. The
hot exhilaration of spying, of knowing that he could be discovered at any time, that his life could be dashed apart if he
wasn't quick enough, clever enough, strong enough. . . . It
was all sweeter than any drug.

They'd assume it was the money—the truly outrageous sums the Xer funneled into his carefully buried accounts. But money had nothing at all to do with it.

So it was that when the courier 'bot appeared at the door to his quarters that afternoon, he relished the familiar kick of excitement that stormed through his blood. Wearing an expression of no more than mild interest, he ordered the door open and let the little globe dart inside.

He knew who it was from, of course. Given this morning's briefing, he'd been expecting it.

The courier was a nondescript little device with just enough juice to manage a time Jump. It could as easily have been carrying a message from his mother.

It stopped in front of his eyes and floated there while it scanned his retinas and confirmed his identity. A moment later, a slot opened in its belly and a tiny capsule dropped into his waiting hand.

He popped the capsule between thumb and forefinger and smeared it across his forehead, leaving a streak of cool liquid on his skin. In seconds, the nanobots in the liquid seeped into his skin and started their voyage to his brain. The 'bots were keyed to his DNA; they would disgorge their message to no one else.

He moved to the bed and lay down, anticipating the disorientation the message would bring. Soft, sibilant, a voice began to whisper in his mind—his spymaster, the mole buried high in the upper echelons of Temporal Enforcement. He had no idea who the mole was, though he meant to find out.

He could use the insurance if everything went to the Seven Hells.

*Holt has infected the primitive Jessica Kelly,* the mole began in that sexless, unidentifiable mental voice. *You've got to kill her now before she activates. Try not to reveal yourself if you can help it, but take care of her regardless. Our Xeran friends consider it a priority.*

He opened his eyes as his eyebrows rose in interested

surprise. They wanted him to kill the girl right under Galar's nose?

A slow, deadly grin of pure anticipation spread across his face.

**The infirmary took** up one entire level of the Outpost, and there were times it needed every centimeter of the space. The offices used by the doctors and nursing staff surrounded a soaring open central ward, softly lit and filled with gentle, soothing music. When Galar walked in, he counted fifteen glowing globes arranged in the ward's center. An unusually high patient count, though admittedly there'd been more after that tourist group had gotten caught in the earthquake.

Each globe held a bed inside a sterile field designed to both protect its occupant from infection and maintain privacy. On the outside of the globes, shifting three-dimensional images displayed the patient's vitals.

He found Chogan standing in the center of the ring of globes, sipping a cup of stimchai with the greedy relish of a woman who has been craving one far too long.

"You seem to have a full house."

Chogan curled a delicate lip. "Two stagecoaches full of tourists collided while being chased by an Apache raiding party. Both of 'em overturned. I was just barely able to dispatch a team to get them back before the whole lot got kacked. It's like I always say . . ."

Galar grinned and finished the sentence for her. ". . . Time travel is not for morons."

"And yet, they always think it's some kind of goddamned game. I keep telling people, the temporals don't play. And this bunch brought kids. I spent the morning digging an arrow out of a ten-year-old."

He winced. "Ouch."

"Yeah. Ouch." She shook her head with a sigh of pure disgust, then straightened her shoulders. "But you're here about your vic. Given the morning's adventures, I haven't had a chance to put in a request to transfer her to the Rehab Center, but . . ."

"We're not sending her to the Center, Doc. She's got a Xeran military assassin after her. We're keeping her here."

Chogan froze with her cup half-lifted to her mouth, staring at him over its rim. "I'm not trained to provide temporal rehabilitation to a native, Master Enforcer. Besides, I've got my hands full as it is."

"Nobody expects you to keep an eye on her." Galar managed not to snarl. "That's my assignment."

"Yours?" Dr. Chogan's iridescent green brows flew up as she regarded Galar in surprise. "Do you have any idea how delicate it is to rehab someone who's been temporally displaced? Besides, I've already started the EDI. She'll be unconscious until it's finished." Almost to herself, Chogan added, "I'd rather keep her out until we transfer her to the Center. She'll find all this traumatic enough as it is."

"Unfortunately, that's not an option." Galar ran a thumb along his lower lip in thought. EDIs—educational data implants—were imprinted directly onto a user's memory. Once the brain integrated the EDI's information, it could be used just like knowledge acquired through reading or personal experience. Galar could download and use EDIs instantly through his computer, but with humans like Jessica, nanobots had to do the cerebral imprinting. "What's included in the basic ed program, anyway?"

Chogan shrugged. "Galactic Standard, an elementary knowledge of twenty-third-century technology and science. The same thing any kid knows by the time he's ten."

"Can you add an unarmed combat routine? And basic weapons use too. I have a feeling she's going to need it."

Chogan swallowed a mouthful of stimchai and meditated over the taste a moment. "Well, yeah, but she's not going to be able to use it unless somebody works with her to get those skills integrated. She doesn't have a neuronet computer like

you Enforcer types to help her absorb what she's downloaded. Somebody's going to have to help her. That's what
rehab is for."

"So I'll help her."

Chogan looked at him. "Oh, yeah. That'll work."

He frowned. "What do you mean by that?"

"Empathy and a delicate touch are vital in rehabing a native. Neither are phrases that leap to mind when I hear the
word 'Warlord.' And *you* . . ." She snapped her teeth together
with a click. "Never mind."

Stung, he glowered at her. "Look, I don't like this any
better than you do, but the Chief Enforcer gave me a mission, and I'm going to carry it out. Implant that combat data
and call me when you wake her up."

Chogan's eyes narrowed. "I'm not one of your subordinates, Master Enforcer!"

He drew a deep breath and hissed it out between his
teeth. "Dr. Chogan, *please* add the combat EDI." Without
waiting to see if she'd agree, Galar swung around and
stalked out.

And pretended not to hear Chogan's muttered "Dickhole."

*The dream was confusing, frightening. Starkly vivid. An
incomprehensible babble of alien language that gradually
became understandable. First a word here, a word there,
then sentences streaming through her consciousness in liquid, musical phrases.*

*Next came images. Strange shapes flashing against the stars,
oddly beautiful forms she suddenly realized were ships. People
with skin colors she'd never seen before—matte black, metallic gold, a shimmering emerald green. Hair like flame,
peacock feathers, or filaments of silver tinsel. Too many
fingers, too many toes. Tails. Aliens that couldn't possibly be
human, and yet were unmistakably intelligent as they stroked*

*controls with delicate frond fingers, their eyes huge and opal-escent.*

*Dragons soaring against a double sunrise, long reptilian tails whipping.*

*The dream darkened then. A brutal face, inches from her own, slit pupils glaring, moonlight glinting off horns. "You're like her now!"*

*The flash of a blade, an explosion of pain . . .*

*Charlotte, standing over her with a knife. Pricking her finger. Blood dripping, one slow, hot drop at a time. . . .*

*A shape screaming toward the curve of Earth, so blinding white, her eyes ached. . . .*

**"Nooo!" Jessica's eyes** flashed wide as she jerked awake.

"It's okay, it's okay." The voice was deep, soothing. "You were having a nightmare."

Cautiously, she turned her head and found a big blond man sitting beside the bed. After a moment of disorientation, she recognized him. The cop who'd saved her. Galen? No. Galar.

Her mouth felt like sand. "Water?" she croaked. The word sounded wrong somehow, but she didn't know why.

"Of course." He stood, and she blinked. She hadn't remembered him being quite so . . . stunning. He had to be a good six inches over six feet, with the leanly powerful build of a professional athlete. The scaled suit he'd worn had been replaced with something in a dark blue fabric, also piped with silver. The stark color called attention to the bright gleam of his blond hair and the translucent gold of his eyes. His face was just as striking, narrow and angular with an aquiline nose and a firm, aggressive chin. His cheekbones were chiseled and elegant, his blond brows thick over intelligent eyes that searched hers intently.

She watched him turn to a console by the bed. He murmured

something to it, and a cup appeared through a small doorway in the console. He handed it to her.

Jess took it, staring at the console with a frown. A word teased her tongue, and she spoke it. "Vendser."

Galar gave her a faint smile. "That's right. It's a food vendser."

But the words still sounded wrong, composed of strange syllables and odd, lyrical grammar. Jessica froze in the act of lifting the cup to her mouth. "We're not speaking English."

"No." He sat down in the chair again and leaned forward, bracing his elbows on his knees.

A shaft of cold stabbed through her. "But I don't speak anything except English."

"You do now."

Words crowded to the tip of her tongue, but they made no sense. She drained the cup in one long, desperate gulp, hoping to clear her befuddled mind. "Galactic Standard." Both hands curled around the empty cup in her lap. "We're speaking Galactic Standard." The knowledge was suddenly right there, but she had no idea what it meant. Galactic Standard? It sounded like something from a science fiction novel.

He nodded. "Yes, that's right."

Fear clicked down Jess's spine on icy claws. Flashes of imagery filled her head, things she could almost understand. Things that made no sense, words she had no frame of reference for.

"Stop it!" Jess didn't know if she was talking to him or to her own suddenly rebellious brain. "I don't know what the hell is going on, but stop it!" She flung the covers aside and rolled out of bed.

Alarm widened Galar's remarkable eyes. He came out of his chair and moved to block her. "Jessica, calm down. It's all right—you're safe."

"Fuck that!" Jess bared her teeth, breathing hard as she fought to control the panic that threatened to send her into pointless flight. "There are things in my head that don't belong there! Did you do this to me?"

"It's just an educational data implant. There are things you need to know if you're going to . . ."

*"Take it out!"* Alien images and strange words flashed through her head, building to a blinding, incomprehensible roar. Panic clawed at her. "Take it out!"

"Jessic—"

She danced forward and slammed a punch right at his chiseled jaw.

**Galar blocked the** punch by sheer reflex—not that it would have hurt him if it had landed. He couldn't help but notice she'd executed it perfectly. Apparently she'd integrated the combat EDI—at least if you pissed her off enough to use it.

Lips peeling back from her teeth, she went for his eyes with clawing nails. He grabbed both wrists and forced her back down on the bed, riding her body with his, trying to control her wild, writhing struggles with his greater weight. "Jessica, calm down, dammit! You're all right! It's just an EDI. It's not going to hurt you!"

"I didn't tell you to put that in my head! I don't want it there!" Fear and rage blazed in too-wide blue eyes. "You've got no right to tamper with my brain!"

Running footsteps sounded behind him. "Move, Galar!" Dr. Chogan snapped.

He twisted aside. The doctor snaked a hand past him and clapped it against Jessica's forehead. Galar smelled the sharp, medicinal scent of a capsule breaking, spilling its drug cargo onto the girl's skin. A moment later, her eyes rolled back, and she went limp under him.

He rolled off her to find Chogan staring grimly at the two of them. "I warned you."

Galar raked a hand through his hair. "Yeah, you did."

Feeling helpless, he stared down at Jessica as she sprawled unconscious on the bed.

She looked delicate in the thin infirmary sleep suit, particularly compared to the lean, muscled strength of the War-fems and female Enforcers he was used to. The memory of her terrified rage made something ache in his chest. He rubbed an absent circle over his heart. "Why did she react like that?"

Chogan sighed. "You and I grew up absorbing implanted knowledge; it's natural to us. But to a temporal native, data implants are an inexplicable mental rape. Some of them even go insane."

Galar stared at her, sickened. "Why in the hell do we do it, then?"

"Because when you take somebody from the past and stick them in the twenty-third century, surrounded by tech they've never seen and don't understand, they don't do well," Chogan explained patiently. "A good rehab specialist can trigger the integration gradually enough that they can cope. Which is why we need to send her to the Center."

"We can't do that, Doctor. The Xeran would kill her, half the staff, and anybody else who happened to get in the way. He's a heavy-combat battleborg. They wouldn't have a prayer."

She frowned at him. "Why is somebody like that after this poor girl?"

"Believe me, we've all asked that question." He rocked back on his heels and ran a thumb over his lower lip, his mind racing. "Do we have a rehab specialist EDI?"

"Probably, but it would take me too long to integrate and use it. Unlike some, I don't have a neuronet combat computer."

"I do."

She stared at him, visibly startled. "You're really serious about this, aren't you?"

"When I'm given a mission, I carry it out."

"Warlords." Chogan scrubbed both hands over her face. "You're all crazy. All right, I'll call it up for you."

He watched her move to the main console and bend to murmur instructions to it. A moment later his computer spoke in his mind. *Infirmary computer offers a temporal rehabilitation specialist EDI. No virus detected.*

*Download it.* He braced himself.

Information poured into his mind in a torrent of words, images, and concepts. He didn't fight it—just let the flood surge through him like a river of light. The kind he'd experienced so many times before.

What would it be like to endure that surging flood for the first time?

Galar opened his eyes to find Chogan watching him. "On second thought," she said, "I'm just as glad I don't have a neuronet comp. I thought for a minute there you were having a seizure."

He rolled his shoulders, trying to banish the knots that had gathered between his shoulder blades during the download. His mouth tasted faintly of copper, and his head ached violently, but he ignored both sensations with the ease of long practice.

As always when Galar absorbed an EDI, everything seemed almost ridiculously clear now. He no longer felt helpless in the face of Jessica's confusion, anger, and pain. Not that helping her integrate her new knowledge would be easy, but at least there were proven techniques he could use, and he understood the psychological processes at work.

There was *nothing* he hated as much as feeling helpless and ignorant.

"It was worth it." Galar gave the doctor a faint smile. "I know how to help her now."

Chogan lifted a brow. "Oh?"

"I need to get her the hell out of here for a few hours. Give her a more familiar situation to deal with."

"Like what?"

"I think the expression was—a date."

**Jessica came awake** to the crackle of a fire and the warmth of a man's arms. She opened drowsy eyes to find the golden glow of a campfire dancing in a circle of stones.

"Feeling better?" The rumble in her ear was deep, calming. The words were English.

She knew that voice. "Galar?" Her tongue felt thick.

"Yeah, it's me."

She frowned, remembering she'd been really pissed at him. Hadn't she . . . hit him? But why? What had . . . ?

As if that question had broken some mental dam, strange words and concepts began to rush into her mind, a chaotic, terrifying flood of information she had no memory of acquiring. Jess stiffened, sucking in a hard breath like a drowning woman.

Arms tightened around her with the faint creak of leather. "Don't think about that."

"What . . . ? You're not . . ." Words crammed their way onto her tongue until she was reduced to helpless stammering, overwhelmed by alien ideas, by thoughts that made no sense.

Men from the future. Spaceships. Strange worlds. Was she losing her mind? "What's happening to me?" Her voice shook, high and breathless.

"Don't think." Galar's voice was low and calm and deep. Soothing, like the big hands that rubbed slowly over her shoulders. "Just breathe with me. In. Out."

Fighting mindless panic, Jess managed to pull in one breath, then two, then three, breathing in time to the muscular chest slowly rising and falling against her back. Gradually, her terror began to abate.

"Yes," he said softly. "Think only about now, about this moment. Look around you. Smell the air. Taste it. Look at the trees, the mountains, the sky. You know these things. You understand these things. You're safe here."

Obeying him, she gazed around the clearing. They lay on a warm blanket on a bed of crackling autumn leaves. Trees surrounded them in a half circle, blazing with the brilliant reds and golds and oranges of October.

Just beyond the colorful branches lay a steep drop-off overlooking the rolling sweep of a familiar mountain range. The Blue Ridge. They were in the Blue Ridge Mountains, not on some alien world in some alien time.

Safe.

Jess took another cleansing breath and felt her panicked muscles relax another fraction. The air smelled cool and deliciously crisp, scented with wood smoke.

Not threatening. Not alien. Familiar.

"There," he murmured in her ear. "That's better."

"Yeah." Abruptly she was aware of him as he half-reclined with her resting against his muscular chest.

*For a man I don't even know, I've spent a lot of time in his arms. . . .*

And it felt good. Good not to fight. Good not to be afraid. Good to be safe.

Jess took another deep breath, conscious now of his scent, equal parts masculinity and leather. She could hear the strong, even thud of his heart as her head rested against his chest.

*But that's an illusion,* unwelcome knowledge warned. *He's not the ordinary man he appears. He's something else. Something not quite human.*

She tensed.

"Shhhhhhhhh," Galar breathed in her ear. "Nobody's going to hurt you."

God, she needed to believe that. Had to believe that. She thought she'd go crazy if she didn't.

"Breathe," he insisted softly. "Don't think. Breathe."

For a long moment, she concentrated on doing just that,

looking out across the fire at the mountains beyond. Until finally, painfully, her fear abated again.

He wasn't going to hurt her, no matter what he really was. He'd saved her. He cared. He held her in his arms and tried to soothe her fears. Those weren't the actions of some kind of cold, alien man.

"Are you hungry?" he asked, his voice a comforting thrum in his chest. "There's food." He gestured, pointing out a basket that stood on one corner of the blanket. Folds of red-checkered fabric protruding from its closed wicker top, and steam rose gently from it, smelling deliciously of fried chicken.

Jess's stomach rumbled; she was ravenous. She found herself wondering how long it had been since she'd last eaten. "That does smell good."

He eased out from behind her, laying her back against a thick pile of pillows. They felt warm, as if heated from the inside. Comforting. She snuggled into them and watched Galar move to the basket and kneel, flipping back the lid.

He was dressed in jeans and a cream cable-knit sweater worn under a black leather jacket. His golden hair blazed in the light of the setting sun, and his shoulders looked very broad. The jeans stretched tight over the long, powerful muscles of his thighs.

He reached into the basket and pulled out a couple of plates, then started loading them with food. Silverware clinked, and fragrant steam wafted into the air.

Looking down at herself, Jessica realized she, too, was dressed in jeans, along with a red fleece sweatshirt under a blue-jean jacket.

Galar knelt beside her again to present her with a plate and a fork, then handed over a cup of steaming tea. She surveyed the meal a little dubiously, then relaxed. Fried chicken, potato salad, corn on the cob, a buttery golden biscuit. Familiar and homey.

Jess picked up the chicken breast and took a bite. It

crunched, flooding her mouth with juice and the taste of tender flesh. Experimentally, she tried the tea next. It was just as perfect to her Southern girl taste, sweet and strong and wonderfully hot.

Galar sat down cross-legged next to her and settled his own plate on his lap. Dubiously, he picked up a chicken leg and studied it as if he'd never seen one before, then took a cautious bite. He blinked in surprise and licked a crumb of breading off his lips. "This is good."

"Yes." Chewing, she gazed out over the mountains. They looked like blue, rolling waves in the orange glow of the sunset. The food and familiar surroundings gave her courage to ask the questions beating so demandingly in her brain. "Why? Why did you bring me here? What *are* you?"

Galar looked up from probing his potato salad with a cautious fork. "A man." He gave her a faint smile. "Just a man."

"No, not just a man. You're from the future." She knew that, though she couldn't have said just how. "You and those other people who appeared in my living room. And that . . . thug. The one with the horns, who stabbed me."

Galar sighed. "Yes. We're from the future."

Hearing that impossible knowledge confirmed threatened to tip Jess back into panic, but she fought off the fear with gritted teeth. "I'm not crazy."

"No. You're not crazy. We gave you a data implant to help you understand our language, our time, but you're having trouble processing it. I'm trying to help you."

"This . . . data implant. That's where all those weird images and words are coming from?"

"Exactly."

"I don't want it." Her heart started pounding again as she felt the pressure of unwanted knowledge. "Take it out."

"I can't. You need it if you're going to survive in our time."

"So put me back where I came from!" The words burst from her, heartfelt and desperate.

"I can't. The Xeran will try to kill you again. And without us to protect you, he'll succeed."

Jess remembered the cold agony of the horned thug's knife. Automatically, her hand went to her stomach, tugged up the hem of her shirt. Her belly was smooth, unmarred. "He stabbed me. Where's the—?"

"Our doctor healed you."

Jess frowned, realizing she must have been unconscious for weeks, judging by the complete lack of any sign of injury. "How long have I been out?"

Galar shrugged. "A couple of days."

"Is that all? Wonderingly, she stroked her fingers over her unmarred skin. A new thought made her frown in puzzlement. "Why did he attack me? I never did anything to him. Was he crazy?"

"He wasn't crazy. But as to exactly why he came after you, we have no idea." He cocked his blond head, studying her face. "Are you ready to talk about it?"

She considered the question cautiously. "Yeah, I need to understand what's going on."

"What do you remember?"

Jess shrugged. "I was asleep. Next thing I knew, this guy grabbed me, jerked me off the bed, and slammed me against the wall. Choked me." She rubbed her arms, feeling again the echo of that icy terror. "The guy . . . What did you call him, a . . . Xeran?"

"That's right."

"Was he an . . . alien?" She felt self-conscious just asking the question, but Galar didn't look amused.

"No. He'd have looked a lot weirder than that."

Jessica snorted. "He was weird enough as it was. Big. Really big. More than seven feet tall." She closed her eyes, calling up the memory of his face with an artist's attention to detail. "Probably about three hundred pounds or so. He had some kind of metal horns protruding from his head. . . ."

"Skull implants. The Xerans decorate their heads with spikes, horns, and hoops."

"Sounds like somebody's compensating for something." She grinned at him, holding her fingers a fraction apart.

Galar grinned back. "Could be."

"Anyway, this guy had a square, kind of brutal face. I could do a sketch for you, if it would help."

"No need. We've already identified him. What else can you remember? What did he say to you?"

He listened intently as she related everything she could remember. His eyes narrowed when she told him the Xeran was looking for Charlotte. It was obvious he didn't like that idea at all. Jess could understand that; she wasn't crazy about it either.

Why did an alien assassin want her roommate, anyway?

## · 5 ·

❦

**"You're sure it was Charlotte he was after?" Galar**
frowned, his golden brows lowering.

"He kept asking where she was." Jessica shrugged. "I
told him I didn't know."

"Where *did* she go? She wasn't in the house—we
looked."

"I have no idea. For all I knew, she was hiding in a closet
or something. She was still home when I went to bed."

Galar nodded, his expression abstracted. "I saw her walk
into the living room before I lost consciousness. When I
came to, she was gone, and the Xeran was in your bedroom."
He ran a thumb thoughtfully over his full lower lip.

"Wait." Jessica frowned at him, putting aside her plate.
"What? You were there *before* the attack?"

"We were watching the house." He said it in an offhanded
way, as if it didn't occur to her she might object.

*"Why?"*

"We knew you were going to be attacked."

Her jaw dropped as incredulous anger stirred. "And you didn't warn me?"

He shrugged impressive shoulders. "We didn't know who the attacker was going to be."

"So? You couldn't have called and said, 'Hey, you might want to get out of the freaking house before the psycho tries to kill you'?"

"No."

"Why the hell not?"

"Because that's not the way it works." His expression was patient, reasonable—and, to Jessica, infuriating.

"Since *when*?"

"It's complicated."

"This entire thing is insanely complicated. No, it's just plain insane. Explain it anyway!"

He rested his forearms across his knees and sighed. "We're not allowed to even attempt to change history. He was supposed to stab you. There was nothing we could do to prevent it."

Jess opened her mouth to blurt something outraged, then slowly closed it as more of that upsetting knowledge burst into her consciousness. "It's not just that you're not allowed to change history," she said slowly. "You can't, can you? At all. It can't be changed." She knew that in the same maddening way she knew he was from the future.

He gave her an approving smile, like a teacher whose student has made a major mental breakthrough. "Exactly."

For a moment she almost understood why, but the knowledge seemed to dance away. Before she could try to drag it back, Galar asked, "You said the Xeran told you he could smell Charlotte's blood on you, and that's when he stabbed you. But when did she cut herself?"

Still groping for understanding, Jess grumbled, "I have no idea."

"Do you remember anything she did that was . . . unusual?"

"No. Charlotte's just a really nice person. A freelance writer. And a lot more successful at her art than I am, because she makes a good living. Why would some time-traveling psycho want to kill her?"

"He knew something. Something about Charlotte, something about you. He said you were dangerous."

Jessica blinked. "Me? I'm a *painter*. I'm about as dangerous as a bag of marshmallows."

Galar arched a blond brow. "Aren't you the same woman who torched a Xeran battleborg?"

"*Battleborg?*" *A genetically engineered Xeran warrior with cybernetic implants,* her mind supplied. This time she found the implanted knowledge more welcome than overwhelming. "He's from a world called Xer, which is the capital of some kind of totalitarian interstellar empire. Kind of quasi-religious. An enemy of your government, the Galactic Union." Thoughtfully, Jess continued, "But both you and the Xerans are descended from humans. Right?"

He gave her another of those pleased smiles. "Right."

She rocked back, thinking. There were so many things she almost understood, yet there were all these frustrating holes in her knowledge. "Why did you save me?"

Galar blinked. "Why wouldn't we?"

"I'm from—what? Three hundred years in your past?"

He shrugged. "About that."

"So what difference would it make if I died? Why go to all the trouble of Jumping through time to keep that Xeran from turning me into sushi?"

He picked up the ear of corn from his plate and took a bite, his teeth very white as they closed on the golden kernels. He chewed, visibly considering what to say, then swallowed. "I'm an agent with Temporal Enforcement. My job is to keep time travelers like the Xeran from preying on people like you."

"In that case, thanks for saving my ass."

"Actually, you saved your own with that turpentine trick."

"Except for the whole bleeding-to-death thing, which is what I would have done if you hadn't gotten me to a doctor."

He inclined his head. "Well, yeah. But still, for a human to accomplish even that much against a battleborg is no mean feat."

Battleborgs. People from the future. "I can't believe I'm having this conversation." Jess watched her breath puff white in the air, though her backside felt toasty against the pile of heated pillows. Her gaze slid to Galar, sprawled on the blanket braced on one elbow, biceps bunching beneath the sleeve of his leather coat, his body long and powerful—and more mouthwatering than the picnic.

He looked up and caught her watching him. His golden eyes crinkled at the corners, and his teeth flashed white against his tanned face.

A man from the future who looked a hell of a lot like the man of her dreams. . . .

**It was working.** Getting her away from the alien environment of the Outpost, speaking English, feeding her familiar food—it was all helping her cope with the flood of strange knowledge. Add to that her natural intelligence and strong will, and she'd already begun to process and accept her situation.

Which was a damn good thing, because the mess she was in was even more complicated than Galar had thought. It had never been about Jessica at all. The Xeran's target had apparently been Charlotte Holt all along.

But why?

"You said you knew this Xeran was going to come after me." Jess looked up from her plate, her gaze sharp. "How did you know?"

"Police report," Galar told her absently. "Anything that involves a famous artist and murder raises red flags with us, particularly when no body is found."

She shook her head sharply, as though not believing her ears. "Okay, wait. Famous artist? What? Me? Since when? And murder? I'm not dead."

"We know that, but the police don't." Tersely, he outlined the conclusions the Claremont County coroner had drawn based on the amount of blood on the scene.

"So they do think I'm dead." Her eyes widened in realization. "Ruby thinks I'm dead!" She rolled to her feet. "I've got to tell her I'm okay. How do I get back?"

He sighed. She wasn't going to like this at all. "You don't."

Jessica frowned at him. "What do you mean? You brought me here, you can take me back."

"No, actually, I can't. As far as everyone from your time is concerned, you're a murder victim. History tells us you were never seen again. That means you don't go back. Ever."

"You don't understand. Ruby's got a record. A couple of minor drug possession charges, a DUI. And there was this bimbo she got in a fight with over a guy. The bimbo went to the hospital, and my sister was charged with aggravated assault and battery. Nothing serious, but it'd be just enough to make the cops wonder if she killed me. The family's always the first ones they look at anyway."

He nodded. "You're right. She and her dealer were both suspects initially. Luckily for your sister, though, twenty people saw them together in a bar at the same time the cops believed the attack took place. They were cleared."

Jessica sagged in relief. "Well, that's something, anyway. But, Galar, I don't want her thinking I'm dead. Our mother passed away a year ago, and it really hit Ruby hard. If she believes I was butchered by some killer . . ." She shook her head. "I don't know what she'll do."

Galar snorted. "Don't worry about her. She'll be fine."

"You don't know Ruby. She seems tough, but . . ."

"Jessica, thanks to you and your art, she became a very rich woman."

Smoky blue eyes blinked in surprise. "Rich? Ruby? She lives in a broken-down mobile home."

"Within six months of your death, she'll sell one of your paintings for two hundred and fifty thousand dollars. And the prices will go up from there."

Jessica gaped. "One of *my* paintings? You're kidding."

"You're considered one of the greatest artists of the twenty-first century. Initially that's why we thought you were targeted. If an art thief could get his hands on historically unknown Jessica Kelly originals, they'd be worth millions of galactors to unscrupulous collectors."

"Millions? Man. Oh, man." She fell back against the cushions. He watched as she started thinking it through. "You think collectors would be interested in *new* paintings?"

His lips twitched. "I can pretty much guarantee it."

"Hot damn, no more ramen noodles!" She grinned a moment, jubilant, before her smile drained away. "But can't I drop by and see Ruby for just a minute? Just long enough to let her know I'm not dead?"

"No, because frankly, I doubt your sister could keep her mouth shut about it. And another thing—that Xeran is still after you. Do you really want to risk bringing him down on her?"

"But he doesn't want me. He wants Charlotte."

"Yeah, well, judging by the knife he stuck in your belly, now he wants you too." He leaned forward and took her hand. "And I don't want him to get you."

"But why?" she demanded. "Why is he hunting us? What the hell is going on?"

"I have no idea, but I'm damned well going to find out."

Before she could think of another question to ask, Galar stood. "You're getting cold. Let's go in."

"In where?" Jess automatically started gathering her plate, cup, and silverware. After tucking them into the basket, she helped him put away the rest of the picnic supplies, then handed him the basket.

"Back into the Outpost." Galar stood, basket swinging from one hand as he draped the blanket over a broad shoulder with the other. Correctly interpreting her lifting eyebrow, he added, "It's our headquarters. Something like a combination police precinct, customs office, hospital, and mall."

"Interesting combo." Carrying the heated pillows, Jess followed him as he strode back up the hillside on those long legs. The view was incredible—and she wasn't thinking about the landscape. The man had a great ass. Regretfully, she dragged her attention away from it. "Where exactly are we? *When* exactly are we?"

He glanced back over his shoulder. "You'd call it the Blue Ridge Mountains of Georgia. As to when—it's December 21, 1532 CE."

"Fifteen . . . thirty-two?" Jess gaped. She wouldn't even be born for almost five centuries. "Why in the hell did you build your headquarters here?"

He shrugged. "It's a good central point, temporally speaking. And the area will be sparsely populated for another couple of centuries. What local residents there are believe this mountain is the domain of evil spirits, so they avoid it."

"I don't blame them," Jess muttered.

They walked up the slope toward a sheer granite cliff, jutting here and there with a few scrubby bushes. She eyed it dubiously, hoping they wouldn't have to scale the thing. Though in reasonably good shape, she didn't think three times a week on a StairMaster qualified her for rock climbing.

Galar walked straight up to the cliff—and *into* it, slipping through the solid rock like a ghost.

Jess stopped in her tracks to gape. A hand reached out of

the rough stone face, closed around her wrist, and drew her in after him.

She looked wildly around to find a pair of doors sliding closed behind them. "Three-dimensional camouflage field," Galar explained, and started up the curving corridor, his booted feet quiet on the thick carpeting.

"Ah. Okay." Jess followed him warily, staring around. The walls spilled a gentle illumination, and a soft, strange music played. Her mind began whispering alien words again, producing images of peculiar instruments, phrases she'd never heard before.

Licking her lips, she fought to control her racing thoughts, her heart thudding with anxiety. *Calm down,* Jess told herself fiercely. *Nobody's going to hurt you. You'll get used to this.*

"Are you all right?" Galar broke step to look at her, concern in those rich, bright eyes.

She rolled a shoulder with a jerk. "Just struggling with information overload. I'm dealing."

He flashed her that admiring smile that made something warm in her chest. "Yeah, you are. Considering everything, you're doing damned well."

She dredged up a smile for him despite her twitching nerves. "Thanks."

They rounded a curve and veered down another corridor. This one was crowded with blue-uniformed men and women, striding along with an air of purpose. Two of them were carrying on a lively argument in Galactic Standard about a grav-ball tournament. Jess's mind produced images of teams of people darting back and forth in weightlessness, slamming at a glowing blue ball with padded gloves.

The association with zero G triggered another mental picture: people in tight space suits, working around some kind of ship. Then a different kind of ship flashed against the stars, its nacelles flaring bright blue.

Images began to pour into her mind faster and faster. Alien

faces, mouths moving in an incomprehensible roar, strange landscapes, impossible creatures. Each sensation triggered others in a confusing cascade, blinding, deafening.

Jess staggered, shaking her head hard, fighting to regain control. Gritting her teeth, she squeezed her eyes shut, trying to close out the flood of alien sensation.

She heard Galar mutter a curse, then he caught her by the arm and pulled her after him. "In here. It's quieter."

A door hissed closed as powerful arms wrapped around her, drawing her tight against a big, warm body. "You're having an information cascade. It's a side effect of the EDI. Just hold on and breathe, like I showed you before. It's all right."

Jess grabbed him back and held on tight, using him as an anchor against the alien flood. Squeezing her eyes shut, she moaned in terror.

"Breathe with me," he murmured in her ear. "In. Out."

Jess obeyed, concentrating on the rise and fall of his chest, the beat of his heart, the warmth and strength of him. The frightening mental flood slowly retreated.

She pressed her face against the wool of his sweater, breathing in his scent. He felt wonderful, all hard muscle, long and lean and powerful. Her body stirred, a purely feminine reaction to his stark masculinity.

The rising tide of desire swamped the last of the alien images, which sank from her consciousness at last. After several long breaths, she dared open her eyes. The room around them was small, dim, blessedly quiet. And empty, aside from racks of thin metal bars attached to the walls. "Where are we?"

"Equipment closet outside the gym. I wanted to get you out of the flow of traffic until you stabilized."

Jess sighed and burrowed closer to his warm strength. He made a slight noise, a soft male growl that brought her gaze to his face.

The heat in his gaze was as unmistakable as the ridge of lust she could feel growing behind his zipper.

**The file had** said physical contact was a quick way to ground someone against an EDI cascade—a flood of unwanted mental associations—so Galar had taken her in his arms. Then she'd wrapped herself around him like climbing ivy, with a sheer, stark desperation that had touched him.

Poor little primitive, trapped in a world she didn't understand, stripped of every friend she'd ever had. Prey to a battleborg assassin.

But even as his pity rose, she'd turned it on its head. Desire had replaced her desperation, so fierce it triggered his own. With no effort at all, she'd set ablaze the hunger that had been simmering since the moment he'd first seen her at her easel.

She felt so damned good as she buried herself against him, slender, soft, deliciously female, fiercely sensual. Better yet, there was no artifice at all in those blue eyes as she looked up at him.

She simply wanted him.

Jessica Kelly was nothing like Tlain. For once, Galar's heart and head and body were in perfect agreement. Besides, he was sick of living like a wary monk, imprisoned by his own vows, his own fears.

How long had it been since he'd had a woman?

*Sixty-two days, six hours, three minutes,* his computer whispered.

*Damn,* Galar thought. *No wonder I'm losing it.*

So he lowered his head and took her lips. Sweet. Goddess Mother, she tasted as sweet as she looked, pure as rainwater.

"Galar," she moaned into his mouth, his name an intoxicating, breathy little whimper that made him harden even more.

He growled as a wild recklessness rolled over him, an impatience with his caution, with years of self-denial and discipline. He didn't think he'd ever wanted a woman like this, with this aching, unheeding ferocity.

The kiss started out feral, a luscious erotic assault of teeth and tongue and lips. Jessica jolted against him with wide-eyed surprise. He instantly gentled, the press of his mouth softening into a caress. She caught her breath, then released it in a sigh and let her eyes slip closed.

**This was nuts.** He was a man from the future, a warrior from a world she couldn't even imagine. And yet—and yet—he tasted so good. So rich. Hot and male and insanely tempting.

She was plastered against him from shoulders to feet now, until it seemed every molecule of her touched a molecule of him. Her senses were abruptly full to bursting with raw masculinity—that tall, brawny body, firm and strong and solid against her more delicate one. His scent, intoxicating and masculine. His taste, dark and rich and just a little alien.

Her nipples gathered in sizzling response, heat sliding into a honeyed ball low in her abdomen. She groaned softly, heard him rumble a dark, hungry response.

And then, reluctantly, Galar pulled away. "As much as I'd love to continue this, I don't want our first time to be in a closet." His smile was dazzling, intoxicating.

So much so, it didn't even occur to her to protest his assumption. "No." Reluctantly, she dropped her arms from around his waist. "I suppose not."

Jess followed as he led the way out of the closet and down the corridor. "We can cut through the gym," he told her, taking her elbow in one big, warm hand and guiding her through another door. "There's a lift just through . . ."

"Die, you bastard!" a voice howled.

Jess yelped a startled little scream. Galar jerked away from her and whirled, putting himself between her and the room beyond. She braced a hand against his broad back as steel rang on steel, voices snarling threats and insults.

Sounded like a knife fight.

Warily, Jessica craned her neck to see around the width of Galar's shoulders. They stood just inside a sprawling room, its ceiling soaring so high it put her in mind of a high school basketball court. Unlike the gym, though, the walls were gleaming white, except for one that appeared to be a solid sheet of glass. The Blue Ridge rolled beyond it, going dark with shades of indigo night.

Another howl of fury. A woman flew through the air in a superhuman bound, knives flashing in both hands. Lips peeled back from her teeth, she shot straight at a huge red-haired man who waited for her with a lunatic grin on his face and blades in either hand. He wore what looked like bright green bicycle pants and nothing else. Sweat streamed from the brawny bronzed torso that gleamed in the overhead light as if oiled.

The woman landed like an Olympic-caliber gymnast, solidly, without so much as a forward bobble. She instantly pounced into a lunge, her knife flashing toward her opponent's throat as she yowled that blood-chilling challenge again. He backflipped, bounding off the floor as if it were a trampoline. Undeterred, the woman charged after him. He hit the ground and whirled to circle with her, their knives clashing in metallic, ringing scrapes as they snarled insults at each other.

Forgetting her fear, Jessica moved around Galar to get a better look. Their speed was inhuman, a blurring exchange of blows she could barely follow. The whole fight looked more like something out of some special effects–laden martial arts flick than anything she'd ever seen in real life. Every time they leaped into one of those stunning bounces or improbable spins, Jess wanted to search for wires.

*Nobody can jump like that.* Her jaw dropped shamelessly open at one fifteen-foot bound. *It's just not possible.*

She was still gaping when the redhead leaped through the air toward the woman, his foot scything into a kick. His target ducked—and he kept going.

Straight at Jess.

*Oh, shit . . .* There was no time to duck, no time to . . .

Broad shoulders suddenly blocked her view. Jessica stumbled back as Galar snatched the redhead out of the air as easily as a man catching a football. He didn't even rock back on his heels.

"Holy shit," she whispered, staring at the two big men in blank astonishment. The redhead had to be six-foot-eight, as solidly muscled as an offensive lineman. Easily three hundred pounds of muscle. Yet Galar had caught him as if he weighed nothing at all.

Now he thrust the redhead back on his feet. "What the Seven Hells do you think you're doing? You could have killed her, you idiot!"

"Sorry, Master Enforcer." The redhead looked mortified as he backed away from Galar's incandescent rage. "We just got a little carried away."

"Sorry isn't good enough," Galar snarled, poking a forefinger into his target's brawny chest. "Whether you're in combat or only combat practice, you maintain awareness at all times of *everything* around you. That's why you've got a battle comp. Use it!"

"It won't happen again, Master Enforcer." The man looked shamefaced. His female opponent hurried over, her expression just as apologetic.

*Damn,* Jessica realized belatedly. *It was only some kind of practice session.* She'd thought they were fighting to the death.

"I am sorry," the redhead told her. "I didn't notice you standing there."

"You should have," Galar said in that same icy tone.

He turned his attention to the woman. "And so should you."

"You're right, of course," the woman said, entwining her fingers with the redhead's. Like the two men, she was tall, but more leanly elegant than massive. She was also breathtakingly beautiful, with a bone structure a fashion model would envy, set off by huge violet eyes. She wore her black hair braided and gathered into a tight coil. A sleeveless one-piece tank suit emphasized the beauty of her body while again reminding Jessica of a gymnast. It was snug and cut high on the leg, the fabric thin and dark blue, with a red rectangle down the left side from breast to hip. She'd tucked those terrifying knives back into a pair of thigh sheaths.

"We *are* sorry," the woman told Jess earnestly. "It's a good thing that Master Enforcer Arvid has such quick reflexes."

"How did you *do* that?" Jess asked in wonder. "Can everybody in the twenty-third century leap tall buildings in a single bound?"

"Nope." Smiling faintly, the woman gestured at her big redheaded companion. "We're cyborgs."

Jessica's EDI spat out a definition that made her frown in puzzlement. "Humans with mechanical arms and legs?"

"Mechanical as in gears and pulleys?" The redhead snorted. "Hardly. The technology is a lot more advanced than that."

"Good to know." Jess turned toward Galar. "So you're a cyborg too?"

He shook his head. "Genetically engineered. But I have sensors and a computer implant."

"Ooookaay. Sensors. A computer implant." She contemplated the steadily shrinking size of computers in her own time and decided she could believe it.

The woman stepped forward and offered her hand. "Enforcer Dona Astryr." She nodded at the redhead. "Senior Enforcer Ivar Terje."

"Jessica Kelly." She clasped hands with the two agents. "People still shake hands?"

"No." Dona smiled. "But you do."

"Oh. Well, thanks."

Galar took her elbow in one big hand. "Let's go." Bad temper still growled in his voice. "I need to meet with the Chief Enforcer and tell him about the Xeran and Holt."

Ivar looked at him, interested. "What's this about the Xeran?"

Galar gave him a glower. "You don't need to know."

Ivar blinked as Jessica lifted a brow at Galar's brusque tone. Galar ignored her stare, tugging her away from the two agents.

"What brought that on?" she demanded.

"I didn't save your ass so one of my own men could break every bone in your body out of carelessness," he gritted.

*And how much of all that anger is sheer sexual frustration?* Jess wondered. That kiss had been pretty damned steamy, after all. She considered teasing him about it, but a glance at his rigid back made her carefully close her mouth again.

Better not.

# · 6 ·

**Dona Astryr watched the Master Enforcer lead the** primitive away, his steps so long and angry, Jessica almost had to run to keep up. She sighed. "I don't think I've ever seen him that pissed off. But I guess we had it coming."

"We?" Ivar shook his head, his expression chagrined. "Don't you mean me? It was my screwup. I could have killed her. Or at least hurt her badly."

It *had* been uncharacteristically clumsy of him. Ivar normally demonstrated an almost superhuman awareness in combat; he rarely put a foot wrong. But he was also competitive as hell, and sometimes his need to win drove him to take too many chances.

Knowing he'd probably browbeat himself about his mistake, Dona gave his beefy shoulder a pat. "Luckily, the primitive's not hurt. And we'll both be a lot more careful the next time."

"I'll try." Ivar's lids lowered as he gave her a molten stare.

One corner of his handsome mouth kicked up in a wicked little smile. "But you can be very distracting."

Her heart gave an eager thump as he drew her into his arms. As always, his kisses seared her right to the soles of her boots. Dona sighed wordlessly into his mouth and twined her arms around his powerful neck.

Even as Ivar worked Dona's mouth with skillful hunger, he considered the implications of his little experiment. He hadn't really expected it to work; he'd assumed Galar would block him before he could do any interesting damage. Even if he'd gotten lucky, at most he'd have broken one or two of the little bitch's bones. Regen would have taken care of that in short order, though the reaction of all concerned would have been entertaining.

As it was, he'd scared the hell out of Galar and the primitive without arousing anyone's suspicions, a neat and thoroughly enjoyable trick.

Besides, the Master Enforcer's reaction had been interesting, to say the least. He'd gotten quite a bit angrier than Ivar had expected. The Ice Lord generally didn't seem to give a damn about much of anything. Yet he'd been thoroughly pissed off at the primitive's close call.

Such intense emotion suggested a weakness Ivar could exploit, given the right opportunity.

And Ivar was very, very good at finding—or making—the right opportunity.


**"This time travel** thing confuses me," Jessica told Galar as they headed down the corridor. She'd decided his still-simmering anger warranted a change in subject. "I know you can't change history, but I don't understand why." Thoughtfully, Jess added, "Though I guess nobody would risk it if there was a real chance of wiping yourself out of existence."

"Actually, at one time, we did worry about that. Quite a

lot. But we've since discovered that's not the way it works."
Something small and bright red blurred through the air toward them. Galar reached out a hand and snagged it with offhand skill before it could dart past.

"Release!" a tiny voice shrilled. "I do not belong to you!"

"Hush," Galar told it.

"What is that?" Curious, Jessica craned her head to look down in his hand. The thing was about the size of a baseball, but it was covered in bright crimson fur fine enough to wave in the air currents. Big, bulging cartoon eyes rolled in alarm. It had no visible nose or limbs, but its mouth was wide and pink, reminding her vaguely of Kermit the Frog.

"It's a 'bot—a toy."

"I'll bite!" the thing squeaked.

"I wouldn't advise it." To Jessica he added, "The perception of time in the twenty-first century is a little off. You think of it as a river, something that moves and changes. But it's not."

Jess frowned, considering the implications despite the headache it was starting to give her. "So everything is predestined?"

"Not predestined. It is what it is." He held up the toy. "Look, our little friend here exists in three dimensions—width, height, length. He's made up of molecules, atoms, electrons, protons, neutrons, quarks."

"Right." Jessica nodded. "We know that even in my century."

"But he also has a fourth dimension, extending from the moment he was created in a factory to the moment he breaks and is put into the recycler . . ."

"Yeep!"

". . . made up of years, hours, minutes, seconds, milliseconds, chronons . . ."

"Chronons?"

"The smallest possible particle of time. Anyway, he's got a temporal structure just as he has a physical shape."

"But what if I went back in time and stomped on him? Wouldn't that change his structure?"

The toy squeaked, a high-pitched peep of alarm. "I do not like you! Get away from me!"

"You could," Galar told her, ignoring the 'bot's struggles, "But it would be a waste of time. We know he's still here." He gestured with the toy. "That tells us you failed to break him. He got away, he was repaired, or someone stopped you. But you can't know what happened unless you actually go back and try it."

Jessica nibbled a thumbnail. "We could ask him."

"Yes, but he might lie. Or he might not even know because he didn't see what stopped you. That's the thing about history: you can never know what really happened—absent some kind of recording—unless you go back and experience it for yourself. Which makes it your future, not your past. Time travel means everything effectively takes place *now*."

She grimaced and rubbed her temples. "I think I'm getting a headache."

Galar nodded. "I know what you mean. I've been a time traveler for ten years, and sometimes these discussions still give me migraines."

"Wulf!" the little 'bot shrilled suddenly, jerking so violently, Galar almost lost his grip. "Wulf, save me!"

"Flybot?" The answering voice was so deep, Jessica felt it more in her bones than her ears. She watched as a figure rounded the corridor. He was a couple of inches shorter than she was, yet he was impossibly broad. Not that there was an ounce of fat anywhere on his massive body. And if there had been, she'd have seen it; he wore one of those one-piece dark blue scaled suits that fit him without so much as a wrinkle. His gloved hands were so enormous, he could have palmed her head like a baseball. His booted feet were even larger.

Despite his imposing proportions, he was surprisingly handsome, though in an angular, starkly masculine way. His eyes had an almond shape that suggested Asian heritage, but their color was a pale, pretty turquoise. His hair fell around those massive shoulders, straight and shining as a length of black silk. "Master Enforcer," the big man rumbled by way of greeting. "Is Flybot bothering you?"

"Just illustrating a point about time travel for my friend here." Galar released the little toy, which darted to its owner with a squeal.

Wulf caught it in a huge, surprisingly gentle hand as it instantly began to babble.

"She said she was going to go back in time and smash me! Evil, evil creature!" Its bubble eyes rolled toward her and narrowed. "Hurt her!"

"Shhhh," Wulf said soothingly, stroking it between the eyes with one thick finger. "No one is going to damage you."

"Evil!"

"You shouldn't talk that way about guests, Flybot." The big man shot her a steely look. "You have no intention of breaking him, do you?"

Jessica swallowed, eying the size of those hands. "Wouldn't dream of it."

"There. You see?" Wulf strode off, still cooing at his pet. "You're completely safe."

Galar watched them go, his lips twitching.

Jessica eyed him. "You're just dying to give him a hard time about his toy, aren't you?"

"Yeah, but he'd break me in half. That man could bench-press a tank. The world he's from has five times Earth's gravity, and he was genetically engineered to be powerful even there."

"Is *anybody* in this place a normal human?" Jessica asked drily.

"Just you."

"Yeah," she said. "That's pretty well what I thought."

As if to illustrate the point, a slender young woman strode

down the corridor toward them, a huge timber wolf trotting at her side. Jess had seen smaller Shetland ponies.

"Ah, Riane and Frieka," Galar said to the two, motioning them over. "Could you give me a hand with something, please?"

"Certainly, Master Enforcer," the wolf said.

Jessica's jaw dropped shamelessly. "He talks?"

The wolf gave her a contemptuous look, then glanced up at his companion. "Primitives. If she calls me a dog, I'm going to bite her."

And it would hurt, Jess decided, eying his impressive fangs. A lot.

Galar shot the big animal a dry look. "Keep your teeth out of my guest, Frieka." He turned to Jess and gestured in introduction. "My fellow Enforcers Riane Arvid and her partner, Frieka. He's a genetically engineered cyborg wolf, so don't call him a dog. He's a little sensitive."

"I'm no more sensitive about that than you are about being called an overevolved ape." Frieka curled a lip in another intimidating fang display.

Riane gave the top of his head a rap and smiled sweetly at Galar. "What can we do for you, Master Enforcer?" Like Dona Astryr, she was taller than Jess, with a lithely muscled build. She looked like the kind of woman who'd never had to watch her weight in her entire life. She also had a truly impressive tattoo running down one side of her pretty face in vivid blue and red, all swirls and intricate lines. One lock of her long red hair was braided and strung with gemstones.

"I need to find the chief and make a report, but I don't want to leave Jessica alone while I do it," Galar told her. "Would you two take her to my quarters and stay with her until I get back?"

"*Your* quarters?" Riane blinked in evident surprise. "You know, we could probably find her another—"

"My quarters," Galar rapped, his tone cold. Riane closed her teeth with a snap.

Frieka's gaze sharpened in sudden calculation. "You think the Xeran's going to come after her here?"

"Let me put it this way—I'd hate to be unpleasantly surprised."

Riane straightened to attention, half-lifting one hand as if to salute before dropping it hastily. "We'll provide any assistance we can, of course."

He gave her a smile that radiated warmth. "Thank you, Enforcer Riane."

Jess blinked, surprised by her own sudden green tide of jealousy. *Where the hell had that come from?*


**Jessica safely guarded,** Galar strode down the corridor toward the meeting he'd scheduled with Dyami. They could have conducted it by com channel, but he felt the need for a face-to-face discussion.

The Xeran situation demanded investigation, but he wouldn't be able to handle it himself if he were guarding Jess. The chief would have to either assign another security detail or send someone else to go after the Xeran.

Galar felt torn. He wanted to do both, but obviously that wasn't an option.

When it came to guarding Jess, he trusted Frieka and Riane more than anyone at the Outpost, with the exception of Dyami himself. After all, Riane was a Warfem, and loyalty was bred into Vardonese Warriors right down to the blood and bone.

From the standpoint of sheer power, Wulf was another possibility, as were Dona and Ivar. The couple might have been careless in combat practice earlier, but they were solid agents. Not Vardonese, of course, but trustworthy enough.

The memory of the combat practice debacle reminded him of that searing kiss. Galar found himself smiling in anticipation.

He was sick of denying himself. If today had taught him

anything, it was that ignoring the attraction was not an effective strategy. It had been too damned long since he'd been with a woman, and his desire for Jess was too irresistible. He'd be better off giving into it instead of letting it distract him at some crucial time.

Such as when the Xeran showed up.

Besides Jess was a damned unlikely source of betrayal. She was too honest, too innocent, despite her smoldering sensuality. In any case, she'd be leaving as soon as they took care of the Xeran, headed for her new life as a celebrated artist.

All of which made her just about perfect for his considerable needs. Anticipation steamed through him on a tide of hot blood.

One way or another, she'd be sharing his bed tonight.

**"He's got a** window," Riane Arvid said with naked envy as she, the wolf, and Jessica walked into Galar's quarters.

"He *is* a senior officer," Frieka pointed out, a string of blue lights flashing in the thick gray fur around his neck. Jessica's implanted knowledge told her those lights must signify some kind of vocalizer. Otherwise he'd be unable to talk, since the anatomy of his throat, chest, and long, fang-filled muzzle were all wrong for speech.

Jess was encouraged that the spurt of new knowledge barely disoriented her at all. Besides, she was too interested in Galar's quarters to worry about it.

Prowling the wall of shelves opposite his sprawling, neatly made bed, Jess eyed his collection of keepsakes. A rapier with a beautiful jeweled basket hilt and engraved blade caught her fascinated attention first, and she walked over to study its graceful, lethal lines.

Then she noticed the trids.

Obviously the equivalent of snapshots back home, they were glowing three-dimensional images that reminded her of snow globes. In one, a very young, very handsome Galar stood with an older couple, both of whom had intricate facial tattoos much like Riane's. The male of the two was as broad and powerfully built as Galar himself, while the woman was a gently muscled blonde. Jess saw a definite resemblance in the line of the man's jaw, in the color of the woman's eyes. "These must be his parents."

"Probably," Riane said, wandering over for a closer look. "This was taken at the Vardonese Military Academy. I recognize it." She gestured at Galar's black uniform. "Looks like a graduation shot." Correctly interpreting Jess's confusion, she explained, "Vardon is our home planet."

Jess turned to study the other woman. Her tattoo was the same color as Galar's father's, a swirl of red and blue, intricate and vaguely Celtic in design. "Are you two related?"

The girl blinked. "No. Why would you think that?"

"You've got the same last name."

"Oh. Arvid is just our House—the Femmat company that genetically engineered us. Most Warriors are raised in House creches and don't have families at all. Galar and I are unusual in having biological parents."

Jess's own father had left when she was only a couple of years old, but at least she'd had a mother. Even so, she'd always felt a deep envy of those with both parents. What would it be like to have no one at all? "Is everybody in the future genetically engineered?"

"Not the general galactic population, no. Though scientists do use genetic engineering when they've got some kind of good reason—like adapting colonists for life on a planet where the atmosphere or gravity would be too much for a standard human."

"So Vardon is like that?"

"Nope. It's just run by hyper-controlling Femmats." The wolf looked up from chewing industriously on his own flank. Reacting to Jess's stare, he added defensively, "What? It itches, and unlike you overevolved monkeys, I don't have fingers to scratch with."

As Jess wrinkled her nose, Riane rolled her eyes. "That's nothing. He also licks his genitals." She gave an elaborate shudder.

The wolf sniffed. "You're just jealous."

"Nah," Jess said. "It's more fun when somebody else does it." As Riane choked back laughter, she asked the wolf, "What's a Femmat?"

"The female aristocracy of Vardon." The wolf sat back on his haunches and scratched with his hind foot. "Damn itch is traveling."

Without being asked, Riane knelt on the floor beside him and started digging her nails into his fur.

"Up some," the wolf instructed. "To the right. . . . Ahhhh! You got it. Bless you, kid."

Jess watched the two absently, her mind working. It seemed that though her EDI was extensive, it didn't include everything. Which only made sense, since there were one hundred and three worlds in the Galactic Union alone.

The only one that really interested her, though, was Galar's home planet. "Women run Vardon?"

"Yep," Riane explained, giving Frieka's muscled ribs an affectionate thump as he lolled back on the floor. "A bunch of scientists wanted to create a utopia a couple of hundred years ago. Theory was that men commit most of the crimes and a lot of the social injustice . . ."

"Apparently they'd never gone to an American high school," Jess muttered.

". . . so they figured they'd use genetic engineering to get rid of sociopathy, ambition, and aggression."

Jess sat down on the bed and cocked her head at the agent. "Why does this sound like a really bad idea to me?"

"Actually, it worked," Riane said. "The crime rate on Vardon is the lowest in the Galactic Union. Thing is, law-abiding people can be a bad thing, depending on the laws they're abiding by."

"Like when the Xer invaded forty years ago," Frieka

added. "None of the civilians put up any fight at all. The bastards would still be running Vardon if it wasn't for us."

"Yeah, I was thinking none of you guys strike me as lacking aggression."

"Exactly," Frieka said. "Soon after they started their little experiment, the Femmats realized that though they might be peaceful, their neighbors definitely weren't. So they created a genetically engineered warrior class." He nodded at Riane. "Warlords and Warfems, they called them, bred for strength and speed, with battle-comp implants and sensors."

"Doesn't sound like a bunch who'd take an invasion lying down."

"Nope," Frieka told her. "In fact, they formed an underground resistance force. It took them five years to drive the Xer off the planet, but eventually they succeeded."

Riane nodded proudly. "My father was one of those fighters. I think Galar once said his parents were members of the resistance too."

Jess studied her with interest. "What about your mother?"

"Oh, she isn't Vardonese." Riane waved an airy hand. "She's a temporal Earth native, like you. My father was sent back to 2004 to protect her from a Xer Jumpkiller."

Jess blinked in surprise. "Your mother was from the past?"

Riane nodded. "Before I was born. She and Dad killed Jack the Ripper."

"The Victorian serial killer?" Jess's jaw dropped as her interest became utter fascination.

"Yeah, only he wasn't really a Victorian. He was a Xer assassin from the future."

"Damn. Those Xer really are bastards, aren't they? And he came after your mom? Why? Why'd he butcher all those women?"

Riane shrugged. "Like you said, he was a bastard. Besides, he'd found a way to make money off the murders. He recorded his crimes for a bunch of equally sociopathic subscribers back on Xer."

"Sounds like he needed killing."

"Oh, yeah, on a lot of levels. He'd been part of the Xer invasion force years before, and he'd done some nasty stuff to my dad that really messed him up."

"But Jane—Riane's mother—helped Baran get over it," Frieka added. "Then they kacked the son of a bitch."

"And ended up falling in love," Riane finished. "It was all kind of romantic."

Damn, Jess thought, wishing she could talk to Riane's mother. How had she adjusted to life in the future? What had it been like, falling in love with one of these superhuman Warlords?

Her gaze tracked involuntarily to the trid of Galar and his parents. He'd looked young then, almost innocent—not at all the hard-edged warrior she knew. "He was so handsome back then, it's almost ridiculous. But you know, I think he's sexier now. He's got more of an edge or something. Makes him more interesting."

"The Master Enforcer?" Riane stared at her blankly. "Sexy?"

Jess lifted her brows. "You don't think he's sexy?"

"Oh, I don't mean he's not attractive," the Warfem said hastily. "But I guess I haven't really thought in terms of sleeping with him. He's a little too . . . cold."

"Cold? Galar?" She remembered how he'd cuddled her in his arms, helping her keep the fear and confusion at bay. "Hardly."

Riane straightened, looking vaguely alarmed. "You're getting hooked on him, aren't you?"

"Riane." The wolf's tone was warning.

She shot him a defensive look. "Well, Jessica needs to know."

"No, she doesn't. It's none of your damned business. Besides, have you forgotten the last time he ripped a strip off you over this? He hates being gossiped about."

Riane's expression turned mulish. "I don't care. She's a nice person, and he—"

"What are you *talking* about?" Jess demanded, exasperated by the cryptic conversation.

"Getting emotionally involved with the Master Enforcer is a really bad idea." Riane tilted her chin in rebellion at the big wolf. He flopped back on the floor in disgust.

"Why?"

"He's . . . got a pretty dark past. See, he got mixed up with this Femmat spy when he was with Military Intelligence."

"A spy? Galar?" Jess blinked. "And I thought you said the Vardonese were nonviolent and law-abiding. That doesn't sound like any spy I ever heard of."

"That's the rest of the Vardonese population," Frieka said, lifting his head. "The Femmats realized good scientists and government officials actually need ambition and aggression, maybe even a little ruthlessness. So they kept those characteristics in the aristocracy."

"Unfortunately, that means some of them occasionally commit crimes," Riane explained. "Particularly the bunch that admire the Xer."

"They *admire* the people that invaded them?" Remembering her own attacker, Jess grimaced. "Are they nuts?"

"There's a faction that thinks the ruling party has gone too far in eliminating negative qualities from Vardonese society. They think the planetary population has become too soft, too spineless," Riane told her. "They want the Xer back so the Vardonese can relearn the so-called 'military virtues.' "

"Yeah, serial killing sounds real virtuous. And Galar was *dating* somebody like that?"

"Oh, he didn't know she was a spy. He thought she was a loyal Femmat intelligence officer. She had a computer implant, you see, which she used to hide her emotional reactions whenever she lied to him. Which was most of the time."

The wolf flicked an ear. "I don't know what the hell he was thinking, falling in love with a Femmat. You can't trust those little bitches. You want to talk cold . . ."

"He eventually realized she was involved in the Xeran spy ring he was investigating," Riane continued, ignoring the wolf. "He confronted her, and she tried to kill him." She shrugged. "But he shot first. Still got most of an arm blown off, though."

Jess stared at the Warfem, appalled. "He did? But . . ."

"It grew back. Regeneration."

"Oh."

"The upshot is that he doesn't trust women anymore," Riane told her bluntly. "Actually, he doesn't trust anybody. He's pretty well ice cold all the way to the bone. You need to stay away from him or you'll get hurt. Badly."

Put that way, Galar did sound like a very bad bet, Jess thought. Thing was, she didn't believe it. "I don't think you're being quite fair to him," she said slowly. "He's been very kind to me. This EDI of mine . . . it's been hard adjusting, but he—" Remembering the heat of Galar's big body, the tender warmth of his mouth, she felt a blush climb her cheeks. "—helped me."

"Yeah." Riane lifted a knowing brow. "I'll just bet he did."

"Riane, I'm going to *bite* you." The growl rumbling in Frieka's chest suggested he meant every word of the threat.

His partner ignored him, a militant light in her eyes. "Warlords can be very seductive. All Vardonese Warriors are engineered for strong sex drives anyway, but the males are especially—"

"Horny?" Jess put in drily.

"Pretty much. Thing is, I've been here a year, and I've never known of Galar bedding anybody. I'm told he's got a thing about sleeping with people he works with. But since he doesn't work with you . . ."

Frieka rose to all fours, his ruff lifting, his lips pulling back from impressive fangs as he stalked stiff-legged toward his partner. "Riane. Shut. Up."

Jess pulled her legs up on the bed away from the cyborg's threatening advance, her eyes widening.

Riane snorted and waved a dismissive hand. "Ignore him. He's all bark and no bite."

"Don't bet on it."

"Umm, that's okay," Jess said hastily. "I get the point." *And I'd just as soon not get Frieka's,* she thought, eyeing those teeth. *All six thousand of them.*

But the two Enforcers ignored her in favor of glaring at each other as though having a silent, ferocious argument. She watched them, frowning.

Was Riane right? Was Galar manipulating her?

## · 7 ·

✤

**Brooding over what she'd learned, Jess rose from** the bed and wandered around the room. Frieka and Riane still seemed to be having that completely silent—and furious—argument, at least judging by the girl's shifting expressions.

Jess's attention fell on what looked like a single sheet of blank white plastic. *Data sheet,* her EDI whispered.

*Hot damn,* she thought, pouncing. It began to glow with a white, even light as soon as she picked it up. *A library!*

The sheet held every book ever published, data densely packed into its every molecule. "Display information on Jessica Kelly, artist," she said to it. Her knowledge might be spotty in places, but it did include how to access a data sheet.

A list of titles appeared on the sheet in Galactic Standard: *Jessica Kelly, Genius and Tragedy*; *Blood and Paint—The Story of Jessica Kelly*; *Dead Too Young*; *Tragic Genius . . .* The list went on, book after book.

Jessica glowered down at the sheet. "I'm sensing a theme here." Shrugging, she flopped down on the bed and touched one of the titles at random. The text of the book flashed on-screen, and she began to read.

**The window took** up one entire wall of Dyami's office, showcasing a breathtaking sweep of stars in the clear night sky. The moon rode high and full among them like a queen among courtiers, spilling a bright glow over the gently rolling mountains below. The light edged each dark tree that jutted from those high slopes as if the branches had been dipped in silver.

All in all, it was one hell of a view, but Galar knew the one from his own quarters would be just as fine. He was looking forward to making love to Jess with that glorious moon breathing a pearlescent gleam over her skin.

He turned his attention back to Dyami, who was briefing Dona Astryr and Ivar Terje. The chief had called the two into his office as soon as Galar had told him the battleborg's real target had been Charlotte Holt.

"Obviously Master Enforcer Arvid can't guard Kelly *and* investigate what the hell is going on," the chief said as he restlessly paced his spacious office, skirting the enormous black desk that put Galar in mind of a star cruiser. "That's where you two come in."

Galar, Dona, and Ivar sat in the informal grouping of low, well-padded chairs beside the window. The two Enforcers had changed out of their combat gear into their dark blue uniforms. Galar felt underdressed in the twenty-first-century clothing he'd worn for his picnic with Jess.

Dona, he noticed, was watching Dyami pace with reluctant fascination. She kept dragging her gaze away, but her eyes always slid back a moment later.

Ivar was watching her watch the chief. Despite the polite attention on his face, there was a marked tension in his massive shoulders.

Hmmmm.

Since the disaster with Tlain, Galar had gotten into the habit of observing his coworkers, checking for emotional undercurrents flowing beneath the surface. The undercurrents roiling between these three raised all sorts of questions. Dyami and Dona had the mutual habit of watching each other when the other's attention was elsewhere. Ivar had obviously noticed, and didn't like it one damned bit. Which probably explained the edge Galar often sensed in the big man.

"You think Marcin has killed the Holt woman?" Ivar asked the chief now, his tone coolly professional. "It would explain why she disappeared from the historical record following Kelly's 'murder.'"

"It's certainly a possibility," Dyami said as he walked by.

Dona's gaze dropped to his ass, then flicked guiltily away.

"Marcin said Jessica was dangerous, that we didn't understand what we were involved in," Galar said. "Maybe he thought Holt was dangerous too. But how could two twenty-first-century women be dangerous to a Xeran battleborg? So dangerous, in fact, he had to Jump through time to kill them. It doesn't make any sense."

"Something else is going on here," Dona said, running a thumb back and forth over her lower lip. Dyami glanced at her mouth as he turned to pace in the other direction, then quickly snapped his eyes away. "We're working on incomplete information," she continued. "And I would lay odds Holt is the key to all this. We need to focus our investigation on her."

"But Marcin's the battleborg," Ivar said, slinging one leg over the other in an abrupt gesture that suggested tightly leashed anger. "He's the killer we have to worry about."

"But Holt may be the motivation for his crimes," Dyami told him. "I want to know everything you can find out about her. Who is she? Where did she come from?"

"She's already been pretty thoroughly investigated over the centuries," Galar pointed out. "Kelly's biographers have always considered Holt a rather suspicious figure, since none of them has ever been able to dig up much about her background. She appeared a few months prior to the murder and then was never seen again."

"Could Holt have been a time traveler?" Dona asked.

Galar shook his head. "I wondered about that, too, so I did a thorough scan of her when we arrived. There was no sign of any molecular traces in her body that didn't belong in the twenty-first century. And she scanned as completely human."

"Well, there's certainly something going on with her," Dona said, sitting back in her chair.

"So go find out what," Dyami ordered, turning to watch them. "Dismissed."

The two Enforcers nodded and rose from their chairs. Dyami's gaze dropped to Dona's ass as they strode from the room. The chief quickly dragged his gaze away—and caught Galar watching him. He lifted a dark, cool brow. "Question, Master Enforcer?"

Galar looked steadily back. "No, sir."

"Then go keep an eye on our little friend."

"Yes, sir." He gave the chief a nod, rose, and walked from the office thoughtfully.

Were Dyami and Dona having an affair? he wondered as he started down the corridor. Considering the question, Galar decided it wasn't likely.

He'd known Dyami for years. The big Warlord had trained him when he'd first come to the Outpost as a rookie agent a decade before. Then-Master Enforcer Dyami had been a damned good partner, intelligent, thorough, and patient as he'd taught Galar the ins and outs of investigating temporal crimes. They'd become close friends, close enough that Galar was strongly tempted to ask Dyami what the hell was going on between him and Dona. But since the man was his superior officer, it wasn't really an appropriate question.

Besides, unless he missed his guess, there *wasn't* anything going on beyond a reluctant attraction. Dyami wasn't the type to make a sexual play for a subordinate, particularly not one who was already in a romance with another of his men.

Galar's eyes narrowed in speculation. Ivar had joined the Outpost staff only a year before, and he and Dona had promptly become a couple. Had Dona gotten involved with him to distract herself from an inappropriate attraction to Dyami?

If so, it wasn't working.

Technically, of course, none of this was Galar's business. But there was an uncomfortable little itch at the base of his neck that told him this situation had the potential to cause trouble. It certainly bore watching.

In the meantime, he had a romance of his own to attend to. His temporal rehab EDI suggested the best way to help a native find her feet was to give her something to do. In Jess's case, that something was obvious. He decided to spend the next couple of hours making sure she had what she needed.

Then, perhaps, she'd be in the mood to give him what *he* needed.

*Jessica's going to* love this, Galar thought in satisfaction as he headed back to his room a couple of hours later.

He walked in to find Jess sprawled on her belly, her chin on her fist, staring sightlessly across the room.

Galar gave her a narrow-eyed glance, then turned to dismiss Riane and Frieka. Both Enforcers slinked out. He watched them go, wondering about their collective air of guilt.

More interested in what was bothering Jessica, he walked over to the bed. She didn't even look up.

Spotting the data sheet beside her, Galar bent and picked it up. His brows lifted as he read the text.

Ahhh.

"You know," Jess said in a low, pain-filled voice, "my murder was the best thing that ever happened to my sister."

Galar winced. She was probably right, but he asked cautiously, "What makes you think that?"

Instead of answering the question directly, she rolled over on her back and stared at the ceiling. "Ruby was a crack addict. Lived with a succession of boyfriends who either beat the hell out of her or were her drug dealers. Or both."

It was nothing more than the truth. "I read your file."

"Yeah. I guess you would have." Jess folded her hands under her head and frowned at the ceiling. "You were right, by the way. She did get rich on my art."

Misery was so plain in those blue eyes, Galar wished he could deny it without lying. Because he couldn't, he only sighed. "That may be, but according to what I've read, she also grieved for you. I don't think she ever got over it."

"Maybe." She was silent for a long moment. "It's ironic, really. Ruby always thought my work sucked."

"Well, she did kick the drugs. Maybe once she was off them, she realized how good you are."

Jess was obviously sunk too deeply in her funk to notice the attempted compliment. "What changed everything was when she got David Sheraton involved. He was this Atlanta gallery owner with a reputation for spotting talent. He said my work was brilliant and started carrying my paintings. They began commanding huge sums of money. Critics started writing articles calling me a tragic genius."

He sighed and sat down on the bed next to her. "Somehow I have the feeling this story is more complicated than that."

Jessica snorted. "You have good instincts. I had an interview with Sheraton three weeks ago. Showed him my portfolio." Her brooding gaze met his. "He said, and I quote, 'I'm not seeing anything special here.'"

Galar winced. "Bastard."

"Which begs the question: Why did his opinion change a hundred and eighty degrees in three weeks? And then I realized—I was dead. I was a pretty girl who'd been mysteriously, horribly murdered. So first there's the morbid curiosity factor, which turned all my paintings into instant collector's items. Sheraton looked at my portfolio and thought, *Ka-CHING.*" Her mouth curved into a bitter smile. "Apparently *that* was special."

Recognizing the deep wounds under that smile, Galar thought, *All right, what am I going to do about this?*

The best way to deal with Jessica's painful realization, he decided, was honesty. He sighed and reached for her hand. Her long, slim fingers felt cool and limp in his. "Unfortunately, that's not an unusual attitude. Another artist was targeted by an art thief assassin last year. We saved him, but the assassin came after him a second time and cut his throat."

That got a reaction. Her brows snapped down. "But why? What did his death accomplish?"

"Had he survived, the value of his original art would have declined because he could still produce new work. So a collector hired the killer to take him out."

"What about the art that will never be produced?" Jessica sat up and folded her long legs under her, glowering. "What about the things he could have said, the way his talent could have grown if he'd been given a chance? Didn't that matter?"

"Not to a man who'd just spent sixty million galactors on a painting that was suddenly worth about half that."

"Money," Jessica snarled. "It was never about the art. It's all about money. All that stuff about my talent in those books—it was all bullshit. My paintings aren't really art—they're collectibles. Like fucking baseball cards."

And here was the heart of her sudden depression. "That might explain your initial popularity, but I assure you, it wouldn't have mattered after the first twenty years or so."

He caught her eyes with his, willing her belief. "Critics have acclaimed your work because it's good. *You're* good."

Her mouth twisted bitterly. "Am I?"

"Yes, you are. Come on." He rolled off the bed, reached down, and drew her to her feet. "I think it's time I remind you just how good."

**Jessica followed Galar** out of the room and down a corridor to another elevator. After a quick, smooth descent, they emerged into a hallway. Depressed as she was, she couldn't help but notice the enticing width of the shoulders that contrasted perfectly to his narrow waist and tight, muscular ass. The view was enough to lift her spirits all by itself.

She was still admiring him when Galar stopped and opened a door. He stepped back, gesturing her through. Curious, Jessica stepped inside.

Into the studio of her dreams.

The ceiling was high, airy, while the floor underfoot was made of some kind of gleaming wood as smooth and polished as glass. One entire wall was a window with another breathtaking view of the mountains.

It faced north, revealing a beautiful starlit sky and moonlight-kissed mountains. For centuries, artists had favored studios with north-facing windows as a source of perfect, even light. The view from this one would provide a stunning backdrop for her work. A long, low couch upholstered in dark green sat in front of the expanse of glass, draped with a deep red cloth.

An easel sat before it, massive oak and sturdy, of the type Jess had always dreamed of, but had never been able to afford. A huge canvas sat on it, stretched over a wooden frame, already primed with gesso.

Beside the easel sat a heavy wooden taboret, arranged with a dazzling selection of oil paints and a set of new brushes of every size and design. Two cans—turpentine and linseed oil—stood among the colorful tubes, unopened. A pile of clean rags waited beside them.

Jessica scanned the taboret with the joyous delight of a child on Christmas morning. "There are hundreds of dollars' worth of art supplies here!" Reverently, she examined the precious tubes. She'd always dreamed of owning oils of such quality, but she'd never had the money.

Wonderingly, she turned to look at Galar. A smile of pleasure curved his handsome mouth—the delight of a man whose gift has been well received. "You did this for me," she said slowly.

Not exactly the act of the cold-blooded bastard Riane had described.

"You're going to be here for a while, and you need a place to paint. Is everything the way you need it? The computer said this is how art studios should be arranged, but if it's not right . . ."

Warmth spread through her chest, feeling remarkably like sunshine. "It's perfect."

"Are you sure? Because I can—"

"It's perfect," Jessica interrupted. On sheer impulse, she stepped over to him and rose on her toes to kiss him on the cheek. He was so tall, she had to brace a hand on his shoulder to steady herself. His cheek felt warm against her lips, angular and firm. "Thank you."

She dropped back to her heels and looked up into his face. Heat flooded those golden eyes with fierce male desire. Jessica caught her breath. Staring into that burning gaze, she swallowed.

No, there was nothing at all cold about Galar Arvid.

Her heart began to pound, and she found herself looking away. Her mouth felt dry as she managed to say, "You don't know how much this means to me."

For something to do with her hands, Jess moved to the art taboret and began to arrange the paints in the order she always used them—flesh tones at the top, then warm earth shades, then the deep blues and greens, then jewel tones. Finally the huge tube of titanium white.

"What would you like to paint first?" Galar asked in that deep, seductive rumble of his.

Jessica turned to look at him, at the angular contours of his handsome face, at the enticing shades of his blond hair. The word was sheer impulse. "You."

He inclined his head in a courtly kind of nod. "It would be an honor. Nude?"

Jessica blinked. There was absolutely no insinuation in his tone at all, but she felt heat spill into her cheeks.

Galar smiled slightly. "My people don't consider nudity an automatic invitation to sex. And I've noticed your studio pieces are usually nudes."

"Yes." Jess mentally cursed the blush. How unprofessional could you get? She'd painted male nudes before, after all. Though none of them had looked like Galar. "And yes, I would like to paint you." Especially with the starlit night providing a perfect backdrop for his blond masculinity. "How about now?" She realized she probably sounded way too eager, but she was itching to paint.

She needed this. Craved it, in fact. Desperately. To lose herself in the paint, in the smell of linseed oil and canvas, in the sweet, heady rush of creation. She wanted to forget what she'd lost, forget the frightening, alien world she'd have to somehow make a place for herself.

How had Galar known? They barely knew each other, yet somehow he'd sensed the perfect thing to pull her out of her funk.

There was more to this man than knife-edged cheekbones and great shoulders, no matter what Riane thought.

Like Jess, Galar still wore the civies he'd worn outside. Now he grabbed the hem of the cable-knit sweater and tugged it over his head, then folded it and put it beside the couch. Jessica caught her breath at the beauty of his sculpted torso, then breathed out in a sigh as he slid out of his jeans. His legs were long and brawny, with big, well-shaped feet. Sometimes muscular men could look a little short-legged, but Galar's big, lean body was in perfect proportion.

Jess tried very hard not to stare between those powerful thighs. Even soft, his sex was impressive—a long, veined shaft with a plum-sized head, the heavy balls covered in wiry blond curls.

"How do you want me?"

*Any way I can get you.* Somehow she managed to keep the words from coming out of her mouth.

A professional model would have known how to arrange his body. Galar, however, was not a professional model, and Jessica found herself guiding him into the pose she wanted.

His square chin felt slightly rough with beard stubble as she angled his head up. She showed him how to bend one knee until his thigh hid that luscious shaft—she knew she wouldn't be able to concentrate with it on display. Jess positioned one powerful arm over the knee, then escaped back to her easel with a sense of relief.

Scooping up a stick of charcoal for the initial sketch, she went happily to work.

**Galar had to** tell his computer to suppress his erection.

Again.

He'd been telling the truth when he'd said his people didn't consider nudity an invitation to sex. Privacy was at a premium in the barracks conditions aboard ships, space stations, and paramilitary installations like the Outpost. It was only good manners to ignore whatever bare skin you saw.

But he hadn't realized how it would affect him to have a woman look at him the way Jessica did. That gaze of hers set his Warlord hunger burning like a torch.

The sizzling intensity that had first drawn him to her was back, blazing in her eyes, coiling through her slim body. She painted in long, furious strokes for more than half an hour, only to abruptly stop.

Galar's mouth went dry as Jessica strode toward him on those long legs. She crouched to stare up into his face, then studied the line of his body. It took every erg of his self-control to keep from dragging her into his lap and devouring that soft mouth.

Just as he was about to reach for her, Jess rose, turned with a roll of her lovely ass, and walked back to the easel. He managed not to snarl in frustration.

Galar inhaled, fighting for self-control. The breath carried the scent of her, richly feminine despite the overlay of paint. He wanted to bury his hands in her hair, feel the long, dark, silken strands against his palms, his fingers. He wanted to jerk up her red sweatshirt and cup those round, pretty breasts, taste her nipples. Were they pink? he wondered. A deep rose? A soft, dusty brown?

He wanted to reach between her legs and find her softest flesh, make her slick and ready.

Her lips parted, and the pink tip of her tongue peeked between her teeth.

*Sweet Mother.*

**Jess had never** seen anything quite like Galar's eyes. First they were a glowing gold, like honey in the sun, shaded with depths of amber and ocher. But as she painted him they began to burn, first with a single spot of red, then with flecks of crimson that had grown until now his pupils were a scarlet blaze.

And the look on his face—intent, almost predatory. Staring at her like a starving wolf looking at a lamb just out of reach. His sensual lips were slightly parted, an erotic flush riding those bladed cheekbones.

If any other man had looked at her like that, she would have gotten the hell out of the room. But this was Galar.

And she could feel herself getting wet.

With every breath she took, the lace cups of her bra gently abraded her stiff nipples. It was amazing she could still paint. Amazing she wanted to, when part of her ached to throw the brush aside and join him on that couch.

But the fact was, she loved what she was doing to them both too much to stop. The luscious heat she felt sizzled onto the canvas like an electric charge, energizing every brushstroke.

His painted eyes stared out of the portrait at her with a stark masculine hunger that reflected a breathtaking reality. Though his big body lay in a pose of mock relaxation, the need that coiled through him was every bit as naked as he was.

Jessica suspected this painting would make her blush when she was eighty. She was also quite sure that it would never appear on anybody's wall but her own.

So she went on painting despite the ache in her nipples, the heaviness between her thighs, the wet heat that built with every stroke.

Despite the burning red blaze in his eyes.

She found herself longing to test the boundaries of his control again. Laying the brush aside, Jess moved toward him as her heart pounded in a jungle drum thump. He watched her coming like a leopard staring at an approaching gazelle.

Waiting for the moment to spring.

She stopped just beyond his reach and sank slowly, gracefully, to her knees, moving like a geisha in a dance. She pretended to study the long, powerful line of him sweeping from chest to waist to hip. Avoiding his eyes. Somehow she sensed that if she met that red-coal gaze of his, his control would snap and the game would be over. And she wasn't ready for it to end. Not just yet.

She stood and walked back to her easel, feeling his gaze burning on the sway of her ass.

When she picked up the brush again, her hand shook.

Jessica studied the tiny vibration regretfully. Much as she loved playing with them both, she didn't want to ruin the work she'd done. It was time to stop.

She looked up. Directly into his eyes. He didn't smile, didn't speak. Just rolled to his feet in one powerful, athletic sweep. He stood there beside the couch, big feet braced apart.

His cock rose to full, breathtaking erection, flushing dark, its shaft lengthening, wrist-thick and breathtaking, his balls drawing tight. As if somehow he'd released some superhuman control he'd had over his body.

"Come here." It was a growled command, brooking no disobedience. Expecting none.

Jessica would have told any other man to go straight to hell.

She went to Galar.

Her mouth was dry, her nipples hard. As she stood looking up at him towering over her, she felt as if her sex were full of heated honey, thick and sweet. His nostrils flared, scenting her. His smile was slow, hungry. Confident. His cock jerked upward, a brush of heat against her belly.

"I want to touch you. I want to see you." Galar reached for the hem of her sweatshirt, pulling it off over her head and tossing it aside. His eyes glittered as he studied her breasts, cupped in lace and silk. He swallowed and went for the front clasp of her bra. Spilled her curves free into his warm hands. "Sweet Mother, you *are* beautiful." He sounded almost reverent.

"So are you." Jessica let her head fall back with a helpless groan as his big fingers rolled the aching tips.

"Undress for me," he said in a rumble.

"Oh, yeah." Swallowing, she reached for the snap of her jeans with eager, shaking hands. The zipper sounded like a surrendering sigh. Jess pushed her jeans down over her thighs, stepped free of them, kicked them carelessly aside.

Galar took a single step back to sweep a burning glance

over her. She shivered under his eyes, feeling small and vulnerable. And delicious.

Her gaze fell on the hard swell of his pectoral, the jut of a tiny brown nipple. Aching to touch him, she reached out. His skin felt hot, hard, smooth. Her hands left a smear of crimson across it like war paint.

"I'd better wash my hands." Her knees shook as she turned back toward the taboret and found a tube of cleanser. She squeezed the thick green gel into her palm.

Big hands reached around her naked waist and closed over hers, stroking the cleanser over her flesh. Whatever the stuff was made of, it stripped away the paint better than anything she'd ever seen, then disappeared like water.

Galar cleaned her hands thoroughly, slowly, until they tingled, clean of paint and aching with the need to touch him back. His fingers felt strong and warm. Her nipples perked. It was hard to breathe.

"You have beautiful hands," he murmured in her ear. The hunger in his voice made her shiver. "So slender. So delicate and small. Feminine."

She swallowed, looking down at his big male hands, with their stark, strong tendons and veins. There was nothing at all delicate about him. Nothing at all feminine.

Galar turned her in his arms, those powerful palms so gentle on her shoulders. Jessica stared up into his starkly handsome features. Up close, the red blaze of his eyes didn't look quite human.

"Why do your eyes glow?" Her voice sounded dreamy to her own ears.

"They do that when I'm in *riaat*." His lids lowered, veiling the glow with thick blond lashes. "Or aroused."

She had no idea what *riaat* was, and at the moment, she couldn't have cared less. All her attention was focused on his mouth, on the movement of his lips, the full, seductive curve of his lower lip, the thinner line of the upper with its little cupid's bow dip at the top.

Galar smiled and lowered his head. Reading her mind.

The kiss was slow and thorough and dizzying. She leaned into him with a helpless groan. His tongue touched the seam of her lips in a delicate request for entry, and she opened for him with a sigh. He slid inside in a delicious mating thrust. She twirled her own tongue around his, and he moaned, a rough, throaty sound. His arms tightened around her, dragging her close.

Big. Hot. Hard. His cock lay against her belly like a lead pipe. She quivered.

By the time he drew back, they both shook with need. He bent, scooped one arm behind her knees and the other around her shoulders, and swept her into his arms. Pivoted with easy strength to put her down on the couch.

Jessica's heart pounded in a sweet, crazed beat as he straightened, sweeping a glowing glance over her before sliding a knee onto the cushion beside her hip. She watched him bend toward the aching tip of her right breast. His hand cupped her, warm and skillful, as his tongue swirled around her nipple. She closed her eyes at the hot storm of sensation that trailed each wet flick and caress. Teeth closed, gently raking, dragging an aroused gasp from her lips. "Galar!"

He rumbled something, deep and feral. Jessica slid her hands up the powerful width of his shoulders to find the cool blond silk of his hair. Her fingers threaded through the short cropped curls, loving the feel of them, the heat of him against her.

Slowly, gently, Galar began to nibble his way down the line of her torso, stopping at her belly button to lick the little indentation until she squirmed and giggled. She felt him smile against her belly, then continue on his way with those sweetly arousing little nips.

He rose onto hands and knees, moving over her, head down as he tasted his way along. His cock pointed toward her body like a divining rod. Unable to resist, she closed her hand around the thick length.

It was his turn to gasp.

The shaft felt like heated silk, veined and hard. She stroked dreamily. Deep inside her, something tightened and clenched.

At last his mouth reached her soft, damp curls. He parted the petals of her sex with his fingers and gave her a long lick. She shuddered at the mind-blowing sensation, the flood of honeyed heat.

A drop of pre-come gathered at the tip of his cock. Jessica eyed it hungrily, then started pushing her way beneath him.

He straddled her helpfully, letting her angle the thick shaft down toward her mouth.

And then he began to feast.

# · 8 ·

Galar inhaled, breathing in the heady musk of her damp flesh. He parted the bright, rosy petals, studying the luscious glisten before he leaned down and slipped his tongue between them. He closed his eyes in pleasure at the taste. A little astringent, a bit salty, but Sweet Mother, there was nothing as intoxicating as the taste of a woman's pleasure.

Even as he sampled her lazily, he felt those soft little hands of hers busy on his body—one hand raking blunt nails across his butt, along his thighs, teasing and maddening, the other stroking between his thighs. The feeling of those long, tapered fingers closing around his cock made him shudder in hot delight.

Her tongue flicked over the head in a long, teasing swirl. He shuddered.

Lady, she was incredible. So delicate compared to the tough, muscular warrior women he was used to, she was long-legged and slim as a willow. And yet there was fire in her, a sizzling sexuality, a toughness that refused to give in, not to assassins, not to despair.

Unease rose in him suddenly, and he froze, his tongue going still, even buried as it was in her luscious flesh.

She was dangerous. She could get to him, work her way under his skin in a way none of the others had been able to. Somehow he sensed he'd never be able to hold her at that easy professional distance he'd always been able to maintain with his lovers.

She could make him vulnerable.

But even as cold breathed over Galar, her hot mouth engulfed his cock, sliding it halfway down her throat. Lust and pleasure clawed him, drowning the voice of caution with no effort at all. He groaned against her sex as Jess bobbed her head, sliding his erection in and out.

He'd worry about his vulnerability later. Right now his Warlord's body demanded he feed its considerable hunger.

With a growl of need, he began to bite and lick and suckle.


**Sensation rippled through** Jess, intoxicating and delicious—the hot, wet flick of his tongue, the warmth of his big hands stroking her thighs, her ass. The satin-and-steel texture of his cock, tasting of masculinity, salt, and the slightly bitter taste of pre-come. She cupped his balls in her hand, enjoying the feel of velvety skin and soft, springy curls. Widening her jaws, she took more of him in. He rewarded her with a deep groan.

A long finger traced along the seam between her inner lips, then found her slick opening and pressed deep. The feeling made her shiver.

Suddenly he pulled away from her as if unable to stand it anymore and turned to face her, hands braced on the couch on either side of her head.

For a moment they stared at each other, breathing hard

with need and pleasure. His angular features looked tight, his mouth full and damp. His eyes shone like a torch.

A powerful thigh slipped between her legs, and she spread herself for him, letting him ease into position. She drew a leg up, enjoying the slide of her skin along his.

"You drive me mad," he said, his voice rough.

She smiled, reaching up to draw a finger down the line of his braced arm, following the ripple of biceps down to the tendons of his wrist. "I can say the same."

"Good." His lids veiled those remarkable eyes, and he lowered his head as he settled over her. She drew in a breath at the sensation of his hard strength pressing precisely against her body—not so hard that she couldn't breathe, but letting her feel his solid power.

Then his mouth found hers in a slow kiss, sampling, brushing back and forth, catching her lip gently between his teeth, giving her a sliding taste of his tongue. She kissed him back, savoring the taste.

But though the kiss started out lazy, wooing, it heated like a pot coming to a boil. He began nipping at her, sliding his tongue deep. She shivered and wrapped one leg around his, sliding it the length of his big body until she could dig a heel against his ass, silently urging him on.

He drew back with a low, hot growl, braced himself on one hand, and reached down with the other. Wrapped it around his cock, angled it, and found her.

They both gasped as he entered, slow, relentless, a gliding thickness that teased her deliciously.

He threw back his head, the long cords of his throat working as he fought for control. Biting down on his lip, he drew out, then pressed deep again.

Jessica wrapped both legs around his narrow ass, then slipped her arms around his massive chest. And held on for dear life as he began to thrust. Deep. Controlled. Filling her more completely than any man ever had.

Lost in heat and hunger, Galar rode her, watching her

exquisite face. Her blue eyes shimmered, her hair spilling around her face in heaps of dark silk. Her skin shone like porcelain, contrasting with the blushing pout of her parted lips.

Each thrust made her pretty breasts dance, full and pink-tipped and impossibly tempting. Her long legs clamped over his ass as she ground up at him, adding the strength of her slender body to his.

Pleasure spilled through him, coiling hot around his balls, tightening, goading him to sweet madness until he thrust faster, deeper in heavy lunges. She gasped in time, surging against his body.

The climax roared out of nowhere, a fountain of blinding fire that dragged his head back. He roared, lost in the honey-eyed flames, in the pulsing grip of her sex around his cock. He heard her scream in raw pleasure as she followed him over.

When the long, delicious spasms finally died away, he collapsed over her, sweating and gasping. Somehow he possessed just enough wit to roll over onto his back and pull her into his arms. She fell against him, panting, limp. Her heart pounded against his chest.

"God," Jessica whimpered, "that was amazing."

That, he decided, was putting it mildly. He'd never had such delicious sex in his life.

At that thought, a little snake of unease slithered up his spine.

<br>

July 21, 2008
Charleston, South Carolina

**The coffee shop** was one of those quaint places that had helped make Charleston beloved of tourists everywhere. The street was cobblestone, shaded with century-old oaks, while the building's exterior was painted cotton-candy pink, with contrasting baby blue Victorian gingerbread. A sign that read "The Loving Cup" hung from a pair of gold-painted hooks.

Her heart pounding, the woman who called herself Charlotte Holt scanned her surroundings warily, too weary and frightened to notice their charm.

The hooves of a big carriage horse clopped on the cobblestone as the beast drew a white landau past. A pair of elderly tourists smiled at her sunnily from its red leather seats. A harried-looking mother ducked around her, towing a three-year-old. The child's face was smeared with the remnants of a chocolate ice cream cone, and he wore an expression of vast contentment.

A big redneck in a gimmie hat drew Charlotte's quivering attention, but a quick scan of his mind showed he was exactly what he appeared to be. Not, thank God, the Xer assassin who'd been dogging her trail like a horror-flick ghost seeking bloody vengeance.

Deciding it was safe, she limped into the coffee shop. Her hip burned with every step, a painful reminder of the wound Marcin had inflicted two days before. If not for her powers, she'd be dead.

Even as she pushed open the front door to the cheerful jangle of a bell, rich scents enveloped Charlotte. Expensive ground beans, chocolate, caramel, steamed milk, whipped cream, the yeasty smell of baking muffins. Her stomach rumbled. She tried to remember how long it had been since she'd eaten. Breakfast yesterday? Or had it been the day before?

But more than the tempting promise of food for her hungry stomach—so much more than that—was the feeling of peace that hung in the shop.

*They* were here.

Every knotted muscle in her neck and shoulders relaxed. Charlotte sighed as fear and tension ran out of her like water.

Eagerly now, she walked toward the counter. Two matronly women worked behind it, moving in the smooth rhythm of long partnership as they waited on a fidgeting teenager listening to a pink iPod. The heavier of the two dispensed a flood of something dark and steaming into a paper cup as her thin coworker rang up the kid's purchase.

The first woman's round face was lined with age, and her body appeared to carry fifty or so pounds it could have done without. Her gray hair was gathered into a tidy bun on top of her head, tied with a garnet ribbon that matched her dark red apron. Her partner was taller, more wiry than round, her hair a shade of black that was a little too dark, as if she'd dyed it herself, badly.

To Charlotte's special senses, both women seemed to radiate tranquility like a pair of matching beacons pouring light into foggy darkness.

Vanja and Ethini.

She'd have died for either of them without hesitation. Had damn near done so more than once.

Charlotte watched the two with an awe and longing she didn't bother to disguise. Vanja looked up, giving her a slow, serene smile, sweet and guileless as a child's. "There you are. Your usual?"

"Yes," Charlotte said with gratitude, leaning wearily against the counter as the older woman moved briskly around pouring two large cups of ice tea. It was too hot for coffee.

Suddenly Charlotte felt exhausted. A combination of hunger, sleeplessness, and fear, she supposed. "And a muffin, too, please." She needed the carbs desperately.

Vanja handed her the cups, along with a blueberry muffin on a paper plate, then exchanged a silent glance with Ethini. The two women smiled as if saying something Charlotte couldn't hear.

They probably were.

As Ethini went back to work, Vanja headed toward the

rear door that led out to a brick courtyard. Charlotte started after her, then paused, frowning. Something seemed to vibrate the air in her lungs, a powerful something that wasn't either of the women.

Instinctively, she scanned the room until her senses zeroed in on a shelf covered with knickknacks—a collection of snow globes, candles, and plates printed with paintings of Charleston landmarks. The kind of kitsch beloved of tourists everywhere, all of it dangling price tags.

One of those tacky little objects was one hell of a lot more than it appeared.

Charlotte shot Vanja an incredulous look. "You brought it here? What if the Xerans—?"

The woman shrugged calmly. "Even if they do, do you really think they'll recognize it?"

She gave the shelf another glance. "No, I don't suppose they would."

Vanja stepped through the door. Shaking her head, Charlotte followed.

The courtyard was empty at the moment, which wasn't surprising considering the suffocating noon heat. Vanja would hardly have suggested they talk here otherwise.

A massive old oak dominated the space, which was surrounded by a brick wall topped with decorative wrought-iron spikes. Planters of colorful peonies nodded in a faint breeze as a bumblebee circled them drunkenly.

Gratefully, Charlotte sank into a chair at one of the wrought-iron tables in the shade of a big garnet cafe umbrella. She sipped her tea, relishing its bracing sweetness, then took a bite of muffin and sighed. For once she wasn't running, wasn't hiding.

Wasn't afraid. Even the pain of her wound faded into the background, no more than a nagging ache.

Vanja reached out and rested a hand on Charlotte's injured hip. Power poured from the plump fingers, tearing a soft gasp from her lips. The pain faded, melting away as the deep knife wound began to heal.

Dark eyes met hers, kind and infinitely deep, as Vanja took her hand away. "Poor Char-lotte." There was a hint of some unidentifiable accent in her soft voice, something that might have been mistaken for a Charlestonian drawl. Charlotte knew better. "You have sacrificed much for us."

Charlotte stared into those fathomless eyes hungrily. "It was no sacrifice. I have gained far more than I lost."

That compassionate gaze dropped to her newly healed hip. "He hunts you still?"

Charlotte shrugged. "Colonel Marcin is not the kind to give up." She dared reach out and touch the other woman's hand. For just a heartbeat, she thought she felt fur under her palm. "And even if I defeat him, there will be others. The Xer mean to kill you and steal the T'lir."

Vanja's mouth curled in a very slight smile. "We are not so easy to kill. Nor is the T'lir so easy to take."

"But they are very good at killing." Her mouth tightened. "And stealing." They'd stolen her life, hadn't they?

Vanja only shrugged.

Charlotte sighed, afraid for her, but knowing by now that not even danger could pierce that smooth serenity. "How is Jessica?"

Vanja's gaze turned distant, abstracted. "Her body changes in its time. Our enemies plot her murder. She will soon face her test."

Charlotte's hands twisted in her lap. "Do you know—have you seen . . . ?"

"You know I cannot tell you that, child."

Her shoulders slumped. "No. I suppose not."

Jessica's test was her own. Just as Charlotte's was.

**Feeling loose-limbed and** relaxed in that way that just screamed "great sex," Jess followed Galar back to his quarters.

She didn't even bother to ask for a room of her own. Hell, after sampling his mind-blowing passion, she didn't want one.

She paused to watch shamelessly as he stripped, enjoying the shift and play of powerful muscle as he moved, admiring the perfect V of his torso, the length and power of his legs.

He cocked a blond brow at her. "Enjoying the view?"

Jess grinned. "Absolutely."

Galar folded his brawny arms, rocked back on his heels, and stared at her in obvious challenge. Jess laughed softly and peeled her sweatshirt off over her head.

His golden eyes flared with approval as her bare breasts bounced free. She caught the waistband of her jeans and rolled her hips in a teasing wiggle as she pushed them down. She grinned at him. "Enjoying the view?"

Galar barked a laugh and swooped down on her, scooping her into his arms as his cock jerked upward into full erection. "What do you think?"

Jess wrapped her arms around his neck. "I think I'm impressed."

"You *think*?" he purred, "Obviously, I'm going to have to work harder."

An hour later, deliciously exhausted, Jessica sighed as Galar pulled her against him and curled his big, sweaty body around hers. She pillowed her head on his powerful shoulder, sighed, and slid quickly into sleep.

*Jess recognized Earth. Blue, wreathed in clouds, the familiar landmasses painted in green and brown and ocher.*

*The ship came screaming in, a flashing shape against the background of space. Even with her new knowledge, it seemed profoundly alien, all curves and sweeping lines that looked somehow as if no human hand had created them.*

*It slammed into Earth's atmosphere and kept going as a protective shield flared bright around it, warding off the friction of entry. As the great craft plummeted toward the ocean, Jess's head tossed against her pillow.* Tsunami, *her mind whispered, conjuring images of people screaming, drowning . . .*

*Instead, the ship abruptly braked and slid into the water with scarcely a splash. It slipped downward through the cold blue, deeper and deeper, until it finally settled onto the ocean floor, a cloud of silt rising around it.*

*The scene shifted. A thrumming sound reverberated through the water, strange and hollow to Jess's ears.*

*The source of the thrumming finally appeared: a nuclear submarine, sliding through the depths like a shark. Lights flashed out from the sub, dancing over the alien vessel, tracing its inhuman lines.*

Damn, it's huge, *Jess thought, startled. The craft was easily five times the size of the sub.*

*At last the submarine cruised away, considerably faster than it had approached. Jess could almost sense its crew's eagerness to report what they'd found.*

*But no sooner had it vanished than the ship slowly went transparent and disappeared. Some kind of camouflage field, Jess realized. But why hadn't the crew activated it sooner?*

*It was as though they wanted to be seen.*

*The scene shifted again. A team of deep-sea divers appeared, only to swim away disappointed when they found nothing but cold and darkness and deep, still water.*

*Shift. Now she was inside the ship. Dim, curving shapes towered around her, lit only by the gentle amber glow of alien instrumentation.*

*It seemed she glided between row after row of transparent eggs, glowing a soft gold. Somehow she knew each of them was bigger than a man. Gazing within, she saw forms,*

*half-seen yet unquestionably alive. Each had six limbs, cov-*
*ered with fine fur, and elongated heads balanced on narrow*
*necks, from which wafted a dandelion puff of mane.*

*As she gazed within one of those eggs, the eyes of its oc-*
*cupant met hers, huge, dark, lit with a profound intelligence.*
*Kind eyes, alien though they were, radiating sweetness and*
*peace. Christian saints might have had eyes like that.*

*Half-hypnotized, Jess floated in the darkness, letting the*
*creature's alien serenity wash over her in gentle waves.*

*Until blue light exploded in the darkness like a lightning*
*strike. Figures flashed into being between the eggs, mas-*
*sive, armored, spikes glinting from shaved skulls.*

*Jess recoiled in horror.*

*Xer!*

*One of the Xerans stepped directly into her view. A*
*woman, delicate rings jutting from her temples. After a fro-*
*zen instant of blank horror, Jess recognized the big green*
*eyes and fragile features, despite their cold expression.*

*Charlotte Holt.*

**Jess jerked upright** with a shout. Heat and light burst
from the center of her chest, illuminating the room. All
around her, she saw objects dance with a clatter, then tumble
from shelves, hitting the carpeted floor in a chorus of
thumps.

"Jessica!" Strong arms closed around her. "Lights!" Galar
snapped. The room filled with a soft white glow, banishing
the last of the alien light.

"The Xer!" Instinctively, Jess dug her nails into his biceps with a strength born of desperation. "They're going to
kill them! They're going to steal the T'lir!"

"Hey! Hey, it's all right," he said soothingly. "You just
had a nightmare."

She scanned the room wildly. Every object he'd had on

his shelves lay on the floor now, as if toppled in a storm of energy. "Are you sure about that?"

And what the hell was a T'lir?

**"We must have** had an earthquake," Galar told her. She'd told him about the dream as they moved around the room picking up and putting away the fallen trids, statuary, and weapons.

Jess stopped in the act of picking up the data sheet and stared at him. "In Georgia?"

He shrugged. "It felt like one to me. The bed shook so hard I almost fell off."

Jess opened her mouth, then closed it again. If she told him she'd done it, he'd think she was nuts. Yet as she'd jolted awake, she'd felt something rush out of her in a burning flood of energy.

No, it must have been a nightmare. Only . . . "What about Charlotte?"

Galar shot her a look as he picked up the sword and put it back in its place on the shelf. "You think she really is Xer? Jessica, it was just a dream."

"But it seemed so real. I've never had one that vivid, and I've had some pretty vivid dreams."

"Charlotte isn't Xer, Jess." Shaking his head, he bent to pick up a fallen trid globe. "I scanned her. She was as human as you are."

"Sensors can be fooled." Or so said her EDI, anyway.

"Not really. You can shield against them, but then they won't pick up anything at all. Charlotte read as completely human. If she'd been shielding, I'd have known it."

She frowned. "I thought Xerans *were* human."

"They came from human root stock, yes, but that was before a couple of hundred years of genetic tinkering. There are significant differences now." He stepped closer to rest a comforting hand on her shoulder. "You had a nightmare, Jess. That's all it was."

*God,* she thought grimly, *I hope you're right. Because if you're not, something really scary is going on.*

**Jess watched her** opponent brandish his knife, a sneer of menace on his face. Muscle rippled up and down his powerful bare chest as he moved.

"You've got to be kidding me."

Galar lowered the knife and sighed. "Jess, that EDI combat file won't do you any good if you don't practice."

"I don't see how it would do me *any* good at all against a Xeran battleborg."

He glowered. "Now there's an attitude just guaranteed to get you killed. May I remind you that you torched his ass the last time you fought him?"

She snorted. "The last time I fought him, he gutted me."

"Yeah, but you fought him off just long enough for us to get to you." Galar gestured with the knife. "That's the whole point of this little exercise. You're right—one-on-one in any extended fight, he'd kill you. That means your job is to make sure you don't get in an extended fight with him. You get the fuck away and give us a chance to save you."

"When am I ever alone long enough for him to get to me?"

Galar shrugged those brawny, distracting shoulders. "If he kills me, you *will* be alone."

Jess stared at him, her eyes going wide as her stomach twisted. "What?"

His steady, calm gaze didn't even falter. "You've got to be ready for any eventuality, Jess."

"I don't want you to die for me, Galar."

"I'm not particularly thrilled about the idea either." He took a step closer, his stare going narrow and fierce. Demanding.

"But if I do end up dead, I don't want it to be for nothing. Do *not* let him kill you. Remember—the Outpost computer will hear you if you yell. You don't even have to dial 911. Just scream for help, and every Enforcer in this facility will be here within two minutes. But you have to stay alive for those two minutes."

She swallowed. "But what about you?"

Galar shrugged. "With regen, there's a good chance they can help me, if they can get to me in time."

Jess straightened her shoulders and sighed. "All right. What do I need to do?"

"Run like hell the minute he shows up."

"I thought I was supposed to fight."

"Not if you can help it. If Marcin Jumps into the Outpost, I'm going to engage him." His mouth pulled into a grim, hard line. "You run. Don't argue, don't stop to watch or help, just get as far away as possible."

"You want me to leave you?"

"You bet your luscious little ass. If you're not in the line of fire, I don't have to worry about keeping you alive. Besides, every Enforcer in the Outpost will be on the way." He smiled slightly. "I don't want you hanging around distracting them from saving my life."

Jess still didn't like the idea of abandoning him, but she had to admit he had a point. "Run like hell. Got it."

"Put barriers between him and you," Galar continued. "He's faster than you are, so you need to give him an obstacle course to deal with. Close doors, throw furniture in his path. Slow him down however you can."

"What do I do if he catches me?"

He grinned. "Get away."

"No shit. Got any suggestions as to how I do that?"

"He's going to expect you to fight like a human civilian—timidly and ineffectively." Galar balled a fist and bared his teeth. "You have to do the opposite. When you hit him, give it everything you've got. Try to drive your fist through his skull." He pumped out a punch, demonstrating.

Jess snorted. "Do I look like a Warfem to you?"

"How much force you can actually generate is beside the point. Even if all you do is startle him, that could be the two seconds you need to get away and stay alive." He gave her a come-on gesture with his fingers. "Hit me."

*This is a waste of time.* She knew better than to say so, though. Biting her lip, Jess wound up and drove her fist right at his bare stomach.

# 9

**The impact jolted all the way up her shoulder as if** she'd driven her fist into a concrete block. *"Ow!"* She shook her stinging hand and blinked tears out of her eyes.

"Not like that." He hadn't even rocked back on his heels, she saw resentfully.

Sliding the knife into the sheath at his waist, Galar turned so he stood in profile to her. "You need to drive from your hips so you're putting your entire body behind the punch, not just the muscles of your arm." His slight sneer told her just what he thought of the muscles in question. He slid his right leg back, cocked his right arm, and threw it forward, twisting his hips to add torque as he did.

Jess was suddenly very glad she was not on the other end of that fist.

"Now you try it." He moved around behind her and put his hands on her hips. "Everything comes from here. Step your right foot back."

Jess obeyed, feeling more than a little awkward—and entirely too aware of his presence at her back. She threw a punch. "Well, that sucked." She grimaced at its lack of force.

"Try again," Galar said patiently, no hint of frustration in his voice.

Jess gritted her teeth and set herself, determined to get it right this time. She gave it everything she had—and damn near fell on her face.

To give him credit, Galar didn't even sigh. "Better, but you need to watch your balance. Let me see your fist. No, not like that. You'll break every bone in your hand." He unwrapped her fingers and showed her how to make a proper fist.

"This brings to mind one of my grandmother's favorite sayings," Jess told him drily. " 'Never try to teach a pig to sing. You'll frustrate yourself and annoy the pig.' "

"The pig's life doesn't depend on her ability to belt out an aria." He frowned. "I don't understand this. Chogan gave you a combat EDI, but you don't seem to be accessing it at all."

She grimaced. "I noticed."

Galar rubbed his jaw, contemplating her. "You're overthinking this. It's like with the basic knowledge file. When did it quit swamping you?"

Jess cocked her head, considering. "When I stopped fighting it."

"I think you're doing the same thing with the combat EDI. If we can get you to start reacting automatically, it will come."

And with no more warning than that, he swung a roundhouse right at her head.

Jess's right arm jerked up, knocking his wrist upward even as she stepped back, pivoting neatly away. She stopped and blinked at him in astonishment. "I did it."

Galar gave her a satisfied grin. "You certainly did."

"Damn good thing, or you would have taken off my head."

He snorted. "Please. I'm a Warlord. I've never thrown a punch I wasn't in total control of."

"Must be nice," she grumbled.

"Let's try that again." His eyes narrowed in a calculating expression.

It was one Jess quickly learned to dread. He gave her no quarter whatsoever, stalking her like a tiger, throwing punches and kicks at what she would have sworn was full speed. Luckily, he wasn't kidding about his control. Even when she missed a block, he never hit her. And at first, she missed a lot of blocks.

But he was right. The rain of attacks gave her no time to think, forced her into pure reaction, leaving her sweating and breathing hard, heart pounding.

"Galar," she panted at last. "That's enough. I need a break."

He peeled his lips back from his teeth and flashed the knife he'd drawn as she'd gotten better. "Marcin won't give you any breaks, Jess."

Anger slid through her, quick and hot. She'd been giving him all she had. Her muscles felt like cooked spaghetti, and she ached all the way to the bone. She was tired, dammit. And anyway, if he was right, no fight with the Xeran would run more than a few seconds anyway. Either she'd get away, or she'd die.

"We've got a word for guys like you," she gasped. "Asshole!"

"Less talking, more fighting." He swung the knife.

Furious now, Jess took one step forward, swung up her left arm to block his attack, and powered her right fist right into his mouth.

Galar's head snapped back from the force of her punch.

**Jessica's instant of** triumph became horror as Galar lifted his fingers and wiped blood off his mouth. She'd split his lower lip. "Oh, hell, I'm sorry!"

He grinned at her, a smear of crimson across his teeth. "Now that was what I was waiting for. I knew if I pushed you hard enough, you'd cut loose."

"You *wanted* me to hit you?" Then she scrubbed a hand over her face as realization hit. "Of course you did—that was the point."

He nodded. "Even after I got you to start using your EDI, you've been totally on the defensive. And that's not the way to win a fight against a Xeran. That's not even the way to *survive* a fight with a Xeran. It's going to take aggression and ferocity to stay alive against that son of a bitch."

"Point taken." She ran both hands through her hair and grimaced. It was as wet as though she'd just stepped out of a shower. "I probably smell like a goat."

"Nah, just a slightly sweaty female." He dropped a big hand on her shoulder. "Let's clean you up."

Jess moaned in gratitude. "Oh, God, yes."

**Ivar had long** since perfected the art of watching and listening without appearing to pay any attention at all. That talent was one of the many things, along with his sociopath's ability to blend, that had made him such a successful spy.

So the entire time Galar had been giving Jess her combat lesson, he'd been working with a gravity bar in a corner of the gym. He'd had the bar on its highest weight setting, but such was his cyborg strength that he could leap and spin and jab with it with only half his mind on what he was doing. The rest was entirely focused on Galar and the primitive.

It had been blind luck that had brought him to the gym at this particular moment. But then, luck was another key ingredient of his success.

Not that he'd need much luck to kill Jessica. Her combat skills were laughable at best. He'd learned that just by watching her. It would be as simple as getting her alone for five seconds and snapping her delicate little neck.

The trick would be not getting caught. The Outpost's security system was formidable. The moment he tried to launch an attack, its sensors would detect his aggressive intent, and it would summon the other Enforcers. His cover would be blown, assuming he even survived.

Though imagining Galar's reaction to finding the little bitch dead, he was seriously tempted anyway. Somehow she'd gotten under the Ice Lord's skin, something Ivar had always assumed impossible. Galar didn't even seem to be putting up a fight against her assault on his heart.

Yes, killing the primitive would be delicious. Especially if he got to watch Galar's reaction afterward. He just had to make sure he didn't get caught.

Ivar's eyes narrowed as he began to pump out another set of repetitions with the weight bar. He had a kernel of a plan, but it would need more development.

First he'd need to hack into the Outpost's security system, which would be tricky. He was confident he could eventually pull it off, though. Ivar had never encountered a system he couldn't penetrate if he put his mind to it.

Which meant the primitive was as good as dead.


**Galar led her** down a hallway lined with doors. Jess followed mechanically on legs that shook slightly with sheer exhaustion. "And I thought I was in good shape." She groaned. "I hit the gym three times a week!"

Golden eyes cut in her direction, but Galar kindly did not express his opinion of her workout schedule. Instead he said only, "It doesn't matter how fit you are. Combat is a whole different magnitude of effort, since it's as much mental and emotional as physical." He swung open one of the doors and led the way inside.

Into an oasis.

Jess stopped on the threshold to stare. There were no walls or ceiling, just a rain forest of bright jungle green. An oval pool lay in the center of a cluster of colorful lilies and feathery emerald ferns. A semicircle of trees curved around the pool, shading the bubbling water with a canopy of leaves. A scarlet macaw eyed her from one limb, its glorious feathers bright as Christmas decorations.

The illusion was perfect, but it was definitely an illusion. The floor under her feet was hard and smooth, not soft jungle loam. "Damn, Galar, how did you do this?"

He shrugged and reached for the waistband of his black snugs. "Same basic technology as the imagizers we use for trids and camouflage." Before she could absorb that idea, he was stripping the pants down his long, beautifully muscled thighs.

Jess blinked at the sight of his bare ass, and suddenly felt a lot less exhausted. "Uh, what if somebody comes in?"

Galar stepped out of the snugs, gloriously naked. "I've told the comp we want privacy. It won't open the door for anybody else." He gave her a slow, predatory smile. "We don't have to worry about being interrupted."

"Oh." She swallowed, her gaze on his cock. It was rising into a truly impressive erection. "Isn't that convenient."

"Very." He lifted a blond brow. "Aren't you overdressed?"

Jess dragged her eyes away from Galar's impressive shaft. "Apparently."

But as she started tugging down her own skintight snugs, the muscles of her arms and thighs twinged painfully. She flinched. "Owww! Dammit, I'm sore!"

"We'd better get you in that water, or you won't be able to move tomorrow." Galar frowned. To her disappointment, she saw his erection dip. "In fact, I think you need a massage."

Jess watched his cock sink regretfully. "So do I, but I don't think I'm going to get the one I've got in mind."

His frown transformed into a rakish grin. "Never underestimate a Warlord, love. We can always rise to any occasion."

She groaned at the pun and took the hand he extended

to help her into the pool. The heat of the bubbling water
was enough to make her start sweating as her feet found the
steps that led down into the big marble tub. A surprisingly
soft padded bench ran around its outer wall, and she settled
onto it with a sigh, sinking to her shoulders in steaming
bubbles.

"Scoot forward," Galar told her. She obeyed, and he slid
off the lip of the pool onto the bench behind her, legs spread
on either side of her hips. She turned her head to watch him
pour a bright blue liquid from a bulb container into his
palm.

"Uetian herbal oil," he explained, rubbing his hands together. "Nothing's better for sore muscles."

His palms, strong and warm, found her shoulders. Jess
closed her eyes and purred as his long fingers dug in, discovering every knot in her muscles with unerring accuracy.
She let her head fall forward. Broad thumbs circled a particularly nasty spot, massaging it skillfully until it melted
away.

*Damn, this is better than sex.* Then she grinned, remembering just how good Galar's lovemaking was. *Well, almost.*

**The skin of** Jessica's shoulders felt fine-grained under his
hands, hot and slick from the combination of the oil and the
water. Looking over her shoulder, Galar watched her pretty
breasts bob, flushed pink by the heat. He badly wanted to
taste those rosy nipples, but he was a patient man, and she
needed the massage.

She'd earned it, too. Galar smiled, remembering her
fierce concentration as she'd fought to block his attacks. To a
man who'd spent his life fighting alongside cyborgs and
Warfems, she'd looked more than a little clumsy.

He wasn't sure why he'd found that so endearing.

Maybe it had been her fierce determination. Jess kept

pushing, kept trying even when she was all but staggering with fatigue. Pissing her off enough to make her swing at him had taken a surprising amount of work. She'd been so intent on getting it right, no matter how deliberately unreasonable his demands. She might not be a product of genetic engineering or some warrior culture, but she was a fighter all the way to the bone.

No wonder he couldn't resist her.

Galar rubbed circles in the center of her palm with his thumb, then began to work his way up the length of each long, tapered finger. He'd already massaged her back and arms so thoroughly, she lay completely relaxed against him, almost dozing.

"Mmmm," Jess whispered. "That feels so good." She gave a sensual little wiggle.

He smiled. "I was beginning to think you'd gone to sleep."

Jess turned her head to give him a wicked smile. "Not with that hard-on of yours pressing against my butt."

He lowered his head to give her ear a gentle nibble. She shivered deliciously. "Should I apologize for keeping you awake?"

"Only if you don't intend to live up to my expectations."

He cupped her breast with his free hand, then began to delicately roll her nipple between oil-slicked fingers. "Oh, you don't have to worry about that."

She smiled, shuttering her eyes in pleasure. "You relieve my mind." He released her hand and started conducting an entirely different massage between her long legs. She arched and caught her breath.

Oiled fingers stroked and toyed with first one hard nipple, then the other, until she squirmed in helpless need. He gave her no quarter, teasing breasts and sex simultaneously while she whimpered.

Galar rumbled in pleasure at her reaction. She felt snug and delicious around his oil-slick fingers. He remembered how it had felt to drive his cock into that sweet, tight channel. His erection bucked, trapped between his body and her hips.

Her answering chuckle sounded distinctly feline.

**As Galar's fingers** teased her nipple and sex, pleasure flowed through Jessica's body like a wave of heated honey, shimmering and sweet. She let her head loll back against his shoulder. After that long, delicious massage, she felt as boneless as a plate of pasta. Even her arousal was lazy, a gently rising heat instead of the urgent storm of lust she'd experienced the day before. Yet it was no less sweet, no less intoxicating.

Leaning back in Galar's strong arms, Jess let herself enjoy his slow, sensual teasing. His cock pressed against her like a wicked promise, and she grinned, anticipating.

"You like that?" he rumbled in her ear, sliding first one finger deep, then two.

"You're the man with sensors. What do you think?"

"I think I want to fuck you." The rough tiger growl sent a shaft of pure lust jolting through her. Before she could stir, he surged under her, sweeping her out of the water and into his arms.

Jess yelped, startled, as he turned and draped her across the side of the pool on her belly. "Hey!" She started to rear up, but he curled a big hand around the back of her neck, keeping her gently in place. "What do you think you're doing?"

"Take a guess." Laughter rumbled in his voice as he stroked a hand over the curve of her ass, then found her opening with two fingers.

She gasped as he gave her a slow, teasing pump. To the outrage of her feminist sensibilities, the feeling of being held down actually increased her arousal. "Let go!"

"No," he said thoughtfully. "I don't think so. I've got plans for you."

"Galar!" Her attempt at a tone of stern warning was probably blunted by the giggle she couldn't quite suppress.

"Jessicaaaa," he purred back, shifting his hold to the center of her back. Water sloshed around her knees as he wrapped his other arm around her thighs.

And buried his face right against her pussy.

"Oh!" She tried to rear up, startled, but his Warlord strength controlled her body effortlessly, keeping her in place for the long, wet lick that followed. "Gaaalaaarr!"

He made a rumbling sound and settled down to eat her in earnest, first circling his tongue around her clit in a delicious, burning spiral, then lapping between her lips, then finally thrusting deep into her core. In and out, in and out, drawing flickering hot patterns that maddened. In seconds, he had her writhing, but the powerful arm around her thighs kept her pinned and helpless.

Jess had never been so turned on, so fast, in her entire life.

He paused in those mind-blowing licks for a series of little nibbles, pressing his teeth gently into her lips and over her clit, careful to use just enough force to make her squirm, but no more. At the same time, he probed her with his free hand, pumping maddeningly deep. Teasing her until it was all she could do not to howl.

"Oh, God!" Jess tossed her head, panting. Every stroke, every nibble, every lick sent another blazing jolt of pleasure through her nervous system.

"You taste good," he growled, an elemental male rumble. "So juicy, so sweet. And you're *tight* too."

She squeezed her eyes shut and panted. She was so damned close to coming, she could feel the fiery nimbus of the climax trembling right on the edge of her consciousness. "Fuck me! God, please *fuck me*!"

He gave her a slow, tormenting stroke with those big fingers. "You sure you're ready?"

"Yes!" It was a scream of pure frustration.

"No." He lowered his head and curled his arm tighter around her thighs. "I don't think you are. Not quite."

"You bastard!" Jess bucked against his hold, maddened.

He only laughed and went back to using that ruthless tongue again, avoiding her clit now, as if knowing all it would take was one tiny stroke to send her over.

Yowling in a combination of pleasure and pure frustration, she hunched and tried to kick, clawing at the floor around the tub, only dimly aware it was smooth tile instead of grassy loam. Out of the corner of one eye, she saw something sail past and bounce off the invisible wall of the chamber. She was far too absorbed in the oral torment to register what it was or what had sent it flying, though. "Galar, damn you!"

"Now," he purred, straightening behind her and dragging her legs apart with both hands. "*Now* you're ready!"

He drove his cock into her in one strong, ruthless thrust. She wailed at the piercing pleasure of being so completely filled.

Galar felt massive, thicker than her fist, and he pumped in and out of her in merciless digs that stretched her deliciously. Almost too much, almost too hard, but not quite. The feral intensity of his ride was just what she needed, shooting her up the sweet, searing curve to orgasm.

Until finally—finally!—Jess came in long, blazing ripples so hot, she literally saw stars.

Galar threw back his head in delight as her tight inner muscles milked his cock with long ripples. Gritting his teeth, trying to hold on just a little longer, he slammed his hips against hers, working the thick shaft in and out and in again. Each honeyed stroke made him shudder at the raw pleasure of possessing her.

He'd never in his life experienced anything as hot as teasing Jessica into a mindless frenzy. He fully intended to do it again. And again.

And again.

Imagining the pleasure to come, he felt the orgasm swamp him in a shuddering liquid blast that tore a bellow of delight from his throat.

**Later, as they** staggered around on shaking legs getting dressed, Galar found the bulb of herbal oil lying all the way by the far wall of the chamber. He frowned down at it, wondering how it had gotten there. He didn't remember throwing it, and he didn't recall Jess doing so either.

Then again, they'd been pretty turned on. Who knew what one of them had done in the heat of the moment?

**Marcin slid the** penitent's rough gray robe on over his naked shoulders. The fabric's stiff fibers pricked at his skin as if with hundreds of tiny claws. He worked to embrace the discomfort, knowing there would be worse to come. Atoning for his failure to apprehend the heretic would require blood. And a great deal of pain.

He'd chased her for the past endless week, getting close only to fail repeatedly as she'd Jump again and again until he'd lose the trail. She seemed to be able to sense his presence even when he was fully shielded, something that should have been impossible.

Those repeated failures weren't just frustrating—they could cost him his life. His stomach twisted in dread, but he ignored it. Fear was an unworthy emotion, he told himself, a barrier on the path to victory.

Marcin walked across the cold black quartzion floor, grinding his heels with every step so the sharp stones dug even harder into his bare feet. An icy sting told him he'd succeeded in his goal. When he looked back, he saw with satisfaction that he'd left bloody footprints glistening on the stone.

Perhaps it would help appease the warrior priest's fury.

Though even if it didn't, he'd embrace whatever punishment he was dealt. That, too, was his duty. Failure had a price, and an honorable man paid it without stinting.

He strode along the stone corridors of the Cathedral Fortress, passing soldiers, pilgrims, worshipers, and priests. A frigid glare repelled any curious gazes that lingered on his penitent's robes and bloody tracks.

The crowd thinned quickly as he found his way to the priests' wing. Tarik ge Lothar's quarters lay at the end of the corridor, in a coveted location in the tower that overlooked the Great Inland Sea.

When Marcin stepped through the unlocked door, the view through the huge window took his breath. The Inland Sea lay in a great sweep of blue all the way to the horizon under the pale violet sky, waves battering the black stone cliffs that formed the base of the Cathedral Fortress.

Leading a cohort of the Faith came with other benefits as well. Though low-ranking monks like Marcin might have bare stone cells with only a few amenities, Warrior Priest Tarik's quarters spoke of battles won and the rewards of victory.

First there was the great fur skin that lay across the smooth marble floor, fully twelve feet long. The creature's six legs were tipped in dagger blade claws. Its massive, bearlike head glared out at the room, snarl exposing tusks the length of a man's forearm.

The colonists on Cambria called the creatures gravediggers for obvious reasons. Marcin would have hated to take on a beast of such size, even with full armor and a beamer.

Tarik had stalked it without armor, using naught but a knife, though it was said he'd spent a full week in regen afterward healing the resulting wounds. It had been one of the tests that had proved him worthy to lead his cohort.

Arranged on the gleaming black headboard shelves of his bed were trophies of other battles: an exquisite bronze of a nude woman looted during the invasion of Vardon; a katana from ancient Japan; an array of priceless objets d'art and weapons, all in gold or marble or encrusted with gems.

But the real centerpiece of the room was the massive cabinet that occupied the place of honor across from the bed. Like the warrior priest's bed, it had been carved from gleaming black Xeran spiderwood. Marcin recognized the distinctive style of the intricate carving as the work of the finest artisan on the Fatherworld. The warrior priest must have paid a great deal for that cabinet.

Skulls lined the shelves, both human and alien, each painted in the dark, dried blood of its owner. Xeran characters described the death blow that had killed each of them, along with words of praise for their courage and combat skills. These were Tarik's most honored foes.

Not a few of them had Xeran skull implants.

Marcin would have liked to examine them more closely, but he didn't quite dare. Instead he moved to the center of the room, where a fire bowl sat on a piece of priceless crimson Takega silk.

Arranged on the silk on one side of the bowl were five silver boxes filled with herbs. Opposite the boxes lay a strand of shining wire studded with sharp thornlike projections.

Marcin knelt on the side of the cloth before the thorned wire, silently admitting his guilt.

Expressing his willingness to pay the price.

# · 10 ·

❧❦❧

**No sooner had he seated himself than Tarik entered** on silent slippered feet. He was dressed in a black silk robe and loose trousers, both embroidered with silver thread in symbols of the Faith so that they had a somber gleam.

The first time Marcin had met Tarik, he'd been surprised to find the warrior priest a smaller man than himself—a full head shorter, built for muscular grace rather than the sheer bull power of a combat 'borg. Yet he would not have cared to meet the priest in battle. Even without the four sets of horns that revealed his rank, there was a stillness about Tarik, a kind of lethal calm. It was the icy serenity of a man who'd been learning the skills of the warrior from the time he could walk. He looked like what he was: the leader of the most deadly cohort in the Xeran priesthood.

Tarik studied him, light glinting on his horn implants. Marcin bowed from the waist, lowering his head to the depth required by Tarik's rank, then a little deeper to indicate his personal respect.

Tarik inclined his head slightly in return. "Thou hast left the blood of thy repentance on the stone." His voice was beautiful, giving the lyrical words of the priestly language a kind of dark music.

"I have not yet killed the heretic. My failure shames me." He lifted his head and met Tarik's eyes with his best calm and level stare. "But I shall succeed."

"It is as well." Tarik sank gracefully to his knees on the other side of the fire bowl. "We have decided we wish to execute the apostate publicly."

The tensed muscles in Marcin's back relaxed fractionally. He might yet get out of this interview with his life, though he knew better than to hope he would not bleed. "As thou will." He inclined his head.

"Of more importance is the location of the Abominations, that they may be destroyed and the T'lir obtained. That must be thy priority." He began to take pinches of herbs from each of the silver boxes, each gesture smooth, graceful, an act of ritual. "If the heretic does not survive thy questioning, do not concern thyself. The Abominations must be eliminated before they spread their poison. And the T'lir— it's the key to the Fatherland's victory over our enemies." He lifted a sparker next, flicking the metal device in the fire bowl to produce a tongue of flame and a curl of glowing green smoke.

Marcin closed his eyes and breathed deeply, drawing the smoke into his lungs. In seconds, he felt his senses sharpening. Beneath his knees, the prickle of his rough robe began to feel like tiny shards of glass digging into his skin. He managed not to grind his teeth or shift his weight.

Opening his eyes, he met Tarik's cool gaze. The pain of the robe's fibers intensified, but he didn't allow himself to blink. Sweat rolled down the small of his back, a silent testimony to his misery. *I am the master of my body,* Marcin chanted to himself. *My body does not master me.*

Another agonizing minute ticked by. Then two. Then three. Then ten, every second bringing more and more pain as his overstimulated nerves reacted to the drug. He never moved.

Until Tarik drew the knife from his sleeve and put it down before him. A faint smile curved the warrior priest's mouth.

Marcin knew that if he'd failed the test, Tarik would have slit his throat with that blade. He didn't allow his triumph to show on his serene face.

Tarik snapped his fingers. A panel opened, and a courier ball flew into his hand. "Here are thy new orders. A trap has been prepared for the other heretic, the primitive Jessica Kelly. You will lend thy assistance before returning to thy hunt for the apostate."

Though a thousand questions flooded his mind, Marcin merely inclined his head. "As thou will."

Tarik paused and lifted a coal black brow. He said nothing, but he didn't need to. Marcin knew what he expected.

He flipped his robe open, baring his groin. Then he picked up the thorned silver wire and began to wrap it around his penis as his sensitized nerves howled in agony.

Approval lit Tarik's icy red eyes.


**The alien ship** was dark and strange, a warren of snaking corridors, oddly-shaped rooms, and bizarre equipment that was obviously not designed for the use of anyone with two legs and ten fingers.

First Scientist Chara va Hol moved cautiously down one of the ship's dim corridors, fascinated and wary as she examined the curving bulkheads. It was more like walking around inside a living creature than a vessel.

Which was actually an apt comparison, since sensor

readings suggested the material around her was organic, similar to a neuronet computer. Was this entire vessel a comp?

Humming in interest, Chara contemplated data from the small flotilla of sensor globes that orbited her like floating silver apples. Her headset projected the information into her mind in a gentle shower of data.

"Any sign of the T'lir?" Warrior Monk Decarro ge Ralit demanded, his armored boots scraping on the deck as he trailed her.

"Not so far."

He grunted. His body thin and hard as a sword blade, his features narrow and pinched, Ralit reminded Chara far too much of her father. Something in his fanatic's eyes made the flesh of her shoulders jerk with the memory of childhood scourgings. She fought to ignore the sensation. She could not afford the distraction.

She had to make the most of this opportunity.

Chara had already scored quite a coup in being the one to discover that the Sela ship had Jumped into Earth's distant past. Which should have been impossible. No one had ever managed to Jump an entire ship.

How had the Sela done it? The Empire would give much for such technology.

If Chara capped that discovery by being the first to learn where the aliens had hidden the T'lir, her future as a temporal anthropologist would be assured.

Unfortunately, there were ten other teams searching the alien ship. Beating them to the prize would not be easy, but achieving victory would be more than worth the effort.

Encouraged by that enticing vision, Chara went back to dictating notes into her headset log. "This ship is ancient. At least a thousand years old, according to my scans. If the Sela were capable of such advanced tech a thousand years ago, why were they living like agrarian primitives when we discovered them last year?"

"Because they are Abominations," Ralit growled in the priest tongue. "And mad. Mind their heresy does not infect thee as it did the expeditionary force." His hand fell to the shard pistol at his hip, fondling its silver butt.

Her shoulders twitched again, but she made no answer. Ralit would not have welcomed comment, for he was of the same sect as her father. He, too, believed that women were by nature weak and lacking in warrior virtues.

Though Javor va Hol had done his best to score those virtues into Chara's flesh with the whip and the wire. . . .

Chara came to an abrupt halt, her attention captured by a discrepancy in the data. "Huh."

"What goes?" the monk demanded.

She lifted a gloved hand to run it across the wall to her left. The sensor globes orbited faster, as if excited. "According to my sensors, this section of bulkhead is five hundred meters thick."

"Shielding for the T'lir?" Ralit asked eagerly before frowning in sudden unease. "Or some weapon?"

Chara snorted. "I doubt it. People advanced enough to Jump an entire ship three hundred years into the past would have better means of shielding than simple mass. No, I think these readings are an illusion. According to the expeditionary force's files, the Sela are certainly capable of such."

He recoiled, his crimson eyes dilating in horror. "They interfere with our minds?"

She made no answer, too busy running her hands over the ridges and swirls of the bulkhead. Just prior to this mission, Chara had downloaded an EDI that contained every bit of data the ill-fated expeditionary force had collected on the Sela before being suborned into heresy.

"I think I recognize this pattern of indentations," she told the monk as she pressed her fingers into them. Two of the marks, however, remained beyond her reach. She growled in frustration. "Curse it, their anatomy is too different; I can't trigger them by myself. Ralit, put your fingers there and there."

Reluctantly, the monk placed thumb and pinkie where she indicated and pressed in at her nod.

The bulkhead slid aside, revealing a vast, echoing space filled with row after row of glowing golden eggs, each bigger than a man. Chara smiled in satisfaction. "The crew."

For a moment, music seemed to fill the air, heard not so much with the ear as in the heart, in the very pump of the blood. Heaven's own aria, sweet and slow and soft. She drew in a breath in pure wonder.

Then the music was gone. Or had she imagined it?

Apparently not. Ralit's hand fell to his shard pistol again, a profound fear in his eyes. "Unnatural!" he hissed.

Chara advanced toward the nearest of the eggs, trailed by her swarm of sensor globes. Through its translucent shell, she could see its occupant, six-legged and richly furred, lying curled and still. She contemplated the data. "They seem to be in some kind of travel sleep."

"Make one of them tell you where the T'lir is," the monk growled, following at a cautious distance. "Then we'll blow this whole cursed vessel and everything in it."

Chara bit back an instinctive protest at the waste. To Ralit, the Sela were not vastly advanced beings, but a proven danger to the faithful. Hadn't they seduced an entire expeditionary force into turning their backs on the Victor? If not for the enticing possibilities offered by the T'lir, the Cathedral Fortress would have ordered the Sela's home world burned to bare rock.

Chara shrugged. Well, waste or not, she had a job to do. The Victor knew this wasn't the first mission to fill her with distaste.

She contemplated the egg, trying to work out how to open it. After a moment, she found the correct position of fingers in indentations, and the whole thing swung open like a clamshell, sighing softly.

*The alien within it stirred and lifted its silken head. Enormous eyes blinked open and met hers.*

*Chara inhaled sharply. She had never met such a gaze in her life, so wise, so compassionate. There was sadness there, and understanding, and—*

*Forgiveness?*

"Use your probe on it," Ralit snapped. "The pain will make it spill its secrets quickly enough."

*Chara shot him a revolted glance. He wasn't even looking at her, his gaze instead focused on the alien, his upper lip drawn up in an expression that was half snarl, half grin. A dark, horrific excitement filled his eyes, almost sexual in its anticipation.*

*He really did remind her of her father.*

What am I doing? *The thought stabbed through Chara's heart like a blade. It had the raw force of a question she'd hidden from herself for years. Decades.* Why am I playing any part at all in this perversion?

*She looked back at the alien. It lay in its egg, watching her quietly, as if waiting for her decision.*

"The probe," Ralit demanded again, licking his lips. "Use the probe."

You want it tortured, you torture it. *The words hovered on the tip of her tongue, but she didn't bother to utter them. Ralit would be afraid to touch the alien for fear its heresy would contaminate him.*

*And because he didn't trust Chara, weak woman that she was, so lacking in Warrior virtues. What would she do while he was . . . distracted?*

"Ah, child," *a voice said in her thoughts. To her astonishment, it sounded female, though power rang in every rolling mental syllable.* "What have your people done to you?"

"Torn me asunder." *The thought flashed through her, more a product of the heart than the mind. And all the more true for it.*

*"Yes," the voice replied. "I see that."*

*Chara found herself reaching toward the alien's muzzle, driven to discover if its fur was as soft as it looked.*

*"No!" Ralit barked. "Do not touch it! It will contaminate thy thoughts with heresy!"*

*Too late. Her fingers had already met that honey-gold fur, thick and impossibly soft. But there was more in that instant of contact, so much more Chara's mind vibrated like a silver bell.*

*There was power.*

*She caught her breath as the creature's consciousness flooded hers. Its mind was unimaginably ancient, radiating peace and understanding. There was no judgment in the Sela's thoughts, no condemnation for Chara's failures, no sense that her softness made her unworthy of life.*

Vanja, *Chara thought in wonder.* She calls herself Vanja.

*And in a moment, Ralit would force Chara to take the probe off her belt and bury it in this exquisitely soft fur. She'd have to watch the Sela writhe and scream as the air filled with the stench of burning flesh. Until Vanja broke under the pain and betrayed her people and herself—and gave the Sela's greatest secret to the Xeran Empire.*

*Which would use it to plunge the galaxy into war.*

*But if Chara did not do these things . . .*

*"Your people will kill you if you try to save us," Vanja warned in that soft mental voice.*

*"I will not tell you again, Chara—draw your probe." Ralit stepped closer, his eyes cold, demanding, his hand on his holstered shard pistol. "And do your job."*

*Fear shot through Chara under his icy stare. Her father had looked at her the same way before every session of "instruction." She reached for the probe.*

*Instead, her hand found the shard pistol next to it. In one smooth motion, she drew the weapon and shot Ralit in the chest. The spray of metal shards took him full on, echoed in reverse by a spray of bright heart's blood. For one shocked*

*instant as he fell to the deck, Chara was reminded of a
crimson flower.*

*Her sensor globes scattered like frightened birds. Off to
report the murder to her superiors, no doubt.*

*Coolly, Chara pivoted and shot them out of the air. They
hit the deck with a chorus of tiny pings. She turned back to
the monk.*

*Looking down into his astonished, blood-flecked face,
she realized it had never occurred to him that she'd find the
courage to kill him.*

*"Oh, child," Vanja said softly. "What have you done?"*

*"Something that's needed doing for a very long time."
Weapon drawn, a cold, lethal determination in her heart,
Chara went to find the rest of the boarding team.*

*Her father's training had made her a very efficient killer.*

**Jess jerked awake** staring at the ceiling, her heart pounding in hard, desperate thumps. Shivering in reaction, she
rolled out of Galar's wide bunk and staggered through the
doorway that led to the bathroom.

As she splashed a handful of water into her face, Galar
stepped into the doorway. "You okay?" He leaned a shoulder against the door frame, studying her with concern. "Another nightmare?"

"Yeah." She straightened and ran her wet hands over her
face. "But it didn't seem like a dream. It was more . . . logical.
More real. Like a memory. Chara's memory."

"Chara?"

"Charlotte. Chara va Hol is her Xeran name." Jess grimaced. "Or at least, it was in my dream."

"Tell me."

As they dressed, she did. "Do you think there's any truth
to it?" Jess asked, as she pulled on a tunic and leggings, both
of which felt silken against her skin. The rich royal blue

fabric shimmered like a gemstone as she sat on the bed to tug on the matching boots.

Galar frowned as he sat beside her. "I suppose it's possible. Could be she slipped you a memory bead."

This, Jess's EDI told her, was a nanobot drug capsule that held a recording of someone else's memories. You smeared it over the skin, much as you did with an EDI.

"I don't remember her touching me like that." Jess reconsidered, then shrugged. "Though I guess she could have done it when I was asleep."

"But that still doesn't account for my readings," Galar pointed out. "Charlotte scanned as completely human. I don't see how she could have faked that."

"It was probably just a nightmare."

"Probably."

She just wished she could believe that.

**Galar lay sprawled** on the couch in glorious nudity, posing as Jess put the final touches on the painting of him.

The door opened behind her and a hearty voice called, "Hey, Master Enforcer!"

Jess cursed as her brush slipped, leaving a crimson streak across the canvas. She turned to glare as the big redheaded Enforcer sauntered into the room.

A twenty-first-century male would have scrambled to cover himself. Galar only looked around calmly, completely comfortable in his nudity. "Yes?"

"Dona and I have been working the Marcin case," Ivar told him as Jess worked to repair the damage to her painting. "We were doing a scan on incident reports when we found an interesting lead. We think we know where to find him."

Irritably, Jessica wondered why they were poking their collective noses in Galar's case, then remembered he'd said Dyami had assigned the two to find the assassin.

The redhead shot him a grin. "I was wondering if you wanted to be in on the takedown."

Galar considered the idea, obviously tempted, then shook his head. "I can't leave Jessica unprotected."

"So get somebody else to guard her for a couple of hours. We could really use you on the team."

He hesitated a long moment. "I suppose I could ask Wulf. I was thinking about asking him to give her a hand-to-hand combat lesson anyway. He's a good teacher. And he's the only Enforcer I know who could singlehandedly wipe up the floor with a battleborg." Galar returned his attention to Ivar. "Tell me what you're planning for the Xeran."

Jessica listened absently as she put the finishing touches on the painting's background. As Ivar spoke, she began to frown. It seemed the Enforcer had found a police report of a bald man with steel horns protruding from his head, running down a residential street. The cop obviously thought the drunk who'd done the reporting wasn't all that reliable a source, but the Enforcers knew differently.

"That does sound like Marcin." Galar, too, frowned, obviously just as uncomfortable with the scenario as she was. "But why would he run around in public without even using a camo field? He'd have to know he'd stand a good chance of some temporal native spotting him and leaving a report for us to find."

Jessica looked around the edge of her canvas. "It's a trap."

"Obviously." Ivar gave her a feral smile. "So we're going to trap the trappers with the best team we can put together." He nodded at Galar. "Which is why I was hoping you'd be able to join us. You're damn good in a fight."

"Thanks." Galar gave him a dry look, then shook his head. "Still, I'm not sure I like this plan of yours. There are too many unknowns. We could all end up shooting straight into the Seven Hells."

"I'm well aware of that, and I don't like it either." The big man spread his ham-sized hands. "Unfortunately, it also may be the best chance we're going to get to take Marcin down."

"I *would* be a lot happier with that battleborg out of the picture."

"But even if you do get him, what's to stop them from sending another assassin?" Jess asked.

"Nothing." Galar shrugged. "But Marcin is one of the most dangerous agents they've got. Odds are, his replacement won't be quite as deadly as he is."

"That's assuming the Xeran military is involved, which we haven't established," Ivar pointed out. "He could be doing this on his own for all we know."

"It's possible, but I tend to doubt it." He ran a thumb over his lower lip. "Then again, if we capture Marcin, we'll have a better chance of finding out what the hell is going on." He considered the question for a long moment, then clapped Ivar on the back. "All right, you convinced me. I'm in."

Jessica frowned at her canvas, wondering why her instincts were clamoring a warning.

**Because Galar had** no intention of letting Jess out of his sight, she found herself sitting in on the planning session for the Marcin mission.

Ivar had assembled a team of ten Enforcers around the massive gleaming conference table. Besides himself, Dona Astryr, and Galar, the rest of the team included Riane and Frieka; a married couple, Jiri and Ando Cadell; a brawny, grim-faced black agent named Peter Brannon; and Tonn "Bear" Eso, the biggest human being Jess had ever seen.

Eso was over seven feet tall, a hulking blond who had to duck when he entered the room. He would have looked intimidating if not for the constant grin he wore, as if he were always thinking of his next joke.

They all listened attentively as Ivar explained the basis of his plan, the reported Marcin sighting. No sooner had he finished describing the incident than Frieka's jaws gaped in a lupine grin from his seat next to his human partner. "Okay, people, all together now. One, two, three . . ."

"It's a trap!" the Enforcers chorused, and broke into laughter.

Ivar shot them all a glare. "Funny. Yes, we know it's a trap. But we don't intend to be caught."

"Well, that's a relief," Jiri Cadell quipped, rolling her eyes. Her husband elbowed her. She grinned and poked him back.

Peter Brannon scowled fiercely. "How stupid do these Xerans think we are?"

"Stupid enough to send only three or four agents to arrest Marcin, instead of the ten we're actually going to send," Galar told him.

Jess frowned, voicing the thought that had been bothering her since she'd walked into the room. "Is ten going to be enough?"

"If we try to send more than that, we'd produce a huge temporal energy spike the Xerans would be able to detect all the way to the present," Galar explained. "But the reverse is also true. Our sensors aren't detecting a spike of Xeran Jump energies at those temporal coordinates either, which suggests they don't have a large party there."

Jess frowned. "But what if they Jumped several groups of ten in earlier and had them wait to ambush you?"

"We'll pop a courier to the Outpost and give a good hearty yell for help," Galar told her.

"At which point Dyami, who'll be waiting with a backup team, will Jump in and save our collective asses," Ivar added.

"What about the local cops?" Jess asked as a new thought occurred to her. "All those people Jumping in will sound like World War Three. You're going to be butt-deep in law enforcement."

Galar shook his head. "No, because modern T-suits generate a dampening field beyond a certain radius. Nobody can see or hear a Jump beyond twenty meters or so."

"So why not get rid of the boom and the light altogether?" Jess asked, interested.

"The engineers did try that," Galar told her. "Unfortunately, there's a lot of energy liberated in a Jump. They discovered that if they tried to eliminate the effects completely, the forces reflect off the suppression field and squash the Jumper like a bug."

Jess wrinkled her nose. "Ewwww."

"Speaking of killing people, how are we going to take out Marcin?" Ando Cadell asked.

Galar gestured, calling up a trid image of what appeared to be a perfectly ordinary twenty-first-century neighborhood, lined with narrow brick ranch houses and small two-bedroom wood frame houses. "I used photos from the time in question to create this trid." A computer-generated image of Marcin appeared, dashing down the street. He looked as real as the photographed houses.

"This is the path we believe the battleborg will follow, based on the incident report," Galar continued. "We're going to break into five teams of two in order to create a perimeter and take him down. Ando and Jiri, I want you two here." He waved, and the image switched to an overhead view. A second gesture created a red dot in the location he pointed out.

One by one, he gave the teams their assignments, making sure they were ready for any trap the Xerans tried to spring.

As Jess watched, the Enforcers settled in to plan in earnest. She found herself relaxing. It certainly seemed Galar had things under control.

**An hour after** the meeting broke up, Ivar leaned a shoulder against the wall of the gym to watch Wulf spar with the combot. Normally the big man fought in a blur of motion and power, using all the great bull strength of a high-grav native. Today he swung with only a fraction of that power, his movements slow and deliberately clumsy.

"What in the Seven Hells are you doing?" Ivar called, though he knew perfectly well.

Wulf ducked the combot's return swing and shot him a look. "Galar's asked me to give his primitive combat lessons while I play bodyguard. I'm trying to make sure this damned combot won't kill her."

It was a legitimate concern. The 'bot Wulf had chosen was built along the typical dimensions of a battleborg. Two meters tall, it looked just like a massively muscled human, and it was programmed to respond as one when you hit it.

Ivar had sparred with it a few times himself; it had a punch like the kick of a soji dragon. If it cut loose against the primitive at full strength, it would kill her.

The 'bot took another swing at Wulf, a fraction too hard, a fraction too fast. He ducked. "Cease!"

It froze in mid-move. Wulf straightened and stared at it in silence for a long moment. Probably using his computer to readjust its programming.

"Again," the big man ordered at last.

The combot swung. He ducked, nodding approval. "Much better."

Ivar turned, whistling softly, and walked away. It was a good thing Wulf couldn't see his smile.


**Since Galar was** the senior officer on the strike team, he spent the next two days working on the plan to capture Marcin. He met repeatedly with the Enforcers as well as with Dyami himself, trying to work out every contingency.

Jess found the process a fascinating experience. Galar was an entirely different man when he was in officer mode, an icy strategist who considered every detail, no matter how small. Whenever he spotted anything he considered a weakness in the plan, he worked on it relentlessly until he found a solution.

But as the planning continued, Jessica's sense of foreboding began to grow again. Something was going to go badly wrong; she could feel it in every cell.

Yet she had no logical reason to believe Galar was headed for trouble. The battle plan he'd put together allowed for every contingency, including fifty Xeran Marines showing up instead of the ten they expected.

Logic didn't seem to matter. The premonition scraped at her consciousness like a sweater made of sandpaper, flaying her nerves until she wanted to scream.

Two hours before he was scheduled to leave on the mission, she snapped.


**Jess lay curled** up on the bed as Galar cleaned his armor and weapons in preparation for the mission. He held his helmet on his lap, steadying it with one hand as he used a buffing cloth to clean the faceplate of any hint of oil or dirt. He was shirtless, wearing only a pair of snugs that clung to his hips. Every move he made sent muscle rippling in his arms and torso. His expression was intent, his profile sharp as he looked down at the helmet. A lock of blond hair fell over his golden eyes. Her fingers itched to smooth it back.

Jessica watched, fighting to contain her brooding restlessness. She jerked her twitching shoulders like a restive horse. "I don't want you to go." The words burst out of her without her conscious intent. "Stay home with me."

Galar looked up from the helmet, quirking a brow. "You know better than that. I organized this mission. I've got to lead it."

Jess sprang restlessly to her feet, unable to contain the need to move. "Something's going to go wrong. Somebody's going to get hurt. Badly."

He frowned, watching her pace. "What makes you say that? If you've thought of something I haven't, I'd like to hear it."

At least he wasn't dismissing her worries out of hand. "I don't know what the problem is, Galar. I just know there is one."

He put the helmet aside and picked up the chest plate, his expression thoughtful. "We've done everything we can to minimize the danger."

"I know that."

"So why are you still spooked?"

"Damned if I know." She frowned, rubbing a palm over her tingling nape as she strode from one wall to the next. "I just have this feeling."

Galar gazed at her, then put the chest plate aside and rose to step up behind her. He caught her gently by one arm, arresting her restless pacing, then turned her around and drew her into his arms. "It's going to be fine, Jessica. I've been going into situations like this for years, and I've always come out on top. Even when the odds were a lot worse than one to one."

For a moment she let herself relax into the warm shelter of his arms. He felt so damned good against her, solid and strong, hard with muscle. Every breath she took carried his scent, spicy and male, with a trace of some alien musk. She sighed and twined her arms around his neck, threading her hands into the cool blond silk of his hair.

He might die today.

The thought skulked into her mind on cold, skeletal feet, and she shivered, tightening her grip around his neck.

She tried to banish it, but she knew that for all his strength and science, he was only mortal.

*He could die today.*

A chilling image flashed through her mind: Galar's face, roaring in rage, a spray of blood painting his skin.

It wasn't just imagination, either—she could literally see it, smell the blood, hear his bellow of pain and despair and fury.

*It was going to happen.* She knew it, could feel the truth of it beyond any hope of denial. If he went out there today, he would suffer for it. Suffer trying to protect her.

*He could die today. For me.*

*No!*

The bottom dropped out of her heart in a sickening swoop of pain. Never mind that she hadn't even known him a few days ago. The thought of never touching him again, never feeling his warm strength against her body, never hearing his deep rumble of a voice or experiencing the tender ferocity of his lovemaking—it all filled her with a bitter sense of loss.

"Don't leave me!" Her fingers fisted in his hair as she closed her eyes against the rise of tears. "Don't go!"

His arms tightened around her. "It's just for a few hours at most. Wulf will make sure nothing happens to you while I'm gone."

"I'm not worried about me, dammit. In fact, take Wulf with you. I'd feel a lot better if he were watching your back instead of mine."

"But I wouldn't." His arms tightened around her. "I want to know you're safe even if everything goes to hell and Dyami has to jump in with reinforcements. Wulf can handle just about anything. At the very least, he can Jump you to safety."

*But what about you?* Her eyes squeezed shut on the furious wish that she could make him stay with her, out of danger. She remembered those fierce moments he'd made love to her and imagined him wanting her so desperately he couldn't stand to leave. Couldn't stand to go among the people that meant to kill him.

Deep within her, a burning core of energy began to swirl and swell, strengthening itself on her fear and the love she had yet to acknowledge. Growing hotter and more intense with every heartbeat.

Until it rushed outward in a sudden furious blast.


**Galar held her** in his arms, surprised by the velvet tenderness that filled him. She felt so delicate, so fragile, yet she held on to him with surprising strength, as if to protect him against whatever it was she feared.

He could almost imagine she loved him. . . .

*Something came pouring out of her.* He felt it storm, tinging, burning, from her chest into his, stealing his breath, freezing his heartbeat.

An instant later his heart began pounding again, in a furious thundering rhythm, as he hardened. His cock jerked and filled with hot blood, his balls going so tight he could only gasp in erotic surprise.

His last rational thought was *What's happening . . . ?*

Then even that was gone, and his awareness flooded with her. The smell of her skin, the soft curves pressing against his abruptly ravenous body.

She pulled away, and her smoky blue eyes met his, shimmering with fear for him—and a ravenous need of her own.

Galar groaned and took her mouth.

# · 11 ·

❧

**Jess opened for Galar, kissing him back, her lips** like sun-warmed rose petals. He thrust his tongue into the wet haven of her mouth, moaning with the desperation of his arousal. She tasted impossibly sweet, yet so intoxicating his head swam.

He had to have more of her. Had to touch her.

Catching the hem of her tunic, Galar jerked it off over her head. Jess smiled up at him with shy hunger, standing there dressed only in thin, flowing trousers and a tiny bra that cupped the pretty hemispheres of her breasts in cream lace.

Unable to resist, he traced the tips of his fingers over the skin rising above the scalloped edges of the bra. "Sweet Mother," he breathed. "You feel like silk."

Jess's pretty mouth quirked as she pressed close, one hand cupping him. "And you feel like granite." Slender fingers explored the shape of his erection through the thin fabric of his snugs, tracing his cock's central vein up to the thick, rounded head. Her thumb smoothed across sensitive skin, and he shuddered in need. Watching his face, Jess licked her lips, her blue eyes going dark and smoky. She was breathing fast, and her heart pounded against his fingertips.

With a low groan, he bent and took her mouth again, kissing her long and deep, fingers stroking her nipples as they tented the lace cups. He could get drunk on the taste of her lips alone. The bold little tongue sliding into his mouth made an animal growl of hunger rumble in his chest.

He ached to taste those stiff nipples, wanted to feel her roll against him like a petted cat.

Breathing hard, she stepped back and reached between the swell of her breasts to flick open the bra's clasp. Lace cups sprang apart. She caught them in her hands, barely keeping the delicate flesh veiled. A teasing roll of her shoulders spilled the straps off her arms, but still her long fingers concealed the pretty tips he ached to see.

Galar reached out and took her hands, drawing them away so he could slip the bra off. The scrap of lace and silk dropped unnoticed from his hand as he stared at her. Sweet, pale mounds tipped by rosy little points that lifted and fell with every eager breath. He inhaled deeply, drinking in the delicate musk of aroused woman as he feasted his eyes on her. "Sweet Mother, you're beautiful." His voice sounded hoarse to his own ears.

Her grin flashed. "You ain't so bad yourself."

"Glad you approve." He leaned down to give one nipple a lick, in the process slipping a hand down the waistband of her trousers and underwear. Her belly drew in under his fingers with a ticklish little flinch, and he smiled around the nipple he was nibbling. Traced a teasing finger around her belly button to hear her giggle.

Smiling, Galar slipped his hand down farther, cupping her softly furred mound, then sliding one finger between her lips. She was already slick there, creaming richly. He thumbed her clit and listened to her sigh.

"Oh, yeah," she breathed. "I definitely approve."

"Then you won't mind if I tell you you're overdressed." He drew his hand from between her thighs, caught her trousers and panties, and slid them down her long, smooth legs.

"I'm not the only one." Jess stepped out of them and kicked them aside before reaching for the waistband of his snugs. She knelt to pull them off, watching his cock bob free, hard and eager. "Yes, that's *much* better."

Giving him a wicked little smile, she closed her cool fingers around the broad shaft. Leaning forward, she took its flushed head into her mouth for a deep, hard suckle that made his eyes roll back in his head. Her clever tongue swirled in hot circles over the very tip, sending whip-flicks of raw delight dancing up his spine. One small, soft palm cupped his balls, gently rolling, sweetly teasing.

If not for the control his computer gave him, he'd have come on the spot. Having no intention of letting it end that quickly, he throttled his reaction back and stroked her hair. It felt like silk in his fingers.

Half hypnotized, he watched his cock slide in and out of Jess's pink mouth. Watched the way she angled her head to take him deeper, dark lashes fluttering down. He'd never seen anything so erotic in his life.

Slowly, she drew back her head until the shaft popped out of her lips. His breath roughened even more as she extended her tongue for a series of slow licks, as if savoring some exotic sweet.

What was it about her? He'd had other lovers—Warlords were never at a loss for partners—but none of them had ever affected him this way. Some might have been more skilled, one or two might have been more beautiful, but Jess was still . . . more.

It was as though those delicate little hands touched more than his body. As though she reached something buried deep inside him, something still and cold and lonely.

Something that stirred and warmed a little more every time she kissed him.

It was the kind of realization that would have scared the hell out of him a few days before. Now all he wanted was—

More.

**Jess had never** much enjoyed giving blow jobs, especially not to the one previous well-endowed partner she'd had. She'd always considered the act a bit boring and unpleasant, especially given her strong gag reflex. In fact, she often found herself wishing her partner would hurry up. *Come, already!*

Galar was different.

He fascinated her: the textures of his cock in her mouth, the shaft so smooth and hot, the nubby velvet of the heart-shaped tip, the softly furred testicles like fat plums.

His reactions were equally delicious. She loved the way that massive body stiffened, muscles jerking in time to her every tongue-flick and suckle. The sense of erotic power was intoxicating. And wildly arousing.

Dreamily, Jess leaned into him as she sucked, running her free hand along his thighs, tracing the elegant shapes of muscle. Her artist's senses adored his body—its textures, its scents, its tastes. The soft clouds of hair at his chest and groin, each narrowing to the little treasure trail that led between them.

She loved his big hands, too, so broad and square, with those long tapering fingers now tangled in her hair. Tough hands, calloused and capable. And so wickedly skilled, like that surprisingly tender mouth and wooing tongue.

She could happily spend hours exploring Galar, getting to know every inch of his superman body and wickedly intelligent mind. Discovering what made him moan and tense and come, what made him throw back that handsome head, corded throat working as he shouted his pleasure.

But she didn't have hours. Soon—too damned soon—he

was going to leave her to go into danger. Those Xeran bastards were going to try to kill him today. And there was nothing whatsoever she could do to protect him.

On a despairing moan, she drew in a hard breath and took him deep, forcing his long shaft as far down her throat as she could. Trying to lose herself in him, drown her fears in his delight.

Forget. Forget and build a memory that would be with her to the end of her days.

"Enough!" he gasped suddenly, voice ragged. Grabbing her by the shoulders, he pulled her to her feet, caught her backside and lifted her into his arms as if she weighed no more than a kitten.

"Galar!" Jess grabbed at his shoulders with a startled little laugh.

The laugh became a moan as he bent her backward. His mouth fastened onto one nipple as if he was starving and she was his only source of food.

And then he began to tease. Gentle scrapes of the teeth, swirling licks, and long, drawing suckles that shot sweet little darts of pleasure along her nerves.

Moaning in delight, she clung to him, losing herself in sensation. His broad shoulders felt warm and smooth under her hands, his flanks firmly muscled against her calves as she wrapped her legs around his butt.

He didn't seem to feel her weight at all.

His cock jutted between their bodies like a promise, hard and hot and satin-smooth. Jess couldn't wait to feel him drive it inside her. Her core ached to be filled, flesh slick and swollen tight. Maddened, she rolled her hips, teasing them both with the friction of her sex against his.

He growled something, his voice rumbling as he licked slow circles around each nipple, pausing to dole out wicked little nips and teasing rakes of the teeth.

She whimpered helplessly and let her head fall back as he closed his mouth over one for yet another hungry suckle.

Pleasure sparked along her nerves like points of shimmering light dancing just beneath her skin.

"Now," she gasped, rolling her hips again, starving for his deliciously searing entry. "I don't need any more foreplay!"

"Yes, dammit," Galar gritted back. "You do!" He closed his mouth over one nipple with such luscious ferocity, she could only writhe. The motion caught his cock beneath her body so it pressed against the seam of her lower lips, tormenting her with images of grinding thrusts.

Maddened, Jess leaned back and reached for the big shaft to angle it for entry.

"No," he growled, tightening his grip on her ass, not letting her have the distance she needed to impale herself.

"Galar, please!" she groaned, squirming.

"Not yet!"

Cunning, Jess reached between her thighs, touched her own wet heat—and traced her glistening fingers along his lips. "Now!" she demanded in a hot whisper.

He groaned, growled, and lifted her to impale her on his cock in one hard, ruthless rush. They both shouted at the pleasure of the sudden penetration.

"God," Jess moaned helplessly, "you fill me so full. . . ."

"Just wait," he growled, and began to roll his narrow hips, working his cock in and out of her fist-tight wetness.

Jessica shuddered and bent backward in his supporting grip, grinding hard to meet him. Clinging to his biceps, she watched him in a haze of furious need. The tendons of his neck stood out in hard relief, and his gloriously powerful torso rolled as he fucked her in those ruthless thrusts.

Each long pump seared her, raked her inner flesh deliciously, sent delight driving through her in hot spikes. But even more glorious was the look on his face, the half-blind ecstasy, the grimace of mingled effort and building orgasm.

Her own climax shivered just out of reach, spurring her onward. Driven, Jess lashed her body in his arms, impaling herself, seeking that last perfect degree of pressure that would . . .

She screamed as it hit in a burning deluge, drowning her in light and fire. He stiffened, throwing back his head in a raw animal roar.

Yet even as the sweet pleasure stormed through her, Jess was aware of a dark whisper of dread.

*The Xerans will try to kill him today.*


**Finally the last** blazing pulses faded away, leaving her clinging to him, panting and sweating as she listened to his slowing heartbeat.

"Seven Hells," he groaned at last, slowly pulling her off his now-limp, sticky cock. "That was amazing. And I'm going to be late." He sat her tenderly down on the bed.

*You're going?* Somehow she bit the words back as she watched him turn and duck into the bathroom. Headed, no doubt, for a desperately needed shower.

*Of course he's going.* The thought held a trace of bitterness. Galar Arvid was not, after all, the type of man who'd let a bout of great sex keep him from doing his duty.

At least his knees were visibly shaking as he walked into the head. That was something, anyway.

Jess thought about joining him and decided against it. She'd only end up begging him again, and she knew better. At least, her conscious mind knew better. Another part of her wasn't quite that smart.

She threw back the covers and slid under them to sit, knees pressed to her chest, a frown of brooding on her face. What had happened, anyway? One minute she'd been making a fool out of herself, and the next . . . *Something* had blown out of her chest and into his, and then he was fucking her brains out.

She'd done that. Somehow. Just like she'd knocked everything off his shelves the last time.

But how?

**Galar strode down** the corridor toward the meeting with
the rest of the strike team. Only Jessica's boot heels clicked
on the flooring; he moved with absolute silence in his armor.
He'd damned well better. He'd oiled and adjusted for an
hour last night until nothing so much as creaked to give him
away.

Galar shot Jess a look. She appeared even smaller than
usual beside his armored bulk, more doll than woman.

There was nothing doll-like about her bleak eyes, though.
She still believed he was headed for disaster, though he
knew she wouldn't say so now. Not with him getting ready
to Jump.

He sighed. "Jessica, humans don't have the ability to see
the future. Some other species do, but we can't do what they
do. Our scientists have done experiment after experiment,
but no one has ever shown so much as a trace of true clair-
voyance. Any stories that say otherwise are nothing but co-
incidence and too much imagination."

"Just like we're not telekinetic." Her voice was toneless.
"Did you ask the Outpost comp whether we really did have
an earthquake the other day?"

Unease slid icily through him. "There was some kind of
tremor, but it was extremely localized."

Blue eyes flashed up to meet his. " 'Extremely localized'
meaning limited to your room."

"I've discussed this with Dyami. We think it must have
been some kind of abortive Xeran attack, but the Outpost's
shields defeated it."

"That makes sense." But she didn't say she believed it.
He wasn't sure he did either, but what other explanation was

there? She'd somehow developed impossible powers no other human had ever had? The Xeran idea was a lot more credible.

"I'm going to be all right, Jess," Galar told her quietly.

She forced a smile and slid a hand through the crook of his arm. "Of course."

Actually, there was something warming about her concern. Her worry was more intense, more personal than that shown by his fellow Enforcers when he was in danger. Almost as if she loved him.

And what an intoxicating idea that was.

He, on the other hand . . . wasn't sure how he felt. Yes, there was an intensity to his emotions he'd never experienced before, not even when he'd thought he was in love with Tlain.

Then again, he'd killed Tlain.

True, she'd needed killing. She'd been a spy, a traitor, while he'd bet his last galactor Jess didn't have a duplicitous bone in her entire body.

Jessica Kelly was, without doubt, the most trustworthy woman he'd ever known. If he was ever going to fall in love again, he could certainly do worse.

If.

**They walked into** the gym to find Galar's takedown team waiting, all dressed in full battle armor. Probably why there seemed to be far more than the ten Enforcers she knew were actually there. They made Jessica feel like a child among a crowd of adults—and she wasn't exactly short, at least by twenty-first-century standards.

Across the room, she spotted Jiri and Ando Cadell. The big male Enforcer suddenly grabbed his wife around the waist and pulled her in for a big smacking kiss. Then he popped her helmet on and dogged it down. She patted his cheek with a gloved hand. He grinned at her and turned to put his own helmet on.

"Remember," Frieka was saying to Riane as the Warfem checked her shard pistol, "I'm in charge of our team. You go when I give the order, not before. Got it?"

"Yes, Mother."

"Do you want me to bite you?"

"Wouldn't be the first time. . . . Hey!" She yelped and leaped back from his snapping jaws.

The corridor door opened and Wulf stepped through, his shoulders almost as wide as the others' even without armor. He exchanged a nod with Galar, who pushed Jess gently toward him. "Keep an eye on her for me, Wulf."

The big man gave him a crooked grin and put an enormous hand on her shoulder. "Don't worry. I'll keep her out of trouble."

Jess lifted a cool brow up at him and said sweetly, "Thank you *so* much, Wulf."

He turned the grin on her, apparently impervious to sarcasm.

Galar lowered his head and whispered in her ear, "I'll be back." Stepping away, he raised his voice. "All right, folks, let's go. We've got a battleborg to bring back alive."

Jessica's throat tightened as she watched the team move off in surprising silence, booted feet not even whispering on the deck.

"Come on, Jessica," Wulf said, steering her through the door and out into the corridor. Even as it closed behind them, the floor shook under her feet with the sonic boom of the mass Jump.

Jess bowed her head, wondering if she'd ever see Galar again.

**Marcin raced through** the night, his armored boots ringing on the primitive pavement, a madman's grimace pasted on his face. His sensors were at full scan, searching the darkness for the drunk who was supposed to spot him.

And the Enforcers who should be drawn out in response.

So far he saw no one at all. The neighborhood he ran through was a rural one, houses spaced far apart, occupants sleeping at this hour. There were no streetlamps, no pedestrian walkways. Nothing but this empty, snaking road and the towering Earth trees that stood to either side.

Some kind of animal—his computer identified it as a *dog*—erupted in a furious cacophony of sound. He shot it a glance as he ran and saw it was straining on the end of a chain tied to a stake.

He ran on, enjoying the sting of adrenaline pumping furiously through his body. Fueling his craving for the battle to come.

Finally, a fight. A break from his frustrating, grueling hunt for that thrice-damned, elusive heretic, Chara va Hol, and the Abominations she was protecting, and the T'lir the warrior priest wanted so badly. An opportunity to shed blood in the Victor's name and prove himself worthy of being a member of Tarik's cohort.

That was, after all, the next logical step in his path to glory. But it wouldn't be easy. Only the elite of the elite were chosen to join the deeply secret Order of the Victor, Xer's ultimate weapon against those who attempted to defy the Fatherworld and keep its people from their glorious destiny. If you were judged unworthy to join, the cohorts might well kill you for your temerity in even applying.

Marcin, however, had so far been judged worthy. Though if he failed against the heretic . . .

Well.

He spotted a man walking along the darkened sidewalk— the drunken primitive who was supposed to report his presence to the police, thereby leaving a record for Temporal Enforcement to find. "You!" Marcin roared in English.

A white face jerked toward him as he charged the man,

bellowing. The drunk whirled and staggered away as fast as his unsteady legs would carry him.

Marcin laughed softly. *That should do it.* He ran after the idiot for a couple of blocks, just to make sure the primitive would head straight for the police.

Finally, deciding the drunk was sufficiently terrified, he turned and loped away into the night. Any moment now . . .

"Halt and drop your weapons!" a voice snarled from the darkness. A man wearing blue Temporal Enforcement armor materialized into his path, apparently having dropped a camo field.

Marcin turned, only to see two more Enforcers racing toward him. His lips curled back in a snarl of satisfaction.

They'd taken the bait.

He wheeled with a roar and lunged right for the first agent, whom his sensors identified as the same big blond he'd fought at the heretic's house. Even better, the man was a Warlord, despite the lack of a facial tattoo.

Killing one of Vardon's hated warriors was a holy act—a fitting sacrifice to the Victor. Marcin had every intention of adding the Warlord's head to his collection.

**Jess stood frozen** in the corridor outside the gym. The sonic boom from Galar's Jump still seemed to reverberate in her bones.

She blinked hard. She was not going to cry in front of Wulf, dammit.

A huge hand fell on her shoulder, and she jumped, glancing around wildly.

"Enough angst," Wulf told her, though his bright turquoise gaze was sympathetic. "It's time for your combat lesson."

Jess had never felt less in the mood for a lesson in anything, much less combat. Her stomach had laced itself into a set of fine, shivering knots. She was seriously tempted to throw up on the big Enforcer's boots.

Unfortunately, if she just stood around waiting for Galar to come back, she was going to lose her mind. A practice fight would at least provide her with a distraction from all this icy fear. "All right," she sighed. "Let's get it over with."

He gave her a wide, white smile and turned her toward the door across the corridor. The sign over it read "Unarmed Combat Practice." "That's my girl. This way."

Reluctantly, Jess followed his broad back as the door sighed open. He stepped aside for her—and she froze in horror.

Marcin stood waiting in the empty room, still, impassive, the bright overhead lighting glinting on his two sets of horns. His booted feet were spread wide apart on the padded floor, his huge hands hanging empty at his side. His black-scaled armor made him look like a biped snake, an effect enhanced by his scarlet slit pupils. If anything, he seemed even bigger and more menacing than she remembered.

She recoiled. "Jesus!"

Wulf snagged one arm before she could whirl and run screaming from the room. "Hey, he's not real. It's just a combot. See?"

Marcin seemed to melt, leaving a big, man-shaped form standing naked before the mirrored wall. Its body was smooth, genderless, reminded her of a really tall department store mannequin. Assuming they'd modeled one on Arnold Schwarzenegger in his Terminator years. Its skin was a kind of icy white, and its doll-like irises were black and glassy.

And more than a little creepy.

A moment later, Marcin was back, complete with horns, red eyes, and chilling expression. She realized the combot must be projecting the Xeran's image over itself.

"Is that really necessary?" Shivering, Jess rubbed her goosefleshed arms, eying the big android. It made a really convincing Marcin.

Wulf shrugged. "Better to confront your fears now. It will be easier if you ever have to fight Marcin in reality."

"Somehow I doubt the words 'easier' and 'Marcin' belong in the same sentence," she grumbled.

**But Jess soon** realized the Enforcer had a point. Exchanging slow punches with the Marcin-bot—stopping periodically while Wulf critiqued—was both grueling and a trifle boring. So much so that the chilling expression in the 'bot's eyes stopped bothering her quite so much.

Panting, sweat streaming from her body, she'd just drawn back a leg to plant a kick in the Marcin-bot's belly when Wulf threw up his hands. "Hold it!"

She lowered her leg and gave the Enforcer a questioning look. "What?"

The big man rolled his eyes. "It's Chief Enforcer Dyami. He's just called me to the main auditorium, where he's got the backup team."

Alarmed, Jess asked, "Is there a problem? Are they going to have to Jump?"

"I don't think so." Wulf scratched his chin, looking troubled. "He said I might as well let you two keep sparring." Turning to the combot, he added, "Keep an eye on her while I'm gone. Dyami said this won't take long."

"Affirmative," the combot said, no inflection in its voice at all, though it still sounded far too much like Marcin.

Panting, Jess braced her hands on her knees and watched as Wulf strode from the room, leaving her alone with the Marcin-bot. She wondered if the thing would let her take a break. Probably not, given the Enforcer's orders.

"Okay," she sighed. "Let's try that kick again." Drawing her leg up, she prepared to drive her foot into the Marcin-bot's rock-hard abdomen.

**Before she could** launch the kick, the combot blurred into motion. Powerful fingers clamped around her throat to dig cruelly into the skin. She gagged and tried to knock its hand away, but it only tightened its grip.

"Hey!" she wheezed in outrage. "That's not the move we're supposed to practice!"

"I know." The Marcin-bot's red eyes didn't even flicker. Spots began to dance before her gaze as its fingers tightened on her windpipe, lifting her agonizingly onto her toes.

"Stop!" she hissed, barely able to force the words past its strangling grip. "Can't . . . breathe!"

"That," it said, "is the idea."

**Galar bared his** teeth and waited as Marcin raced toward him, lethal determination in narrowed red eyes. As he ran, the battleborg brandished a Xer Sevik, one of the long, lethally sharp knives the bastards favored. He wore full temporal armor, which meant the shard pistol Galar carried would be useless.

Galar drew his own blade, a Vardonese machete the length of his forearm. Tossing the weapon in his palm, he contemplated the bastard's armor. To get a blade through the supple, tough material, he'd have to batter it long enough to break down its molecular cohesion with repeated impacts. Which meant this was going to be a long, hard fight.

Which was just fine with Galar. He was in the mood for a brawl. He roared his battle cry and stepped into Marcin's charge.

They met in a jarring clash of steel, knife ringing on knife, the impact sending them spinning apart again like a pair of dancers. Galar whirled back toward Marcin, lips peeled away from his teeth, *riaat* singing its lethal song in his blood. He swung the machete at the Xeran's throat, but Marcin jerked clear, then struck like a snake. The deadly point of the Xer Sevik scraped across Galar's chest, glancing harmlessly off the armor's slick blue scales.

Galar retaliated with a short, brutal punch that snapped

the Xeran's head backward and sent him stumbling. Galar lunged, ramming his machete into the off-balance Warrior's belly with such force, Marcin's feet left the ground. Only his armor saved him from being gutted.

The Xeran hit the ground on his back, flipped like an acrobat, and swung out in a furious kick. His armored boot slammed into the side of Galar's helmet, sending him spinning to the gritty pavement.

Though stunned—Damn, but the cyborg bastard could kick—Galar still managed to turn his fall into a roll. He skidded to a stop on his back to see Marcin falling toward him like a rock. The Xeran landed astride his chest, slamming the air from his lungs as he prepared to drive his Sevik into the underside of Galar's jaw. Fighting to drag in a breath, the Warlord slammed his wrist against Marcin's, knocking the blade away.

Undeterred, the Xeran rammed his armored left fist into Galar's helmet, once, twice, again. The tough visor creaked and crackled, threatening to shatter under the cyborg's inhuman strength.

"Get . . . *off*!" Galar grabbed Marcin by one horn and flipped him off over his head. The Xeran hit the ground with a grunt. Galar twisted around, still maintaining his grip on that jutting horn, and tried to grab its twin with his free hand, planning to break the Xeran's neck. Marcin swung his knife and jammed its point into a nerve bundle in Galar's forearm. The blade didn't break through the armor, but his arm went numb to the shoulder. He lost his grip and Marcin tore free.

Both men scrambled to their feet, breath heaving, thoroughly pissed now and ready to do some killing. Out of the corner of one eye, Galar saw Jiri and Ando Cadell watching, their own blades drawn as they waited for an opening to join the fight. Galar waved his left hand at them in an *I don't need help!* gesture as he and Marcin circled.

Unease flickered through his mind. Where the hell was

Marcin's Xeran backup? The bastards should have sprung their trap by now. Galar's remaining Enforcer teams were still maintaining position, camouflaged and invisible, waiting for Marcin's nasty little friends to make their move.

"You seem distracted." Marcin bared his teeth. "Waiting for something?"

Galar gave him a vicious grin. "Just getting a little bored." He lunged, his knife scraping against the Xeran's Sevik with a metallic ring.

But before Galar could make another attack, a chilling, ululating howl shattered the night. Even Marcin jerked his head around at the sound.

The howling man appeared in Xeran Temporal armor, melting out of the night at Jiri's back like a ghost in black scales. She whirled, instinctively bringing up her blade even as her husband leaped to block the attack.

They were both too late.

Still howling, the Xeran swung the sword he held in both hands. Jiri's head spun away, helmet and all, blood flying in a fine crimson spray.

"Jiri! Nooooo!" Ando's scream of despair and rage was the chilling distillation of a soul's death. He lunged for the Xeran, knife raised.

Coolly, the man pivoted and slashed, taking the Enforcer's knife hand off at the wrist. Ando screamed again as he fell back, gripping the stump with his remaining hand. The Xeran's next thrust drove right through the center of his chest, penetrating armor and rib cage alike as though they were warm butter.

The agent was dead before he even hit the ground.

*Shit! Shit, shit, shit!* Galar blocked Marcin's slash at his own head by sheer reflex, backpedaling furiously. *Enforcers!* He sent the broadcast ringing out over their shared com channel. *Agents down!*

The others were already appearing, dropping their camouflage fields with roared battle cries. Even as they closed on the Xeran and his impossible sword, four more enemy warriors materialized out of the surrounding night. Their swords made a strange, high-pitched ringing sound, chilling and alien, as they raced toward the Enforcers.

What the fuck were those things? How did they cut through full Temporal armor as if it were rice paper? It wasn't even possible.

And yet, all too obviously, it was. Because the Xerans were doing it.

Blocking another flashing knife attack from Marcin, Galar felt his blood turn to ice. Unless he did something now, he and his agents were headed right for slaughter.

**Black sparks flashed** in front of Jess's eyes as she fought to draw in a breath. She grabbed the Marcin-bot's thick wrist in both hands, trying to relieve the vicious pressure on her throat. "Let go . . . of . . . me!"

Red eyes didn't even flicker. "No."

"Stop it!" She swung a desperate foot at the thing's belly, but it didn't even flinch.

"No."

If this was some kind of test, it felt entirely too damned real. Her head was swimming, her vision graying around the edges. "What the hell . . . are you trying to do?"

"I am killing you." Its voice was utterly calm.

It had lifted her until her toes no longer touched the ground. She raised both legs and slammed them into the bot's chest with every ounce of her failing strength, but its grip didn't loosen.

*Fuck,* Jess realized blearily, *it's Marcin. He must have programmed it to kill me!* Sucking in a desperate breath, she wheezed, "Outpost! Help! Help . . . me!"

There was no response. No sirens, no sound of feet running to the rescue, no nothing.

Something was wrong. *Oh, holy God,* she thought, staring

with bulging eyes into the Marcin-bot's merciless face. *He got to the main computer too. The Outpost has been hacked. And I'm screwed.*

Had Dyami even asked for Wulf at all, or was that just a diversion to draw her big protector away?

Jess tried to kick the combot again, but she couldn't even lift her legs. Weak. Too damned weak.

The black spots dancing before her eyes were getting thicker, the light dimmer. She could no longer even see the combot's face, could barely even feel the thick fingers squeezing tighter and tighter around her neck. Choking her so brutally, so slowly, spinning out her suffering instead of just snapping her neck.

An image suddenly bloomed before her eyes. Galar, splattered with blood, fighting Marcin, their blades ringing against each other. His eyes burned with *riaat*—and something else: a black and awful grief.

Even as he struggled with the big battleborg, another Xeran charged him from behind, lifting a sword that chimed like a silver bell.

*The cowardly fuck was going to kill Galar.*

Even half-suffocated as she was, a wave of fury rose in Jess, cutting through the ice of approaching death. "No," she wheezed. *"Dammit . . . no!"*

# · 12 ·

**Even as Jessica's body went limp in the Marcin-bot's** grip, the bubble of heat and rage expanded in her chest, burning hotter, brighter. Building into a flare of energy that exploded out of her in a single searing flash.

The hand around her neck simply disappeared.

Jessica hit the ground on her back. The fingers clamped around her throat were gone, but her chest felt frozen, muscles paralyzed. Her grayed vision began to go completely black.

*Suffocating . . .*

Abruptly her diaphragm spasmed into action, and she sucked in a breath of blessedly cool air. Rolling onto her side, she gagged weakly and concentrated on dragging air in and out of her abused, burning throat.

Where the fuck was the combot? It seemed to have disappea—

*No, wait,* she thought foggily. *Is that a hand?* Struggling to focus her eyes, she saw there was indeed an arm lying on the floor inches from her nose. Looking around, she saw— thank you, God—no blood. However, some kind of oily blue substance covered the walls, the floor, and Jess herself, and there were several . . . parts lying here and there. Some of which looked entirely too human.

The door slid open. "What the Seven Hells?"

Jess looked up to find Wulf rushing across the room toward her, an expression of horrified amazement on his broad, handsome face. "About time you got here," she told him, and vomited on his boots.

**The bastards had** murdered Jiri and Ando.

*No,* Galar thought, parrying Marcin's strike at his head. *He'd* gotten them killed. He'd prepared for everything but swords that could slice through combat armor like a cleaver through a boiled egg.

And if he didn't pull his head out of his ass now, he was going to lose the rest of his team too. Even as he drove a *riaat*-propelled fist into Marcin's face, his sensors reported the desperate battle going on around him.

Bear Eso, Peter Brannon, Ivar, Dona, Riane, and Frieka were trying to fight off five Xerans armed with those impossible blades. One of the swordsmen plunged at Bear, who instinctively tried to parry with his big Bowie-like blade.

The sword cut the knife in two. Only Bear's instinctive backward jerk saved his hand from being sliced off at the wrist. The big man retreated just short of a run as the swordsman stalked him.

"You've lost," Marcin hissed to Galar, his vicious grin bright. "I'm going to take your head and win a place in the cohort! And the skulls of all your precious Enforcers will decorate our trophy cabinets. . . ."

"You haven't won yet, you bastard," Galar snarled, ducking the kick the other aimed at his chest.

*Attack from behind!* his comp shrilled. A sensor image flashed through his brain—one of the Xer swordsmen, pivoting suddenly away from Riane and Frieka, bringing his sword around in a hard diagonal slash aimed right at Galar's back.

Galar dropped to one knee. Blood spurted across his visor. He looked up.

Marcin stared down at his own torso, an expression of stunned horror visible on his face. The Xeran's blade was lodged in his right hip. It had entered through his left shoulder.

He toppled. In two separate pieces.

Galar snarled, uncoiling from his kneeling position, driving his blade straight up at the man who'd tried to stab him from behind. It pierced the underside of the Xeran's jaw in the one place not protected by helmet and body armor. The swordsman made a gurgling noise as the knife pierced his brain.

Galar wheeled as his second opponent toppled. He grabbed the sword from the man's hand before it even hit the ground.

"Seven Hells," Frieka gasped. "Remind me not to piss you off."

"Out of the way!" Galar growled, and charged between the wolf and Riane.

Bear Eso was backpedaling from the flashing blade of a short, muscular Xeran grimly intent on killing him. Galar stepped between them and parried. The two swords chimed together like bells, an oddly pure sound.

*Retrieve our dead and prepare to jump,* he sent over the command com channel that linked the Enforcers' comps. *I'm not leaving these bastards any trophies.*

"Get your hands off that sword!" the Xeran snarled, outrage in his voice. "You're not worthy to touch it!" He lunged.

This time, Galar's parry was a fraction too slow. Though

it knocked the Xeran's sword off-line, the big blade still slid right through Galar's right hip. He felt it grate on bone.

Bear Eso's big hand closed around his shoulder and jerked him back. His stolen sword fell from his hand. The Xeran swooped after it.

Galar reeled away. They had to jump. Now. Before they lost anybody else. He spotted something round and dark and snatched it up.

Jiri's helmet. Which wasn't empty. Teeth clenched against the pain, he looked around. Peter Brannon had Ando Cadell's body in a fireman's carry, while Ivar cradled the rest of Jiri. Riane, Frieka, and Dona were covering their retreat.

"Jump!" Galar bellowed, and hit the button on his belt.

**Grimly, he limped** into the infirmary after the two body tubes and three regenerators. Eso had taken an ugly gut wound, and one of the Xerans' blades had caught Dona in the chest, narrowly missing her heart.

Galar still cradled Jiri's helmeted head in his hands, though he could have put it into the body tube with the rest of her. Her death was his responsibility, after all. He'd failed her. Failed all of them. It had been his duty to lead them safely, but the Xerans had outmaneuvered him. His culpability scoured his consciousness with a pain that dwarfed the sword wound in his hip.

"Galar." Chogan met them in the doorway of the ward. Compassion gleamed in her eyes as she held out her hands. "Give her to me, Master Enforcer. I'll take care of her."

Feeling numb, he handed her the helmeted head. She took it tenderly and carried it after the float tubes.

He looked down at his own body. He was covered in blood—Jiri's, Ando's, his own, Marcin's, and probably that of the Xeran he'd killed.

He did wish he could have held on to that damn sword long enough to get it analyzed and reverse engineered.

Which was no doubt why the Xeran had been so intent on getting it away from him.

Galar rubbed his aching, bloody side. He should probably clean off all this gore. Before or after he gave Dyami his report?

"Galar?" He turned to meet Dyami's appalled gaze as the big Warlord stepped through the ward's double doors. "What the hell happened, Master Enforcer?"

"I underestimated them," Galar told him baldly. "They had some kind of new sword that sliced right through body armor." He shook his head in weary defeat. "There were only five of them, plus Marcin, but we couldn't do anything against those swords. We lost Jiri and Ando Cadell. Dona and Eso are in regen, but my comp says they're not badly hurt."

Dyami studied him in the penetrating way Galar associated with a sensor scan. "Why in the hell aren't you in regen with them?"

"I'm not that bad."

"The hell you're not." Dyami grabbed him by the shoulder and steered him into the ward. "I need a regen tube here!"

Galar gritted his teeth as an unwary step sent pain lancing through him. "I need to finish making my report."

"Report later. Regen now." Dyami's tone did not brook argument.

"Galar!" Jessica burst through the wall of one of the ward's privacy bubbles. Her expression turned to outright terror as she registered the blood glistening on his armored body. "You're hurt!"

"It's not as bad as it looks."

"Yeah, right," Dyami growled. "Medtech!"

Galar ignored him, frowning as a question surfaced in his bleary mind. "What are you doing in the infirmary, Jess?"

"She damned near got killed by that fucking combot,

that's what." Wulf stepped from the privacy bubble after her. "She just got out of regen. Jess, go lie down. Chogan hasn't finished the scans."

"Scans?" Galar pulled away from the medtech who was trying to hustle him toward the regenerator she'd just guided over. "For what?"

"Double-checking some odd readings." Wulf frowned, his gaze shifting uneasily toward Jessica. "I'll explain later."

Jess ignored him, instead moving closer to Galar as she examined him anxiously. "You're pale as milk. Where are you hit? You're covered in so much blood. . . ."

He started to touch her shoulder, then hesitated as he registered the darkening crimson covering his fingers. He dropped his hand. "Most of it isn't mine."

"Too much of it is," the medtech said, a frown on her pretty face. "Get in the regenerator please, Master Enforcer."

"Go on, Galar." Jess caught his upper arm, ignoring the blood that coated it as she turned him toward the tube. "I'm worried about you."

Even as weary and dispirited as he was, he felt warmed at the concern he could see in her eyes. He managed a smile for her as the medtech popped the tube lid. "All right."

Jess rose on her toes and pressed a warm kiss to his bloody cheek. "Thank you."

As he pivoted painfully to climb into the tube, his gaze caught Dyami's face. Galar frowned, registering the unease in the big man's eyes as he watched Jessica.

What had Jess done to worry Dyami?

**Jess lay on** the privacy bubble's bed, staring glumly at the ceiling. She badly wanted to get up and find Galar to make sure he was okay, but she knew Wulf had no intention of letting her leave.

"Is he still in regen?" she asked abruptly. *And if he is, what does that say about how badly he's hurt?*

"No, he's out," Wulf said tonelessly. He was watching her with an intensity that made her feel more than a little uneasy. He'd said he was staying with her to protect against another murder attempt. Given what had happened with the combot, she certainly couldn't argue with that. So why did she have the chilling feeling he was acting less like a bodyguard and more like a prison guard?

"How are the other agents?" She bounced her foot restlessly.

"Why do you want to know?"

Jess lifted her head to stare at him, startled by his suspicious tone. "Because they got hurt trying to make sure I wouldn't get killed. Some of them gave their lives trying to make sure I wouldn't get killed. Why would you think I *wouldn't* care?"

"I definitely agree you should." But his skeptical gaze seemed to suggest that he doubted she did.

Stung, she sat up and swung her legs over the side of the bed to glare at him. "What's your problem? Or have you forgotten I almost died in that gym?" *While you were off chasing wild geese.*

As Jess had suspected, whoever hacked the combot had faked the call from Dyami to draw Wulf away.

She frowned. Wulf had seemed so apologetic and worried when he'd found her after the attack. Yet his manner had grown steadily more chill since then. Why? What was going on that she didn't know about? Did it have anything to do with all the medical scans Chogan had been conducting?

"What did happen in that gym, Jessica?" His eyes were cool, watchful.

She gave serious thought to throwing the bedside vendser at him. "Exactly what I said happened. Exactly what the recording says happened. You saw the trid, Wulf. That combot came within two seconds of crushing my windpipe."

"Until you used some kind of mental powers to blow it apart."

Jess ground her teeth at the skepticism in his voice. "Well, something sure as hell blew it up."

"Yeah, something did."

"You saying I'm lying?"

"Are you?" The voice was deep, velvety, and devastating.

Jess turned as Galar stepped into the bubble. He'd cleaned the blood off, and he looked fit and handsome in his dark blue uniform. She gave him a sunny smile, too relieved to worry about his odd question. "You look as if you're feeling better."

"Somewhat."

Jess frowned, a chill sliding over her. He was studying her with the same wary expression Wulf was. As if she were a stranger, as if they'd never touched, never kissed, never made such sweet, overwhelming love.

Chief Enforcer Dyami entered behind him, just as narrow-eyed and skeptical.

Jessica's heart began to pound, her stomach lacing itself into an icy knot. "What's going on?"

"Did you think we wouldn't notice?" Galar's tone was emotionless, but hell burned in his eyes. They were literally glowing, a coal-red shimmer threading across his irises.

"Notice what? What the fuck is going on? I'm the one who almost died!"

"Jiri and Cadell did die." The red blazed even brighter as his icy expression cracked into a snarl of fury. "What did you tell the Xerans, Jess?"

Jess blinked at him. "Tell the . . . ? The Xerans are trying to kill me! Why would I talk to them? Hell, *how* would I talk to them?"

"That is the question." Dyami lifted a dark brow. "You don't have a communication implant, and no courier 'bots have come to you. You haven't used the com unit that we've been able to determine, and we've got trids of every move you've made since you arrived."

"You've had me under surveillance?" She stared at him in shocked outrage.

"Actually, no. The Outpost records everything that goes on here, though we usually can't access that information without a legal reason."

"So why did it do nothing when that combot was strangling the life out of me?" She knotted her hands into fists. *"I screamed for help, dammit!"*

"I know." His expression didn't change. "We discovered the hacker altered the Outpost's programming to keep it from sending agents to your rescue."

"Are you suggesting I hacked it? Some kind of elaborate suicide attempt, perhaps?" She curled her lip at him in sarcastic fury.

"Or," Galar said distantly, "some kind of attempt to make us believe you're a helpless target of assassins."

Jess fisted both hands in her hair and pulled in sheer frustration. "Why in the hell do you think that? I'm from the twenty-first century, dammit. I wouldn't know how to hack a computer in my own time, much less in this one!" She pointed a shaking hand at the bedside console. "I barely know how to program that vendser!"

"No? Yet you've got Xeran genetic material in your cells. Particularly your brain." Galar walked over to a sensor console at the foot of Jess's bed and waved a hand over the device. A trid image of a human brain appeared, rotating slowly. "This is the first scan Chogan did of you right after you arrived. Everything is just what we'd expect in a twenty-first-century human." He gestured again, and a second image appeared beside the first, showing a sprawling area of bright blue in the frontal cortex. "This is the scan Chogan just made." He pointed at the blue area. "Neurons in this part of the brain show signs of profound mutation, with an accompanying explosion in synaptic growth—new connections between the cells."

Jessica stared at the scan, her stomach going icy. "Is it . . . cancer?"

Galar's blond brows lifted. "Cancer?"

She licked suddenly dry lips and managed a nod. "That looks like something that could kill me."

His expression seemed to soften for a moment before it hardened again. "It's not cancer, Jess. And even if it was, it probably wouldn't kill you. Cancer is rarely fatal in the twenty-third century. Not as long as it's detected in time, anyway."

She breathed out, slumping. "Oh, man. Good." Then she frowned. "So if it's not some kind of cancer, what is it?"

"Chogan believes it has something to do with the Xeran DNA in the mutated cells."

"Charlotte," Jess said grimly. "Charlotte did this. Marcin said I smelled of her blood. It must have something to do with that."

"Charlotte scanned as human."

"Yeah, well, a few days ago, I scanned as human. Now you're saying I'm some kind of Xeran spy." She lifted a bitter brow. "Obviously, you don't know what the fuck is going on."

**"The primitive's right,"** Dyami said grimly. "We don't know what's going on. And that's just not acceptable."

"I do know one thing." Galar scrubbed both hands wearily over his face. "She wasn't lying." His sensors had told him she was feeling outrage, hurt, and fear, but there had been none of the telltale signs of deception.

What's more, his heart insisted she couldn't be a Xeran spy. Unfortunately, his heart had been wrong before.

"It's not that hard to fool sensors," Ivar pointed out.

"Only if you've got a computer implant capable of controlling your involuntary nervous system," Galar replied. "Jess doesn't."

Ivar lifted a red brow. "Considering she just blew a combot into its component parts, we have no idea what your little friend can do."

Dyami turned to Chogan, who sprawled wearily at the opposite end of the table. Between the wounded and the dead, she'd had her hands full. "Did your sensors pick up any unexplained energy spikes during the questioning?" Such a spike might indicate Jess was exerting influence on the Enforcers' brains.

Chogan shook her head, green hair sliding around her shoulders. "Nothing. Certainly nothing like the kind of spike when she blew up the combot. Which reminds me." She pivoted her chair toward Dyami. "Chief, I've been thinking."

He tilted his head, the beads in his braid clicking. "Yes?"

"If she could produce a blast like that, why did she wait so long? You saw that trid. She'd stopped struggling. She'd gone limp. I really thought she was dead. Then . . ."

Galar winced, remembering the recording he'd already sat through half a dozen excruciating times.

Jess's eyes had flashed wide in her darkening face, and her mouth had screamed a word she hadn't had the breath to produce.

Galar's name.

Then the Outpost's sensors had picked up a shock wave that had originated from a point six centimeters from her forehead. The blast had shot through the air in a tightly focused beam that ripped the combot apart like a sonic grenade. No human had ever been recorded doing anything like it.

At first they'd thought the combot had simply been programmed to explode, but if so, the blast should have killed Jess even as it demolished the 'bot. Computer simulations showed the blast had unmistakably come from her.

"You know, you've got a point," Dyami said thoughtfully. "Why wait? Especially considering how desperately she fought that thing."

Galar shifted in his seat, remembering her frantic kicks

and punches, the helpless terror in her eyes, her pleading calls to the Outpost computer he'd sworn would protect her.

He'd never watched anything as painful as Jessica fighting for her life while he was five centuries away, getting his ass handed to him.

"Maybe she was faking it," Ivar suggested. "If it was part of some kind of elaborate scam to make us think the Xerans are targeting her . . ."

"She wasn't faking it," Galar growled. "You saw those life scans. Her heart stopped right before that blast."

Ivar sat back and spread his big hands as if to ward off Galar's glare. "Hey, just playing devil's advocate."

"Find yourself another devil." Never mind that he'd wondered the same thing. Had his experience with Tlain made him too paranoid, or was he letting himself get suckered by yet another pretty face?

"I really don't think she knew she *could* do it," Chogan said thoughtfully into the tense silence. "What if it was some sort of desperate, last-ditch reflex?"

"Outpost," Galar said suddenly, remembering a similar incident. "Replay the possible seismic event I've inquired about before." As Dyami he explained, "This is the incident we discussed last week."

"Oh, yeah, I remember that. We decided it was some kind of abortive Xeran assault, defeated by the shields."

A trid image appeared of Galar's quarters, Jessica curled against him under the coverlet. At his silent command, the comp enhanced her face so that the image appeared to zoom in. She was frowning in her sleep, eyes flicking back and forth behind closed lids. An expression of horror crossed her delicate face.

Abruptly she jerked upright. "Charlotte!"

Every object on Galar's shelves danced backward, hit the wall behind it, bounced off, and fell to the deck with a fusillade of crashes.

"I thought at first it had to be some kind of earthquake, but the Outpost said whatever it was occurred only in my room," Galar told the other Enforcers. "But what if Jess did it?"

"Looking at it in light of what happened with the combot, it certainly appears that way." Dyami ran his knuckles over his jaw. "I'm beginning to think we've been criminally stupid about all this."

"To be fair," Chogan pointed out, "the human brain is not supposed to be able to produce these kinds of energies. Xerans aren't even supposed to be able to produce these kinds of energies." She hesitated, frowning, lost in thought. "You know, I think I want another look at those scans I just did. That foreign DNA may be largely Xeran, but there are traces of completely nonhuman genetic material in it too. What if it's the alien traces that caused the development of these new abilities?"

"Run some simulations and see what you find out," Dyami told her. "And keep me posted about your conclusions."

"Of course."

"So what are we going to do about Jessica?" Galar asked. "Do we assume she's a Xeran spy or an innocent victim of some kind of unusually impenetrable Xeran plot?"

The Chief Enforcer sat back in his seat, a dark frown on his handsome face. "Well, she's been the target of at least two murder attempts that came pretty damned close to succeeding. We have to assume she'll be a target again." He hesitated a long moment. "I'm not inclined to believe she's a spy, but on the other hand, I'm not comfortable completely dismissing the idea either." He rose from his seat and began, restlessly, to pace. "So we arrest her. It'll put pressure on her, maybe give us some leverage to get the truth out of her if she's lying."

Galar's stomach knotted. "But what if she's not?"

Dyami looked at him, his expression steely. "The brig is the safest place on the Outpost. We'll put her under twenty-four-hour guard to make sure there are no more murder attempts. She is not to be left alone."

Chogan shook her head. "She's not going to like that, Chief."

"No," Dyami said. "But she'll be alive."

Galar rose to his feet. "I'll do it."

The chief looked startled. "That's not necessary. Ivar can—"

"She's my responsibility," Galar told him tonelessly, despite the nausea already churning his stomach. "I'll do it."


**Jess sat in** frozen silence, ignoring Wulf, who sat by her bedside like a stone monolith. Weary anger tightened her belly and knotted her neck.

They thought she was a Xeran spy. After everything she'd been through—including almost being murdered not once but twice by those bastards—the Enforcers really thought she was one of them.

*Galar* thought she was one of them. That's what hurt. He'd made love to her, touched her more profoundly than any man ever had, and yet he still believed she was working for the Xerans. That, in fact, she'd somehow betrayed them all, in the process getting Ando and Jiri killed and the others badly wounded. Including Galar himself.

Hadn't he been listening when she warned him he was heading into a chain saw? She'd even seduced him in a futile, instinctive effort to get him to stay home. A real Xeran agent would have been shoving his ass out the door.

*Dammit,* she thought, grinding her teeth, *I am not going to cry in front of Wulf.*

*But God, it* hurts.

# · 13 ·

※❀※

**Wulf's head lifted, alerting Jess. She looked around** just as Galar strode through the bubble chamber's wall. He looked big and coldly expressionless. Only his eyes held heat, glowing with some fierce emotion, like a pair of coals. He stopped just inside, his feet wide apart, his expression watchful. "Jessica Kelly, you're under arrest on charges of espionage. Come with me, please."

On one level, she'd been expecting this. So why did it feel like a body blow? She managed to draw in a breath against the pain. "Do I get an attorney?"

"Not at the moment." His handsome face looked as if it had been carved out of a solid block of ice.

What were her legal rights here? She had no idea, but she'd better find out. "I want a lawyer."

"You'll get one after you're transported to the twenty-third century."

"When will that be?"

"I'm not sure, but you'll be notified. Come along."

She blinked her stinging eyes hard, savagely determined not to cry. She was damned if she'd give him the satisfaction. "Where?"

"The brig." He didn't even flinch.

"Damn you, I'm not a spy!" The words burst from her, futile but uncontrollable. "I haven't done anything! I'm the victim here! I'm the one Marcin's trying to kill!"

"Marcin's dead." Galar said the words as if he were announcing the weather report. "I killed him with a little help from a Xeran who was trying to stab me in the back."

A faint relief penetrated her outrage and fear. "Well, that's something, anyway." Unfortunately, it didn't mean the Xerans weren't still after her. Ignoring the spurt of panic that thought inspired, Jess rose from the bed and braced her shaking knees. Squaring her shoulders, she stalked past him. "Let's go."

**Jessica walked ahead** of Galar like a queen, her delicate back straight, her steps unhesitating even as he directed her into the wing that held the brig.

Every instinct he had howled a protest as they started down the corridor between the cells. *She hasn't done anything to deserve this. She's not a spy.*

But could that gut feeling be trusted? What if he were wrong again? Ando and Jiri had already paid for his mistakes with their lives tonight. He couldn't afford another fatal error in judgment.

Besides, Dyami was right. Jess would be safe in here, particularly if he was watching her. Between that and Marcin's death, the Xerans should have a lot more difficulty getting at her. Assuming she really was their target.

His instincts insisted she was in serious danger, and he

wasn't inclined to doubt them. The Xerans' murder attempts had been a little bit too sincere for window dressing.

Then there was the question of who had hacked both the Outpost computer and the combot. Not Marcin; the Outpost's cybernetic defenses were too strong to be defeated from a distance. You'd have to be on the Outpost to do it.

Unfortunately, there'd been more than a thousand people on the Outpost when the attack had taken place, any one of whom could have been the hacker. Besides the Enforcers themselves, there was the facility's technical support staff, not to mention all the tourists and shopkeepers. Though that lot was basically confined to the concourse level, it wasn't completely impossible for one of them to have been the culprit.

He'd prefer that to the alternative—that one of his fellow Enforcers was a spy. They'd certainly have the technical ability for the job, as well as the inside knowledge of the Outpost's workings to pull it off.

But if an Enforcer was behind the attack, it meant one of his own people was working for the Xerans. And that, in turn, meant that Jessica was not the only possible target.

They all were.


**Ivar walked back** to his room, carefully maintaining the same grim expression he'd seen on the faces of Dona Astryr and the rest of his fellow Enforcers. But inside, behind his careful mental shields, he was grinning in triumph.

True, Jessica had survived his murder attempt and destroyed the combot assassin. On the other hand, two Enforcers had died in the battle with the cohort, so it wasn't a total loss. Most delightful of all, Jess was now under suspicion for the very acts of espionage that Ivar himself had committed. And that smug bastard Galar was walking around as if he had a meter-wide hole in his chest. It had

been all Ivar had been able to do not to laugh in his agonized face.

*Take that, you fucker. Two dead Enforcers, your girl-
friend in the brig, and a spy working under your very nose.*

The only thing that would have made it any more delicious
was if he'd actually managed to kill the primitive.

No, on second thought, putting her under a cloud of suspicion was sweeter. Though he supposed he could still arrange
her death. . . .

No. Too risky. Galar and Dyami weren't stupid, after all.
They had to realize hacking the Outpost comp had been an
inside job. If he attempted it again in order to get at the girl
and kill her, his chances of getting caught would be unac-
ceptably high.

He'd just have to be content with the knowledge that the
girl was in the brig and Galar was eating out his own heart
while doubting himself and her equally. God, that was
sweet.

*Senior Enforcer?* the Outpost computer said into his mind.
*A courier has arrived for you.*

Ivar went tense, feeling adrenaline spike through his
body in a delicious chemical cocktail of excitement and fear.
It was probably his spymaster. He'd taken the chance of
sending the man a report when they'd returned from the
mission.

He keyed open the door and stepped into the hall, waiting
impatiently while the courier verified his identity and spat
out the data bead. Escaping to his bed with it, he cracked the
bead between his fingers and smeared its nanobot contents
over his forehead.

*"Fool!"* hissed the spymaster in his mind. *"The point of
this entire trap was to kill the primitive! Failure is not acceptable. Kill her. Kill her now, or the Xerans will be coming
after us both next!"*

Silently, viciously, Ivar began to curse, knowing the spymaster was right.

Despite the risk, something had to be done about Jessica.


**Jess sat on** the narrow cot, her chin resting on her knees. Her eyes ached, swollen from the crying jag she'd finally indulged in once they'd given her some degree of privacy.

As cells went, it was a relatively comfortable one, she supposed. There was a vendser set in the wall, though it was programmed to provide food and drink only on a rigid schedule. There were no obvious bars in the doorway. In fact, there didn't even seem to be a door; the opening framed a sun-dappled forest clearing which she knew to be a trid. In reality, a couple of Enforcers were stationed out in the corridor just beyond the field barrier. A barrier, she'd been warned, that would deliver a painful electric shock if she blundered into it. Being in no mood to get jolted, she'd kept her distance.

At least the guards could see her, even if the trid kept her from seeing them. When the image had blocked her view, she'd gone cautiously to the doorway and called to make sure the Enforcers were still there. She'd been relieved when they'd responded. Never mind the lack of privacy or the fact that they were presumably there to keep her in. She just didn't want to be alone if another assassin showed up.

Though she *had* saved herself last time. . . .

Unfortunately, Jess had no real idea how she'd done it. Brooding, she let her head fall back against the wall behind her and stared at the ceiling. What would happen if she blew a hole in it?

The Enforcers would probably be pissed. . . . But she needed to figure out how to use her powers deliberately. Next time she might not have time to get angry enough or desperate enough to produce a blast before some thug snapped her neck.

What had she done the last time? She closed her eyes,

trying to call up the memory in sufficient detail so that she could re-create her actions. The Marcin-bot's steely fingers had been clamped around her throat, squeezing with slow, brutal power. Black spots had flooded her vision, dancing and swelling until she could no longer see the android's emotionless face.

And then she'd had the vision. Galar, covered in blood, an armored Xeran racing toward his back with a strange chiming sword lifted in both hands. . . .

Terror and rage had flooded through her dying brain, a fear not for herself but for Galar. Energy had swelled in her chest in a huge, hot bubble until it had exploded out of her and blown the combot apart.

Now she tried to re-create that feeling, that bubble of blazing force.

Nothing happened.

Jess gritted her teeth and glared hard at the spot over her head, fighting to generate that hot burst. *Make a hole,* she chanted mentally. *Make a hole!*

Nothing.

The thing was, she realized, all that desperate energy seemed beyond her now, plunged into darkness as she was. Galar had turned his back on her, had left her locked helplessly in here.

Galar, the man she loved.

She squeezed her eyes shut at the stinging power of the revelation. *Yeah, I love him. It wouldn't hurt so damned bad if I didn't.*

Jess remembered Riane's warning about Galar's distrust of women because of Tlain, the Femmat who had betrayed and shot him. He'd killed her, but he'd still spent weeks in regen growing back the arm she'd blown off.

Now he was convinced Jess was a Xeran spy too. And Jess—Jess was trapped in a world she knew nothing about, knowing no one, having lost the only family she had left, facing God knew what charges. If she was convicted of espionage, what would be the penalty? Historically speaking, spies were often executed.

"Jessica?"

Her eyes flashed open with a kind of desperate hope as Galar entered her cell. Had they discovered she was innocent?

Dyami followed him in. Both men were dressed in the dark blue uniforms of Temporal Enforcement. Both looked big, powerful, and almost overwhelmingly male. And both wore identical expressions of cool, distant professionalism.

Jessica's heart sank. She curled a lip, weary anger surging through her. "I gather you still think I'm the Mata Hari of the Outpost."

"We just have a few questions," Galar told her.

"Why bother? You're not going to believe anything I say anyway."

Dyami lifted a dark brow. "Try us and see."

She sighed. "I am not Xeran. I don't work for the Xerans. The Xerans have tried to kill me twice. I'd think that pretty well says it all."

Galar folded his powerful arms. "Then why is there Xeran genetic material in your cells?"

"I have no idea. I was born in 1983, and I'm pretty damn sure neither of my parents were Xerans."

Galar leaned forward and fixed her in a hard, flat stare. "Did you tell the Xerans about our combat plans?"

Jess met his eyes without flinching. "No."

He lifted a brow. "That's it? Just no?"

"Well, I could point out that I have no way to contact the Xerans, even if they weren't trying to kill me, and even if I didn't think they're all a bunch of psychos. I could also point out that I warned you yesterday's mission was going to be a bloody disaster, and you ignored me." Jess snapped her mouth closed to stop the flood of angry words.

Considering she was currently in a cell with a target

painted on her back, she really couldn't afford to vent her furious hurt.

He glared back at her. "You said you had a 'feeling.'"

"I told you," she snarled back. "I saw you covered in blood. I begged you. Hell, I even seduced you trying to get you to stay with me. And all you said was that humans aren't clairvoyant."

"They're not." His golden eyes narrowed. "But maybe you did know. Maybe you knew because the Xerans told you."

"Do you really think that?" She felt her chin begin to tremble and fought to steady it as she glared at him through stinging eyes. "Do you really think I could betray you and your people and let you walk into a buzz saw like that? You think I could know that your people were going to die—and do nothing? *What the hell kind of monster do you think I am?*"

"Jessica . . . ," Dyami began, his tone placating, his eyes uneasy.

She ignored him, too angry and hurt to care what she revealed. "I made love to you, Galar. I don't know what that means to your people, but I know what it means to me!"

"What *did* it mean to you, Jessica? Tlain and I made love dozens of times, and she still tried to kill me."

"I'm not Tlain! Tlain was a sociopathic bitch, and she deserved what she got."

"All right, enough," Dyami growled, pushing away from the wall with an expression of distaste. "This isn't an interrogation—it's a lover's quarrel."

"For us to have a lover's quarrel," Jessica snarled bitterly, not looking away from Galar's hot gaze, "he'd have to give a fuck."

"Maybe if *you'd* given a fuck, Jiri and Ando wouldn't be dead."

Dyami clamped a grip on Galar's shoulder and dragged him through the door. "I said *enough.*"

*Dammit,* Jessica thought as the two men vanished behind the trid field, *I am not going to cry. He's not worth it. He's not worth it.*

But he was, and she knew it.

**Dyami hauled Galar** into the corridor under the astonished gazes of Jess's two Enforcer guards. "Dismissed," he snapped, pushing Galar back against the wall.

The men turned and fled, apparently recognizing the chief's dangerous expression.

Instinctively, Galar braced to military attention under his commander's gaze. Heat flooded his cheeks. *Kill that,* he ordered his computer. His face cooled again, despite the shame scalding his thoughts.

"I've changed my mind," Dyami said, with a slight, surprising smile. "I want my ice-cold Galar back."

Ignoring that sally, Galar forced himself to meet the big man's gaze. "She didn't do it. She's not a spy. You saw her reaction to what I said."

"Yeah." Dyami sighed. "You can't fake sensor readings like that. So you were *trying* to goad her?"

"I wanted to eliminate any possibility she might be dissembling."

"Well, you did that." The Chief Enforcer studied him. "You've established her innocence to my satisfaction—and presumably your own. Especially given that Chogan is now convinced that the psychically active parts of that foreign DNA are more alien than Xeran. So now what?"

"That's up to you. Are you going to let her out?"

"And do what with her? It's for damned sure she's not going to want to go back to your quarters with you."

Galar flinched slightly, knowing his commander was right. He'd hurt Jess badly. She might never forgive him for this night's work. "There are other quarters than mine."

"But she's probably safest in the ones she's in."

"Granted, but do we want to leave her thinking she's still facing espionage charges?" Galar hated the thought of her spending the night wrestling with that particular fear, especially on top of all the others she was dealing with. He remembered the bitter betrayal in her eyes and felt sick.

"Good point." Frowning, he gave his jeweled braid an absent tug, eyeing Galar. "All right. I'll turn her loose and get her a couple of bodyguards for the night. In the meantime, go get some sleep. You look like hell."

Galar hesitated, then nodded wearily. He wanted to apologize to her, but he knew he'd probably be better off giving her some time to cool down. "Thanks, Chief Enforcer."

Dyami waved him off. "Go. Sleep. And give yourself a break from the guilt. We'll get this mess figured out and make those bastards pay."

He managed another nod and turned away, knowing even as he started down the corridor that he'd be getting no sleep this night.


**"Jessica?"**

She looked up warily as Dyami stepped back into the cell. Tensing, she waited for Galar to follow.

The chief's perceptive black eyes studied her. "I sent him back to his quarters. He looks like shit."

Jess slumped in relief. At least she wouldn't have to deal with another verbal acid bath from her former lover.

"You owe him, you know."

Her head jerked up as she stared at Dyami in astonishment. "For what?" *Ripping my heart out of my chest?*

"Convincing me you're not a Xeran spy, DNA or no DNA." He leaned a brawny shoulder against the wall. "That was the whole point of that ugly little show of his, by the way. He knew if he goaded you enough, you'd demonstrate your honest outrage beyond even my capacity to doubt."

"Wait—you're saying he didn't really mean those things?"

The icy needle of pain lodged in her chest began to melt. "He doesn't believe I'm a spy?"

Dyami shrugged. "I'm not saying he didn't have his doubts. But he figured if he pissed you off enough, you'd show us the truth. And you did." He shook his head. "Besides, the Xeran explanation never quite played for me anyway. Especially since Chogan now thinks that foreign DNA of yours isn't just Xeran."

Knotted muscles began to relax as relief flooded her. "So I'm no longer under arrest?" *And Galar doesn't believe I'm a spy!*

"No, you're cleared. As soon as your bodyguards get here, I'm sending you off with them." He searched her face. "Would you like them to escort you to Galar's quarters?"

She swallowed, contemplating the gossamer thread of hope growing in her heart. Yes, he'd hurt her, said things she was going to have a hard time forgiving. But if he'd been motivated by a desire to prove her innocence, she could understand that a bit better. "Let me think about that."

"He's a good man," Dyami said softly. "A hard man in some ways. Certainly hard on himself. But I consider him someone I can count on. I think you can count on him too."

"I think . . ." She took a slow, deep breath. "I think maybe you're right."

"Chief Enforcer?" The soft alto voice sounded as Dona Astryr stepped into the cell. "Reporting for duty, sir."

"Ah, there you are." Dyami nodded at Jessica. "Please escort Ms. Kelly wherever she wants to go."

She rose to her feet. "I think I want to go to Master Enforcer Galar's quarters, please."

Dona nodded. "Of course."

Her big, redheaded partner stepped into the cell, looming at her back. "It would be our pleasure," Ivar Terje told her with a broad, charming smile.

Jessica, feeling almost giddy now, returned his grin. She

stepped between the two agents and headed eagerly into the corridor.

She and Galar had a lot to talk about.

**Jess strode along** the hall, scarcely aware of the Enforcers trailing her.

The real key to this whole thing was Charlotte. Charlotte, whom Jess knew was a Xeran, Galar's sensor readings notwithstanding. It was Charlotte who'd planted that Xeran genetic material in her cells, Charlotte who had been Marcin's primary target. *"Blood—I can smell her blood on you,"* the Xeran had growled just before he'd stabbed her. *"She's made you one of them!"*

Blood. That was where the Xeran genetic material had come from. But why had Charlotte given her that material? And what was its connection to Jessica's new abilities?

Galar had said Xerans didn't have such powers any more than humans did. And in truth, Jess had never seen any evidence that Charlotte had powers either. She'd always seemed like a perfectly ordinary person.

Yet Marcin had called Charlotte a dangerous heretic. He'd feared her, though presumably he could have broken her in two, at least physically.

*Questions,* Jess thought, frustrated. *All I have is questions.*

Questions. Charlotte had said something about questions once. What had it been again? Jess frowned, fighting to remember. They'd been looking at the painting Jess was working on. Charlotte had turned and given her an odd, piercing look. *"This is the kind of painting you'll find answers in, when you're ready to look for them."*

She froze as her heart began to pound. It hadn't been a casual comment. Charlotte had meant it literally.

There were many ways to store a message in a painting in the twenty-third century. Ways Charlotte, as a Xeran, would be fully aware of.

Jess needed to get her hands on that painting. Literally. Even if it meant she had to travel in time to do it.


**Dona Astryr frowned** in unease as she followed the primitive. The woman seemed lost in thought, less aware of her surroundings than Dona would have been in her shoes. Had she forgotten the Xerans wanted her dead?

But if Jessica was taking the threat lightly, Ivar definitely was not. Dona slanted a look at her lover. The big man strode along, his face impassive, but her sensors told her he was drawn tight as a bow under that professional facade. She'd fought alongside him long enough to know he was preparing for an attack.

*What's wrong?* she commed to him, alarmed. *Have you picked up something?*

*What?* He shot her a look. *No, nothing like that. Just making sure I'm ready if a threat does materialize.*

Dona heaved a sigh of relief. *Good.* She turned to scan the approaching corridor junction.

Ivar struck in a merciless blur. One huge fist slammed into the side of her head, detonating an explosion of light and pain. Dona went flying, slamming headfirst into the wall in another burst of agonized stars. She hit the floor with a thud she barely felt.

His armored boots rang on the deck as he walked toward her. *Get up get up get up!* Tears of shock and pain stinging her eyes, Dona fought desperately to scramble away.

Ivar fisted one hand in her collar, grabbed her weapons belt with the other, picked her up, spun around, and rammed her headfirst into the opposite wall.

Everything went black.


**Jess stood frozen** in shock as Ivar dumped the body of his lover on the floor. Suddenly all too much was all too horribly clear. "It was you," she blurted. "You're the spy! *You* hacked the Outpost and the combot."

He bared his teeth at her in a wild, chilling grin and flexed his massive hands. "Oh, yeah. I've been working for the Xerans for years."

"You *bastard*, you got those Enforcers killed!" Her lips peeled back from her teeth as pure and bracing rage punctured her paralysis. Her hands curled into fists. *"You sold out Galar!"*

"And I'm going to kill *you*." He lunged for her.

Jess tried to duck away, but he was just too damned fast for her. He swatted her like a mosquito, sending her spinning to the floor, stunned. Blood rolled hot from her nose, her mouth. Her jaw went numb.

"Galar!" She screamed it, roared the name in her mind, a desperate, terrified howl.

"Sorry, sweetheart, he can't save you." Ivar drew back a huge booted foot. "You're dead."

# · 14 ·

❧

**Jess watched that enormous boot swinging at her** head, and knew it would shatter her skull. She threw herself into a roll and flung up her hand, focusing her fury, her desperation.

*Crack!*

The blast knocked Ivar stumbling backward to fall flat on his back.

She rolled to her feet and scrambled away. Her head swam.

"Bitch!" He reeled upright, blood covering his handsome face. *Good.* "You're going to pay for that!"

He took a menacing step toward her. . . .

Dona grabbed his legs, wrapping herself desperately around his ankles. He went down again with a howl of fury. "Run!" the woman yelled, scrambling astride him to aim a furious punch at his face. "Get to safety!"

Safety. Was *anywhere* on the Outpost safe? What she needed was that damned painting. . . .

The flare of hot white light filled her eyes with a thunderous crack. *Oh, shit,* Jessica thought, realization dawning. *What did I just . . .*

**Galar! The raw** terror in the mental scream froze Galar in his tracks.

Then he whirled and started to run, racing down the corridor back toward the brig.

It had been Jessica's voice in his mind. Jessica, who didn't have a com implant, yet had just touched his thoughts with that mental howl.

Galar didn't even bother thinking that telepathy just wasn't possible. He'd already realized that terms like "impossible" did not apply to Jessica Kelly. Assuming she was still alive, since it sounded like somebody was trying to kill her. Again.

He rounded a corner to find two uniformed figures writhing on the floor, fists and feet swinging as they fought in the middle of the corridor.

Ivar and Dona? What the hell—? And where was Jess?

"Galar!" Dona yelled, her voice choked. "Ivar's the spy!"

"No, it's Dona!" Ivar's fist cracked into her face with such violence, her head banged against the floor with a thud that echoed down the hall. The female Enforcer went limp under her partner's big body. "She just tried to kill the primitive!"

Ivar rolled off her, panting. Galar's sensors told him she'd been knocked cold by that last double impact of fist and floor.

"Where's Jess?" he snapped.

Ivar shrugged his massive shoulders. "Ran off, I guess."

Galar threw himself into a vicious spinning kick that slammed into Ivar's jaw. The redhead went down like a felled ox. Before he could recover, Galar dragged him off the floor by his collar, drawing back a fist.

"Fuck." The big man spat blood, staring at him, dazed. "How'd you know it was me?"

"I didn't." Galar slammed his fist into his face again. "But I do now."

**"How *did* you** know?" Dona asked as they waited for the medtechs.

Galar shrugged, shaking his stinging hands as he sat astride the big man's unconscious body. He'd just worked out quite a bit of frustration on Ivar's rock-hard head. "I figured one or the other of you was the spy. Since you were already unconscious, I decided to knock Ivar out and sort out who was what later."

"Ruthless of you," she grunted, probing her swollen face delicately. "But effective."

He pulled a set of force cables from his belt and started tying Ivar's thick wrists together. "Did you see where Jess went?"

"I think—maybe she Jumped." The female Enforcer frowned, looking uneasy.

"What?" Galar stared at her. "Where'd she get the T-suit?"

"She didn't have one." Dona shrugged. "Last I remember, Ivar was about to hit her. I tripped him and screamed at her to run. There was a flash and a sonic boom, and she was gone."

"That's . . ." He closed his teeth over the word "impossible." "Never mind, we're talking about Jess. Apparently anything's possible where she's concerned."

The question was, where the hell had she gone?

**Jess's legs buckled** as she materialized, and she collapsed, knees hitting the thinly carpeted floor with a tear-inducing crack.

"Jesus H. Christ!" a female voice yelped, but Jess was otherwise occupied with the violent nausea and thundering headache that were currently vying for domination. Squeezing her eyes shut, she concentrated on breathing.

"Jess?" Ruby's voice quavered with both stark terror and dawning hope.

Swallowing hard to contain her rebelling stomach, Jess opened her eyes.

Her sister was staring at her across the width of the single-wide trailer, half-cowering against the scarred, wood-paneled wall. Ruby was pale as skim milk, her red-rimmed eyes wide, her bloodless mouth pulled into an O of shock. Her painfully thin body trembled. For once, Jess didn't think it was withdrawal.

"I'm not a ghost," Jess rasped. "If that's what you're worrying about."

"Where . . . ?" Ruby stuttered. "How . . . ? There was lightning. In my house!"

Oh, yeah. It wasn't just the ghost thing. Ruby had just gotten her first up-close-and-personal taste of a temporal Jump. Between the sonic boom and the light show, it was a wonder she hadn't run screaming from the trailer.

This was going to be a bitch to explain.

Jess cleared her throat. "Sorry about that."

Ruby took a cautious step closer, her muscles coiled, as if ready to bolt. "Jess, the cops said . . . they said you were dead."

"They were wrong." Deciding her stomach was going to stay put after all, Jess rose wearily to her feet.

Her sister reached out a cautious hand and brushed her arm with shaking fingers. "You *are* real!"

"Well, yeah. I . . ."

To Jess's astonishment, her sister jerked her into a hard, fierce hug. "I never thought I'd see you again! I thought that bastard Billy Dean'd had you killed!"

Surprised, touched, Jess patted her sister's thin back.

"Billy Dean didn't have anything to do with it. It was . . . somebody else."

Ruby pulled away, her gaze narrow and fierce. "Who? Who did this to you? We need to get the bastard locked up! You gotta talk to the cops."

"Uh, the cops can't do anything about this guy. Besides, he's dead."

Ruby's brows flew up and she blinked in astonishment. "*You* killed him?"

"No, my . . . uh . . . lover did."

"You've got a lover? Get out! Since when?" Blue eyes narrowed. "Is that what you've been doing while I was locked up? They thought I killed you, by the way."

"Yeah, I heard. I'm sorry. I would have come sooner, but I . . . couldn't get away."

"Couldn't get away? I thought you were dead, Jess! How could you . . . ?"

"They wouldn't let me go." Spotting the stained velour armchair printed with birdhouses standing in the corner, Jess staggered to it and collapsed with a weary groan.

"*Who* wouldn't let you go? I don't understand any of this." Ruby wandered to the matching couch and fell onto it. Hands shaking, she searched through the litter of beer cans and wadded Kleenex on the scarred coffee table. Finally she found a packet of Virginia Slims and a box of matches.

The familiar ritual of lighting the cigarette seemed to steady her. She took her first deep draw, eying Jess through the smoke. "Your blood was all over the apartment." She sounded like she was beginning to think again. Which, knowing Ruby, might not necessarily be a good thing.

"Yeah, I got stabbed. But then I got better." Jess rubbed her aching forehead. Her EDI had warned that Jumping without a T-suit was unpleasant in the extreme. It wasn't kidding.

"Where the hell have you been?" Ruby's eyes flicked over Jess's clothing, taking in the emerald-green fabric that draped softly over her body. It sure wasn't polyester. "And where did you come from?"

Jess winced, anticipating her sister's reaction. Unfortunately, she didn't think she could get around telling her the truth. "The future."

"Yeah. Right." She snorted a plume of smoke. "Seriously, where have you been?"

"Hello? Remember Mr. Lightning Bolt?" Jess demanded tartly. "How do *you* think I beamed in like Captain Kirk? I'm not exactly hiding David Copperfield up my sleeve."

Ruby stared at her for a long beat. Slowly, her jaw dropped, and she started going pale again. "You're serious."

"As a heart attack." Jess sighed. "Look, this is going to be hard for you to believe, but give me the benefit of the doubt." Maybe she should take a look at the painting first, though, just in case Ruby decided to get difficult. "Where did you put my paintings?"

"Your paintings?" Tweezed brows drew together. "I don't have your paintings. The cops took everything."

"Damn." Her heart sank. How was she going to get a look at that piece if it was in police custody?

"Look, what's all this shit about you being in the future? Could you *please* tell me what's going on?"

"You're going to think I'm nuts."

Ruby's lips twitched. "I've *always* thought you're nuts."

"Yeah, I know," Jess said drily.

Her sister sighed and took another long pull on her cigarette, eyeing her through the smoke. "Let's drop the sibling rivalry for a minute, okay? Just tell me who tried to kill you and where you've been. *And what's with the lightning bolt?*"

So Jess took a deep breath and told her the whole thing. It took more than an hour. An hour of looking into her sister's eyes and watching disbelief and wonder go to war there.

Wonder finally won. "Holy shit," Ruby breathed when she finished.

"That's putting it mildly." Jess leaned forward and braced her elbows on her knees, staring into Ruby's stunned face. "Listen, you can't tell anybody you saw me. Including the police. They have to go on believing I'm dead."

Ruby frowned. "Why?"

"Because . . ." *Oh, hell, this is way too complicated to explain.* Ruby hadn't even passed her high school biology class. She sure as hell wasn't up to a lesson in twenty-third-century temporal physics. "Because if they find out I'm still alive, the future will be changed." *Never mind that you couldn't really change history.* Jess had learned years ago that if she wanted Ruby's cooperation in anything, she had to make it about Ruby. "*Your* future would be changed."

"*My* future? What do I got to do with this?"

"Actually, it's about my paintings. You've got to get them back, Ruby. They're going to be worth a lot of money."

"But . . ."

"Yeah, I know nobody was interested in them before," Jess interrupted, "but that was before I was murdered. Now they're collectors' items. Or they're going to be. In six months, you're going to sell one of them for two hundred and fifty thousand dollars."

Ruby's jaw dropped. "Two hundred . . . thousand?"

"Two hundred and fifty thousand. A quarter of a million dollars. And the price will go up from there. You'll be rich."

"Me? But they're your paintings!"

Jess shook her head. "I told you, baby. As far as the world is concerned, I'm dead. The paintings are yours now, and so is the money."

"Money." Her expression dazed, Ruby stared around at the single-wide trailer with its shabby furniture, scarred 1970s-era wood paneling, and worn shag carpeting. "God knows I'd love to be rich. I'd love to move out of this rat hole. I'd love not to be . . ." She broke off, but Jess knew the rest anyway. *I'd love not to be a crack addict and a whore.*

Her chapped lips compressed. "But it's not right. What are *you* going to do?"

"Build a new life in the future. That's where I belong now." Jess hesitated, then said softly, "There's a guy."

"The same guy who killed the one who stabbed you? Your lover?"

"Yeah. His name is Galar Arvid. He's . . . incredible."

Ruby's gaze softened. "He's not just a lover, is he? You love him."

"Yes," Jess said simply. "I love him."


**"Ivar always said** he could hack any computer," Dona said. "Apparently it wasn't an empty boast."

"Apparently not," Dyami growled, eyeing the female Enforcer. Anger seemed to sizzle off him in waves of heat.

She met his stare without flinching, her face expressionless, though Galar could sense her misery.

Dyami had ordered her to join him and Galar in his office as soon as Chogan had released her from regen. She'd spent an hour in the tube, healing the skull fracture Ivar had given her.

"Fucker damned near killed her," Chogan had growled to Dyami.

The chief had actually paled at the news, his eyes taking on a cold, murderous glitter.

Galar suspected Ivar was lucky he was safely in the brig, espionage charges or no.

Now Dyami studied Dona as if he barely knew her at all. Galar would give him one thing: the man could act. "So when did you realize Ivar was dirty?"

"When his fist hit the back of my head." Her lips twisted in a bitter smile.

Galar sat back in his seat, eying the two with sympathy. Even now, some of the tension between them had a distinctly sexual edge.

It was particularly easy to detect in Dona's case, since she was making no effort at all to control her emotional reactions. She'd even deactivated her computer implant. Without it, any attempt to lie would light up her brain like a com console.

Dona apparently wanted to make it very clear to everyone that she was telling the complete truth.

Evidently the truth wasn't pretty, though, because shame and anger seemed to dominate her thoughts. Along with one other emotion. "You're feeling pretty guilty," Galar observed. "What about?"

"I should have realized what was going on." Dona tilted up her chin and looked him in the eye. "I knew Ivar kept his computer implant active almost all the time, but it didn't occur to me it was because damn near every word coming out of his mouth was a lie. Instead, I believed him when he said he . . ." She didn't drop her gaze, though color spilled into her cheekbones. "I believed him when he said he loved me. But a man who loves you doesn't beat you half to death so he can kill an innocent woman." Her eyes went bleak. "My gullibility cost Jiri and Ando their lives, and damned near got Jessica and me killed."

Dyami sighed, his broad shoulders slumping, the hostility draining from his face. "You're not the only one he suckered, Enforcer. I thought he was aggressive, competitive, and intelligent, but I would have sworn he was honest. And certainly loyal to the Galactic Union." His voice took on an icy note. "Instead, he's a sociopath who isn't loyal to anybody or anything."

"It's safe to say we all bought the act," Galar agreed. "He's good."

Damned good, at any number of vicious little skills. Not only had Ivar sabotaged the Outpost's computer during the combot's attack on Jess—along with the combot itself—he'd also hacked the comp again when he'd been sent to bodyguard her. That's why the Outpost had ignored the assault on both Jess and Dona.

Galar and Dyami, using their respective comp implants, had determined how he'd pulled that little trick off and plugged the security holes in the Outpost's mainframe. He wouldn't be doing it again—and neither would any other potential Xeran moles.

Another worrisome issue was the courier 'bots who'd visited Ivar so often. There was no way of knowing what those couriers had told him . . . or what he'd told them. The 'bots were supposedly from legitimate sources: family members, officials with Temporal Enforcement—but the Enforcers were going to have to backtrack to find out if those people had indeed sent them. Galar had the distinct feeling they'd discover otherwise.

At the moment, though, he was much more interested in another question altogether: where had Jessica gone?

And was she being hunted there too?

**Ivar sat in** his cell, clenching and unclenching his big fists. They'd disabled his computer implant and left him with only enough power to his cyborg limbs to let him walk and feed himself. He doubted he could win a fight with a newborn kitten right now.

Bastards. They didn't deserve to win. He was faster, better, smarter.

If he could get his hands on that bitch Dona, she was dead. He was going to kill her for betraying him like this. Tripping him. Keeping him from doing his job and killing that stupid primitive.

He'd put Dona to the test, and she'd failed him. So much for her claims of deathless love. When push came to shove, she'd chosen her career over him. Hell, she'd probably been fucking the chief behind his back, too, the little whore.

He was going to make her pay for that. Somehow.

Unfortunately, he had no idea how he was going to pull off that neat little bit of revenge. They'd stolen his power.

The deafening sonic-boom crack of displacing air brought his head up with a jerk. Male voices bellowed—his guards, yelling for help from Outpost Security. Both men cut off in mid-shout. Warning Klaxons began to howl.

He managed to reel to his feet just as the trid field vanished from the cell doorway. A hulking battlebot stuck its glossy gray, vaguely humanoid head through the opening. "Come."

Ivar smiled, vicious and triumphant. It seemed he wasn't done yet.

**Galar raced down** the corridor toward the brig with Dyami and Dona Astryr at his heels. He'd gone to *riaat*, and the berserker state's biochemical storm was a hot, burning song in his blood.

Shouts rang out, along with a familiar rippling snarl and vicious barks. Frieka was on the scene, making life difficult for the bad guys.

They rounded a corner to find a knot of Enforcers fighting a unit of battlebots. A fast head count told Galar there were fifteen of the hulking, glossy gray androids slugging it out with an equal number of their own people. Somewhere in the midst of the group, his sensors told him, Ivar and another of the 'bots were fighting Frieka and Riane.

*"You can be damn sure that 'bot has a Jump unit,"* Dyami told the two Enforcers through their implants. *"We've got to get to them before it transports Ivar out. I don't want that son of a bitch getting away."*

From the corner of one eye, he saw Dona snarl. *"Over my dead body!"*

The nearest of the 'bots spun toward Galar, swinging up a shard rifle. Galar threw himself into a forward roll as Dyami ducked aside. The barrage of metal fragments hissed overhead like a deadly rain. The 'bot danced backward, smoothly shifting its aim to follow Galar's roll. He kicked out, catching the android across the thighs, and it fell. Its weapon hit the deck and skittered right into Galar's waiting hands.

He swept up the rifle, rolled to his feet, and fired into the 'bot's head. The 'bot jerked, tried to rise, and he fired again. The second blast took out what was left of its command system. It fell back, its skull spitting sparks and blue smoke.

Galar turned to see Dyami heave one of the 'bots over his head, roaring a battle cry as he hurled it at another. The androids collided with a deafening crunch and a flurry of sparks.

Never piss off a Warlord in full *riaat*, Galar thought in grim satisfaction.

Spotting another 'bot drawing a bead on Dyami's dark head with a shard rifle, Galar opened up with his own weapon, sending the android stumbling back under a hail of shards.

As his opponent fell, Galar turned to see Dona forcing her way through the crowd, trying to get to Ivar. The traitor had both hands locked around Frieka's furry throat in an effort to keep the wolf's snapping teeth from his own jugular.

Just beyond them, Riane, also in *riaat*, traded punches with another of the 'bots. Riane's booted foot hit a puddle of blood and skidded out from under her. As she fell to one knee, the 'bot drove a kick into her face, slamming her backward. She landed hard on the deck and didn't move.

Galar cursed and lifted his rifle, but another Enforcer staggered between him and the Warfem's victorious opponent. He bellowed at the man to step aside.

Too late. The 'bot grabbed Frieka by the scruff, tore him away from Ivar, and hurled him across the corridor like a stuffed toy. The wolf's yelp cut off as he hit the wall hard. The 'bot jerked Ivar to his feet.

"Get me out of here!" the traitor yelled.

Galar cursed and adjusted his aim, trying to get a clear shot at Ivar's head.

*BOOM!* The blinding light and rolling thunder of the Jump shook the deck beneath Galar's boots. When his vision cleared, both Ivar and the 'bot were gone.

"Seven Hells!" Galar snarled.

The nearest combot turned toward him and said, its tone oddly polite, "I am programmed to warn you we will now self-destruct. You have thirty seconds to clear the area. Twenty-nine . . ."

"Twenty-eight," another 'bot said.

"Fuck!" Dyami roared. "Retreat!"

Ignoring him, Galar raced past the 'bots to grab Frieka by the scruff of the neck. Hauling the beast into his arms, he turned to find Dona Astryr draping an unconscious Riane over her shoulder. "This way!" he snapped, and galloped up the corridor with the women at his heels.

Glancing back, Galar saw Dyami running the opposite way, carrying a wounded Enforcer as if he weighed no more than a pillow. The other agents sprinted after him.

"Five . . ."

"Four . . ."

"Three . . ."

"In there!" Galar roared at Dona, and dove at her, Frieka tucked under his arm. His lunge carried all four of them into an open cell. With any luck, its reinforced walls would . . .

The battlebots began to detonate in thunderous booms that shook the floor under them. Galar, Dona, Frieka, and Riane went down in a heap of fur and uniformed flesh. Galar covered the others' bodies with his and threw both arms over his head.

The explosions seemed to go on forever, blast after deafening blast. Until finally silence fell, broken only by the *whoop* of the Klaxon and the *whoosh* of foam as the Outpost's fire-suppression system activated.

"Bloody hell," Galar said, barely able to hear his own words through the ringing in his ears.

"Yeah," Dona said bitterly. "That about sums it up."


**Jessica paced the** shabby living room, chewing a thumbnail. "I need that painting."

"Why?" her sister asked, watching her from the couch. "What good is it?"

"Charlotte told me it holds the answers I'm looking for. I'll bet if I can just touch it . . ." She turned toward Ruby. "You think you could ask the cops to let you see it?" Then she grimaced and waved a hand, dismissing the question. "Never mind. They'd just say no and get suspicious of you again. Where the hell would they be keeping it?"

"Probably in the evidence room." Reading her astonished glance, Ruby shrugged. "Billy Dean was always talking about this fantasy he has of breaking into the county evidence room. That's where they keep all the drugs."

"Probably every drug dealer in the county has the same fantasy." Jess grunted. "Along with every murderer, rapist, and pedophile who'd like to destroy the evidence against him." Which implied that the room would be both heavily guarded and equipped with a formidable security system. Not the kind of place she'd want to try to break into, even with her new powers. Particularly since she wasn't sure she could really control them.

So the evidence room was out. She supposed she could Jump to the time when the cops returned the paintings to Ruby. Except she had no idea when that would be.

Her eyes narrowed thoughtfully. Or she could go the other way, and get to the painting before the Xeran's attack even occurred. No, better not. What if she ran into herself?

Except she hadn't. She'd certainly remember meeting some mirror image of herself babbling about men from the future.

That could mean she'd successfully gone back and gotten her hands on the painting without getting caught. Except what if she got to the painting before Charlotte left her message in it?

Or . . . she could Jump to the period after the Enforcers left with her past self, but before the cops showed up. She'd probably have a couple of hours to get done whatever she needed to do.

Yeah. That would work.

"I'm going to have to go," Jess said, swinging toward Ruby. "Remember what I told you. When they give you the paintings back, go to David Sheraton at the Sheraton Gallery in Atlanta. He'll put the whole thing in motion."

"I'm not going to see you again, am I?" Ruby's lower lip trembled.

"No." Jess's own eyes stung. "I've got to be dead from now on."

"I've been such a bitch to you. After they told me you . . . died, that's all I've been able to think about. What a bitch I've been." Her shoulders shook.

"You're not a bitch." It wasn't strictly true—Ruby had been pretty damned nasty at various times, particularly since acquiring that crack habit. But still, when the girls had been younger, they'd been close. "I love you, sis. The other stuff—that doesn't matter. Not anymore."

Her sister threw herself off the couch and grabbed her in a hard, fierce hug. "I love you, too, Jess. I wish . . ."

"Just get off the drugs, baby." She wrapped both arms tighter around her sister. "You do that for me, you hear? Once you kick the crack, you'll be fine."

"I'll try." She stepped back, grief and guilt flooding her eyes with tears. "But what if I can't do it? I've tried so many times. . . ."

Jess grabbed her by her thin shoulders and met her eyes fiercely. "You can. You will. You have the strength, you hear me?" Somewhere inside her, a bubble of warmth began to expand. She caught her breath, feeling it suddenly burst free and flash from her body to Ruby's. The younger woman's eyes widened as she jerked rigid.

"Oooh," Ruby breathed, the sound a long, fading sigh. A smile suddenly flashed across her tear-streaked face, white, confident. "You're right. I can do it, can't I?"

"You can do anything," Jessica told her fiercely. "All you have to do is want it."

"Yeah." Ruby's smile became a grin. "And I want this. All the shitty things I've ever done, I want to make right. I want you to be proud of me."

"I am proud of you," Jess told her around the knot in her throat. "Because you're going to be amazing. And your son will be a great artist."

Ruby's eyes widened. "I'm going to have a son?" She broke off, frowning. "Wait—how do you know this?"

Jess gave her a grin that was rapidly getting a little watery. "I've read some of my own biographies. They talked about you." She had to swallow at the lump growing in her throat before she could continue. "You're going to meet a good man, Ruby, and you're going to fall in love. You'll have a son, and he'll be a great artist in his own right. You'll have grandchildren, and great-grandchildren. And you'll be happy." Tears swam in her eyes as she realized she'd never get to meet any of the people who would enter her sister's life. Not the handsome husband, not the artist son.

Because she'd never see Ruby again.

Her sister reached out and cupped her cheek. "But I'll never forget."

Jess choked and dragged her into another hard, fierce hug. For a long moment they stood wrapped around each other, knowing it would be the last time.

# · 15 ·

✥⚘✥

**Galar rolled off the pile of fur and flesh that was**
Dona Astryr, Riane, and Frieka, suppressing a curse at the
vicious ache in his head. The wolf whimpered, and one of
the women groaned. *Comp, scan the other Enforcers for
injuries.*

*Sensors indicate Riane has suffered a concussion, while
Frieka has a fractured foreleg. Dona's injuries are minor.*

*Anything life-threatening?*

*Negative.*

Well, that was something, anyway. "Hey, Dona, you conscious?"

"Yeah, yeah. Has anybody ever told you that you weigh a
ton?"

He grinned. "Sorry about that. Normally I keep my weight
on my elbows."

Dona snorted, recognizing the double entendre, and sat
up herself. "Hey, Riane." Bending, she scooped red hair out

of the Warfem's face. The girl looked up at her, a little dazed. "Up and at 'em, kiddo."

"Frieka!" She jerked upright, then swayed dizzily. Obviously ignoring her own injuries, Riane reached for her furry partner. "You're hurt!"

"Just my foreleg." He yelped. "Don't touch it!"

"I'm not going to touch it, I'm just scanning you. Calm down, you big puppy."

"I'm going to bite you." The wolf considered her with pain-filled eyes. "Or I would if you hadn't put a dent in your thick ape skull. You do realize you need a regenerator more than I do?"

"I'm fine."

"You're not fine. Would you lie back down before you fall and put another crack in your head?"

Since everyone was healthy enough to squabble, Galar returned his attention to his comp. *What's the status on the fires?*

*Extinguished.*

Better and better. He limped to the doorway and stuck his head outside, then winced at what he saw. The Outpost's ventilation system was hard at work drawing off the blue pall of smoke that still swirled in the corridor's air. The floor was covered in foam, with several thick humps of it that apparently marked the remnants of the 'bots. Anything not covered in white foam was charred black from multiple blasts. There were several irregular areas showing through the foam where the explosions had damaged the walls and floor.

*Did we lose anybody?* he asked the comp.

*Negative. The Outpost comp reports that medtechs are on the way for the wounded.*

*Good. Tell 'em we've got a couple for them here.*

*In process.*

He saw a tall figure round the curve of the corridor and limp toward him. It was Dyami, a thin stream of blood dripping down his face from a cut on his forehead, the red obscuring the green and gold of his tatt. The big man wore a grim expression as he scanned the damage.

"I'm going to kill that fucker Ivar," he growled as he drew close enough. "And whoever sent that 'bot team to bust him out when I find out who it was."

"At least they warned us they were self-destructing," Galar sighed. "We'd have had a lot more dead if they hadn't."

"Unfortunately, there's an ugly implication to that warning," Dyami told him grimly.

"Yeah?" Though he had a bad feeling he already knew what Dyami was going to say.

"By law, 'bots manufactured in the Galactic Union have to warn they're going to self-destruct, even combat models. Xeran 'bots don't. Remember the howls of outrage from the military when the Council of Legislators came up with that little gem? But it saved our butts this time."

"And it also means somebody from the GU sent that team." Galar scrubbed a hand over his face. "We've got another mole. Which is why they self-destructed. Whoever it was thought we might be able to trace his identity if we captured one of the 'bots intact."

"Dona?"

He considered the question, then finally shook his head. "I don't think so. Judging by my sensor readings, she was as unpleasantly surprised by the self-destruct announcement as I was."

"Which at least clears her, if nothing else." Dyami fisted his hands on his hips. "Unfortunately, that still leaves me with just about every other Enforcer on the Outpost as a suspect."

Galar lifted a brow. "Including me?"

"Fuck, no. Jessica would be dead by now if you were the mole. You're too damn good to screw something like that up."

"Thank you," Galar said with elaborate sarcasm.

Dyami flashed him a toothy grin. "You're welcome."

"I just wish I shared your confidence. If I *was* that good, I'd know where Jess had . . ." He broke off, realization dawning. "Oh, shit."

The Chief Enforcer lifted his dark brows. "I gather you just figured it out."

"Her sister. Jess was devastated when I told her she couldn't tell Ruby she was still alive. If she suddenly figured out how to transport herself, you can bet she'd head right for her little sister."

"This is the drug addict, right?" Dyami sighed. "Perfect. Go get her before somebody really does kill her."

Galar nodded and turned to lope up the corridor, passing Chogan, her medtechs, and a procession of regenerator tubes. He'd need his T-suit for this.

**Ruby sat on** the couch where she'd been when all this started, torn between joy and sorrow. Joy that she hadn't gotten her sister killed after all—she'd just *known* Billy Dean had ordered Jess's murder to get revenge on her.

But almost as strong as that joy was grief that she'd never see Jess again. She kept thinking of every rotten thing she'd ever said, every cutting little comment born of her jealousy of her brilliant sister. The sister who had never been an addict, never been a punching bag for every abusive bastard in the county. Never whored for the money to buy crack.

*Well,* she told herself. *I'll never do that again either.*

It wasn't the first time she'd promised herself she was done with self-destruction. Hell, there'd been times she'd made that promise every day. *This is the last time. Tomorrow I'll start over.*

Now she actually believed it.

The boom of displacing air and the blinding flash of light tore a startled scream from her throat. She bounded off the couch, her heart pounding with shock as she blinked away the purple flashes from her vision. *Jess is back!*

But the figure who stood warily scanning her shabby living room was not a woman. He was tall, blond, broad-shouldered—and as handsome as any movie actor she'd ever seen.

Ruby took one look at him and thought, *Jess's cop.*

He frowned at her. "Where is Jessica?"

Ruby swallowed. Damn, he was gorgeous. No wonder her big sister was willing to turn her back on her career and all that money to be with him. "She . . . just left."

He frowned, studying her intently. "Did she say where she was going?"

Ruby hesitated nervously. What if this wasn't the cop? What if it was the guy who'd tried to kill her? Jess had said the cop had killed him, but . . .

"Look, she's in danger," the big man said impatiently. "There are killers after her. I need to find her before she gets hurt."

Ruby had her flaws, but she also had a well-developed people sense. This man, she knew, meant exactly what he said. "She went back to her apartment to the time right after she was . . . attacked."

"What?" He stared at her. "Why?"

"She said she needs the painting she left there. I don't have it, so . . ." She shrugged.

He frowned. Even that looked good on his angular face. "What does she need the painting for?"

"She thinks her roommate left a message in it."

"In the painting?" He cocked his head, considering the idea. "Yes, I suppose it's possible. Thank you." He hesitated, giving her a narrow-eyed look.

Ruby knew what he wanted. She sighed. "I won't tell anyone either of you were ever here."

A smile flashed over his face, one so dazzling she found herself staring. "Thanks."

The crack of the sonic boom rattled every dish in her cupboard. When Ruby blinked away the purple flashes, he was gone.

"Damn, Jess," she muttered. "Some girls have all the luck."

**Both palms braced** on the carpeted floor, Jessica blinked away purple afterimages and fought her rioting stomach. She felt as if she'd been turned inside out.

When she identified the wet substance saturating the carpeting under her hands, she damned near lost the battle. With a cry of revulsion, she jerked back on her knees, staring down at the blood.

Her blood.

Gut twisting, Jess stared around the shambles of her former living room. The Enforcers had evidently left the lights on after they'd rescued her. The easel lay on its side beside the painting she'd been working on. Tubes of paint were scattered around it, along with the can of turpentine she'd emptied on the Xeran. The scorch mark where she'd burned him was gone now—apparently Galar's friends had cleaned it up. Probably in order to leave no evidence that wasn't part of the historical record.

She turned her attention to the painting again, rising cautiously to her feet.

What if she was wrong? What if Charlotte hadn't left her a message in the painting? Or what if she had, and it proved to be something Jess didn't want to know?

*Well, whether I want to know or not, I need to know.*

Ignoring her pounding heart, she walked across the living room, bent, and picked up the painting. It looked no different than it had the last time she'd worked on it, a subjective eternity ago.

An odd realization penetrated her consciousness: the paint was still wet. Of course. From the painting's standpoint, it had been only a couple of hours since she'd stopped work. Never mind that, to her, it had been days.

Dizzying thought, that.

Jess drew in a deep breath, steadied her courage, and touched the still-tacky paint with a finger. And waited.

Nothing happened. She wrestled her impatience back under control. Waited some more.

Nothing. The refrigerator hummed in the next room, a familiar sound, oddly homey in a room that smelled so disturbingly of fresh blood.

"I knew you'd come," Charlotte whispered.

Jess dropped the painting with a clatter and whirled.

Her friend stood behind her, looking as solid and real as she had the night she'd disappeared.

With some half-formed thought of keeping her from getting away, Jess grabbed for her arm, but her fingers swiped right through Charlotte's wrist as if she were a ghost. "What the hell—?"

"This is a recording, Jess. I'm not really here."

"Figures," she grumbled, one hand to her chest with its thundering heartbeat.

"By now you know what I did to you. I want to tell you I'm sorry for the pain I've caused you. Sorry for drawing you into my war with my former superiors. . . ."

"So I was right—you are Xer."

"Sorry you'll be hurt by Marcin," the image continued.

"You knew what was going to happen?" Jess demanded hotly. "Why the hell didn't you warn me?"

"You're probably wondering why I didn't warn you, but I couldn't. There are things going on I can't explain. We both have our tests, and this is part of mine. We have to prove ourselves worthy."

"What tests?" Jess muttered in frustration, knowing even as she asked the question that the recording wouldn't answer. "Worthy of what? And who do we have to prove it to?"

"I know you have a great many questions. If you pass

your tests, you'll get the answers you're looking for. If you don't . . ." An expression of anguish flashed across Charlotte's delicate face. ". . . well, you won't need them. For now, you're here, and that means you've come far enough to receive this next gift. Good luck, Jess."

A rainbow blast exploded behind Jess's eyes, knowledge slamming into her mind so fast and hard, there was no way to process it all. Images, sounds, color—all blended in one seething mental detonation. Jessica's brain seemed to pulse under the bombardment.

*Too much! Too much! Stop!*

But it didn't stop. It went on and on, burning, blinding. Until, in sheer self-defense, her mind went dark.

**Galar shook his** head hard, trying to clear his dazzled vision and the ears that still rang from the sonic boom of his Jump. When he could see again, he first registered the bloody shambles of Jess's living room, with its tumbled furniture, paintings, and easel.

It took him a moment to realize the bundle of blue fabric on the floor was actually a body. Jessica, lying sprawled and still.

"Jess!" Galar's heart shoved its way into his throat as he dropped to his knees, scanning her frantically.

There were no obvious wounds, no blood, but that might mean nothing. A head injury . . .

*Is she all right?*

*Unconscious,* his comp replied. *She seems to be in some kind of shock.*

*Any reason I shouldn't move her?*

*Negative.*

There was no time to waste. Galar scooped her into his arms, cuddled her close, and Jumped.

He'd wanted to transport directly into the infirmary, but the delicate equipment there didn't take well to sonic booms.

Instead, he materialized in the closest Jump chamber—heavily soundproofed and shielded to contain any temporal radiation. As he carried Jess through the door, he sent a message to the infirmary. *"Jessica's been hurt."*

*"How badly?"* Chogan's voice demanded.

*"I can't tell. She's unconscious, in shock."*

*"Bring her."*

As he strode into the infirmary, the doctor met him and pointed toward an open and waiting regenerator. "What happened?" she demanded.

"I don't know." Galar lowered Jess carefully into the transparent tube. "I got a lead she'd gone back to the scene of the attack, sometime right after we left with her the first time. She was lying on the floor of the living room, unconscious. There was no sign of any attacker."

He stepped back as Chogan closed the tube lid and started the program. The device began to flood with pink healing mist as the doctor studied readouts and pushed buttons. "Hmm."

"What?" Galar demanded, frustrated.

"There's no sign of physical injury at all. But . . ." Her frown looked troubled.

"But?"

"Those brain changes we saw earlier have intensified." She gestured, bringing up trids of three brain scans.

"Seven Hells," Galar breathed. The scan with today's date was almost solid blue with new synapse growth.

"What's more, the ratio of alien material is increasing," Chogan told him. "It's as if the Xeran DNA acted as a base to give the alien material a foothold." She nibbled on a thumbnail, her brows drawn down in worry. "I don't mind telling you, Master Enforcer—I don't like this at all."

"What's it doing to her?" A chill spread over him. "Do you think it's going to . . . hurt her?"

"I have no idea," Chogan said bluntly. "Luckily her auto-immune system doesn't seem to be attacking the new material, so we don't have to worry about her body killing her own nervous system." She returned her attention to the tube's readouts, frowning and pushing buttons.

Galar waited, controlling his impatience until she finally stepped back away from the tube. Was it his imagination, or had her expression lightened with relief? "Well?" he demanded.

"Physically, Jessica seems perfectly healthy. Exhausted, which isn't surprising considering what she's been going through the last few days. Needs a couple of good meals too. Her blood sugar's too low for my taste. Other than that, though, everything's fine."

He blew out a breath in relief. "So why's she unconscious?"

"Good question. Come to think of it, these readings . . ." Chogan's eyes narrowed. "Actually, they look rather like an EDI reaction. I've seen this kind of thing before with patients in the aftermath of a particularly traumatic download. Let me see if I can bring her out of it. . . ." Delicate fingers danced over the tube controls. The mist stirred, then slowly began to thin. Chogan popped the lid. "Jessica? Wake up, Jess!"

Jess's blue eyes fluttered open, and she began to cough. "What . . . happen'?" Her voice firmed as her gaze began to sharpen with its customary intelligence. "Dr. Chogan? Galar? Where did you . . . ?"

"Ruby told me you'd gone back to your house." Galar took her hand and helped her sit up. "I went after you and found you out cold on the floor. What happened?"

Jess coughed again and leaned both elbows on the edges of the tube, looking a little dizzy. "I remembered Charlotte had said something about one of my paintings having the answers I needed. So I went back to check. Sure enough, she'd left some kind of nanobot message in the paint."

Chogan shot Galar a look. "I wonder if that was all that was in that paint."

"You think Charlotte slipped her something that accelerated the neural changes?"

"Could be."

Jess frowned at them both. "What the heck are you talking about?"

Chogan displayed the brain scans for her. Galar watched her pale in alarm. "Holy shit."

"That about sums it up," the doctor agreed, then went on to explain her findings in more detail. "The good news," she concluded, "is that you seem healthy otherwise. So far you're not suffering any ill effects, but I want you to keep me posted on anything—and I do mean anything—that strikes you as weird."

Jess gave her a dry smile. "Like blowing up robots with the power of my mind?"

"Yeah. Like that."

She snorted. "Believe me, you'll be the first to know."

Galar scratched his chin thoughtfully. "What did Charlotte actually say in her message?"

Jess shrugged. "That she was sorry about what she'd done to me, but we both had tests we had to pass. That we had to prove ourselves."

"Prove what? To whom?"

"Exactly what I was wondering. Unfortunately, she didn't say. Then she triggered this . . . psychic bombardment. It was like the EDI, but worse. Knocked me out completely."

"Do you remember anything about it?"

Deep lines grooved between Jessica's fine brows as she seemed to struggle to remember, then shook her head in frustration. "Nothing I can make any sense of. Just . . . this wild confusion of colors and smells and sounds."

"If it's anything like a regular EDI, your brain will have to incorporate the information you've downloaded," Chogan told her. "Give it time, and it'll start surfacing as you integrate it."

"Assuming we *have* time." Jess gnawed gently on a knuckle. "I have an ugly feeling everything's getting ready to go straight to hell."

Galar snorted. "You mean it's not there already?"

"Yeah, the concept of this getting worse boggles my mind, too, but that was the implication of Charlotte's little psychic candygram."

"Candy what?" Chogan looked puzzled.

Jess sighed. "Never mind." She turned to Galar as a new thought occurred to her. "Please tell me you've found out Ivar was your mole. And is Dona okay?"

"She's fine. And yes, we did. Unfortunately, no sooner did we put Ivar in the brig than someone sent a team of exploding battlebots to break him out."

She blinked at him. "Exploding battlebots? That sounds . . . not good."

"That's putting it mildly. We now have craters in the brig."

"Anybody killed?"

"No, but Ivar escaped. Dyami has dispatched every available Enforcer to track him down. I almost pity the bastard when the chief gets his hands on him."

"I wouldn't mind a crack at him myself."

Galar curled his lip in agreement. "I owe him for Jiri and Ando." Something dangerous flickered in his eyes as his voice dropped to a menacing growl. "And you."

"So what do we do now?"

"That's a good question." Chogan rocked back on her heels, eyeing Jess. "I could keep you here for observation, but I think what you really need is some food and a good night's sleep. Charlotte's EDI would be more likely to surface if we give you some peace and quiet—which you won't get in an infirmary bed with various things beeping at you all night."

Jess grimaced. "That's a pretty safe bet."

Chogan aimed a stern look at Galar. "That goes for you, too, Master Enforcer. How long has it been since you've slept?"

He blinked. "Well . . ."

"Go. To. Bed."

"Yes, ma'am," he said with suspicious meekness.

"What are you waiting on? Get out of my infirmary."

"Yes, ma'am," Jess and Galar chorused as he helped her out of the tube. Together, they made a fast escape as Chogan shook her head and went to search out Dyami to make her report. She knew the big Warlord wasn't going to be happy about this situation.

At all.

# · 16 ·

**The Outpost's cafeteria was deserted at this hour,**
since it was between the mid-watch's dinner and the late
watch's early-morning meal. Galar and Jess had the dining
area to themselves, so they found a choice table beside the
enormous window that took up most of the room's rear wall.

Stifling a yawn, Jess stared out over the moonlit mountains, listening absently as Galar put in their order with the
table's vendser. Five minutes later, a panel slid open and two
steaming plates appeared, accompanied by the appropriate
flatware and a couple of glasses. Galar parceled everything
out and they settled down to eat.

Jess paused, fork lifted, as she stared down at her plate
dubiously. She couldn't identify a single substance on it,
though she thought the purple thing with fronds was some
kind of vegetable.

"It's safe to eat," Galar told her, pausing with his fork
halfway to his mouth. "I promise it won't even bite back."

She poked a dark brown substance. "Are you sure? What *is* this?"

"Vardonese *keflir*. It was my favorite meal when I was a boy. My father's *keflir* was incredible." He took a bite, chewed thoughtfully, and swallowed. "This isn't quite that good, but it's not bad."

She warily cut a forkful and bit into it. It was covered with something that had a nutty kind of crunch. The meat inside flooded her mouth with delicate juice and a taste reminiscent of lamb. "It is good." Emboldened, she tried the purple thing. It wasn't much like any other vegetable she'd ever had, but she decided she liked it anyway. She turned her attention to a fluffy green pile with little red bits scattered inside it. "Kind of slimy," Jess said after a bite. "Reminds me of boiled okra. You could probably fry it though. . . . Then again, Southerners can make anything edible by breading it and covering it in ketchup." She forked up another bite of purple frond.

"I never liked gedira either," Galar admitted. "But it's good for you."

She snorted. "It would be."

They ate in companionable silence for several moments before Galar spoke again. "I wanted to apologize for what I did to you." He stirred his fork through what was presumably some kind of vegetable, his expression brooding. "Those things I said. I know I hurt you."

Jess looked up from cutting another bite of keflir. "Dyami told me you were trying to clear me."

"Yeah." A muscle flexed in his jaw. "But there was more to it than that. Tlain . . . Who told you about her, by the way? I know somebody did, because you threw her name in my face."

"Ahhh. . . ." Trapped, she stared at him, remembering she'd sworn not to rat out Riane. But if she lied, he'd know it. "I promised not to tell you."

One corner of his mouth curled up. "Never mind. I think

I can guess. No wonder Riane and Frieka looked so guilty when they slunk out of my quarters the day I asked them to guard you."

"I have no idea what you're talking about," Jess said with dignity.

He snorted. "Please."

She gave up and grinned. "There's a definite downside to"—*loving*—"dating a man with sensors. No little white lies."

"Never stopped Tlain. Then again, big black lies didn't stop her either."

The bleak, angry pain in his eyes made her draw in a sharp breath. "You really did love her."

"I thought so at the time." Galar shrugged his broad shoulders, then gave her a faint smile. "Lately I've come to a different perspective on that."

Her heart leaped. What did he mean by that? Don't ask, dammit. "Ria— My source said she did quite a number on you."

"You could say that." His gaze turned inward. "She had a computer implant, so she had pretty good control over her own brain function. Gave her the sociopath's trick of believing her own lies."

"Ivar must have done the same thing."

"Oh, yes. Otherwise we'd have tripped to what he was doing soon after he arrived at the Outpost months ago. Dona said she'd noticed he used his implant constantly, even in casual conversation, which should have been a big red warning flag. But I can't blame her for only seeing what she wanted to see. I committed the same sin."

"You don't think Dona was in collusion with him, do you?" Jess asked, alarmed. "Galar, she didn't hesitate to jump him the minute she realized he was trying to kill me."

"I know. She got badly beaten for her pains. Ivar is a great deal stronger than she is."

"The prick."

"But I," he said silkily, "am a great deal stronger than Ivar is, at least in *riaat*."

"Kick his ass when you catch him."

"Oh, I will. If Dyami leaves me anything to kick. I gather he has some rather violent plans for the bastard."

"I wouldn't mind giving Ivar a little bit of what I gave that robot, myself. Except I can't." She fell silent as realization hit, her eyes widening.

"What? Why not?"

"That EDI Charlotte gave me just told me I can't use my powers to kill people. Run away, yes. Destroy property, yeah. And I did give Ivar a good sock in the mouth, but that's about as far as I can go."

Galar went very still, apparently realizing she was trying to tease more information out of her recalcitrant brain. "Why?"

Jess blinked. "Because they're not my powers. They come from the T'lir, and the T'lir won't allow the use of lethal force. That's why the Sela had to run." She sat back in disgust as the information abruptly dried up again. "Run where? From whom?"

"Who—or what—are the Sela?" His tone carefully lacked any urgency at all.

"The fuzzy people in the eggs. The ones I saw in that dream I told you about. The Xerans call them Abominations, and they want to kill them all."

"Maybe it's the Xerans the Sela are running from," Galar suggested.

"Yeah." She sounded almost dreamy to her own ears. "Yeah, that's it. It's the Xerans. They want the T'lir, and the Sela can't allow them to have it. We'd all be lost then. The People would only be the first to die."

"And what is the T'lir?" His voice was very gentle.

"An hourglass," she said, feeling as if she were floating. "Everything pours through. Everyone." Jess giggled, suddenly giddy. " 'Like sand through an hourglass, so are the days of our lives.' " Her consciousness snapped back into full focus, and she buried her frustrated face in her hands. "Fuck. I lost it in the intro to one of Mom's old soaps."

"What are you *talking* about?" Galar demanded, his tone sharpening as he evidently realized she had stopped drawing on the EDI.

"Soap operas," Jess explained. "Daily television serial dramas. There was one called *Days of Our Lives* my mother loved when I was a kid. That line about sand through the hourglass was part of the intro." She stopped. "And it means something, but damned if I know what."

"Don't try to force it," Galar warned. "You'll just drive it deeper into your subconscious. It'll come back out when you trigger another association. Probably by accident."

"Great," she growled. "We're at the mercy of television jingles."

"And on that note," he said, pushing his empty plate aside, "I think it's time we go to bed." He stopped, a trace of—was that pain?—in his eyes. "I can find you other quarters if you'd rather."

Jess put a hand on his. It felt warm and strong under her palm. "I want to sleep with you." She grimaced. "Though I won't guarantee we'll do much more than sleep. I'm whipped."

He gave her a smile that made his handsome face even more striking. "I'd be delighted to simply sleep with you."

They dropped their plates into the vendser recycler—Jess noted with bemusement that she'd absently cleaned her plate, including the slimy okra-like vegetables. "I must have been hungrier than I thought."

Another flash of that breathtaking smile. "And you didn't even have to fry anything and cover it in ketchup."

"Hey—don't mock the ketchup. It's one of the Southern food groups. Along with grits, fatback, collard greens, and pig's feet."

"Pig's feet?" He took her hand as they started out of the mess. "You are really very odd."

"Hey, I didn't say *I* ate them. Though if you covered them in ketchup . . ."

*"Pig's feet?"* His tone of utter horror made her laugh.


**Jess and Galar** returned to his quarters at last. She watched, looking a bit bemused, as he walked around lighting the beeswax candles he'd once acquired with the vague thought of using them during some future special seduction.

And if a seduction had ever needed to be special, Galar decided, this one was it.

He turned from lighting the last candle to see her sliding her loose, forest green top off over her head. Galar swallowed, suddenly dry-mouthed, as she stepped out of her pants, then paused, boldly, sweetly naked.

"Goddess, you're beautiful," he managed, his voice hoarse, as he stared at her pretty tip-tilted breasts with their hard, sweet little nipples.

She gave him a cocky little smile, though a blush pinkened her cheeks. "You're not so bad yourself." The soft delta between her thighs was all mysterious shadow in the dancing golden candlelight. Her eyes cast back tiny flame reflections, half hidden in the long, straight fall of her hair.

Galar suspected his own eyes glowed like coals with the force of his desire. He knew his cock jutted against his uniform trousers, urgent and demanding.

He ached to show her what he'd tried and failed to express at dinner. His regret had seemed too huge, too complicated to put into words. Instead he'd let himself be diverted by trivialities—Ivar, the Sela, this T'Lir of hers.

Or at least, they felt somehow trivial in the face of this swelling thing in his chest. A distraction from what his hindbrain insisted was truly important, no matter what his reason said.

This was not the time for reason.

The rest would have to be dealt with—questions answered, problems solved. But not now. Now he had to repair the gulf he'd created between himself and Jess.

She rocked back on a bare heel and lifted a brow. "That thing I said about you being not bad yourself. That was a hint."

Somehow he'd lost the thread of the conversation. "A hint?"

Shaping the words very slowly, Jess elaborated. "You. Are. Wearing. Too. Many. Clothes." Then she grinned wickedly. "Get nekkid."

He grinned back. "Oh." Slowly, he started pulling up his uniform tunic. Perhaps a seductive striptease . . .

"You're just taking too damned *long.*" Jess grabbed the hem of his tunic and whipped it off over his head. "Now that's how you're supposed to take your clothes off for me. Fast. Like you're unwrapping a birthday present. A really *big* birthday present." Leaning forward, she found his hard, flat brown nipples with her soft mouth.

The first pass of her tongue made him gasp. "Jess . . ." His voice sounded hoarse, pleading. This was supposed to be for her, his apology for his blindness, his ingrained suspicion.

Her eyes glinted up at him. "Shhhh." A swirl of her tongue, wet and breathtaking.

"But I . . ."

"No." Her fingers feathered down his chest, tracing the ridges and swells of muscle, combing through chest hair, dipping teasingly into his belly button. "This time is mine."

He swallowed. "That's fair."

Her eyes glinted. "I don't care if it's fair or not. You owe me, buster."

And how did she intend to collect? Intriguing thought. . . .

Galar found out when one smooth hand slid down the waistband of his trousers, slipped between briefs and skin, found his thick erection. Her skin felt cool against the fevered heat of his. Blunt nails gently raked, and his cock jerked in ferocious arousal.

"Hmmm," she purred. "What have we here?"

He smirked. "If you don't know, I've been doing something wrong."

"Smart-ass." Her bright gaze focused on the urgent ridge of his erection. He saw her eyes widen as they flicked to one of the pouches hanging from his weapons belt. "Ahhh. I think I know just how to take the wind out of your sails."

"Isn't that counterproductive?"

She snorted and pulled the exploring hand out of his pants to run a finger up the length of the hungry ridge. "Not as long as you've got this oar."

His laugh cut off as she opened the belt pouch and pulled out a length of restraint cable. "Now what," he said, his mouth going dry, "do you intend to do with that?"

"What do you think?" She unwound it with a flick of her wrist and a grin of sensual anticipation.

"I usually do the tying up."

"Then it would do you good to be on the receiving end. On your back, cop." She planted a palm on the center of his chest and gave him a teasing backward push. Galar let himself go over, knowing the bed lay directly behind him.

Feet spread wide, the cable dangling from one hand, she eyed him with all the arrogance of a conquering queen. His cock bucked under her stare.

"Assume the position."

Slowly, he stretched his arms up over his head, pressed his wrists together. And gave her a deliberately taunting grin. "Now what?"

Jess's reply was a smile every bit as feral as his own. She pounced like a cat, landing lightly astride his thighs, then put the cable between her teeth and began to crawl up the length of his body. His gaze flicked from her swaying, tempting breasts to her wicked eyes, dark and mysterious in the candlelight. At last she stopped, straddling the width of his chest. "Hands." She gave him an imperious gimme wave.

Galar lifted his crossed wrists, and she circled them with the restraint cable. The golden coil touched his skin and promptly tightened as she wound it around.

"Little snug there," he said. It wasn't, not really, but it would also hold him, even in *riaat*.

She smirked. "Good. Wouldn't want you to get away."

He lifted a brow at her. "So now that you have me, what are you going to do with me?"

Jess rocked back on her heels and surveyed him, her pretty mouth taking on a deliciously evil curve. "I'm sure I'll think of something." She contemplated his belt, then reached for the clasp. "I'm very creative. Shouldn't take me long to arrive at some suitable punishment."

"Punishment?" Both brows flew up.

"Yeah. You've been bad, Galar. Very, very bad." Slowly, she drew off his belt.

"I trust your plans don't involve that." He dropped his voice to a menacing growl.

"Oh, no." The belt sailed across the room to land with a clunk and a rattle. He winced at the sound of his holstered shard pistol thudding against the wall. "Though a spanking might do you a world of good."

He narrowed his eyes at her. "I wouldn't recommend it."

"I'm sure you wouldn't, but I'd love to have that magnificent ass draped across my lap."

"I could say the same. And I suspect I can spank considerably harder than you can."

She gave him a mock glare. "Mustn't threaten the mistress, Master Enforcer." Leaning down, she raked her nails slowly down his ribs. He sucked in a breath and squirmed.

Her eyes widened with delight. "Are you *ticklish*?"

He glowered. "Don't even think it."

Jess laughed. "My big, tough *ticklish* Warlord." She started to go for his ribs again.

In one smooth movement, Galar threw his legs up, encircled her waist, and rolled her beneath him as he braced on his knees astride her. He started to lower his bound hands to her flat little belly for a good tickle. . . .

"Uh uh!" She gave his butt a stinging slap. "Off! I'm in charge this time, remember?"

"You sure about that?"

Her eyes narrowed in threat. "You know," she purred, "I think I'm beginning to feel sleepy. Too sleepy for sex."

"I'll bet I could wake you up." He wiggled his fingers.

"Off!"

It was tempting to demonstrate a Warlord's idea of sexual dominance, but he supposed she was entitled to extract a little payback.

"All right." Galar threw himself back on the bed. "But don't be surprised when I take my turn."

"I know you weren't threatening Mistress Jessica. Again." She ran her tongue over her teeth. "Because there'd be consequences."

"Really." Slender hands curled around the thick, flushed shaft of his cock. Her smile sent a quiver of anticipation through him.

**Galar lay looking** up at her with hunger and challenge in his eyes. His powerful wrists were wrapped in that restraint cable, hands clasped on his chest, but his rock-hard erection did not suggest submission of any kind as it pointed at his chin. Her artist's eye admired the beauty of his long, powerfully graceful body. Her woman's body heated in response. And her heart . . .

Turned over in her chest.

She bent over him, wanting to touch, stroke, kiss all that masculine magnificence. Climbing astride his thighs, she ran both hands down his body, tracing the ripples and ridges of muscle, enjoying the texture of smooth skin and soft chest hair. His lids dipped as though he enjoyed her touch like a cat being petted.

Here and there she paused to thumb a nipple or cup the heavy weight of his balls, absorbed in him, in his body, in the way it reacted to her. Skin drawing tight, darkening with engorging blood, the rapid thump of his heart under her palm.

A bead of pre-come formed on the tip of his cock like a tear. She bent her head and licked it away, listening as he drew in a hard inward breath.

"Jess . . ." He groaned, sounding strangled. His bound hands tangled in her hair, and his back arched. "Sweet Mother, Jessica . . ."

Rolling her eyes up to his face, Jess watched him shiver as she gave him another swirling lick. There was pure intoxication in the idea that she could affect this strong man with such power. She felt hot inside, all cream and honey. She was tempted to go down on him again.

But no. He really did owe her for letting Dyami lock her in that cell. And as she eyed his hungry expression, she decided she knew exactly the way she was going to collect.

Slowly, teasingly, Jess lifted her head, letting his cock slowly slide from her mouth with a wet pop. He blinked up at her, panting. "Now," she announced, crawling up his torso, "it's your turn."

His blond brows lifted as she knelt straddling his head, carefully supporting her weight on her knees.

"In college," she told him, "we called this the mustache rodeo. Except I intend to last a hell of a lot longer than eight seconds."

"But I don't have a mustache." Galar gave her an innocent blink. "And—rodeo? Eight seconds? I have no idea what you're talking about."

"Guess," she growled.

"Hmmm." He pretended to think, then extended a curving tongue. "Perhaps . . . this?"

Jess gasped as he swirled that tongue around her clit with wicked, seductive skill. "Yeah. You've got it."

His eyes glinted in a wicked smile. "Good," he purred, and began to lick in earnest.

Damn, he was good with his mouth. He used his teeth and lips as well as that amazing tongue, nibbling her clit with careful delicacy, tugging tender flesh here, lapping there. In seconds he had her nerves sparking, her thigh muscles twitching.

Panting, she gazed down into the upper half of his face—all she could see with his mouth between her thighs. Golden eyes glinted, watching her face with absorbed attention. Two hot points of *riaat* red burned in his pupils.

She shivered at the slow, seductive slide of his tongue along the seam of her sex. He paused to swirl his tongue over an especially sensitive bundle of nerves she hadn't even known she had.

Bound hands touched her backside, stroked gently. Moaning, suddenly starved for penetration, she lifted herself just enough and rolled her hips invitingly. One finger slid up her sex, stroked gently as he lapped her clit. Jess groaned at the extravagant pleasure.

Then the forefinger of his other hand found a second opening. Circled it lazily.

Jess had never sampled that particular variant, and her eyes widened in alarm. "Uh, Galar . . ."

The finger slid deep. Exotic pleasure danced along her nerves, shocking her right to her good little Southern girl soul. "Galar!" she squeaked.

He only rumbled like a big cat enjoying a particularly tasty meal.

Oohhhhh, it felt good. His tongue swirling, one finger in her sex, the other in her ass. . . . *Oh, damn!*

Her orgasm detonated in a sweet, blinding flash, liquid pulses shooting through her body with every lick and thrust he made.

Until finally he lifted his head and met her eyes. "Fuck me!" His blazed like a torch.

Dazed, hot, she rose from him on aching legs and managed to edge her way back down his body to his jutting, impressive cock. With trembling hands, she angled the shaft toward her tight, swollen core. And sank, impaling herself deliciously.

Galar made a choked sound, a strangled half-shout of arousal. "Release my hands," he gasped.

She grabbed for his wrists and unwrapped the cable. He promptly pulled her head down to meet a devouring kiss.

It went on and on, that kiss, his tongue delving almost as deeply as his cock. He tasted of keflir and alien spices, intoxicating and delicious and maddening.

Slowly, almost unconsciously, he began rolling his hips up at her, thrusting in and out. Jess moaned into his mouth, overcome by the sensation of his width, his length, the delicious push-pull of cock in cunt.

And Galar's hands, exploring and stroking, touching just the right places to heat her liquid desire even more. Galar's mouth, making love to hers with slow thrusts of his tongue, gentle nips of her lower lip, tasting, spinning a slow and delicious spell of need.

Desire flared through her, so hot and bright she could resist it no longer. With a gasp, she pulled away from him, leaned back and grabbed her ankles. Fierce in her need, she started driving up and down on his cock in hot pursuit of more stimulation. More pleasure. More Galar.

He slid a skillful hand under her sex between one stroke and the next, touched just the right spot, and lunged upward. Once, then again, then again, in precisely judged strokes that jolted her head on her neck.

And set off a wave of flame that tore through her hungry body. She came with a scream, lost and blinded, overwhelmed.

Even as he roared out his own climax.

# · 17 ·

**The three remaining men of the cohort stared at** Tarik ge Lothar's swaying erection with a sort of fascinated horror as he paced his chamber.

Which was, of course, precisely the reaction Tarik had been looking for when he'd wrapped it in the Penitent's Braid as a sacrifice to the Victor for the failure of their mission. The three lengths of wire formed an intricate, bloody cage, spines digging savagely into his organ. Blood dripped with every pace, in time to the ferocious pain that jarred through him. The hebeer he'd drunk kept him fully erect despite the pain. He used the blend of agony and arousal to sharpen his rage, his determination that this failure would be the last.

The sight of his remaining cohort intensified that anger. Only Yunti, Ket, and Wevino were left now. Jebat and Marcin had both been lost to that hell-cursed Warlord. The thought that one of the despised Vardonese had killed his men angered him past all bearing.

To put the final, galling cap on Tarik's rage, that fool spy had even failed to kill the primitive. And still the heretic, the Abominations, and the T'lir eluded them. Such a black and utter failure would not please the Victor. Indeed, it was perilously near enough to wipe away the string of successes Tarik had laid at the god's feet.

He wanted to howl in frustrated fury.

"The people have turned from the Way of the Victor," Tarik growled as blood from his abused penis dripped on his striding feet. "They forget that pleasure is meaningless without discipline. What worth is delight if one has never known pain?"

"It is as dust," the cohort chorused.

"But *we* of the Cathedral Fortress still remember the way." Tarik narrowed his eyes, letting the ancient words roll from his mouth. "We are faithful."

"We are faithful," his men responded, their voices blending in a masculine chant. "We are disciplined. We are strong. We shall lay our triumphs at the Victor's feet for his exaltation."

Tarik was pleased by the grim light of fanaticism that burned in their faces. He'd spent years building his cohort man by man, choosing each new warrior with care, nurturing and training until they become the perfect embodiment of his will, a well-honed weapon to please even the Victor's hand.

Or they had been. The loss of Jebat's steady strength was a terrible blow. And he'd had such hopes for Marcin.

The Warlord would pay for that.

Tarik stopped his restless pacing and turned to face them as they knelt. Curls of rich, fragrant smoke rose around them, designed to hone their concentration to a fine, cold edge. He breathed in deeply, drinking the drugged smoke like wine, though it heightened his awareness of his pain. "The Fatherworld began its long slide thirty years ago when we were driven from Vardon. The Victor was disgusted by our failure, our weakness. He has allowed us to flounder in darkness to force us back to the Way. But now, out of his kindness, he has provided us with a weapon—if we can but lay our hands upon it. The T'lir will provide us with the means to bring Vardon once more under the Fatherworld's control. And after it, the rest of the . . . ," he curled his lip, "Galactic Union. Their worlds will yield their riches to us, their rightful conquerors, and they will come to know the discipline of the Victor."

He watched his men raise their faces to his, eyes shining with the power of the vision he'd created in their minds. "And we will be avenged," they chanted.

Despite the pain, Tarik smiled.

Nails scratched softly at the door to his quarters. "Warrior Priest Tarik? I have news," the monk called through the door.

Tarik's muscles tightened in anticipation. "Enter."

The monk slipped inside on silent feet and dipped a low bow. His black robes whispered on the marble floor. "The Temporal Scan Team has word of the heretic. Since she does not use standard Jump technology, we have been able to isolate the energy patterns of her leaps. We have determined she has gone three times to the same location."

Tarik's lips peeled back from his teeth. "We have her."


**Charlotte approached the** coffee shop with light steps. The street around her was lit by headlights and scented with the reek of gasoline, yet she thought it had never looked more beautiful or welcoming. She had seen Marcin's death in a vision, and it had filled her with a terrible relief. It was a sin to find joy in the assassin's fate, yet knowing that she'd finally escaped him made her want to dance. Now, at last, it was safe to return and bask in the sweet peace of the Sela's presence.

Perhaps Vanja would finally tell her she'd passed the last

of her tests. It would be so sweet to put her burdens down and simply rest.

Bells jingled cheerfully as Charlotte pushed open the coffee shop door, unlocked despite the "CLOSED" sign in the window. She'd known it would be. She could sense the two Sela waiting beyond it. Vanja and Ethini would know she was coming.

She heard the terrible chiming of the quantum blade first. For an instant she thought she was dead, but the chime stopped just short of her throat. "Move one step, heretic," a deep male voice growled in the ancient language, "and lose thy head."

Horrified, Charlotte stared past the warrior priest's shoulder. Two even bigger priests held Vanja and Ethini in cruel, choking holds. The two Sela, still in their guises as human women, wore expressions of terror on their lined faces. Charlotte glanced around wildly, only to see seven more heavily armored priests, all with swords, all watching her with malevolent intensity from around the room. Eleven to their three.

Bad odds. Very bad odds.

Brutally strong fingers closed over her arm and dragged her before the two women. "You will tell me where the T'lir is," the priest demanded in heavily accented English. "Or I will cleave this one in two."

Charlotte squeezed her eyes shut in icy anticipation. Vanja and Ethini would not surrender the T'lir to these monsters, and she would not want them to. She had always known she might have to give up her life for the Sela. Now it seemed the time had come.

But Gods and Goddesses, she didn't want to die knowing the two Sela would pay the price too.

**"Charlotte!" Jessica jolted** upright in bed, her cry of horror echoing in the darkened room.

A powerful male form hit the floor beside her in a combat

crouch. Terrified, she shot off the opposite side of the bed with a scream of shrill terror.

"Lights!" Galar snapped. Jess's fear faded as they flashed on. "It's all right," he told her soothingly, moving around the bed to take her into his arms. She went with a muffled sob, taking comfort in his warm strength. "It was just a dream."

"No." She swallowed hard. "No, not this time. It was another vision. The cohort has captured Charlotte and two Sela." Stepping back, Jess quickly recounted what she'd seen: the coffeehouse, Charlotte walking in to find the cohort holding the two women hostage. "They're going to torture them to force them to give up the T'lir."

Jess waited tensely, searching his gaze to see how he'd react. Before, he'd denied the reality of her visions. What would he say this time?

Galar frowned in concern. "What do you want to do?"

She blinked. "You believe me?"

"I've sworn off disbelieving you. Regardless of whether I can explain what you do, I can't deny you do it."

Jess drew a deep breath. "Thank you for that."

"Do you know where this coffee shop is?"

She considered the question. There seemed to be a faint, cool tug deep inside her chest. "I'm not sure, but I think I can find it."

"Good." He frowned. "After what happened the last time we went up against those Xeran bastards, I'm not inclined to take them on alone. We're going to have to talk to Dyami."

"It's the middle of the night," Jess pointed out.

Galar shrugged. "He's a cop. It won't be the first time I've had to wake him up."

"But given that we're talking time travel, does it matter when we go?"

"It's time travel as long as those bastards keep their captives in the past. The minute they take them back to our time, all bets are off. I don't want to leave those women languishing in the hands of torturers any longer than we have to."

She frowned, confused. "But couldn't we arrive in your future at the same time they do, before they have a chance to hurt the Sela or Charlotte?"

"If we knew when that was, yes. But if we got there too late . . ." He shrugged. "You can't change history. If they kill your alien friends before we get to them, they're dead. If the Xerans do something horrific to them, it's done. Do you really want to take the chance?"

Jess shuddered. "Let's go wake up Dyami."

**Jess sat tensely** next to Galar in the office in Dyami's quarters, side by side in a pair of curving chairs upholstered in dark blue. She found herself wishing the chief would put on a shirt. Dressed only in a pair of black snugs, he paced the room, muscles flexing and working along the length of his big body.

Jess might be in love, but she wasn't blind. And Dyami looked far too sexy, with his long black hair flowing around his shoulders and the colorful tattoo painting one side of his face. She dragged her eyes away and focused on Galar's long, strong fingers, twined around hers. His grip tightened in a squeeze. She looked up to see his lips quirk into a half smile. He leaned in and purred in a low voice, "I don't do threesomes."

She felt herself go scarlet and choked out, "Neither do I!"

"And I certainly don't," Dyami said drily.

"Warlord hearing," Galar said, by way of explanation.

Jess buried her face in her hand. "Just kill me now."

"That, as it happens, is what I'm trying to avoid," Dyami said. "I agree that we can't risk leaving those women—or whatever they really are—in the hands of the

Xerans. It's possible you were only dreaming, but given your demonstrated abilities, I don't want to take the chance. Can you give us a day and time of this attack? Even a location?"

She frowned in anxiety. "No, but I know where it is. I can Jump there. I . . . feel it. I think I can take a few of you with me."

Biceps gave a distracting bunch as Dyami ran both big hands through his hair. "With all due respect, I do not want to trust my agents' lives to psychic abilities I don't even understand. I want us to Jump using our own technology."

"Well, can you just follow me, then?" Jess asked. "Trace my Jump energies?"

"That shouldn't be a problem, particularly since you're not trying to lose us." He frowned heavily. "However, there's another very large problem with that plan. You're a civilian, and I'm less than thrilled about the idea of taking a civilian into a possible firefight with Xeran fanatics who've already killed two of my people."

"She can always Jump clear again once she's led us there," Galar pointed out.

"But if we're following her, there's likely to be a few seconds when she's alone with the Xerans," Dyami told him. "I don't want to give them another hostage."

"I don't have a problem with letting her use her abilities to transport me."

His commander searched his face. "Are you sure about that?"

Galar's golden gaze hardened. "I'm not leaving her alone with those bastards, Chief. Not even for a few seconds."

Dyami scrubbed his hands over his face as if to force blood back into his tired skull. "I really don't like this." He dropped his hands. "But all right. I'll gather a team. Galar, get her a T-suit. Even if she doesn't use it, there's no reason for her to endure Jump sickness."

"Armored?" Galar asked, rising to his feet.

"Definitely." The chief's expression turned grim.

**Less than an** hour later, Jess waited for the rest of the team with Galar and Dyami, running nervous fingers over the scales of her new suit. It was a soft civilian dove gray, unlike the blue and silver uniform armor of the Temporal agents. Galar had even given her a shard pistol and drilled her in its use until he was sure she could hit what she fired at. Thanks to the combat EDI he'd had Chogan give her, she was a pretty good shot.

Frieka and Riane were the next to walk into the gym. The Warfem looked alert and bright-eyed in full armor, almost bouncing in her eagerness. The wolf, on the other hand, flopped down on the floor and shot Jess a look that was almost human in its grumpy sleepiness. "This was your idea, wasn't it?" He yawned hugely. "I'd bite you if it wasn't four in the morning."

Wulf came in next, accompanied by the towering cyborg Enforcer Tonn "Bear" Eso, and Peter Brannon, the grim-faced, dark-skinned agent who'd also been in on the last fight with the Xerans.

Dona Astryr entered last, her eyes circled with sleeplessness and grim resolve.

Jess left Galar's side to talk to her. "How's it going?"

She shrugged. "We're still trying to track down Ivar and whoever sent in the battleborg team to break him out of the brig. TE Headquarters has sent an internal security team to investigate. I spent the morning getting run through the wringer by a couple of hard-asses who thought every word out of my mouth was a lie."

Jess winced. "I'm so sorry, Dona."

Dona spread her slender hands. "It's not your fault, kiddo. I'm the one who was too dumb to realize I was fucking a spy and a liar. I'm lucky Dyami's letting me come along on this mission at all." She laughed, a short, ugly bark. "I guess he figured he'd better give me a chance to kick some Xeran butt before I punched one of those IST pricks in the teeth."

Before Jess could think of anything comforting to say, Dyami lifted his voice. "All right, folks, line up. I've had the tech boys working overtime on some new equipment. Looks like they've got it ready."

Sure enough, a yawning man in civilian clothes entered, pulling an antigrav pallet behind him piled high with gear. Visibly intrigued, the agents lined up as he started passing it out.

"Shields and axes?" Wulf asked, accepting one of each. "I thought we were heading for the twenty-first century, not the eleventh."

"We did an analysis of the sensor data the first team collected when they fought the Xerans," the tech explained, holding up one of the circular shields. "The swords they used generated quantum fields. The physics would be a bitch to explain, but the long and short of it is that these units generate a blocking field. You click the thumb switch here as you block." He demonstrated with a clumsy swing. "It'll keep the swords from cutting through."

"That'll come in handy," Dona observed, picking one of the shields off the pallet and examining it.

"The axes have been in development at headquarters for some time," the tech continued, lifting one of the massive weapons with difficulty. "Again, they generate a field designed to break the molecular bonds of body armor. Takes more strength than most humans have, but that's not a problem for you guys."

"Nice." Wulf gave his axe a testing swing, then rotated his wrist to give the weapon a blurring silver twirl. "Good balance."

The agents collected their new weapons and spent several chaotic minutes practicing, getting used to them. Axes and shields met with a strange, musical chiming sound Jess found rather chilling. So was the cheerful bloodlust in the Enforcers' battle cries.

*What the hell am I doing here?* She watched Galar and Dyami circling, whaling away at each other. *I'm just an artist. I don't know a damn thing about combat.* Her stomach coiled itself into an uneasy knot. An even grimmer thought made her go cold to the marrow. *What if I get these people killed?*

Dyami and Galar separated at last, and the chief lifted his voice in a shout. "Enough fooling around, boys and girls. Let's get this done. Gather around and listen up."

Jess obediently moved closer with the others and listened as Dyami ran over the combat instructions. "If Jess is right, they've got at least three hostages, all of whom will appear to be human. She thinks at least two are actually aliens called the Sela."

Brannon spoke up. "How do we know she wasn't just having some kind of nightmare?"

"We don't," Dyami said promptly. "But since she just blew the hell out a battleborg with her mind alone, and had a vision about that Xeran disaster that might have saved lives if we'd only listened to her . . . Well, let's just say I'm inclined to take her seriously. Other questions?"

There were a couple, crisp and professional, asked in technical jargon that flew over Jess's head. After answering them, Dyami turned and gave her and Galar a nod. "Make your Jump. We'll be right on your heels."

Galar lifted his axe and shield. "Ready," he told Jess crisply.

At those words, her anxiety coiled even tighter. She fisted her hands to hide their shaking.

Galar dipped his head and whispered, "You can do it, Jess." His gaze met hers, so warm with trust and confidence her eyes stung in pure gratitude. She ached to taste that handsome mouth again, but it wasn't the time or the . . .

"Oh, what the hell," Galar said, and ducked in for a kiss that managed to curl her toes, interested audience or no.

"Get a room!" Frieka hooted, triggering a wave of laughter and good-natured catcalls. Galar lifted one hand in an obscene gesture and went right on kissing her.

By the time he stepped back, her heart was thumping in pleasure instead of terror. She managed a cocky smile. "Let's go kick some ass."

He flashed her an approving grin. "That's my girl."

Jess drew in a deep breath, laid one hand on his brawny shoulder, and reached for the cool point of alien energy deep within her chest. Concentrating, she called up the memory of the dream—Charlotte, the Sela, all those Xerans.

The power detonated in a rainbow of light and the thundering force of a tsunami, almost ripping Galar from her grip. Frantically, Jess grabbed for him, and the power obediently caught the Warlord up and swept him along in her wake.

They spun helplessly together like autumn leaves in a tornado, a terrifying whirl of light and force and sound. Jess couldn't even draw breath to scream.

Suddenly there was floor under her feet again, and she staggered. Her ears rang with the boom of displacing air as nausea twisted her stomach mercilessly. Blinking, half-blinded, she braced herself against something straight and strong and warm. Galar, no stranger to time travel, stood behind her like an oak.

A furious male voice roared, "Warlord!" Something rushed toward them, half-seen in the blizzard of purple sparks that filled her vision from the Jump. Jess recognized the deadly musical chime of a quantum sword. . . .

Galar thrust her behind him and threw up his shield. The sword's chime buzzed into a discordant rasp as the weapon bounced against the blocking field. The Xeran swordsman cursed.

Desperate blinks cleared the spots from her vision, and Jess could see again.

Galar and the warrior circled, weapons at the ready,

stalking each other like something out of *Gladiator.* Instead of the Roman Colosseum, though, they were surrounded by the tables and chairs of a surprisingly large coffee shop.

A long red marble counter ran across the rear of the shop, two towering coffee machines on either end. Beneath the counter stood a glass bakery case piled with muffins, cookies, and fresh-baked pies. They gave the air a sweet and homey smell that was somehow chilling, given the three terrorized women who cowered against the case like hurricane survivors clinging to a rooftop.

Charlotte Holt knelt with her arms protectively curled around two older ladies in white dresses and red aprons. One was plump and matronly, the other thin and wiry. Jess's special senses told her neither was human.

The Sela.

A knot of Xerans surrounded them, swords in hand, fanatical hate twisting their hard faces as they glared from their captives to Jess and Galar. Obviously not just ready to kill, but eager for blood.

Six more Xerans prowled across the room toward Jess, Galar, and the man he was fighting. All the warriors wore the same black-scaled armor Marcin had. And all of them carried quantum swords.

"Dammit, Jess, why are you still here?" Galar roared at her, blocking a sword swing aimed at his head. "Jump your pretty little ass back to the Outpost!"

Before she could object, the room rocked as the rest of the Temporal Enforcers arrived. The thunder of the mass Jump was deafening. Jess ducked, squeezing her eyes shut against the glare.

*Damn good thing those T-suits dampen sonic booms,* she thought, blinking the spots out of her eyes, *or every cop and firefighter in Charleston would be running this way to find out what exploded.*

The Enforcers didn't waste any time. With roared battle cries, they charged the Xerans, who howled and ran to meet them. Swords and axes rang a peal of violence as the two forces collided.

*I should do something,* Jess thought, staring in dazed fascination. *I shouldn't just be standing around here with my thumb up my ass.*

Despite what Galar thought, she did know how to fight. She'd waded into more than one brawl over the years, defending her mother from some pissed-off boyfriend, or her sister from drunken rednecks, jealous girlfriends, or debt-collecting drug dealers. She might not be a Warfem, but she could grab the nearest beer bottle and swing it at a deserving head.

But this was different. These people moved as if gravity were less a law of physics than a suggestion. Spinning, leaping, their bodies moving with impossible speed and agility as they dodged blows or launched attacks. Those twenty-pound axes might just as well be made of balsa wood, the way the Enforcers tossed them from hand to hand or sent them flying through the air. And the Xerans were just as powerful, just as insanely skilled with their chiming quantum swords.

Jess wasn't a coward, but she wasn't crazy either. This wasn't a fight a mere human had any business trying to join.

After that, her perceptions seemed to dissolve into chaotic flashes of terror and stark desperation.

A chair went flying from somebody's kick, slamming into Dyami's shoulder. He batted it aside like a fly and went on hacking at his opponent.

A spray of blood arched in a crimson parabola. For an instant, it seemed to hang in the air as if frozen. Then it hit the ground and splashed, leaving a Jackson Pollock splatter on the black and white tiles.

Wulf leaped at one of the Xerans with a joyous berserker bellow, smashing the man into the table behind him. It snapped under the impact, dumping them both on the floor.

Undeterred, the two men went on flailing at each other with fists, feet, and blades, a blur of deadly motion.

Riane and her furry partner harried a Xeran. Frieka had apparently taught the Warfem to fight like a wolf, because she danced in and out like one, her axe describing deadly silver arcs.

The Xeran roared in frustration. Every time he tried to close with her, Frieka charged in to bite and snap. Finally the distracted man's foot slipped in a puddle of blood, and he fell to one knee. The two Enforcers pounced. Jess looked away, wincing.

But it was Galar who kept drawing her eye in the chaos, magnet to her steel.

She'd seen him as tender lover, patient teacher, cool-eyed leader. But Galar in battle was another man entirely, his face set, almost expressionless, in stark contrast to the red *riaat* blaze of his eyes that gave him a faintly demonic air. His big body didn't so much move as flow through the patterns of attack and defense, seemingly without any effort at all.

Her artist's eye was fascinated by the bunch and play of muscle under his skintight armor as he and the Xeran fought. There was something almost erotic about the battle, about the two men so utterly focused on each other, about the ring of steel and the grunts of effort.

One of them was going to die today. And unless Galar was lucky as well as good, it might just be the man she loved. A chill spun over her, and she looked away.

Right into Charlotte Holt's desperate, pleading gaze. *Help us!* The woman's mental voice rang in her mind, borne on a wave of power from the T'lir.

Jess snapped to attention as she took in the situation. Frieka and Riane, having dispatched their first opponent, were trying to rescue the three women. Only two men guarded the captives now; the other Xerans had joined the battle with the Enforcers.

Now the wolf was attempting to draw the pair away so Riane could shepherd the women to safety.

Jess's eyes narrowed. Maybe there was something she could do after all. . . .

*Riaat* burned in Galar's veins, a hot, furious storm of power and rage. He ached for revenge—for Jiri, for Ando, and most of all, for Jess.

The Xeran spun, swinging the quantum sword right at Galar's face with vicious speed. Galar thrust his shield into the path of the blade, deflecting it, as he came around with his own axe. The Xeran leapt back, a snarl flashing dimly through the visor of his black faceplate. "This time you die, Warlord dog!" he spat.

Galar ignored the insult as he scanned for an opening, in no mood to bandy words with the bastard. He suspected this was the same man who'd taken the quantum sword from him before, the one who seemed to be the leader of this crowd.

Which made the Xeran a very choice target, indeed.

Narrow-eyed, Galar circled with the warrior, testing him in the course of attack and counterattack, in the deadly, circling dance of axe, sword, and shield. The bastard was good, Galar had to give him that. He might be shorter, less powerfully built, but he was fast and agile, as well as astonishingly skilled.

Maybe even better with a blade than Galar himself.

The Warlord's senses sharpened as time seemed to slow to a honeyed crawl. He was aware in a distant way of the other Enforcers battling the Xerans: the chiming ring of quantum blades, the heavier clunk of axes, the gasps and grunts of effort and pain.

Once he glimpsed the hostages, huddled in a terrified knot by the rear counter. A Xeran with a sword had one fist wrapped in the hair of the older, plumper of the three women. He was trying to force Riane and Frieka to keep their distance, but the two kept trying to snake past his guard. One feinted at him as the other attempted to snatch his hostage to safety. The warrior raised his sword threateningly over the woman's head, and the two Enforcers reluctantly retreated.

But the sight that made Galar's blood run cold was Jessica, edging along the wall toward the Xeran's back, an expression of mingled terror and determination on her face.

What the fuck was she doing? He'd told her to Jump for home the moment she'd guided them in!

Seven blazing Hells, she was going to get herself killed trying to rescue those damned fuzzy aliens of hers. . . .

# · 18 ·

Jess licked her lips as she edged along the wall toward the Xeran who held Vanja's hair fisted in his hand.
The woman—that was what she appeared to be, anyway—
knelt on the floor, one hand wrapped around the warrior's
thick wrist as she tried to relieve the pressure on her hair.
Charlotte and Ethini hovered nearby, unable to flee with
their leader in danger.

*Dammit, don't just stand there,* Jess thought furiously, *do
something!*

Charlotte's gaze flicked to hers. She could sense the angry, helpless frustration boiling off the other woman. *There's
nothing I can do.*

*Why the fuck not?*

Charlotte lifted one shoulder in a tiny, helpless shrug.
Jess growled. *All right, dammit, then I'll do something. I
have no idea what, but I'm not just going to stand around
and wait for someone to kill you.*

She wasn't sure, but she thought Charlotte winced.

Jess stared at the three hostages, eyes narrow and grim. If she could just get her hands on them, she could Jump all three to safety. (And why the hell hadn't Charlotte or the Sela already done that? They were just as capable of Jumping as she was. What was going on with them, anyway? Had the Xerans blocked their powers somehow?)

Without the hostages to worry about, Galar and his Enforcers could mop up the Xerans.

She badly wanted to simply blast both Xeran bastards the way she had that battleborg, but the T'lir wouldn't allow its power to be used to take a life. Which was damned stupid of it.

On the other hand, she might be able to use the power indirectly.

Jess looked around for something to use as a weapon. Her eyes fell on a shelf just above her head. Kitschy snow globes stood there in a line, each with dangling price tags attached. Apparently the shop sold tourist junk along with caffeine fixes.

Jess scooped one of the globes off the shelf, reached into the core of energy buzzing in her mind, and shot it into the globe. Then she wound up like a fastball pitcher and sent the little orb sailing toward the Xeran's helmeted head.

The power blast detonated as it hit him, shattering his helmet and knocking him sideways. He lost his grip on Vanja, and Riane and Frieka leaped on him. The Warfem's axe rose and fell.

Jess shot across the room and grabbed Charlotte's wrist. Vanja scrambled to take her free hand. Jess turned toward Ethini, but instead of joining them, the wiry Sela ran right past her.

Confused, Jessica whirled. The woman sprinted for the shelf of snow globes.

"Ethini!" Vanja cried. Her friend ignored her, reaching for one of the globes.

From the corner of one eye, Jess saw a Xeran warrior charging toward them, Galar at his heels. With a surge of effort, Galar shoved him aside and ducked between him and the women. But even as the Warlord threw up his shield to protect them, the Xeran spun like a bullfighter, danced forward, and swung his sword.

And cut Ethini in two.

She came apart in mid-stride, blood flying like a dark rain, wetting the walls, her killer, and Galar himself. Half her torso slammed into the shelf, which tumbled off its brackets, spilling the globes to smash on the floor.

The alien's chest landed on the limp tangle of her lower half with its too many legs, a small, profoundly alien creature, the illusion of humanity shattered. More blood welled from the sundered halves, not red, but a kind of dark blue vaguely reminiscent of blueberry syrup.

Vanja screeched. It was a piercingly high, profoundly alien sound, heard not so much with the ears as with the soul. A shattering psychic cry that flayed the spirit, made the breath catch, the eyes tear.

Between one blink and the next, Vanja's human form vanished, replaced by something dark and quick that skittered over the floor to crouch over her friend's pitiful little corpse. The sound she made raked at Jessica's mind with claws of pure, wrenching pain.

And Jess found herself standing over her mother's body as it lay wasted and small in the hospital bed, mouth gaped open, eyes staring, flesh pulled thin over stark bones. Grief exploded through her, just as fresh as it had been the day cancer had taken Tina Kelly a year ago. A grief not just for her mother, but for the closeness they'd never had. A grief at the bitter knowledge that her mother had never truly loved her.

Jess keened as she crashed to her knees, the sound echoing Vanja's screech.

And the pain got worse. And worse. *And worse.* Growing

with every instant, increasing into a crushing spiritual pressure, unendurable and black.

Distantly, she heard other voices crying out, some deep and masculine, some female, all ringing with that terrible pain. Even the wolf howled.

"Noooo!" Galar bellowed, the anguish in his voice chilling Jess to the marrow.

Over the cries, over the anguish, she heard the Xeran laugh. "Weaklings," he sneered.

*What's happening?* Jess wondered in desperation. With an effort, she turned her head to look at Charlotte. Charlotte knew the Sela better than anyone. She would know.

*Psychic . . . feedback,* Charlotte told her, mind to mind. *The Sela are mentally linked. The death of one . . . devastates the others. And anyone else in range. The pain of one feeds the pain of the others, so it grows.* She stopped to pant, her eyes glassy.

*Oh, sweet Christ,* Jess thought in horror. It was going to get worse, the grief and anguish increasing with every passing second like a microphone feedback screech. So intense, so severe, that not even hardened warriors like the Enforcers could resist.

The Xerans were moving between their fallen opponents, swaggering as they gazed down at them in contempt.

*Why are those bastards immune?* Jess wondered suddenly.

*Their helmets block Vanja's cry,* Charlotte explained. *Took us . . . months to develop the technology. The first time one of the priests killed a Sela, the effect almost killed him.*

*The Xeran leader knew,* Jess realized. *He knew what killing Ethini would do to Vanja. He intended to render us helpless.*

The killer moved to stand over Jess and Charlotte, who still clutched her hand. He raised his sword over their heads. "Tell me where the T'lir is, and I will kill you now, cleanly," he told Charlotte, "and the pain will end."

But it wouldn't end. Jess knew that. It would just keep getting bigger and darker and more all-consuming, feeding off Vanja's horrible grief and that of those around her.

"Vanja," Jess croaked aloud in desperation, "stop!"

But the Sela didn't seem to hear the plea over her own keening. Each rising uluation drove through Jess's head like a spike.

Helpless. They were helpless, delivered into the hands of the Xerans, who would kill them all and take the T'lir, and with it, the secret of the Sela's power.

Unless . . .

Emotion. *The key was emotion.*

With a vast effort, Jess turned her head. Galar lay beside her, cut down where he'd tried to shield them from the Xeran. His eyes were lost, wide as he relived whatever horror Vanja's powers had brought crashing over him.

Jess licked dry lips and crept her fingers toward his face. Her hand felt like a chunk of solid lead, but somehow she forced it across the inches separating them. Touched his cheek. He jolted, blinked, seemed to swim up out of the nightmare. His helpless gaze met hers.

"Emotion," she rasped. "Use your comp. Stop the . . . emotion."

**Galar's eyes widened** as he immediately grasped what she meant. They were all drowning in defeat and despair and choking grief. But they didn't have to. *Computer, blank all emotional reactions.*

Instantly, a blessed numb coolness spread over him as the dreadful pain eased. *It's the emotions!* He broadcast on the Enforcers' communication frequency. *Shut them off!*

Galar's hand closed tight around the axe he still held. His eyes narrowed on the Xeran who crouched over Charlotte Holt, trying to force her to give up the location of the T'lir.

Silently, Galar rolled to his feet, took a deep, hard breath, and spun, swinging the axe with both hands. The jolt of impact rolled up the length of his arms.

And the Xeran's head sailed across the room.

The bastard's body collapsed in a boneless sprawl of arms and legs, blood pooling from its severed neck. Just like the poor little Sela he'd killed.

A Xeran shouted in shock and rage. Galar turned to see the man racing toward him, sword lifted. Dona rose behind the Xeran like a ghost, took one step forward, and cleaved both his helmet and head in two. There was no expression at all on her face as she watched him fall.

The other Enforcers were up, too, springing at their foes with implacable ferocity. Feeling nothing whatsoever, Galar strode across the room to join in.

**Dazed, Jess watched** as the Enforcers fell on the Xerans with a cold ferocity. Two of the enemy went down in that first hard rush, but the others recovered quickly.

Galar fought in a blur of male power and overwhelming strength, his axe flashing around him, his shield blocking the Xerans' swords.

Behind him, a Xeran wheeled toward him, saw his back was turned, and charged, lips pulled back in a soundless snarl. Embroiled in another fight, Galar didn't seem to see the man coming.

Jess rolled over and scrabbled through the shattered glass from the fallen shelf, found the one intact snow globe, and started to send her power pouring into it.

And froze, staring at it in shock. Santa's red-nosed face grinned back at her through the glass.

It was the T'lir!

*This was what Ethini was trying to get to!*

She could feel the globe's power surging within it like a miniature sun. And she knew exactly what to do with it. She touched the cool, glowing point within her own chest. . . .

And power blazed into her from the globe's glass depths, fierce, exhilarating, wiping away her grief, her insecurity, her lingering guilt over her mother's death. With a savage smile, Jess sent that energy lancing around the room.

Everywhere it touched, the Xerans' helmets burst, popping like lightbulbs, yet leaving the men inside them uninjured.

And unprotected from Vanja's psychic screech.

They went down howling like animals to writhe on the floor, drowning in the Sela's grief.

Galar and his Enforcers did not give them the opportunity to recover. Axes swung with brutal efficiency—and a total lack of emotion.

Jessica carefully did not watch the carnage.

Instead she turned and walked across the room to lay one hand on Vanja's furred, oddly shaped head. Closing her eyes, she sent the T'lir's soothing energy rolling over the Sela. The keening stopped.

"You could have saved her," Jess said softly, knowing it was true. "You had the power. Why didn't you?"

The Sela looked up at her, infinite sadness in her huge, liquid eyes. Her face was almost catlike, almost human, but was not quite either. "It was your test, my dear. She gave her life to administer it. What could I do except honor her sacrifice?"

"Did you know she was going to die? Did *she* know she was going to die?"

Vanja angled her furred head in a gesture reminiscent of a shrug. "There would have been no test otherwise."

Jess threw Charlotte a look. The woman was sitting up, wiping away tears. Her shoulders slumped with weary grief. "That's why Charlotte didn't do anything either. You told her not to."

"Yes."

"What kind of test?" Galar demanded, flicking blood from his axe as he walked over to them. His expression was stony. "Are you saying you could have prevented all this?"

Vanja looked up at him, her eyes liquid and wise. "Can history be changed, Master Enforcer?"

He opened his mouth, then closed it again, looking chagrined. After a moment he tried again. "What's the purpose of this test? What are you trying to learn? And why test us and not the Xerans?"

"We did test the Xerans," Vanja told him, rising to all six legs. "They failed. As for your other questions—well, learning those answers is a test for another day."

Dyami loomed at his shoulder, glowering down at the little alien. "What gives you the right to test us at all?"

Vanja tilted her head. "You'll figure it out—or perhaps you won't." She turned and took the T'lir from Jessica's unresisting fingers.

Holding the globe over Ethini's body, the alien closed her enormous eyes. Snow swirled up in the globe, bursting from it in a rain of golden sparks that drifted down over the small corpse. Her fur began to glow with a sunny light, each soft hair shining brighter and brighter, until the body flared like a star and disappeared. Nothing was left but a few bright, drifting motes and the smell of cinnamon.

Jess's eyes stung. She drew in a breath and knuckled the tears away.

Vanja sagged on her six legs, for a moment, then sighed out a soft, musical sound before turning back to Charlotte. She reached out a furry, long-fingered hand. "Come, my dear."

Charlotte nodded and rose on her own visibly unsteady legs to take the offered hand. "I want to go home," she said, longing and grief choking her voice.

"I know, dear. But you have more to do yet. There's another test."

"Wait," Jess began. "What are . . . ?"

Light burst in a soundless explosion. When Jess blinked away the purple afterimages, both Charlotte and the Sela had vanished.

# · 19 ·

❧❧❧

**The Blue Ridge was at the height of its autumnal** beauty, its rolling mountains clothed in shades of fire under the afternoon sun.

A smile playing around her mouth, Jess watched a pair of eagles circle each other in an updraft like skaters in a couples' competition. The sun shone warm on her bare breasts, and she tilted her head back, basking in the light. By all rights it should have been far too chilly to stand around naked in the mountains, but Galar had produced some twenty-third-century blanket that generated a warming field. She curled her bare toes into the bright purple fabric. "Damn, nobody's trying to kill me," she said as that happy realization hit. "I almost forgot what that was like."

She turned to find Galar, just as naked as she was, doing something with the covered container that was apparently a Vardonese version of a picnic basket. She'd thought he'd been busy with debriefings all morning while she'd been taking her desperately needed nap, but apparently he'd made time to arrange another lovely meal.

Not the least of which was himself. She leered at him happily. He'd folded his uniform with his customary neatness and stacked it beside her own things, his armored boots lined up with her own soft, flexible shoes.

He sat tailor-fashion on the blanket preparing his picnic, an expression of intense concentration on his face that seemed a little over-the-top, considering his task. His bronzed body seemed to glow golden in the afternoon sun, all brawny power and long, elegant muscle ridges.

Thick biceps bunched as he swung four large trays out of the silver container, each shaped like a pie wedge and covered with tiny bite-sized goodies. Beside the container stood a kind of ice bucket that contained three different bottles of wine.

"Why, Master Enforcer," Jess said, sitting down next to him on the blanket, "are you planning to get me plowed?"

He cocked his head as he poured one of the bottles into a fragile, curving goblet. "Is 'plowed' a twenty-first-century euphemism for 'sex'?"

"Nope. It means drunk."

"Then no." His grin was downright wicked as he handed her the wine. "In fact, I want you fully aware and appreciative of every last thing I'm going to do to you."

"You're a bad, bad man, Galar Arvid." She took a sip of the wine. It seemed to burst on her tongue in a flurry of bubbles that reminded her more of apples than grapes. "Oh, that's nice!"

He cleared his throat, suddenly looking a bit awkward as he announced, "It is so sweet and intoxicating, it reminds me of you."

Jess gave him a bemused blink. "Uh, thank you."

Galar reached into one of the trays and lifted out a cube of meat on a tiny skewer. He presented it to her mouth, but pulled it away when she reached for the skewer herself. "I'm supposed to feed you."

Jess hastily dropped her hand and let him put the cube between her teeth so she could bite it off the skewer.

"Like you," he said, "this is tender and hot."

Jess chewed, considering him. The meat was just as delicately juicy as he said, with an exotic taste she found she liked. "It *is* delicious."

He sighed. "I sound like an idiot, don't I?"

"No, no." Actually, his awkwardness was kind of sweet, particularly in such a relentlessly competent man. "I'm just wondering what we're doing. I don't seem to have a copy of the script."

"It's a Vardonese . . . ah, lover's repast. The male is supposed to purchase the most delicious, exotic tidbits he can find. Then he feeds them to his lover, while he tells her how each one compares to her beauty, wit, and intelligence." He shook his head. "Unfortunately, I don't seem to have a talent for the required lyricism."

"Well, that's a relief."

"Oh?"

Jess smiled and took another sip of her wine. "You're almost ridiculously talented at everything else."

"There, you see?" Galar shook his head in admiration. "You would be very good at giving a repast." He reached into the tray and chose a delicate pale morsel. She leaned forward and took it between her teeth. "Now this," he said, "is soft and creamy . . ."

"Like me?" Grinning, Jess chewed. "What is this, cheese?"

He nodded. "Made from *getcari* milk. I bought it in one of the more upscale shops in the Outpost concourse."

Jess savored her bite. "Yeah? I figured all this came from a vendser."

Galar stiffened in offense. "I would never get a lover's repast from a vendser. It would be an insult to us both."

Ooops. She'd just accused him of being tacky. "Oh. Sorry."

Jess eyed the trays with new respect as he chose something colorful out of one of them. Meats, cheeses, fruits, tiny little pastries . . . How much had he spent on this repast of his, anyway? It would definitely be tacky to ask, but everything looked expensive.

He extended a bright red little globe and cleared his throat. "This *carita* fruit is very juicy, with a sweet, delicate taste."

*I am not going to giggle. I am not going to giggle.* Jess leaned forward and lipped the fruit from his fingers to give her mouth something else to do.

Galar eyed her sternly. "You're laughing at me."

Mouth full, she shook her head desperately, eyes going wide.

"Goddess, you look like a chipmunk." He threw his head back and roared with laughter. The threatening giggle burst from Jess's mouth, and she almost choked on her *carita*.

When their laughter finally died, Galar said, "I'm lucky I'm good in bed, because I have no talent for romance."

Jess whooped at this bit of unself-conscious arrogance, then clamped both hands over her mouth. After a moment, she managed to wheeze, "Yep, you're good in bed, all right." She cleared her throat. "Very good. Very." She coughed.

He froze, eyes widening with sudden hurt doubt.

"Oh, cut that out," Jess said tartly. "How many screaming orgasms have you given me?"

Galar relaxed. "Well, that's true."

When she started whooping again, he picked up another *carita* and threw it at her. It landed on one breast with a wet plop. Galar pounced, bearing her backward on the blanket, and nipped the fruit off her skin. As she laughed, batting at him, he scooped up a handful of fruity delicacies and smeared them all over her body, painting her with juice and bright, colorful shapes.

"Hey, I thought you were supposed to feed me!" Jess protested as he went to work licking and nibbling at the sticky mess.

Galar looked up at her, *riaat* flames burning in his eyes. "But I'm *hungry*."

Jess's breath caught. Suddenly she was no longer in the mood to laugh.

He returned his attention to her fruit-smeared body, lapping slowly, pausing here and there to swirl his fingers in juice and spread them over her nipples or clit.

Every few minutes he paused in his licking to feed her some bite from one of the trays. Eyes shuttering in delight, Jess relaxed into the warm blanket, relishing his attentions.

Pleasure unfurled in her body like some exotic orchid, trembling and soft. His hands were warm, his mouth lusciously skilled, his body a feast of hard-muscled strength. And each tidbit he fed her seemed to flood her mouth with a new taste, a new sensation. She moaned softly and let herself float.

**Galar watched her** as she sprawled beneath him like a queen allowing a supplicant to pay just tribute to her beauty. Her long, dark hair spilled over the warming blanket, the sun painting it with shimmering highlights. Her blue eyes shone through her thick, half-closed lashes like gemstones nestled in feathers. Her mouth curved into a lazy smile.

*Goddess Mother, I love her so, my very heart aches.*

He froze in mid-lick as his mind registered the truth of that realization. For a moment, he waited to panic, but then he realized he felt no fear at all.

Jess, beautiful, courageous Jess, would keep his heart safe.

Though keeping *her* safe would be a full-time job. The next time Charlotte or her Sela friends called for help, Galar knew Jess would be ready to Jump to the rescue again. And the Goddess help him if he dared to protest.

She'd come so close to dying today, his stomach clenched in cold fear at the thought. Nor was the danger over. That idiot Ivar was still out there somewhere with his fellow spies, probably still plotting to kill her. And though the Enforcers had slain one crop of Xeran fanatics, an entire planet of them remained. Galar was going to have his hands full keeping them all at bay.

Luckily, he was more than up to the task. "They are not going to touch one hair on your precious head," he growled at her.

Jess blinked at him. "Who?"

Galar made no answer. He was suddenly in the grip of a ferocious need to take her. He wanted to surround her, possess her, feel her sex gripping his, her small, silken body bucking against his harder, bigger one.

With a soft growl, he rose to his knees, scooped her little backside into his hands, and positioned his cock at her opening. He drove inside in a ruthless lunge, drawing in a breath as her tight, luscious flesh gripped his.

"Galar!" Jess gasped, her eyes going adorably wide, pink lips parted.

With a groan, he settled over her and took that pretty mouth with his. Still kissing her, he began to pump, seating his cock to the balls with every thrust.


**Jess clung to** Galar's powerful shoulders, stunned at the abrupt ferocity of his entry. She was more than ready—that wicked mouth of his had seen to that. But she'd figured he'd insist on driving her crazy for at least another hour or so.

Instead, he'd looked up her body and met her gaze, and an expression she'd never seen before had flashed over his face. Half wonder, half stark terror, followed by narrow-eyed determination.

And then he'd rolled over her like a storm, all ferocious desire and stark male demand.

Now he worked his big shaft inside her as he kissed her, his tongue sweeping in and out in thrusts that mirrored his cock's. Each stroke of that thick organ tugged her inner walls with a lush, sweet friction. She could feel her orgasm gathering strength.

Moaning, she dug her nails into his broad back and curled her legs around his waist, holding on as he rode her with that wild desperation.

Suddenly he tore free of their kiss to stare into her face. *Riaat* had turned his eyes to a solid sheet of flame. She'd never seen the red glow so intense. "I love you," he growled. "Love you. Love you, love you!" With every chant, he thrust faster, harder, deeper.

"Galar!" The orgasm exploded with greater speed and force than she'd ever known, a storm of burning pleasure that set her every nerve on fire. *"I love you!"*

"Jesssicaaaaa . . . !" He convulsed against her, his angular face gloriously lost.

And the fire swept them both away.

**They lay together** in a dazed and panting pile. Galar was breathing like a stallion run to the end of his endurance, sweat slicking his skin. Along with, Jess noticed, lingering sticky smears of fruit. She smiled against his shoulder. "We're going to need a bath."

"I lied."

She stiffened in sudden hurt panic and met his gaze.

"No, not about loving you!" Galar said, alarmed, evidently reading her mind. "I meant about the meal being called a lover's repast."

"Oh." Her brows drew down. *And you thought it was necessary to scare me witless about this, why?*

He pulled away from her with some difficulty—they

*really* needed that bath—and fiddled with his Vardonese container again.

"I'm really not hungr—" Jess began, just as he turned back toward her. She broke off.

There was a small, blue velvet box in his hand.

"We actually call it a 'betrothal repast.'"

"Oh." She couldn't seem to think of anything else to say.

Galar licked his lips. "I downloaded an EDI on your marriage customs. It said the male in your time gives the woman a ring." A flick of his thumb opened the box, revealing a glorious ruby surrounded in a cluster of diamonds on a silver band. "So I went to twenty-first-century New York, to that store they call Tiffany, and I bought this."

Jess stared at the ring, speechless.

"I had it all planned," Galar told her. Was that nervousness on his face? "You were going to be stunned by my eloquence and suitably wooed by my food selections." He shrugged impressive shoulders. "So much for that plan. I'm afraid romance isn't my . . ."

She threw himself against him, hooking both arms around his neck as she swooped in for a kiss. "Oh, the ring is beautiful. And your dinner was delicious, and I—" Tears stung her eyes. "I will love you until the day I die."

He cupped her face in his free hand. "Marry me."

"God, yes!" She dove in for a kiss, laughing, crying.


**It was some** time before they came up for air and Galar managed to slide the ring on her finger.

Jess extended her hand, admiring the way the sun threw glints from the diamonds and ignited fire in the heart of the ruby. "God, that's glorious."

He nodded. "Almost as pretty as you are."

Jess dimpled at him. "And you say you're not romantic."

Galar's mouth curved into a smile as he caught her hand in his and began to play with her fingers. The smile drained away. "Do you know what I saw when Vanja caught us in that psychic feedback loop of hers?"

Jess blinked at the unexpected topic change. She shrugged. "I figured it was probably the moment when T'lain shot you."

He shook his head. "Not even close. It was the look on your face when I arrested you. For the first time, I realized just how much I'd hurt you." Galar looked up from her fingers, his expression intense, demanding. "And I wondered—how could you just forgive me the way you did?"

"Maybe because—I dunno—I love you?" Jess snorted. "Dumb question, stud."

"But, Jess, I knew you were innocent," he told her earnestly. "In my soul, I knew it. But I was so determined never to be fooled again, I didn't let myself believe in your innocence. It was raw pride. Ego. Why did you forgive me?"

She blinked. "I . . ." And stopped as abrupt understanding filled her. *White trash*. "Because I didn't believe I deserved anything better."

He caught her chin, tilted it upward. "But you do. You deserve all the love I can give you." His golden eyes narrowed. "And I'm going to spend the rest of my life proving it to you, until you believe it. I will show you just how much you mean to me, just how much you *are* to me. Until you see it, feel it, taste it." A smile flashed over his face, white and wide. "Until you bust my ass whenever I step out of line."

A grin spread slowly across her face. "Okay, you talked me into it." She leaned toward his mouth. "The tasting part sounds especially good."

The kiss went on a long, long time.

Turn the page for a special preview of

# ENFORCER
### by Angela Knight

**Available soon from Berkley Sensation!**

**Punching the senior investigator in the mouth would** be a very bad idea.

For one thing, Dona's titanite-reinforced fist would probably shatter his jaw. For another, Alex Corydon was the leader of the Internal Security Team investigating her, and he already thought she was a spy. Knocking out a few of his teeth would virtually guarantee her a very unpleasant stint in the Gorgon Penal Colony. And a treason conviction was nothing to laugh at, particularly in the twenty-third century.

So Dona Astryr pasted an expression of polite attention on her face and straightened the fingers that wanted to curl into fists. *I'm not going to hit him. I'm* not *going to hit him.*

"You're telling me you had no idea your lover was a spy?" Corydon lifted his upper lip in contemptuous disbelief. His teeth shone very white against the inky blue-black sheen of his skin as his eyes narrowed into slits of metallic gold. Hair the color of flame was bound in a severe braid that emphasized the height of his perfect cheekbones. The dramatic coloring made him look intensely alien, though in reality he was nothing more than human. His purebred DNA was yet another reason he hated Dona's cyborg guts. "You worked with Senior Enforcer Terje for more than a year— even slept with him—yet your sensors never once told you he was lying to you?"

How many times had she explained this? Ten? Fifteen? She'd lost count. Fighting to control her irritation, Dona looked out the wall-length window at the rolling, tree-covered flanks of the Blue Ridge Mountains as they dozed in the sunlight, painted with indigo shadows. It was a beautiful view, one that normally never failed to soothe.

Today it barely kept her from breaking Corydon's exquisite nose. *I know how this works, dammit,* Dona thought. *I've interrogated more than my share of subjects. Pissing them off is all part of the game. An angry criminal makes mistakes.*

But she was no criminal. She was a Temporal Enforcer. She'd spent eight years chasing killers and thieves through time, and she didn't deserve Corydon's suspicion.

Taking a deep breath, Dona returned her attention to the senior investigator, who sat behind Chief Dyami's massive black desk as if he owned it. Her commanding officer had loaned Corydon his office for these relentless interviews of the Outpost staff.

The bastard was convinced someone there helped Ivar commit his crimes. And his favorite suspect was Dona herself.

"Ivar apparently used his internal computer to hide his reactions whenever he lied," she said with careful patience. "There were no physiological changes for my sensors to detect." Dona had an impressive array of them implanted throughout her body, alongside the nanobot units that enhanced her strength to superhuman levels. Titanite-reinforced bones allowed her to use that power without shattering her own arms or legs. A neuronet computer wound through her brain in a molecule-thin network, giving her control of the whole complex system.

"You told Chief Dyami *your* lover's computer was active even in casual conversation. You never even entertained the thought that he might be a traitor?"

"Do you ever wonder if *your* friends are traitors?"

"Actually, yes, I do." Corydon's tone was icy. "I'm always alert for signs of treason."

*I'm not surprised.*

"Your commanding officer told me he considers you an intelligent and capable agent." His chin set at a contemptuous angle. "Your . . . naivete suggests otherwise."

"I'm aware of that." Dona's cheeks heated furiously. Under normal circumstances, she'd tell her comp to control the bright blush staining her cheeks, but she knew Corydon had a sensor array aimed at her. He'd probably take any action by her comp as an indication she was lying. "I assumed he was preoccupied with whatever case we were working at the time." God, she hated to admit this to the smug bastard, but if she wasn't completely honest, he'd hang her out to dry. "But you're right—I should have realized Senior Enforcer Terje was working for the Xeran Empire. Had I done so, at least two good agents would still be alive."

"Ah, yes, Enforcers Jiri and Ando Cadell." Corydon's metallic eyes flicked down to the comp slate sitting at his elbow, either reading sensor data or reminding himself of some detail from her file. "I believe one of the Xerans beheaded Jiri, then ran Ando through when he tried to defend her. After cutting off his hand." The chief investigator shook his head. "Ugly way to die."

The memory of that night raked claws of pain and grief across her mind. "Yes, it was. Very ugly."

"They were married, weren't they?"

"Yes, sir. Almost forty years." Dona remembered Jiri's crow of triumph as she'd won that last hand of Kirilian poker the night before she'd died. "They were good friends of mine."

*"All couples fight,"* Jiri had said once when Dona bitched about her latest row with Ivar over his jealousy. *"It's a great excuse for make-up sex."*

Yeah, right. The last time Dona fought Ivar, he'd damn near beaten her to death. The only thing she wanted to do with him now was to shove a shard pistol into his mouth and pull the trigger.

"Does it bother you, I wonder," Corydon asked softly, cruelly, "to know you got those good friends killed?"

"I have nightmares about it. Damn near every night."

The investigator curled a skeptical lip. "That is too bad." He made a show of studying the comp slate again. "Your record doesn't seem to indicate any real incompetence. You've been an agent of Temporal Enforcement for eight years now. Decent case-solved rate. Adequate string of commendations—even a Silver Dragon for bravery under fire." He sniffed. "But then, you *are* a cyborg. I'd imagine it's easier being courageous when you're so hard to kill."

Her mouth tightened. "I was awarded that for chasing a berserk Tevan cyborg through twentieth-century Chicago after he murdered my previous partner. I managed to keep him from killing any temporal natives, but I damned near died doing it. The medtechs had to resuscitate me twice after they got us back."

"A Tevan?" Corydon's aristocratic nostrils flared. "Tevans have no business time-traveling to Earth. They can't pass for human."

"Since they're eight feet tall, scaled and orange, no. And this one was completely insane. That's why we were chasing him."

"An impressive arrest, I suppose." He glanced down at his comp slate. "Of course, it would have been more impressive if you were human."

*I'm* not *going to hit him.*

* * *

**Corydon finally let** her escape more than an hour later. Dona decided to take a stroll around the Outpost to walk off her anger and anxiety.

She had good reason to worry. The bastard meant to charge her with treason, and he'd dig until he found an excuse to do it. Never mind that Dona was innocent. She wouldn't put it past Corydon to manufacture evidence if he couldn't find any legitimately.

Given the state of computer simulation, it would be easy to create a very convincing recording of her doing something she'd never done. And Corydon was rabidly self-righteous enough to do whatever it took to see she got "justice."

Frowning darkly, Dona strode along the Outpost's broad, ruler-straight corridors, winding her way through crowds of techs, fellow Enforcers, and wandering tourists.

It was a sprawling facility, one of five located in various continents in various eras. Galactic Union officials had chosen sixteenth-century Spirit Mountain as the site for its North American headquarters. In this time, the surrounding area was sparsely populated by Native Americans, who had witnessed enough strange lights and loud noises to consider the mountain haunted.

The Outpost itself was located deep within the core of the mountain, where it housed Temporal Enforcement, a well-equipped infirmary, and a sprawling concourse packed with a wide variety of shops.

Dona headed for the latter. She'd always enjoyed window shopping and people watching in the concourse, where tourists and scholars bought whatever they'd need for their trips through time. Clothing for any era could be synthesized in the stores, along with the appropriate currency and enough supplies for extended temporal excursions.

There were also banks of Jump tubes that would take

time travelers wherever they needed to go with a minimum of discomfort. Unlike Temporal Enforcement agents, tourists, and scholars weren't permitted T-suits, which would have allowed them to Jump around the time stream at will. The Galactic Union preferred to control where civilians went, and what they did when they got there.

Dona passed a bearded, long-haired man dressed in filthy buckskins, his face gaunt, his eyes shadowed from weariness and lack of sleep. He was also in desperate need of a bath. She figured he was probably an anthropologist or historian, back from a long trip experiencing life as a seventeenth-century fur trapper.

Next her attention fell on a man and woman talking earnestly to a patient, cool-eyed tour guide Dona had met before. Beside them, a young boy literally danced with excitement. All five wore late eighteenth-century colonial American dress.

Dona knew the guide to be a thorough professional who prided herself on bringing her charges home without any serious trauma. Her round face was unmemorable with its button nose and blue eyes, and she wore her graying hair in a tightly braided bun. Relatively short and sturdy of build, she specialized in United States historical tours. Her deliberately nondescript appearance ensured nobody would take a second look at her, regardless of what time she visited.

"I just don't think it's a good idea to take a ten-year-old into a war zone," the guide said, eyeing the kid critically. "Flintlocks can kill you just as dead as a tachyon beamer."

"My son is very mature for his age," the man told her earnestly. "We'll keep him out of trouble."

Idiots.

Dona was about to stop and add her authority to the tour guide's when her gaze fell on a tall, dark-skinned man staggering down the corridor. His brown eyes were blank and stunned, and his rough homespun shirt was bloody, hanging in shreds around his thin waist. Just beyond him, a tourist stared in horror at his back.

Dona swore and strode toward the man, barely reaching him in time to catch him as he toppled. At her touch, he yelped in agony and fear, one knobby fist glancing off her chin in a wild swing. "It's all right, you're safe," she told him, ducking another awkward punch. "I'm Enforcer Dona Astryr. I'll get help."

With a moan of relief, he went limp in her arms. Lowering him to the floor, Dona used her comp to message the infirmary. *"I need a regen tube in Concourse Area 3–12B. Flogging victim."*

She helped the man roll onto his belly and winced at what she saw. The entire length of his back was covered in blood and finger-width welts, bruises, and gashes, many of which were deep enough to show glints of white bone and torn muscle.

"She seemed like such a nice woman," the man said, his voice cracked with pain and tears. "So religious, so soft-spoken and sweet. How could she order sixty lashes . . . ?"

"Yeah, they always seem like nice people," Dona told him grimly. "Unfortunately, their version of 'nice' doesn't extend to anybody they consider property."

"I'm not going back." He began to cry in great, wracking sobs. "I can't. I just can't. What am I going to do with the rest of my life? My doctoral thesis . . ."

"Don't worry about that now." She turned her attention to a horrified store clerk staring at them from the entry of a nearby shop. "Bring me a blanket, dammit. He's going into shock."

"Oh. Right. Of course." The woman hurried to her station and began punching buttons. The vendser unit obediently spat out a folded quilt, and she ran back to Dona with it bundled in her arms.

They got him covered and waited tensely. A few moments later, a medtech raced up, towing a long transparent tube. The tube lowered to the floor, sprang open like a clamshell, and slowly edged beneath the man. He whimpered as it jostled him while scooping him into its confines. The medtech crouched beside it, pushing buttons as it flooded with a pink healing mist.

"He'll be all right," the tech said, shooting Dona an acknowledging nod. "But he wouldn't have been if you hadn't gotten to him as quickly you did. Wonder why the hell the Jump tube staff didn't call the infirmary when he arrived. Morons. I'm putting somebody on report. . . ." Grumbling under his breath, he stood and led the regen tube away.

In a day or two, the man wouldn't even have scars to show for his taste of slavery. At least, no physical ones. Dona figured the nightmares would take a lot longer to fade.

"I can see tourists," the store clerk told her, looking after the tube with a shaken expression. "I can see assuming the identity of a nobleman or maybe even a servant. But why in the Seven Hells would anybody pose as a slave?"

"To find out whether history exaggerates." Dona got to her feet as a small swarm of cleaning 'bots arrived to absorb the blood that had spilled on the floor. Round, silver, and about the size of an orange, they landed on the edges of the sticky red pool, which quickly vanished. "If anything, it understates. Anyway, time travel is never really safe. Not even for tourists."

As she turned away, she spotted the little family and their guide. The boy was staring after the tube, his face sheet-pale under his freckles.

His father swallowed and looked at their guide. "Maybe you're right. How much did you say you'd charge for that trip to Disney World?"

**Getting pissed at** a temporal native for bigoted viciousness was a waste of energy. As far as the slaveholder was concerned, she'd committed no crime in ordering a man flogged until he was half-dead. The bitch was a product of a centuries-old system run by a wealthy class too cheap to pay for labor, a system that had to terrorize its victims in order to maintain control. A system that died more than four hundred years before Dona was born.

That was the thing about time travel—the crimes of the past didn't stay in the past.

Dona growled under her breath and stalked into the Enforcers' training gym. She needed to hit something. Hard.

But even as the doors closed behind her, she almost turned and ran out again.

The chief was here.

Chief Enforcer Alerio Dyami stood in a corner of the gym holding a grav bar, pumping out repetitions with a Warlord's effortless strength. He wore only a pair of black snugs that left most of his big body deliciously bare. His black hair fell in a thick mane to his broad, sweating shoulders, one lock of it braided with a string of gemstones that were actually combat decorations on his home planet. An intricate tattoo in vivid shades of gold and green covered the right side of his face, stretching from above one arching brow halfway down his elegant cheek.

Each part of the swirling pattern meant something; she'd looked it up once. The gold and green color of the tat represented House Dyami, the company which had genetically engineered him and implanted the neuronet computer in his brain, giving him access to bursts of fantastic strength. The triangular design running down his cheek meant he was a Viking-class Warlord, the most physically powerful subclass of his warrior people.

And the empty circle that lay directly underneath that meant he was unmated. Which intrigued Dona entirely too damned much, considering that male Vardonese Warriors were renowned for their sex drive and erotic skill.

*He's your commanding officer, you moron,* Dona told herself impatiently. *Eyes off.*

She jerked her head away and mentally stuffed her fascination for her chief back into its box. She'd been infatuated with Dyami since joining the American Outpost two years ago. Which was why she'd gotten involved with that treasonous asshole Ivar Terje. When the big redhead had been assigned as her partner last year, she'd thought he was the perfect antidote for Dyami. He was even taller and more massively built than the chief, with a handsome angular face, cool green eyes, and a talent for making her feel she was the center of the universe.

Instead, the bastard turned out to be a spy for the Xeran Empire. And now Dona herself was under suspicion.

Oh, yeah. She definitely needed to hit something.

Luckily, she spotted just the distraction she needed to take her mind off the chief, Ivar, Corydon, and that vicious little slaveholding bitch.

**Sweet Mother Goddess,** Dona just walked in. With an effort, Alerio managed to keep his eyes from drifting in the cyborg's direction as she strode across the gym on those long legs of hers.

It was a time when genetic engineering had made beauty commonplace, yet Dona was lovely even by those standards. Tall and lean, she had the long, strong build of a fighter, and there was more than enough curve to her breasts and ass to draw his hot-blooded attention. She usually wore her long, dark hair in intricate braids that called attention to her striking violet eyes. Her features were precisely sculpted, cheekbones high and rounded, with a firm chin and a soft, sensual mouth.

That mouth had been the focus of far too many of his most erotic dreams.

It was an entirely inappropriate attraction, and he knew it. She was his subordinate, dammit. Though it wasn't against Temporal Enforcement regulations to take a lover from among one's staff, doing so was a very bad idea. How was

he supposed to maintain objectivity about a woman who'd
obsessed him for the past two years?

To make matters worse, Dona returned his interest. She'd
never said so directly, of course—she was as aware of the
inherent problems of a relationship as he was. But her powerful female response to him was entirely too clear to a man
with sensor implants.

Unfortunately, he wasn't the only one who'd sensed her
interest.

At first, he'd been relieved when Dona had gotten involved with Ivar Terje. Terje, however, had proven to be a
jealous son of a bitch who'd made Dona's life hell even before he'd revealed himself to be a spy. Alerio had itched to
call the bastard out for a Warlord-style hand-to-hand duel
for the way he'd treated her. As the couple's commanding
officer, however, that hadn't been possible.

Now, though, if Alerio ever got his hands on the treasonous bastard, he meant to give Terje the beating he'd been
begging for.

Brooding, he rotated the grav-bar, ignoring the ache of
his straining arms. The bar basically functioned the same as
an antigrav unit, but in reverse. Its actual weight was only a
kilo or so, but he'd adjusted its field generators until its mass
was closer to four hundred. Controlling that mass deserved
every bit of his attention and strength, but it was all he could
do to keep his gaze from drifting to Dona.

She was talking to Riane Arvid, one of Alerio's fellow
Vardonese Warriors. The young Warfem was currently
aiming punches and kicks at a combat practice 'bot. The
big, vaguely humanoid machine circled with her, trying
to avoid her furious blows while getting in some of its
own.

As the two sparred, Riane's cyborg wolf partner, Frieka,
lay watching them with intent blue eyes. The big timber
wolf was basically a four-legged library, his considerable
intelligence enhanced by a powerful internal computer. His

loyalty and love for Riane, however, was bred right into the bone and blood of his canine nature.

"That bastard Corydon!" Riane spat, sweat-damp red hair straggling around her flushed face as she danced around the combot. "I just found out he's the same son of a blood demon who tried to kill my mother!"

"Your mother?" Dona rocked back on her heels. "Why did he do that?"

Frieka lifted his head from his paws and yawned as if faintly bored. "Jane was a temporal native. Corydon thought that damned Xeran Jump killer was supposed to slice her into bacon. When Riane's father saved her, Corydon's first response was to try to kill her himself."

Dona blinked. "Again, why?"

"Because he thought the world would end if he didn't. That was the theory then—if you did something in the past that wasn't supposed to happen, the fabric of space time would unravel like a cheap scarf. *Boom-yow.* Baran, of course, refused to let him kak her, and made him transport all four of us into the future instead. Five, counting Jane's cat." The big wolf snorted. "To Corydon's vast surprise, the universe survived."

Oh, yeah, that's right. After Baran Arvid and Jane Colby's Jump, physicists had taken a second look at the math and concluded history couldn't be changed. Anything time travelers did in the past was supposed to happen. Temporal Enforcement had changed its policies to allow temporal tourism and scholarship. Over the twenty-five years that followed, a whole industry had grown up around time travel.

"But you can just imagine how thrilled Corydon was when he found out I'm Jane and Baran's daughter," Riane snarled, hitting the combot so hard, it staggered backward a few paces. "He's just aching to prove I'm some kind of Xeran spy. Yeah, right. The daughter of the Death Lord, working for the Xerans. Not very damn likely!"

"Since when did Corydon let a few facts get in the way of

blind prejudice?" Frieka drawled. "Want me to bite him for you?"

"Hell, I want to bite him myself!" Riane slammed a foot into the combot's knee.

The machine promptly collapsed in a vaguely humanoid heap. "End combat!" it squawked. "This unit has sustained serious damage. Repairs needed."

Dona cocked her head and grinned at the Warfem. "I think you broke it."

Riane aimed a sneer at the damaged combot. "Yeah, you'd better stay down, you mechanical wimp."

Moving to put his grav bar away, Alerio concealed a smile. No matter how grim a situation was, the comedy team of Riane and Frieka was always good for a grin.

*Com message request received from Senior Investigator Alex Corydon,* Alerio's comp suddenly announced.

Speak of the devil. *Open communications,* he told the computer implant. *"What can I do for you, Senior Investigator?"*

*"My team has a lead on the location of your spy, Chief Enforcer,"* Corydon's voice announced in his mind. *"He seems to have taken refuge in twenty-second century New York. Please assemble a take-down team to make the arrest."*

Alerio's mouth drew into a savage smile. *"Believe me, Senior Investigator, it will be my pleasure."*

He dumped the grav bar into the rack with its fellows and started toward the door. "Riane, Frieka, grab your t-gear and assemble in the conference hall. We've got a lead on Terje's location. We're going to take the bastard down."

"Yes!" Riane crowed, and trotted for the door, the big wolf at her heels.

Dona, for her part, stepped into Alerio's path. "I want to go with you, Chief." Her clear violet gaze met his, level and demanding. "I want—no, I need—to help take him down."

He sighed. "You know better than that, Astryr. You haven't been cleared in this mess yet. It's a conflict of interest."

Her delicate jaw firmed. "You don't really think I'm involved in his plot, do you Chief?"

"No, but Corydon certainly does. It's his show, Astryr, and he's not going to want you along for the ride." Besides, there was another concern. Terje had tried to kill her once before, and Alerio knew damned well he'd try again if given the chance. It would be just like him to cut her throat on his way down. And Alerio had no desire to watch Dona Astryr die.

Violet eyes narrowed. He had the uncomfortable feeling she was reading his thoughts right off his face, and he mentally swore. She'd gotten to know him entirely too well.

"Let me play bait, Chief."

"Forget it." With an uncompromising slash of his hand, he stepped past her and strode toward the door. She followed him with long, angry strides.

"Ivar's obsessed with me, Chief. If he's focused on me, that'll give the rest of you a golden opportunity to take him out."

"And give him a golden opportunity to kill you. Forget it." But his steps faltered. She had a point. If she'd been any other Enforcer than the one who haunted his dreams, would he let her take the chance?

Alerio winced. Yeah, probably. If he kept her off the team, would he be putting the rest of his men in danger to protect her?

Shit. This was exactly why he had no business getting involved with her.

"Chief?" she asked at his shoulder.

"You're in. If Corydon lets you go." Without looking back, he strode out the door, silently cursing himself and the woman who had become his obsession.

ALSO BY
# ANGELA KNIGHT
# WARLORD

Angela Knight's futuristic,
genetically engineered warriors return
in this special collection that contains
her classic romance *JANE'S WARLORD*
and the novella *WARFEM*.

*WARFEM*: In the distant future,
two genetically engineered warriors
overcome their painful past to forge
a future together. But will the long-
kept secrets and betrayal destroy their
chance at happiness?

## "PAGES THAT SIZZLE IN YOUR HAND."
—J. R. Ward,
*New York Times* bestselling author

penguin.com

ALSO BY
# ANGELA KNIGHT

# JANE'S WARLORD

The sexy debut
from the author of
## MASTER OF THE NIGHT

The next target of a time-traveling
killer, crime reporter Jane Colby finds
herself in the hands of a warlord
from the future sent to protect her—
and in his hands is just where she
wants to be.

## "CHILLS, THRILLS...[A] SEXY TALE."
—EMMA HOLLY